The Return of Hester Lynton

The Return of
HESTER LYNTON

Ten New Detective Mysteries

TONY EVANS

LUME BOOKS

First published in 2021 by Lume Books
30 Great Guildford Street,
Borough, SE1 0HS

ISBN 978-1-83901-285-3

Typeset using Atomik ePublisher from Easypress Technologies

www.lumebooks.co.uk

Contents

Introduction

Several years ago my friend and former employer, Miss Hester Lynton, published an account of some of the most noteworthy cases that she had encountered during her career as a consulting detective. Given my own intimate connection with those investigations, I read them with great interest and found them to be both informative and entertaining. That they were intended to be her sole venture into literature was clear from the title she chose, *The Complete Hester Lynton Mysteries*.

However, after an approach from her publisher – and numerous appeals from an admiring public –

Miss Lynton has kindly agreed that another collection of her cases should be published, with one proviso: that it is I who should undertake the telling, not Miss Lynton. Her reasons cannot be argued with. Due to the increasingly tense and dangerous political situation developing in continental Europe, my former colleague agreed some time ago to interrupt her retirement and to serve – at the request of the highest authority – the pressing needs of His Majesty's Government in Whitehall.

More than that I cannot say, except to add that Miss Lynton has entrusted me with a precious tea chest containing all the written records and other memorabilia of her long and distinguished career. I have chosen a selection of cases that span that period, and hope only that the result – now in the hands of my readers – produces as much pleasure for them as it did for me, as I revisited the happy years that Hester and I spent at 12 Newsome Street, where our housekeeper, Mrs Parsons, would regularly usher into our rooms clients with tales from every arcane byway of human nature and human folly.

Ivy Rogerson (*née* Jessop), 12 May, 1914

1. The Case of the Fanshaw Inheritance

It was inevitable that the majority of the cases Hester and I encountered involved criminality in all its most varied and lurid forms. Nevertheless, some of the most noteworthy had little to do with law-breaking, being the kind of conundrums that the official police force had neither the time nor the duty to investigate. One such was the intriguing puzzle brought to us early in our partnership, not much more than a year after Hester had invited me to join her – as secretary and companion – in her practice as a consulting detective at 12 Newsome Street.

Hester had received a letter from her client three days before his visit, and as we awaited his arrival that Saturday afternoon she extracted it from its buff-coloured envelope and passed it to me. It comprised the sum total of what we knew of him to date.

Greystones Manor, Woking, Surrey

Tuesday 11th April 1882

Dear Miss Lynton

I have taken the liberty of writing to you after your confidential services were recommended to me by my friend, Mr Abel Johnson of The Beeches Preparatory School, Chiswick (a man of whom it can truly be said is 'amicus certus in re incerta') whom I understand you were able to assist last year.

My query concerns a confidential family matter. I am in London this coming Saturday 15th April, and will call upon you at 12 Newsome Street at 3pm. Should this not be convenient, I would be most grateful if you could write to me and specify a time on Saturday 22nd or Sunday 23rd April when I could pay you a visit.

Yours respectfully,

Albert Fanshaw M.A. (Oxon)

'What do you make of our mystery correspondent?' Hester asked me, with a twinkle in her eye. I knew her well enough to gather that she had made certain deductions herself, and I decided that I was not about to be outdone.

'Well,' I began, 'the address is certainly suggestive, and the handwriting is educated. Mr Fanshaw is likely to be a country gentleman of some means – and he is an Oxford man, to boot. The Latin phrase shows that his college studies have not been forgotten. Perhaps he is a scholar. I am afraid I do not have his command of Latin. Can you translate his quotation for me?'

Hester nodded. 'Ah yes; "*amicus certus in re incerta*" – "a good friend in time of trouble" would convey the sense best, I think. Cicero quotes the phrase, used by an earlier writer whose name escapes me. We could ask Mr Fanshaw to elaborate, although I suspect he will have more pressing things to discuss with us.'

'And what do *you* make of his letter?' I asked.

Hester took the white sheet from me, rubbed it between finger and thumb and held it up to the window.

'This paper is of distinctly inferior quality,' she said. 'Hardly what one would expect an affluent country squire to be using. To enclose it in an ill-matched buff business envelope is also most unfashionable. It suggests a need for economy somewhat at odds with being the owner of a country estate. And as Fanshaw seems only able to come to London at weekends, he evidently has a job of some kind which requires his presence in Kent during the week. Fanshaw might perhaps be a butler, bailiff or some other employee of the house, but his college degree makes that unlikely. I see Abel Johnson recommended him to us. Do you remember him? A teacher in a small preparatory school, wrongly accused of pilfering. Teaching is a perfectly respectable profession, but not one where Johnson might be expected to be a close friend of a prominent country gentleman. I would hazard a guess that Albert Fanshaw may also be a school teacher, a resident master, and that Greystones Manor is his school. It evidently not one of the leading public schools, or we would recognise the name. His modest salary would explain his economical taste in writing paper. Note also the declaration of his Oxford degree, and the gratuitous insertion of the Latin tag; both characteristic of a schoolmaster sensitive of his tenuous status in the lower reaches of academia. However, I see that it is almost three o'clock. If Fanshaw is indeed a master, then the punctuality characteristic of his profession should ensure his imminent arrival.'

I was about to reply to Hester when the distant ringing of the electric doorbell confirmed that our visitor had arrived. Shortly afterwards, Mrs Parsons ushered him into our room.

The man who entered our sitting room was no more than thirty years of age, but his receding hair and thin features already showed the marks of one who has had to work hard for a living, and has enjoyed little in the way of luxury or leisure. His tweed lounging jacket and trousers seemed chosen for durability rather than fashion, an impression reinforced by the patches of leather sewn into the elbows. He carried a briefcase which, when new, would have been an expensive item of luggage, but was now worn and shabby.

'Mr Albert Fanshaw?' Hester asked, rhetorically. 'I am Miss Lynton, and this is my assistant, Miss Jessop, before whom you may speak in complete confidence. If you would care to take a seat, Mrs Parsons will return with some refreshments shortly. I suggest we have some tea before you tell us how we may help you.'

Once the tray had been brought and tea poured, our visitor commenced his story.

'For the last six years I have been employed as classics master at Greystones Manor,' he said. I noticed that Hester was unable to suppress a glint of satisfaction before Fanshaw continued.

'My parents – a clergyman and his wife, who made considerable sacrifices to secure me a university education – are sadly deceased, and my only relatives until very recently were my uncle, Mr Edgar Rothwell, and my cousin, Mr Joshua Bulmer. Then last month my uncle – a widower – passed away. As Joshua and I were Edgar's closest relatives, I had some expectation of benefiting from his will, particularly as he was a very rich man.'

'And were your expectations realised?' Hester interjected.

Fanshaw smiled, ruefully. 'That remains to be seen. Last week I had a letter from my late uncle's solicitors, Prendergast and Kirby. I have it with me, but I can summarise the contents very easily. Mr Kirby explained that they had been directed by their client, my late uncle Edgar, to send written instructions to me and to my cousin Joshua. These instructions explain how to locate a document, contained in a silver casket. Whoever finds the document first – either Joshua or myself – must deliver it in person to Prendergast and Kirby, and will then become the sole beneficiary of Edgar's entire estate. Can I add that I was not entirely surprised by the content of the solicitor's letter; nevertheless, I went up to London last Saturday and spoke in person to Mr Kirby, who confirmed that his letter to me – and the enclosure – were genuine. I have spoken of this matter to no one. It may be that nothing will come of it.'

Fanshaw made as if to retrieve the documents from his briefcase, but Hester gestured him to wait. 'I will examine the papers very shortly, but I have one or two questions for you first, if I may. What manner of man was your uncle? And was he on good terms with you and your cousin Joshua? I would urge you to speak as frankly as possible. You may trust in our confidentiality.'

I could see that Fanshaw seemed rather discomforted, but Hester's words seemed to reassure him.

'Edgar Rothwell married my father's sister, and was, at the time of his death, a widower. There were two children, but both died in infancy. It was not a match the family greatly welcomed, but they could hardly disapprove, since Rothwell was a wealthy man with a respectable position in society. He was the owner of several flour mills and sauce factories in Lambeth, and had a reputation as a hard-headed businessman. The last time I saw him was when my cousin Joshua and I met him in London three months ago, in early January of this year. Edgar was in town on business, and had invited us for dinner at the Grosvenor Hotel. He more or less told us then that he had little respect for either of us: "ineffectual young men" was how he described us. He said that it was hard to decide which of us was the least inadequate, but that he would have to do so at some stage, as he had no one else to whom he could leave his money.'

'My goodness, he sounds a very – erm – forthright character,' Hester said. 'I can see why you were not surprised by the somewhat eccentric way he plans to allocate his legacy. But what of your cousin? Tell me about Joshua.'

Once again, Fanshaw appeared reluctant to reply, but had little alternative to answering Hester's question. He spoke in the awkward manner of a patient about to reveal an intimate and embarrassing condition to his physician.

'Joshua is a year older than me – he is thirty-two – and has had a somewhat chequered career. He was originally destined for ordination, but after some unfortunate incidents he left theological college and joined the Rhodesian police force. We have never had much to do with each other, and have only met once since his return to England. He thinks little of my profession, which did not prevent him trying to borrow £20 from me. He came back to England suddenly two years ago – I believe that there had been some difficulty over police funds – and since then has been an assistant manager at the Kasovot Club in Mayfair.

'Ah yes,' I said. 'I believe that it has been called "a gentleman's club for those who are not gentlemen." Not that I wish to cast any aspersions upon your cousin.'

Fanshaw shrugged. 'I doubt you could damage Joshua's reputation, since he has none. So there you have it. Edgar evidently considered me to be an unambitious schoolmaster, and my cousin to be a confirmed reprobate. The task he has set is evidently designed to detect which of us is the least undeserving, and to provide him with some anticipatory amusement into the bargain. As you will have gathered, I have come here today to seek your professional assistance in solving the puzzle before my cousin does so.'

Hester smiled. 'Thank you for your frankness. If you could now pass over the letter and instructions you received, I shall see what challenge your uncle has set us.'

The solicitor's covering letter was as Fanshaw had described. The attached instructions were not lengthy, and I reproduce them below in their entirety.

Look in the first appearance of the Island of Despair

1719, 112, 20, 5, 77, 5, 14, 236, 17, 8, 11, 2, 15, 7, 25, 3, 200, 30, 12, 98, 22, 4, 14, 3, 5, 14, 5, 15, 12, 1, 1, 170, 5, 11, 173, 30, 4, 175, 28, 11, 230, 7, 8, 211, 36, 15 98, 22, 14, 80, 26, 3, 16, 11, 11, 270, 35, 14, 13, 33, 6, 158, 20, 12, 22, 36, 8, 311, 21, 13, 99, 11, 7, 91, 18, 12, 46, 12, 5, Crowstead

Hester scrutinised the enclosure for a few moments, then passed it to me.

'Forgive me for stating the obvious,' I said, 'but this is clearly some kind of coded message. The word at the end seems familiar – a place name, I think?'

Albert smiled ruefully. 'As you can imagine, I have puzzled over this conundrum for hours, and that is the only part I understand. Crowstead is a small village in Kent, a few miles south of Sevenoaks. As for the "Island of Despair", it certainly does not feature in any atlas that I can find.'

'A most intriguing problem,' Hester said. There was nothing my friend liked better than an intellectual challenge, and I could sense her enjoyment of the prospect of the task that faced us.

'I hope you will allow me to make a copy of this document,' Hester continued. 'I would not wish to deprive you of the original. There is little to deduce from it, other than that the author was evidently self-educated and had little formal schooling, was meticulous in his habits and valued the finer things in life.'

Although I was well-used to seeing the effect that Hester's uncanny deductive abilities had on her clients, I could not help smiling at the puzzled look on Fanshaw's face.

'But you have characterised my uncle exactly!' he exclaimed. 'Edgar left school when he was eight years old, taught himself all he knew, was the most conscientious of men and enjoyed the fruits of his success. Is it possible that you have met the gentleman?'

'By no means. However, we may safely assume that he drafted the document himself, given its confidential nature. The non-cursive handwriting style of the preliminary sentence is typical of the unschooled writer. This is also a fair copy, based on an earlier draft; the exact spacings between the numerals could only be achieved in a second version, characteristic of the industrious mind. As to his love of luxury – this is the finest cream laid paper that money can buy. We can safely assume that it will be no simple conundrum that Mr Rothwell has set you. When the copy is made, I suggest that you return to your school. You have been wise not to speak of this matter, and should not mention to anyone that you have seen us. With your cousin as competitor, the fewer who know, the better. I will let you know of any progress; meanwhile, please contact me if you have any concerns.'

Fanshaw frowned. 'There is one thing. I am not a rich man, and would be grateful if you could let me know the details of your professional fees.'

'Please do not concern yourself on that front, Mr Fanshaw,' Hester said. 'Let us first see if I succeed in securing your fortune. If not, the puzzle you have set us will be reward enough.'

Four hours later, I gazed wearily at the sheets of paper strewn across the table. Despite those hours of labour, Hester and I and could find no correlation between the strings of numbers and the alphabet, and the elusive Island of Despair was absent from our considerable collection of works of reference. It was then, as I was sipping my coffee and gazing vacantly at the lines of numbers, that a thought struck me.

'Hester, have you noticed that when the larger numbers appear, they are almost always followed by two smaller numbers? That is, apart from the very large number at the beginning, 1,719.'

Hester put down her cup and bent over the puzzle.

'You are correct. If we put aside the first number – yes, the numbers can be grouped in threes. Pass me the foolscap, and I will write them out as a column.'

Picking up a pencil, and dividing the page into vertical columns, Hester wrote:

112	*20*	*5*
77	*5*	*14*
236	*17*	*8*

… and continued until she had transcribed all twenty-six triplets.

'There is a pattern there,' I said. 'All the numbers in the first column fall between seven and 236. The range in the second column is from one to thirty-six, and the third from one to fifteen.'

Hester stood up abruptly, clapping her hands together.

'Of course!' she cried. 'I have been a fool. It should have been obvious – it is a book code!'

Observing my puzzled expression, she continued. 'A book code is a somewhat laborious cypher to use, but extremely hard for a third party to solve. The principle is simple. Two people – you and I, say – each have the same edition of some substantial volume, *David Copperfield*, for example. If I wish to send you a coded message, such as "come quickly", I merely locate those two words somewhere in the text and refer to them using an agreed system. The example we have in front of us seems quite straightforward. The first number in the triple is evidently the page; the second is the line (counted from the top to bottom of the page) and the third is the word (counted from left to right of the line). The book in question therefore has at least 236 pages, each page has no less than thirty-six lines, and there are some fifteen words on each line. We can assume that "Crowstead" is written in plain English because the word cannot be found in the book that was used.'

'Then we have only to identify the book we need to use, and the puzzle is solved,' I said.

'Perhaps. However, that may not be easy. In addition, the large number at the beginning is still unexplained. But let us assume that "Look in the first appearance of the Island of Despair" directs us to the book in question. I cannot say the title is familiar to me. It sounds metaphorical – like the Slough of Despond in *The Pilgrim's Progress*. Perhaps we should look in that book for the island?'

I chuckled. 'One of the advantages of being a clergyman's daughter is that I know Bunyan's allegory extremely well. There is a Giant Despair, but no island of that name. Besides, if memory serves me right, it was published in 1678. Would Fanshaw's uncle not have chosen something more modern?'

It was immediately apparent that my words had made a considerable impact. Hester jumped to her feet, her expression full of excitement.

'That must be the significance of the first number in the code!' she cried. '1719 will the book's publication date! A text of that era is very likely to contain an island allegory. *Gulliver's Travels*, perhaps. Let me see …'

Hester strode to the bookshelves and took out a volume of the *Encyclopaedia Britannica*.

'English literature – eighteenth century – major works – no, *Gulliver* appeared in 1726. Here we are! *The Life and Surprising Adventures of Robinson Crusoe*, first published in 1719. That must be it.'

I quickly scrutinised our bookshelves. 'Unfortunately it is not a volume that we possess – we will have to get a copy tomorrow morning.'

'Not necessary, my dear Ivy. Our housekeeper has an excellent collection of the popular classics. I will descend immediately and ask Mrs Parsons if she has a *Crusoe* we can borrow.'

Five minutes later Hester reappeared, brandishing the book in triumph. She settled herself where the gas jet was brightest, and turned to the first page.

'I pride myself on being able to scan a text very speedily,' she said. 'If there is an Island of Despair in this work, it shall be found within half an hour.'

In the event, it was not ten minutes before Hester gave a cry of triumph. Placing the book on the table she pointed to the opening lines of Chapter 5, which I reproduce below.

> *September 30, 1659. I, poor miserable Robinson Crusoe, being shipwrecked during a dreadful storm in the offing, came on shore on this dismal, unfortunate island, which I called 'The Island of Despair'; all the rest of the ship's company being drowned, and myself almost dead.*

'This is the book, undoubtedly,' I said. 'Pass me the code, Hester – let me transcribe it now.'

Hester shook her head. 'You would not be successful. A volume like this will have been published in many editions over the years. However, I believe that the original instructions provide a clue: we are told to look in the *first appearance* of the Island of Despair. I suspect that the first edition, published in 1719, is needed. We will call at Appleton's antiquarian book dealers in Cheapside first thing on Monday, to see if they can supply us with a copy.'

'Why not the British Museum Library?' I asked. 'We have our readers' tickets.'

'Excellent though that institution is, there is often a delay of half a day in obtaining one's order – and it is also possible that their copy is out at another reader's desk. Time is of the essence in this matter – we can always turn to the library afterwards, if Mr Appleton cannot help us.'

Hester's usual blend of affability and determination soon persuaded the deputy manager to usher us into the presence of Mr Appleton at just after nine that Monday morning. Hester – having given him our cards – explained her purpose very succinctly. She asked if he possessed a first edition of *Robinson Crusoe*, and if so, that we be allowed to examine it – in his presence – for ten minutes or so.

Mr Appleton was a member of that disappearing species of old-fashioned businessmen who might have stepped straight from the pages of *Great Expectations*; benign, pink-faced, bewhiskered and with a traditional black frock coat and high collar.

'Indeed!' Appleton said. 'You intrigue me, Miss Lynton. Of course I would be very happy to oblige, but alas, we do not have a 1719 edition of that work. My memory is clear on the matter, since we sold our two first editions last year. One went to an American collector and one remained in London. I would be happy to give you the purchaser's name, on one condition. I would need to know a little more about the reason for your request. You can rely on my discretion.'

Somewhat to my surprise, Hester told Appleton the whole story, keeping back only the names of the protagonists.

Appleton's eyes gleamed with pleasure. 'How very droll! Yes, I think I can tell you that the purchaser was Sir Robert Noakes, the well-known philanthropist and bibliophile. He resides at 15 Courtney Street, off the Strand. Sir Robert is a somewhat reclusive figure, so do allow me to write you a short note of introduction, which should obtain you a meeting. No, do not thank me – you have injected some welcome variety into my mundane working day, and I shall enjoy telling my dear wife that I have had a fascinating encounter with a consulting lady detective and her companion … without, of course, revealing the details of your mission.'

Hester and I did not find obtaining an interview with Sir Robert to be quite as straightforward as our access to Mr Appleton had been. Sir Robert's butler might have been mistaken for a sergeant major, had we been unaware of his calling, and it was only through the greatest assertion of Hester's authority that our cards and Appleton's note were eventually sent up.

Fortunately, Sir Robert Noakes – a tall, genial man in his late fifties – turned out to be nothing like his servant.

'You must forgive Jefferson,' he said with a bow and a smile. 'As a philanthropist. I have many supplicants keen to importune me, and Jefferson has been trained to repel them. But I see from Mr Appleton's note that you wish merely to examine some references in my 1719 *Crusoe*. Your name seems familiar, Miss Lynton. I believe you were the young woman who was able to assist Lady Berensfield last year? She holds you in great regard.'

An unmistakable flush of pleasure suffused my friend's features.

'Well, I am glad to hear it. If Miss Jessop and I could examine your copy of the book, we would be very grateful. We can do so here, if that is acceptable.'

Sir Robert smiled. 'You are very welcome to take it home with you and to borrow it for as long as you wish – I insist. Incidentally, my *Crusoe* seems much in demand at present. Last week – on Wednesday morning – I had another visitor who also wished to examine it. He was most aggressive when Jefferson was reluctant to show him up, and in the end I had to intervene. He made up some unconvincing story about needing to look at the book in order to settle a bet, and even had the temerity to offer me £20 to see it. Of course I refused, and sent him on his way.'

Hester caught my eye, and I could tell that the same thought that had entered my mind had suggested itself to her.

'This is interesting, Sir Robert,' Hester said. 'Tell me, was your importunate visitor an elderly, white haired gentleman?'

'By no means, Miss Lynton. He was in his early thirties, with a distinctive short black beard. Now, I will ask you to excuse me, as I have another appointment very shortly. I will ring for Jefferson to show you out. And please retain my book for as long as you wish.'

As soon as we had hailed a hansom and were on our way back to Newsome Street, I asked Hester about Sir Robert's parting words.

'Do you think it is possible that Joshua Bulmer has already deduced that the puzzle is a book code, and that it refers to the first edition of *Crusoe*?' I asked.

Hester frowned. 'I am afraid that is only too likely. The fact that Fanshaw's cousin is a reprobate does not mean he lacks intelligence. In my experience, the most feckless of people are often also the cleverest. Unfortunately, he is sure to find a copy of the 1719 edition eventually – meanwhile, we must keep try to keep one step ahead. He does not know of our involvement in the case, which is an advantage. Now, I suggest we resist the temptation to decode the cypher until we get home – then we can examine it at our leisure.'

On our return to Newsome Street, the transcription of the code thankfully proved to be straightforward, even if the result was puzzling. We both sat at the table and read the result.

> *The message can be found guarded by the knight and his lady who share an ancient dwelling with the tenor and his five musical companions in Crowstead*

I picked up the paper upon which we had recorded the message and handed it to Hester. 'I dare say that you are about to ask me what I make of the message. However, on this occasion I insist that you offer your opinion first – not least because I have no hypothesis to offer.'

Hester smiled. 'Then we are equally ignorant. I think that a journey to Crowstead is now in order. Pass me our *Bradshaw*, and I will look up the train times from Charing Cross. It should not take us more than an hour. However, I suggest you take your overnight bag, in case we are obliged to stay there this evening. Who knows – we may be fortunate and find that a Sir and Lady Somebody occupy a venerable manor house on the edge of the village, and have accommodated a choral sextet for the summer.'

As it turned out, the journey took a little longer than Hester had anticipated, as there was no branch line from Sevenoaks to Crowstead, and we therefore hired a horse and trap from the Station Hotel to complete our journey. By just after two o'clock that afternoon we found ourselves in the centre of the small and picturesque village. A respectable-looking public house occupied a prominent position opposite the market cross, and Hester and I were able to secure a private room in which to take a late luncheon, after leaving our horse with the ostler.

It was the landlord himself, Mr Croker, who served our roast shoulder of mutton and boiled plum pudding. After the usual exchange of pleasantries experienced by the traveller in England – regarding our origin, destination, and the probable state of the weather for the rest of the week – Hester turned the conversation in the direction of our cryptic clue.

'Tell me, Mr Croker, do you have any very ancient houses in the village, or nearby? Miss Jessop and I have a great interest in antiquities – of an amateur nature, of course.'

'Well, Miss Lynton – let me see – there's Knole House, of course, but that's some miles away. Then there are the weavers' cottages off the High Street – they go back a hundred years or so, I believe.'

'Thank you, we shall certainly visit those. And do you have any knights of the realm hereabouts? Our friends told us that a Sir someone or other lived here, but I am afraid we have forgotten the name.'

'Knights? The aristocracy, you mean? There was Lady Woodford who lived in the Old Vicarage, but she passed away last year, and Dr Richards and his family have the place now. No, I can't say that there are any titled people actually in the village nowadays.'

'I see. Now, there is just one more thing that I should like to ask. Are there any musical gentlemen – or ladies – resident in Crowstead, to your knowledge? Operatic singers, for example?'

The landlord seemed puzzled. 'None that I know of, Miss Lynton. Old Tom Sheppard sometimes obliges us with a comic song or two in the public bar, but I dare say that's not what you have in mind. Maybe our vicar can help you – the Reverend Willis. He likes opera, and so on. Now, can I help you ladies to a little more custard?'

There seemed no more to be gained from our landlord, and shortly afterwards we found ourselves once more in the High Street, having negotiated with the ostler to retain our horse until we needed him. A short stroll to the outskirts of the village soon brought us to the parish church, where we thought it could no harm to act on Mr Croker's suggestion and seek out the vicar. The lychgate opened on to a path of deeply worn flagstones, shaded by tall yew trees that isolated St Martin's church and the surrounding graveyard from the highway.

'What a charming church!' Hester exclaimed. 'Of Norman origin, I would imagine, although much altered since. Let us look inside – if the reverend is not in attendance, perhaps some other church official might help us. I would imagine that there is little the verger or churchwarden does not know about the village.'

As we walked towards the church porch, the clock in the church tower struck the hour of three. The chime was surprisingly loud, so close to the building, and Hester smiled to see me start suddenly.

'The clock is evidently of that type that makes ingenious use of one of the set of bells in the tower,' Hester said. 'A much more satisfactory arrangement than having a little bell of its own. It sounded like the treble – not deep enough for …'

Before completing her sentence Hester swung open the heavy oak door – and stopped suddenly, so that I almost stepped on her heels. She maintained her frozen stance for a second or two, then stepped inside and closed the door after us.

'Ivy, I believe that I have the answer. Remember the book code reference to "the tenor and his five musical companions"? That is surely a reference to a ring – or set – of six church bells. The tenor is the deepest note, and the treble the highest of the set.'

'And are there always six bells in a church?' I asked.

'By no means, although it is a common number. But we can easily find out, provided the door to the belfry is not locked. Let us see – if we cannot gain entry, we will need to seek out the verger.'

The interior was silent and deserted, with that ineffable atmosphere of cool and musty antiquity that always pervades an English church. Although there was no question of being overheard, we nevertheless lowered our voices in the manner that seems almost obligatory within a holy place.

'The bell tower must be this way,' Hester said, pointing towards the baptistry. When we reached the baptismal font, the entrance to the tower could be seen in the far corner. With Hester taking the lead, we climbed the stone spiral staircase of thirty-three steps to the lower part of the belfry. Once inside the small chamber, we could see the bell-ropes looped above us; there were six in all.

I turned to Hester, repeating the puzzle, which I knew by heart: '"The message can be found guarded by the knight and his lady who share an ancient dwelling with the tenor and his five musical companions in

Crowstead." This, then, is the ancient dwelling. But where are the knight and lady who guard the message?'

'If I am not very much mistaken, we will find them in the church,' Hester said with a smile. 'If my hypothesis is correct, there is no danger of their leaving the premises before us. Lead the way, Ivy.'

Once we had descended into the main body of the church, it did not take Hester long to find what she had been looking for. In a recess on the west side of the nave there lay a well-preserved tomb monument, with a life-sized knight in armour. He was lying on a plinth, next to a female figure wearing a veil, long gown and mantle. The knight had a lion at his feet, and the lady a dog at hers. A brass plaque was fixed to the wall opposite:

This monument depicts Richard Fitzwilliam, 9th Earl of Chalton (d. 1377) and his wife Eloise (d. 1374), moved to St Martin's church following the dissolution of Chalton Priory in 1538. May they rest in peace with God.

'Here are the knight and lady,' I said. 'But where is the message that they guard? There is no inscription other than that plaque. Does it offer us a clue?'

Hester shook her head. 'That plaque had been there for many years – see how the screws that fix it to the wall have corroded. It has not been placed there by Edgar Rothwell. No, the message must lie elsewhere. I wonder ...'

As she spoke, Hester dropped to her knees and took out her large magnifying lens from her bag. She examined the large flagstones that surrounded the plinth, then stood up, dusting down her dress.

'These stones have lain undisturbed for many years,' she said. 'There is nothing hidden there.'

The stone plinth upon which the two effigies lay had a lip around its upper edge, like a table top laid upon a large chest, and as Hester was speaking I ran my hand around it. To my surprise, my moving fingers encountered a slight obstruction. I bend down and peered under the lip – to see that a small, slim envelope of brown paper had been placed underneath. It came away in my hand as I pulled it, leaving some particles of paper behind; it had evidently been stuck to the underside of the stonework with some kind of strong glue.

'My goodness, Ivy, you seem to have scored a hit!' Hester exclaimed. 'What inspiration caused you to look under there? No matter – you must have the honour of opening the packet.'

With a feeling of exhilaration, I carefully tore open the brown paper. Inside was a carefully folded sheet of cream paper, identical to the one upon which the book code had been written. It contained the following words, written in the same rather unformed handwriting as that of the code handwriting that I could safely assume was that of Edgar Rothwell.

Look where your uncle can be found like Amon.

My exhilaration quickly dissolved. 'Another cryptic clue!' I exclaimed. 'And even more opaque than the last.'

Hester chuckled. 'Do not be despondent, Ivy. You have done very well to find it. The answer it contains must certainly be penetrable to a strong mind – Rothwell would hardly have chosen something impossible to solve. We have got all we need from this charming village. Let us return to the inn, reclaim our horse and trap, and drive to Sevenoaks station. I suggest that when we reach London we forget all about clues and puzzles for what remains of the day – my brain for one requires a rest. What do you think of a box for *La Traviata* at Covent Garden, preceded by dinner at Renaldo's?'

I happily agreed with Hester's suggestion for the evening, and so it was not until after a late breakfast the following morning that we turned our attention to the mysterious message we had obtained from the monument tomb. However, before we examined it there was another matter I needed to raise with my friend.

'Last night, when we took a cab home from Covent Garden, I noticed a young man – he looked not much more than thirty – standing in the crowd opposite. He appeared to be looking intently in our direction, although of course there were any number of people near us who might have been the subject of his gaze. I thought little of it at the time, but when I woke in the night I remembered that he had a distinctive jet black beard, neatly trimmed. You will remember that Sir Robert Noakes described a similar young man who enquired regarding his first edition of *Robinson Crusoe*. Do you think we should send a telegram to Albert Fanshaw, asking for a description of his cousin Joshua?'

Hester thought for a few moments before replying. 'I do not think you should concern yourself too much, my dear Ivy. Whilst it certainly seems likely that the man who called upon Sir Robert was indeed Joshua Bulmer, there is no reason to suspect that Joshua knows of our involvement in the case. If my reading of Fanshaw is correct, the man is far too scrupulous to have mentioned to anyone that he has consulted us. There must be a good number of young men with neat black beards in London! My hope is that we found the note in St Martin's church before Joshua had a chance to read it – after all, if he had solved the conundrum first, he would hardly have replaced the message for us to find. If I am correct, he has lost the scent completely. As for contacting Fanshaw – his cousin may well be clean-shaven and have adopted the beard as a somewhat clichéd disguise, in which our enquiry would be pointless.'

I nodded. 'Very well. And now to consider the clue from the tomb – let us hope that night's sound sleep has refreshed our minds.'

I placed the brief note upon the table in front of us, and somewhat redundantly read it aloud: 'Look where your uncle can be found like Amon.'

Hester bent forward to scrutinise the words more closely. 'Let us remember that Edgar Rothwell is addressing his clue to his nephews,' she said, 'so it would be reasonable to interpret the instruction as "Look where your Uncle Edgar can be found like Amon."'

An idea struck me. 'Perhaps it is a reference to a photograph or picture?' I suggested. 'If there was an image of a family relative or friend called Amon in Rothwell's house, the document – or yet another clue – might be inside the frame.'

'Ingenious, but I am afraid it won't do,' Hester said. 'Amon is not a Christian name I have encountered in this day and age. Besides, Rothwell chooses his words carefully. If the clue had said "Look where the document can be found *with* Amon," your idea might be credible. No, I think that we must start with the identity of Amon. The word has a classical ring to it – or perhaps biblical. Now, I bow to your superior knowledge of the scriptures, my dear Ivy. Does "Amon" seem familiar to you?'

I thought carefully. 'There is a Book of *Amos* in the Old Testament, but that is not the same as Amon,' I said. 'Let me see – why, I have my father's copy of Cruden's *Concordance* to the King James Bible on my bookshelf! If there is a reference to Amon in Holy Scripture, we should find it there.'

I blew off a heavy coating of dust from that little-used volume. It turned out that there were nineteen cross-references to 'Amon', and after placing my copy of the Bible on the table before us, Hester and I looked up every instance listed.

None of the references appeared at all promising, until we were directed to the Second Book of Kings, Chapter 21, Verse 23:

21:23 And the servants of Amon conspired against him, and slew the king in his own house.

'See what comes later,' Hester said, pointing to verse twenty-six.

21:26 And he was buried in his sepulchre in the garden of Uzza: and Josiah his son reigned in his stead.

I could sense Hester's excitement, but struggled to understand it. 'Surely, we are not expected to travel to the Holy Land to find the garden of Uzza, wherever that may be?' I asked.

Hester laughed. 'Hopefully not. I think we can rely on a more reasonable interpretation of the clue. We now know that Amon can be found buried in his sepulchre. Therefore, if Fanshaw's uncle can be found "like Amon," Rothwell can also be found buried in *his* sepulchre – and the clue can be interpreted as an instruction to "look in Edgar Rothwell's sepulchre". No doubt that is where we will find the silver casket, and the document it contains.'

'And supposing Edgar Rothwell's coffin was interred?' I asked.

'Then my theory will be disproved, and we shall have to think again. However, the matter is easily resolved. I will walk to the Wigmore Street post office immediately, and send a telegram to Fanshaw asking him where his uncle is buried, and to specify the nature of his resting place in detail. Our next move will be dependent upon his reply. Why not come with me? It is a fine morning, and the air will do us good.'

It was not until late that evening that the answer to Hester's telegram arrived. She opened the envelope and read the message out to me.

'Uncle Edgar is buried in the Rothwell family mausoleum with his wife and infant daughters. St Hilda's churchyard, Thames Street, Vauxhall – well, that is very clear, at any rate. I suggest we visit St Hilda's tomorrow at mid-day, in order to avoid any church service. Hopefully, we shall find someone to admit us to Rothwell's last resting place. However, I will pack a few necessities in my valise in case a more direct approach is needed.'

At noon the next day we started on our short journey, and our cab was soon crossing Vauxhall Bridge and proceeding along the Albert Embankment. When we turned east down a much smaller highway and arrived at our destination, Hester paid off the driver, and we walked through the churchyard gate into the cemetery.

It was evident that St Hilda's churchyard was one of those venerable metropolitan burial grounds that had spread far from its original point of focus – a small and ancient church could be seen in the distance, surrounded by a scattering of memorials, some dating back to the early sixteen hundreds, their inscriptions eroded by time and the elements until barely legible. Had we been searching for a single gravestone, our task would have been almost impossible; however, the mausolea were located together on the north side of the churchyard, barely visible behind a dense screen of yew trees which had no doubt once provided some welcome greenery, but now towered ominously over all that lay around them.

When we got closer to the squat, fortress-like buildings, Hester tugged at my sleeve.

'As Fanshaw's uncle was a self-made man, I would imagine that his family mausoleum was built to his instructions – probably no later than thirty years ago – rather than inherited from his own forebears. Let us examine the newer sepulchres in this collection.'

Hester's supposition proved to be correct. Ignoring the older and visibly decrepit constructions, it was not long before we came to a much more recent example; it did not require much in the way of deduction to realise that this was the edifice we sought, since the name *ROTHWELL* was carved in large capitals over the pair of embossed bronze doors. The mausoleum was constructed of grey granite in the style of an ancient Egyptian tomb, with lotus leaf columns and sphinxes each side of the doorway; it was clear that no expense had been spared, although the uncharitable might have found the building ostentatious to the point of vulgarity.

We both looked at the doors in more detail; there was a large central keyhole, and the latch bolt could just be glimpsed where the doors joined in the middle. The same thought occurred to both of us, but Hester voiced it first.

'It could take us days to obtain the key – even if Rothwell's solicitors allowed it. I will break open the doors. If we succeed in obtaining Fanshaw's inheritance, he will not object to the cost of repairs. If not, I will pay the repair bill myself.'

As she spoke, Hester opened her capacious bag and drew out a short, heavy jemmy, of the type favoured by burglars the world over. She inserted one end into the door opening, and leant upon it with all her strength. There was a sudden sharp crack, and the bronze doors flew open.

The interior of the tomb would have been a disappointment for any *aficionado* of Gothic romance, as dust, cobwebs and mysterious shadows were conspicuously absent. I realised that it had probably been cleaned quite recently, in readiness for the arrival of Rothwell's remains. Wide stone shelves were built on each of the longer sides, no doubt waiting to receive the coffins of future generations of Rothwells; rather poignantly, only four deceased were in residence, two of them in the pathetically small coffins of children. Another, older, coffin was presumably that of Rothwell's wife, and the splendid mahogany casket furthest from the entrance – its gilded handles not yet tarnished by the damp atmosphere – was clearly that of the late Edgar Rothwell himself. Some short lengths of heavy timber leant against one wall, no doubt used to help lift the heavy coffins into position.

I repeated the clue that we had discovered in St Martin's church: '"Look where your uncle can be found like Amon." Well, here we are in his sepulchre, as directed. If the document we seek is here, we have been told that it is in a silver casket. But unless I am being singularly unobservant, there is no such casket here!'

Hester looked sombre. 'I fear that we may have to look a little closer into Rothwell's final resting place. It is unfortunately necessary to open his coffin. I suggest you wait outside whilst I do so.'

'Not at all. Thus far we have investigated this case together – if there is some unpleasant work to be done to secure its resolution, we will tackle that together also.'

'Very well. If you can hold that corner of Rothwell's coffin, to make sure it will not slip from the shelf, I will insert my jemmy under the lid. Hopefully, it has not been screwed down too rigorously.'

This time, it took Hester rather more effort to achieve her aim than she had expended when breaking open the doors. But eventually – accompanied by a good deal of splintered mahogany – the lid was forced to one side.

A corpse that has lain in a coffin for a month or more will never be the prettiest of sights, but the nature of its impact upon the observer will be much affected by whether or not it has been preserved. Evidently, an embalmment of some kind had been undertaken on Edgar Fanshaw's body, since the miasma that arose from his remains was astringently chemical rather than offensively putrid; likewise, the rosy flush upon his cheeks belied the process of decay, and had no doubt been achieved by a funereal cosmetic rather than any natural process. However, our immediate attention was drawn not to the body, but to the small silver box that lay between his feet. Hester picked it up and took it into the centre of the mausoleum. The lid opened with a simple catch and hinge, and with a gasp of delight my friend withdrew the contents – a slim manila envelope.

Before I could voice my congratulations, a most unexpected sound came from directly behind me, causing me to jump with surprise. Hester also started violently and looked up. I turned to see a young man, who had knocked with his fist on the open bronze door to attract our attention.

As we stood, dumbstruck, our visitor stepped over the threshold into the tomb. He was a youthful clergyman, wearing a well-cut charcoal grey suit with a black shirt and clerical collar. There was a small, recent cut upon his chin, and his features had something of the pallor of one who spent too little time outdoors.

'Miss Lynton ... Miss Jessop – do forgive me,' he said with a pleasant, open smile. 'If you will bear with me for a few moments, I will explain my unexpected appearance. My name is the Reverend Horace Kinsman – as you see, an ordained minister of the Church of England. I am an old college friend of your client, Albert Fanshaw – we were at Oxford together. I received a telegram from him saying that I would find you here, and asking me to offer you every assistance. This is not my parish, but of course as you have technically carried out a trespass ...' he looked pointedly at the open coffin 'you may well need my intercession with the authorities on your behalf.'

Hester smiled. 'Why, that is most kind of you, Reverend. So, you and Mr Fanshaw were at Emmanuel College together?'

'Yes indeed! A very happy three years. Now, shall we see if dear Albert's hopes have been realised? I see that you have not yet opened the envelope that will grant him his inheritance. Shall we examine the contents?'

As he spoke, he took a step towards Hester, and held out his hand as if to take the document she had extracted from the casket. Hester's reaction astonished me. She took a sudden pace back, and thrust the envelope deep into her bag.

'Not so fast, sir!' she cried. 'You may look at the contents if you are able to answer one simple question. How were you able to spend a happy three years at Oxford with your cousin at Emmanuel College, when that institution is in actuality part of Cambridge University, not Oxford at all? Ah, I see you have no answer. Let me advance an alternative hypothesis; you are in fact Mr Joshua Bulmer, Albert's cousin, and you are no more a clergyman that am Ivy or I.'

At Hester's words, a sudden transformation overcame the young man's features. His benign expression was replaced by a vicious curl of the lips, his head thrusting forward like an animal about to pounce.

'You're a little too clever for your own good,' he said. 'Well, I can assure you that two meddlesome ladies will not stand between me and my rightful inheritance! Hand that envelope over to me, or I will take it from you.'

Hester laughed. 'Hah! So you intend to use force? You need to think very carefully exactly where that plan might lead you – in my opinion, very probably to Dartmoor prison or a similar establishment. I assure you that it will not be as easy to overcome us as you might think. However, if you are successful, you will certainly need to leave us both injured – or worse – and the subsequent police investigation will lead straight to you.'

As she spoke, Hester took up the iron jemmy, which she had put down next to coffin after prising off the lid. At the same time I picked up one of the lengths of timber that rested against the wall next to me. Bulmer took a step towards Hester, his fists clenched – then turned around, and seeing me with the improvised cudgel in my hand, he again stood still.

Hester and I have since speculated upon the outcome of the confrontation, had it in fact led to a violent conclusion. However, as it turned out we were spared the experience by an intervention that was as welcome as it was unexpected.

A man's figure stepped through the doorway into the mausoleum, and cried out loudly.

'Stop, all of you! There is no need for this. No harm needs to come to anyone. Please stay still, and listen to me carefully.'

The new arrival was none other than our client, Albert Fanshaw, dressed – as far as I could tell – in the same tweed jacket and trousers he had worn when he had called upon us on Saturday afternoon.

Bulmer gave a scornful snort. 'Oh, I see that my cousin Albert is here to add his two penn'orth! I am surprised that your headmaster has given you permission to leave the premises on a Tuesday afternoon. Well, you are welcome to try your luck, along with the ladies, but I still mean to get hold of that document, whatever the consequences.'

Fanshaw stood calmly, fixing Bulmer in his gaze. 'I overheard Miss Lynton's last words,' he said. 'Let me add to them. Before coming here this morning, I deposited a sworn affidavit with my London solicitors, Merrick and Hughes, which I drew up yesterday evening. It describes the peculiar conditions of our uncle's will, states that I have retained the services of Miss Lynton and the friend and expresses my concern that the other claimant – you – might seek to use force to gain his ends. Even you, my dear Joshua, must surely see that any violence suffered here today will swiftly be traced back to you. However, let me propose another solution. I have here a deed of gift in my own handwriting which Mr Merrick himself helped me to compose. It requires only my signature and the date, and the signature of two independent witnesses – Miss Lynton and Miss Jessop would do very well. Shorn of the legal terminology, it pledges that when I receive my inheritance from the estate of my uncle, half of the value – including money, property, shares or anything else of worth – will be given by me without conditions to my cousin, Joshua Bulmer. Of course, I do not know exactly what the total inheritance will be, but as everyone knows that Edgar Rothwell was a very rich man, half will be ample for my needs. Think carefully, Joshua – by taking away this deed you will make yourself wealthy without running any risk from the law. Here, read it for yourself.'

Bulmer took the proffered document from his cousin's hand and read it through carefully. Then he stood for several seconds, deep in thought. Finally he spoke, smiling ingratiatingly.

'Well, Albert, you are clearly not the nincompoop that I have always taken you for. This seems a fair suggestion – with one proviso. Let the four of us go together to deliver our uncle's document and casket to his solicitors, Prendergast and Kirby. Then I can be sure there has been no last-minute trickery.'

Fanshaw shook his head. 'I cannot agree to that. What would then stop you stating that it was *you* who had discovered the document first, and are due the entire fortune? I appeal to you – please do not let your innate greed and dishonesty triumph over what vestiges of common sense remain to you. My offer is this: you may observe whilst I sign the deed of gift, and the ladies witness it. Then you may take it to your own solicitors, for use in the event of my breaking my word.'

Bulmer's face had reddened at this cousin's summation of his character, but he kept his own counsel.

'Very well,' Bulmer said. 'Sign the da**ed thing, and give it to me. And if I don't get my fair share after all this, the three of you will be the worse for it.'

Bulmer left quietly with the signed pledge as his cousin had requested, and after a short interval we hunted out a cab and drove directly to the Great Portland Street offices of Edgar Rothwell's solicitors, where the legal processing of Fanshaw's claim upon his uncle's inheritance was soon initiated. Our offer to take Fanshaw to Charing Cross Station was politely refused; instead he told us that it was his intention to delay his return to his school until the following day – and instead invited us to dinner that evening at the Grosvenor Hotel, where he planned to take a room for the night.

Later that evening, after indulging ourselves with an excellent dinner for which Fanshaw insisted on paying, Hester, our client and I occupied a small private lounge where coffee was brought to us. I was amused to see that, in the few hours before our rendezvous, Fanshaw had managed to purchase a smart new suit of clothes. They were ready-made by necessity, but far superior to the crumpled tweed jacket and trousers he had previously worn. His features, too, seemed much improved; his air of anxiety now replaced by a look of calm satisfaction.

By collective assent we had agreed to postpone any discussion of the case until after we had eaten, and I could see that Hester was now curious to resolve those parts of the puzzle that remained.

'Tell me, Mr Fanshaw, what made you decide to visit your uncle's grave after I had sent you my telegram? You could hardly have known that your cousin was for some reason on our trail.'

Fanshaw looked a little embarrassed. 'I am afraid that I have not yet told you everything. On Monday evening, at Greystones Manor, I returned to my study at half past seven, having finished supervising lower school prep. I found that my door was open – although I could have sworn that I had locked it – and that all my personal papers and belongings had been disturbed. However, nothing at all had been stolen. Even the few pounds that I keep in my desk drawer had been untouched. I naturally assumed that it was an unpleasant schoolboy prank, and informed the headmaster. However, his usual informants amongst the pupils had nothing to report, and so no culprit was identified.

'It was after your telegram was belatedly passed to me by the school secretary yesterday evening – and I had sent my reply – that an unpleasant thought struck me. I remembered that I had made an entry in my diary detailing the appointment that I had made with the two of you at Newsome Street last Saturday. What if had been my cousin who got into my room, using a skeleton key or lock pick? He would have read my diary and known that you were assisting me. I realised that in that case he might be following you, and could track you to the mausoleum. Knowing his ruthless character, I set off to warn you. I decided to go directly to the graveyard today, rather than run the risk of missing you at your house.'

Hester turned to me. 'Ivy, I owe you an apology! The man whom you observed staring at us at Covent Garden – no doubt that really was Joshua Bulmer, despite my scepticism.'

'Hopefully, we will never know,' I said with a smile. 'However, whilst on the subject of mysteries, you seemed very certain that the emollient vicar who accosted us in the mausoleum was Joshua Bulmer. What made you suspect him?'

'His beard was the first thing that alerted me – or rather, the lack of it!

Did you notice the cut upon his chin? A very probable result of a speedy removal of a heavy growth of facial hair. His skin also had a pallor characteristic of the freshly shorn. In addition, his grey suit was a most suitable colour for a clergyman, but of a bespoke cut and quality, which those in that profession can rarely aspire to. By the way, Mr Fanshaw, I assume that your story about calling in to your solicitors this morning to deposit your affidavit and to draw up a deed of gift was an inspired fiction? You drew up the deed yourself on your train journey from Woking to Charing Cross, if I am not mistaken.'

I was amused to observe on Fanshaw's features the bemused expression typical of the recipients of Hester's deductive observations.

'You are correct in both respects. But how could you know?'

'It is very simple. Solicitors are not in the habit of drawing up legal documents at a moment's notice. They invariably ask for a week or two, to justify their excessive fees. And from my glimpse of your deed of gift, its inferior handwriting – compared to the original letter that we had from you – is typical of a draft composed in a moving cab or railway carriage. You do realise, I suppose, that the lack of professional assistance may well mean that the wording of your deed of gift is not legally valid? You may be able to claim the full amount of the inheritance after all.'

Fanshaw smiled. 'By no means. I can assure you that my cousin will receive his half of the money come what may. I have every hope that when he is a rich man, he will have no more to do with me.'

'And what of your own plans, Mr Fanshaw?' I asked. 'Will you go back to Greystones Manor school?'

'I will be returning tomorrow, Miss Jessop, and will offer my services until the end of the academic year, if the headmaster wants me – that is only fair to my pupils. After that, it is my intention to see something of the world. For the last ten years I have laboured dutifully at an occupation which has given me little pleasure. It would not be unreasonable to spend some time redressing the balance. And now, Miss Lynton, as Rothwell's solicitors have kindly provided me with a generous cash advance in anticipation of my inheritance, I would be most grateful if you could name your fee, so that I can settle my account immediately.'

2. The Case of the Stolen Leonardo

Inspector Albert Brasher sat back in our most comfortable chair and stretched out his hand to take the tumbler of whisky and water that Hester held out to him. Her cousin was scrupulous in his avoidance of strong drink when on duty, but on this occasion he had finished his official labours for the day and was clearly in need of a stimulant.

'I don't mind telling you, this is as rum a business as any I've come across,' he said. 'And that's saying something! I'm seeing Superintendent Wilcox tomorrow morning, and for the life of me I don't know what to say to the fellow. Foggy doesn't even cover it. This case is more like wading through treacle – or a sago pudding.'

Hester chuckled. 'You may wish to spare your superintendent the metaphors, entertaining though they are. After such an introduction, please tell us all about the case, before Ivy and I die of curiosity.'

'Very well. Yesterday morning, I was called out to the Ronsard Gallery, off Portland Place. Do you know it? It's less than a mile from here.'

We shook our heads, and Albert continued. 'It's a very select establishment – the owner is the Honourable Arthur Clifford, the younger son of the Earl of Richmond. The gallery specialises in the sale of old masters – some very valuable paintings and drawings go through their hands. At eight o'clock on Tuesday morning, Clifford unlocked the door to the main gallery area as usual, to allow his conservator to enter. This man – Amos Clegg – went into the gallery to collect a painting that needed some repairs to the frame. Clifford remained outside, talking to the attendant. After no more than one minute – everyone is in agreement on this point – Clegg came rushing out, to state that a Leonardo was missing. Clifford ran back inside and sure enough, there was just an empty space on the wall where it had hung the day before. He's certain he would have noticed if the painting had been missing when he locked up at six o'clock on Monday evening.'

'You say "everyone was in agreement" about the time Clegg spent inside,' Hester said. 'Who exactly was present?'

'Arthur Clifford, Amos Clegg and the attendant, William Hepworth. There is an attendant's desk outside the inner door. A team of attendants are on duty there for every hour of the day and night, in addition to another who attends *inside* the main display area during opening hours. When Clegg entered the room, Hepworth was at the desk. Hepworth works the night shift – six o'clock in the evening until eight in the morning. His replacement did not arrive until a few minutes later. The inside gallery attendant does not arrive until nine thirty, when the gallery is open to the public. Only one person holds the key to the door: Arthur Clifford.

'Of course, my first thought was that Hepworth must have removed the painting during the night, possibly after letting in an accomplice. But that idea doesn't hold water. Firstly, Hepworth has worked at the gallery for twelve years and is hardly the criminal type. He's sixty-three years old, a family man, Crimea veteran and holder of the Distinguished Conduct Medal. I reckon I'm a good judge of character – I've spoken to the man and I'd bet my pension he knows nothing about it. Secondly, I don't see how Hepworth could have got hold of the key. Clifford keeps it on his person, and never lends it out.'

'I would imagine the door lock is of good quality?' Hester asked.

'You're right. A Ballister-Smythe deadlock, with tamper-proof cylinders. It would be impossible to force without causing considerable damage, and the door appears to be unharmed.'

Hester got to her feet. 'Very well. This seems a most promising case. Ivy and I will visit the Ronsard Gallery tomorrow morning – shall we say ten o'clock? If you could arrange for the owner to be present, I would be grateful. I will also need to speak to Amos Clegg, but there is no need to give him any prior notice. I will, of course, keep you fully informed of any progress we make.'

After Albert had left us, I sat thoughtfully for some moments. Something he had said had sparked a distant memory.

'Hester – I seem to have heard of the Earl of Richmond before. I believe there was a report in the newspapers some years ago. Can you recollect anything?'

'I am afraid my interest lies more in the court reports than the society pages,' Hester replied with a smile. 'Perhaps Mrs Parsons can help you. She has a comprehensive knowledge of the English aristocracy.'

Then it came to me. 'I remember now! The earl was badly affected by death duties. He had to liquidate most of his estate, and move into his gamekeeper's cottage. That must be why his son has turned to trade, albeit of the most genteel variety.'

As it was a very pleasant day for early October, the next morning Hester and I decided that we would walk the short distance to the Ronsard Gallery. Albert had given us the address.

The Honourable Arthur Clifford was awaiting our arrival in the foyer. He was a large, robust man, well above the average in height and dressed in an elegant lounge suit. Whist clearly an urbane man of the world, his manner betrayed an understandable anxiety. After the usual exchange of greetings he led us upstairs to the gallery, where we paused at the end of a corridor, out of earshot of the uniformed attendant who sat at his desk.

'I understand that Inspector Brasher has told you all that we know,' Clifford said. 'The attendant that you see is Jefferson. The man who was present when we discovered that the painting was missing was Hepworth, who works the night shift. I can arrange for you to speak to him, if you wish.'

'Thank you, but that is not necessary at present,' Hester said. 'But please tell me more about the painting that was stolen.'

'Of course. It is by Leonardo da Vinci, *Portrait of Catherine Nogarola*, painted around 1490 in oil on a wooden panel. It measures sixteen by thirteen inches. Not one of the artist's best-known works, but valuable all the same. It was displayed in a substantial wooden frame.'

'And is the painting the property of the gallery, or are you selling it on behalf of a client?'

Clifford appeared impressed. 'I see you have an understanding of the art business, Miss Lynton. In this instance we are selling for a client. I would prefer not to reveal that person's name unless absolutely necessary – it is a sale to fund a marriage settlement. The catalogue price is £5,000.'

I caught Hester's eye – I guessed that we shared the same thought, that

Clifford was hoping to recover the painting before informing his client of the enormous loss.

'Thank you,' Hester said. 'And now, I should like to see the gallery.'

Once inside, Hester paused to examine the door and lock, then with Clifford to guide her she walked to the far end where the Leonardo had hung. It occupied a space not directly visible from the entrance. The gallery was large and airy, with a floor of polished oak boards that had the dark patina of many years' usage.

Hester's first act was to ask the proprietor to point out a picture with a frame similar to that used for the missing Leonardo. Then, after pacing the length of the gallery, she stopped under one of the row of six large windows that lined the outside wall. Vertical and horizontal metal rods, of about the thickness of a candle, were fixed outside each window. At the base of each window a tilting glass panel allowed a long narrow vent to be opened a few inches, no doubt to provide some fresh air in the warmer weather.

'Mr Clifford, have these windows been examined?' Hester asked.

He nodded. 'Very thoroughly, I assure you. They cannot be opened, apart from the vents, and the bars are all firmly fixed. For a painting to be passed out of a window, it would need to be no bigger than three inches square.'

Hester pulled down on one of the handles that operated a vent, and it opened towards her like a hinged letter box cover in front of the iron bars. As she did so, I looked out of the window nearest to me. We were three floors above ground level, and the smooth brick walls overlooked an enclosed yard at the back of the building, containing a small pile of lumber and some old sacking. It hardly seemed likely that the Leonardo could have been removed from that direction, even if the window had provided no barrier.

'Mr Clifford, what were your first actions when your conservator announced that the painting was missing?' Hester asked.

'I told Clegg to stay where he was. Then I asked him to remove his outer clothing, until he stood in front of us in his underlinen. The Leonardo is not a large painting – it was just conceivable that Clegg could have concealed it upon his person, and be attempting to smuggle it past us.'

Hester laughed. 'Admirably quick thinking, sir! Although sadly to no purpose, as it turned out. Now, if you will excuse us, Ivy and I will spend ten minutes or so examining this room in a little more detail. Then I should like to speak to Amos Clegg, if that is possible.'

'Of course. I shall be in my office on the first floor when you need me.'

After he had left us, Hester spoke to me. 'I have no doubt that Albert's men have already inspected the windows, but I would be grateful if you could also do so, to be absolutely sure that they are as solid as they look. Meanwhile, I will check the walls and floor. Trap doors and secret passages are usually the stuff of fiction rather than real-life detection, but it is as well to make sure.'

Whilst I was confirming that the windows were fixed firmly in their frames, Hester made a circuit of the room, tapping all the walls carefully. She then took her large magnifying lens out of her capacious leather handbag, dropped to her knees and looked closely at the floor boards below the place where the Leonardo had hung.

'It is a shame that I was not called in immediately after the painting was found to be missing,' Hester said. 'These large footprints undoubtedly match the boots of Albert's officers. Wait – now, what is this? Do you have a tweezers, Ivy?'

I was able to produce tweezers from my handbag, and bent down next to Hester. The edge of a piece of thin card could just be seen protruding from the gap between two floorboards. Hester grasped it with the tweezers, then got to her feet and brought it to the light.

'Now, what do you make of this?' she asked.

The scrap was about the size of a postage stamp, though irregularly shaped. One side was plain white, the other coloured mainly red, with a streak of blue along one edge.

'Perhaps a fragment of wallpaper?' I hazarded.

Hester frowned. 'This is too thick for that.'

She took out a manila envelope from her bag and carefully dropped the piece into it. She then walked to the window nearest to where the Leonard had hung, and pointed to the floorboard below it.

'Do you see those marks?' she asked. 'They seem to have been made recently.'

I peered closely, and saw a number of dark spots on the brown patina of the floorboards, each about the diameter of a pea.

'Some kind of stain – when the windows were cleaned?' I suggested.

'Very possibly. Now, I think we have seen all we need to here,' Hester said. 'Let us see if Mr Clifford can take us to Amos Clegg. It will be interesting to hear his account of last Tuesday.'

As it turned out, we were not destined to speak to Clegg that morning after all. Clifford was most apologetic: his conservator had sent in a note, which had just been received by the gallery. Clegg had a head cold, and had decided that he had better stay at home for a day or two, for fear of the chilly October weather turning his complaint into something worse. Clifford seemed remarkably indulgent as an employer – he did not react to this news with any annoyance.

The reason for his generosity was clear when Hester asked if we could see Clegg's workshop. It was apparent the conservator was an excellent craftsman. An oil painting occupied a prominent position, displayed on an easel. It had been heavily damaged – by water, it seemed – and Clegg's partially-completed restoration was masterly.

'A Renaissance Madonna and Child,' Hester said. 'A Filippo Lippi, perhaps? I am afraid my knowledge of art has not been informed by any systematic study. Do you see how the missing arm of the child has been restored? Clegg has matched the skin tones exactly. And here, the edge of the Madonna's robe … the man is rather wasted as a conservator.'

Further examples of Amos Clegg's work were laid out on a number of large tables, which were placed under the light from two large windows and included several frames that were undergoing restoration. As we walked round the room, Hester pointed to a set of brass weights that stood on one of the open shelves, between a jar of brushes and a bottle of turpentine. They were stacked one upon another, and clearly designed for kitchen scales.

Hester picked up the first three from the pile. 'Do you see, Ivy?' she said. 'The half-pound weight is missing from the set. How curious.'

'It has probably been lost at some time,' I said.

'And yet these weights are very new – the brass is as bright as when they were cast. And where are the scales to go with them? No doubt Clegg uses them for holding down items when he is repairing them, or for some similar purpose.'

When we had finished our tour of the workshop, we returned to Clifford's office and took our leave.

'I shall call upon Mr Clegg this afternoon,' Hester told him. 'If he feels too ill to see us, he can always send us away. There is just one further area I wish to examine – the enclosed yard directly under the gallery windows.'

After Clifford led us to the yard we told him that we would make our own way home afterwards, and would contact him later if we had anything to report. The yard was enclosed by a low brick wall, and we could see the row of tall, barred gallery windows three floors above. There was no pipework running down the wall, and the route to the windows looked even more inaccessible than it had from my perspective in the gallery.

'Even Poe's orangutan would baulk at that climb!' Hester exclaimed, pointing up to the windows. 'However, this yard may have something to tell us. Luckily the heavy rain last Monday ceased before midnight, and we have had none since. Let us see what we can find.'

I stood still whilst Hester walked gingerly around the side of the yard furthest from the wall, until she stooped and pointed to some footprints. The dirt and detritus washed over the yard by the rain had provided an excellent medium to preserve them.

'See, Ivy? Police boots again. One of Brasher's men has been here and found nothing. But what have we here – what do you make of these?'

I looked at the smaller prints, which ran back and forth a few feet from the wall.

'These look like women's shoes.'

'Indeed. And do you see this mark?'

Next to the shoe prints, the muddy flagstones bore an irregular indentation the size of my palm.

'Did the owner of these footprints slip and throw out a hand?' I asked.

Hester bent down and peered closely. 'Quite possibly. At any rate, I think it is now time for a brisk walk home, or we will offend Mrs Parsons by missing our luncheon. We will need something fortifying before calling on Mr Clegg this afternoon.'

Later that day our cab delivered us to Amos Clegg's pleasant terraced house in West Holloway. Although small, it seemed a more superior residence than one would associate with an artisan of Clegg's social position, and the impression was reinforced when the door was opened by a young and neatly-turned-out servant. She took our cards inside and we were soon shown into the front parlour, where the maid told us that 'the master will be with you very shortly.'

The room was not at all what I had expected. Instead of the usual array of well-known reproductions, family photographs and unexceptional ornaments, it was full of fresh and original art, including paintings, drawings, and decorative items. One wall was half covered by framed watercolours, including some well executed contemporary London street and park scenes; oil paintings showing ancient views of Venice and Rome were also displayed. One painting, in a prominent position, was of a handsome young man in an undergraduate gown, standing outdoors in front of a venerable stone building – I guessed an Oxford or Cambridge college. It was expertly executed in a naturalistic manner, and from the evidence of the young man's clean-shaven features and fashionably narrow trousers, it had been painted quite recently. Open shelves each side of the fireplace held an assortment of brightly lacquered boxes in the Japanese style.

Before I could comment on this unexpected treasure trove, the door opened and Amos Clegg entered the room. He hardly looked the part of an artisan prised from his sick-bed. I judged him as being no more than forty-five years of age, a little below the medium in height and with a neatly trimmed moustache. He wore matching waistcoat and trousers and a clean – but collarless – white shirt.

After Hester had introduced us, she apologised for visiting Clegg when he was unwell.

The conservator coughed – somewhat ostentatiously – into his handkerchief.

'Not at all – I feel a good deal better this morning. I apologise for my appearance – I wasn't expecting visitors. I'm afraid my wife cannot join us, as she is visiting her mother in Torquay and will not return until next week. Am I right in thinking that I am speaking to the same Miss Lynton and Miss Jessop who were responsible for the recovery of the Rampur Diamond? If so, I can guess what brings you to my house. Let us hope that you have as much success in finding my employer's Leonardo.'

As Clegg was speaking, I caught Hester's eye. She was doubtless thinking the same as I – that Amos Clegg's diction, appearance and manner denoted a member of the middle classes, rather than a skilled workman.

'You are correct,' Hester answered. 'I have been engaged by the Metropolitan Police to assist with this case, with the owner's approval. However, in this instance I hope we will be able to keep the affair away from public. Tell me, Mr Clegg, when was the last time that you saw the Leonardo? You must forgive me if the official police have already asked you that question.'

Clegg frowned in concentration. 'Let me see – it would have been about mid-afternoon on Monday last – the seventh of October – I'd gone up to the gallery to collect a picture that needed reframing. It was hung quite close to the Leonardo, and I am sure I would have noticed if the painting had been missing. Then late on Monday afternoon – at about six o'clock – I went upstairs to speak to the attendant, but I didn't go into the gallery. While I was there Mr Clifford arrived to close up for the day. He went into the gallery for a few minutes to check that everything was as it should be, then he came out and locked the door behind him.'

Hester sat in thought for a few seconds, then continued. 'I would like you to think very carefully. What was Mr Clifford wearing that evening?'

I could not see the purpose of my friend's question, but had learned over the years that Hester's queries – however trivial – were always to the point. Clegg also seemed surprised.

'Wearing? Why, his Inverness cape coat. It was a wet and cold evening, and cabs are not always easy to come by so early in the week.'

'Thank you,' Hester said. She waved her hand towards the wall of framed paintings. 'Would I be right in thinking this is your own work, Mr Clegg?'

'Indeed it is, Miss. Mr Clifford is a good employer, but of course my salary – wages, I should say – as a conservator are only modest. I supplement my income by producing paintings and other little *objets d'art* for the commercial market – mainly to provincial dealers. My *papier-mâché* boxes sell particularly well. I have a small workshop in my back garden, and this room serves as my shop window, as it were ...'

I could not help interrupting. 'And what of this excellent oil painting?' I asked, pointing at the picture of the young student. 'Is this your work also, or that of Mr Frith, perhaps?'

The conservator smiled. 'Mine alone, but thank you for the comparison. That is my son, Steven, painted last year. He is now in his second year at Balliol College, Oxford.'

Hester looked surprised. 'Really! Ivy and I know one of the Fellows there quite well – Dr Marriot. We were able to help him when some examination papers … but I must not betray a confidence. Tell me, how is your son finding university life?'

For the first time in our interview, Amos Clegg looked discomfited. However, he quickly regained his composure. 'Oh – on the whole – he manages quite well, I believe. Of course his life there is very different from what he has experienced at home. He is studying law, and should have a successful career to look forward to.'

'You and your wife must be very proud,' Hester said. 'And are you a college man yourself, Mr Gregg?'

'Hardly. My father was an impoverished school usher. It was my wish to study art and become a professional painter, but that world is closed to those other than the privileged few – or those willing to live on nothing a week. Instead, I served an apprenticeship as a gilder and sign writer, then by self-study became a journeyman painter, restorer and maker of gewgaws for the masses. I've no complaints, however. My wife and I have our health, our son and enough to live on, which is more than many can say.'

That was all the information were able to gain from Amos Clegg. On our way back to 12 Newsome Street, I thought carefully about what he had told us.

'Clegg seemed rather uncomfortable when you asked him about his son,' I said. 'Or was I imagining things?'

'Not at all, Ivy. I see we are almost at the Marylebone post office. If you would like to come in with me, I will send a telegram to Dr Marriot, asking him to write to us immediately with any information he might have about young Steven Clegg. With luck, we will receive his letter tomorrow. Marriot knows us well enough to trust that we will break no confidences.'

As it turned out, the first communication that we had the following morning was not a letter from Dr Marriot, but a large brown envelope which, Mrs Parsons assured us, had been pushed though the letterbox before she had risen at seven. It had clearly been delivered by hand, since the only words on the cover were *MISS LYNTON*, scrawled in very badly printed capital letters. Hester drew out the contents – one sheet of foolscap paper – and placed it on the table between us.

I drew in my breath with surprise. The short message had been constructed by cutting out printed words and letters from a newspaper or magazine, and spelled out the following, in an ungrammatical mixture of upper-case and lower-case letters.

Clifford has took the painting to sell for his self

Without commentating on this dramatic turn of events, Hester took out her powerful magnifying glass and gave the lettering thorough scrutiny. She then prised off the first letter, C, and held it up to the window. Hester then passed the sheet, envelope and separated letter to me.

'What is your opinion of this message?' she asked.

'If it is true, then of course the case is solved,' I said. 'However, I fail to see how or why Clifford would have stolen his own picture.'

'Oh, the how and why are easily explained. Firstly the "how": I am sure that you remember that Amos Clegg told us his employer was wearing an Inverness cape coat when he came out of the gallery and locked the door on that wet Monday evening. An Inverness is an excellent guard against bad weather, but in this case, Clifford may have chosen it for another reason. He is a big man, and the Leonardo is not a large painting: it measures sixteen by thirteen inches. He could easily have constructed a poacher's pocket on the inside of his cape coat, and carried the Leonardo away in it, unobserved. As to the "why": you remember that Clifford is selling the painting on behalf of a client, so if he fakes a theft, and secretly sells it on his *own* behalf, he stands to make a handsome profit. He may well need the money – remember that he has no family wealth to fall back upon. However, such speculation is pointless, since the message is obviously false, and designed to mislead us.'

'You surprise me!' I exclaimed. 'How can you be so sure?'

'The author has been rather too clever. They have tried to disguise themselves with semi-literate orthography – "has took" and "for his self". And yet the message has been gummed onto fine paper, and the letters themselves have come from a quality magazine. An ignoramus with a scanty grasp of English grammar would surely have constructed the message from newsprint and mounted it on cheap writing paper. Evidently, we have frightened someone into using this diversionary tactic.'

Hester rose and put the message into her writing table, then took up her box of cigarettes. It was evident to me that she felt the need to assist her mental processes with the stimulation of nicotine.

'Those lacquered boxes of Amos Clegg would make a fine receptacle for your cigarettes,' I said. 'You should ask him where they are sold. Although perhaps *papier-mâché* would be too insubstantial to preserve that strong Turkish flavour that so often permeates our rooms – or to survive Mrs Parsons' enthusiastic dusting.'

Hester was in the act of placing a cigarette into her ebony holder, but as I spoke she paused in a frozen tableau that was comical to observe. After a few seconds had passed, she spoke.

'Ivy, I have been a fool. The answer to this case has been in front of me the whole time. Where is my coat? I must …'

She was interrupted by a knock on the door. Mrs Parsons had brought us Dr Marriot's reply, which had arrived in the second post. Hester tore open the envelope and spread the letter in front of us. After the usual preliminaries, Marriot came quickly to the point.

> *… Steven Clegg is a capable student, but has found it difficult to adjust to Oxford life. His solution to his sense of inadequacy has been, I am sorry to say, to join a very fashionable set and attempt to buy his way into their favours. The result is that he is now in serious debt, even to the extent of bailiffs calling upon him in the college. I am sad to say that I anticipate his having to leave Balliol – and Oxford – unless some solution cannot quickly be found. Please treat this information in the strictest confidence …*

Hester rubbed her hands with satisfaction. 'That is the final piece of the puzzle. The case is now complete! Ivy, you will excuse my not revealing all, but time is now pressing. I am sure that I now know how the Leonardo was removed from the gallery – and by whom. However, a more urgent matter is to prevent it leaving the country. Has it occurred to you how difficult it is to dispose of such a well-known item?'

I thought for a moment. 'It would need to be sold to a private collector – one who did not exhibit his art to the public – possibly a foreigner.'

'Exactly, but in the first instance that would require a go-between. There are many dishonest men – and indeed women – willing to pay thieves for their valuables, but the market for stolen old masters is an esoteric one. There are only three people in England who would be capable of managing such a transaction. One of them lives in Yorkshire, so can probably be discounted in this instance. Another has recently returned from a spell in Dartmoor prison, so is likely to lie low for a while. The third, however, is likely to be our man: Count Otto von Salzburg. He is a minor Austrian nobleman, whose clients and contacts include some of the richest – and some of the most unscrupulous – men in Europe. He has made his home permanently in London, and has a splendid house in Hanover Terrace, overlooking Regent's Park. We must go there immediately, and hope that he is at home.'

'And will such a grand personage deign to see us without an appointment?' I asked. It seemed to me that in this case even Hester's fund of self-assurance might prove insufficient.

'When he reads what I will scribble on the back of my visiting card, I am sure he will,' Hester said with a smile. 'Ivy, while I summon a cab, would you please ask Mrs Parsons to prepare a simple dinner for four people, for seven o'clock this evening? With a bottle of the '76 Burgundy if we have any left in the cellar.'

'Are we to bring the count and his wife home with us?' I asked, facetiously.

Hester chuckled. 'I think not. Our linen and cutlery would hardly pass muster. If my scheme goes to plan, we will have more congenial guests to entertain.'

It was after mid-day by the time we reached Hanover Terrace, and I had visions of the count being dragged from his dinner to meet us – unless his servants sent us away first. This indeed seemed the most likely outcome after Hester marched up the marble steps that led to number 26. The door opened to reveal a butler of imposing size and even more impressive manner, reminiscent of a bishop about to admonish a lowly curate for drunkenness.

Hester held out her card, which he ignored.

'I am afraid it is not possible to see the count without an appointment,' he said. 'Perhaps you would like to write to his secretary, Mr Torridge, at this address.'

Hester smiled. 'Nevertheless, you will take our cards to your master immediately. Mine has a message written on the back. If, when he reads it, he wishes us to leave, then by all means return and tells us so.'

The butler appeared nonplussed, as if the presence of a determined and confident woman was alien to him. He did not invite us in, but left us on the threshold until he returned shortly afterwards, somewhat chagrined.

'Count von Salzburg can give you a few minutes of his time – if you will follow me, the count will receive you in his study.'

The butler led the way up three flights of a magnificent staircase, each landing surmounted by a glittering chandelier.'

I whispered to Hester. 'What did you write on your card?'

'Just a line asking von Salzburg if he had a Leonardo for sale,' she said.

I was puzzled. 'But if the count has obtained the painting, surely he would have ignored your message? Agreeing to see you is close to an admission of guilt.'

'The count will want to find out exactly what we know, even if his interest excites suspicion.'

The butler ushered us into Count von Salzburg's presence. He was sitting behind a desk of dark mahogany, and the same material had been used to line all four walls with bookshelves. He rose in his seat almost imperceptibly as we entered, pointing to two chairs at one side of the room, as Hester introduced us both by name.

'Do be seated. I must ask Miss Lynton: what is the meaning of your extraordinary message? If I *did* have a Leonardo painting to sell I would be delighted, but unfortunately that gentlemen is no longer taking commissions.'

As von Salzburg was speaking, I scrutinised him carefully. There was something unmistakably foreign about his appearance. It was an effect derived from a combination of his jet black, glistening hair, liberally coated with Macassar oil, a small, clipped goatee beard and a quilted velvet smoking jacket, of a shade somewhere between puce and purple.

Hester sat up in her chair. 'I know that you are a busy man, so will get straight to the point. Last Tuesday morning – three days ago – a Leonardo was found to be missing from the Ronsard Gallery, near Portland Place. Leonardo worked in many different forms, but a moment ago you correctly identified the missing item to be a *painting*: the *Portrait of Catherine*

Nogarola. I believe that it is very likely that this painting was passed to you for disposal, and so we have come to you with a proposition. I suspect that you still have the painting, as a buyer for such a work is not easily found, even for someone with your enviable connections. I am here to request that you return it to me – in exchange for the money you paid for it. After all, the transaction will not leave you out of pocket.'

The count rose from his chair and stepped towards a red and gold bell rope, no doubt to summon his imposing butler. 'If that is what you have come to tell me, Miss Lynton, there is no point in prolonging this interview. Even if I *did* possess the Leonardo – which I deny – why would I give it back to the seller, and forgo the opportunity to make a handsome profit?'

Hester got to her feet. 'Because I am sure that I can persuade the person that sold it to you to have a change of heart, and admit the whole transaction to the police.'

The count shook his head. 'That will not do, Miss Lynton. You play a poor hand of cards very well, but you hold no trumps. I could simple deny such an accusation, as there is no evidence against me.'

'There is one thing more – your supplier will also confess to another crime – he took your money under false pretences.'

The count looked perplexed. 'I do not understand.'

'You were not given the stolen Leonardo. The painting you received was a clever forgery.'

'Nonsense!' the count cried. 'I examined it carefully. It is oil on wood, and the wooden board was ancient.'

As the count spoke, he retreated to the chair behind his desk, having evidently decided not to ring the bell after all. Hester continued.

'I am sure that the *board* is genuine,' Hester said. 'The forger probably sacrificed another Renaissance painting – hopefully a much inferior example – and painted over it. Of course, you could employ an expert to determine the matter for you, but it would be difficult to explain how you obtained the picture, were it found to be genuine. And more importantly, think what will happen when word gets out – and I will ensure that it *does* get out. Who will want to buy the Leonardo from you, when there is a question mark over its provenance?'

Count von Salzburg shuffled the papers on his desk as if abstracted. When he looked up, his voice had taken on an unpleasant tone.

'This is all very clever, Miss Lynton. It is clear that your reputation is not unearned. But there is one further matter for you to consider. If your meddling results in my losing a very substantial profit, that is not something which I could ignore. There are many dangers in London to threaten the unwary. Why, you might fall into the path of a carriage – or under the wheels of a train – or be attacked by a common street-robber. Think of your safety before you proceed any further in this matter.'

I was shocked by this blatant threat to my friend's welfare. Clearly, von Salzburg was a far more dangerous man than he at first appeared. However, I need not have worried: Hester's combination of strong nerve and quick wits proved more than enough for him.

Hester spoke calmly, her eyes never leaving the count's face.

'Really, Count von Salzburg, I am surprised that you resort to such bluster. It has convinced me that the Leonardo is in your possession. I suspect that you are unaware that I am the cousin of Inspector Albert Brasher, an inspector in the Metropolitan Police, and his only living relative. Now, the English police have a well-earned reputation for always acting within the law, however great the provocation. Nevertheless there is one exception to this rule which is well understood by the criminal classes. Any violent assault on a police officer – or a member of his family – is dealt with in summary fashion, without troubling judge or jury. I assure you that Albert knows all about my visit to you today. He will say nothing about it to his superiors. However, were any kind of harm conveniently to befall me, then I would not wish to be in your shoes. You would be arrested, ostensibly for questioning, followed by – for example – a fatal fall down a flight of stone steps to the cells, or a regrettable suicide via a convenient upstairs window. So, here is my proposal once more. I will bring you the money you paid for the forged Leonardo – hopefully later tonight – you will give me the painting, and with luck we will never have to meet again.'

The count stared into the middle distance, his eyes unfocused and a look of subdued resignation on his face. 'Very well. It seems that I have no alternative. If you can give me your word that my part in this affair will never be revealed, I will give you the Leonardo when you call upon me with the money. I wish to God I had never set sight on it, fake or genuine.'

In the hansom on the way back to 12 Newsome Street, we sat quietly for some minutes, until I broke the silence.

'Hester, I have to say that you have excelled yourself! Count von Salzburg seemed to have aged ten years in as many minutes. If he was not such a despicable man, I would feel sorry for the poor fellow. But tell me, was the Leonardo he purchased from the thief really a forgery? And have you told your cousin about your suspicions of the count?'

Hester leant back in her seat with an expression that could only be described as self-satisfied.

'Thank you for the compliment. I must say, that was a very satisfactory interview. But to answer your questions: there is no reason to believe that the Leonardo that he has obtained is anything other than genuine – my suggestion was only a ploy to disturb his equanimity. There is nothing that frightens an art dealer – honest or dishonest – more than any suggestion of forgery. As to my cousin, I have not spoken to him since he asked us to look into the case. Now, I see we are almost home. Our day has been somewhat hectic thus far – I suggest a quiet afternoon is in order, before our visitors arrive.'

When we reached home, Hester asked the cab driver to wait while she scribbled a note, which she then asked him to deliver for her. I guessed it was the invitation to our mystery guests, but I refrained from asking Hester who was coming to supper. I was well used to her love of theatrical surprises – one of her very few foibles. Given her declaration earlier in the day – that the case was solved – I anticipated an interesting evening.

A minute or two after the appointed hour we hear the distant ringing of the electric doorbell, followed shortly afterwards by the sound of footsteps on the stairs. I could only guess that Hester had invited Albert Brasher and Arthur Clifford, in order to expound her solution of the case, but that theory tuned to dust as the door opened and Amos Clegg walked in, looking around him anxiously. A moment later he was followed by a woman of about his age, whom I had never seen before. She wore a tailor-made costume of dark woollen cloth, more suited to a business meeting than an informal dinner, and seemed rather more at ease than her husband.

Hester stepped towards the woman with a welcoming smile. 'Mrs Clegg – let me introduce you to my friend and colleague, Miss Ivy Jessop.'

I spoke without thinking. 'Oh – I thought you were in Torquay – that is ...'

'A small misunderstanding,' Hester interrupted. 'Now, Mr and Mrs Clegg, I must admit having indulged in a certain subterfuge. You were invited for dinner at seven o'clock, but I have asked Mrs Parsons to serve our meal at half past seven. I thought we should settle any little matters between us before we sit down – I am sure that we will enjoy our meal all the better for it.'

'Hester, we are forgetting out duties towards our visitors,' I said. 'Can we offer you any refreshment? Port, sherry, whisky perhaps?'

'I will thank you for a sherry,' Mrs Clegg said. 'And if I'm right about your purpose in bringing us here, perhaps Amos should have a whisky to fortify himself. A large one.'

I looked at Mrs Clegg with new-found interest – she was clearly a woman of spirit. I could not help wishing that Hester had given me some hint of what was about to come, but doubtless all would soon be revealed.

As soon as I had handed round the drinks, Hester began.

'As you may have guessed, I have asked you both here to discuss the disappearance of the Leonardo painting that went missing from the Ronsard Gallery last Tuesday. Firstly, I have an important question for Mr Clegg. If anything can be done to help you and your wife in your current difficult situation, it is important that you answer me truthfully. How much were you paid by Count Otto von Salzburg in return for the Leonardo painting – and just as importantly, how much, if any, of the money still remains in your hands?'

Amos Clegg took a large swig of the whisky which his wife had prescribed so presciently, then set his glass back on the side-table with a heavy thud. 'It seems your reputation is well deserved, Miss Lynton. I suppose you know everything? The count gave me £200 in bank notes, and that's the honest truth. I received them from him on Tuesday night, and the money is still in an envelope under the carpet in our spare bedroom – I counted it, of course. Dorothy – my wife – will confirm what I say.'

Mrs Clegg nodded. 'You see, the money was not for ourselves, Miss Lynton. The fact is, our son Steven has behaved foolishly, and is heavily in debt.'

'And Mr Clegg had planned to go up to Oxford and pay off the debts in person?' Hester asked. 'I dare say you felt that if Steven received it directly, it might never reach the intended destinations.'

At this point my growing impatience became too much for me.

'Forgive me,' I said with a smile. 'I believe that I am the only person in this room who does not know how the business was managed. Unless Mr and Mrs Clegg have supernatural powers, I do not see how the Leonardo was abstracted.'

'Let me explain,' Hester said. 'Our guests can correct me if I am wrong in any particular. Firstly, it was clear that the painting must have left the gallery by way of one of the windows – in fact through the window that was nearest to the place where the Leonardo was hung. Ivy, do you remember the dark spots on the floorboards under that window? They were droplets of oil. Whoever had planned to push the painting through the vent wanted to make sure that it opened silently, and had previously oiled it. Now, I realised that it was impossible for the stolen Leonardo to be removed in that fashion. Therefore, the painting that was stolen was not the Leonardo – it was a cleverly constructed copy which was designed for that very purpose. You will recall the *papier-mâché* boxes in our guest's house.'

I began to understand. 'You mean it was a *papier-mâché* painting?'

Amos Clegg interrupted. 'Not the painting – the frame only. The painting was done on a sheet of thin card, in oil. It took me six weeks to do, and I must admit I was sorry to have to tear it up.'

Hester continued the explanation. 'Mr Clegg had less than a minute to remove the fake painting, and executed the task perfectly. After pulling the fragile frame to pieces he ripped up the card and stuffed everything into a suitable receptacle.'

'A tubular cotton bag – I sewed it myself,' Mrs Clegg interjected with a distinct note of pride in her voice.

'Precisely. Unfortunately, in his haste, your husband let a scrap of painted card fall to the gallery floor, where I later discovered it. Your plan was an excellent one. It was fortunate that after we had visited you, Ivy made a comment about the fragility of your boxes, which made me realise that a similar structure could have framed the missing painting. You were careless in one thing, Mr Clegg – you needed a heavy weight to ensure that the cloth bag fell straight down from the window when you posted it through the window vent, and bought a set of scales for the purpose. Your mistake was to leave the remaining weights in your workshop. The weighted bag left a distinctive mark on the muddy yard below – as did your wife's footprints.'

The rest of the Clegg's ingenious scheme was now clear to me.

'So Mrs Clegg was waiting in the yard under the gallery window?' I asked.

'I was indeed', she replied. 'Fortunately it is overlooked only by offices, and we gambled that no one would be peering out at that time in the morning. Incidentally – it was Amos who decided to say that I was away from home when you both called to see us. He hoped that if his crime was discovered, he could keep me out of it. But I've told him – I must take my punishment was well as him. Have you informed the police, Miss Lynton? If so, I'm surprised we are not already under arrest.'

Hester leant forward and placed a reassuring hand on Mrs Clegg's arm.

'I hope that will not be necessary. No harm has been done. I take it, Mr Clegg, that you were responsible for the anonymous note stating that Arthur Clifford had taken the painting to sell for himself? You are fortunate that your attempt to throw suspicion upon your employer was unsuccessful. It would have thought that such a mean-spirited action was beneath you. Fortunately your clumsy attempt to masquerade as an illiterate was very obviously a fake. This is what I propose. I already know that Count von Salzburg is prepared to give the Leonardo back to me if he receives his £200. In fact, he is expecting me this evening. Therefore, after our dinner I will travel back with you to West Holloway for the money, then on to Hanover Terrace to collect the painting. Tomorrow I will inform the Honourable Arthur Clifford that the painting has been mysteriously returned to our doorstep. And that can be the end of the matter.'

My friend's announcement came as little surprise to me. There had been several occasions in the past where we had found that a crime had been committed, but where none had suffered in consequence, and the harsh penalties of the law would have seemed excessive. In addition, it seemed hardly likely that Mr and Mrs Clegg would ever offend again.

'I don't know what to say ...' Amos Clegg stuttered.

'Then there is no more to be said. There is nothing to be gained by ruining your lives, when you were acting only with your son's welfare in mind. Amos must remain in his position at the gallery, and you must both never speak of this unfortunate episode again.'

'But what of our poor Steven?' Mrs Clegg said quietly.

Hester stood up and rand the bell to summon Mrs Parsons.

'Take my advice, and let young Steven suffer the consequences of his actions. If you had paid off his debts, what lesson would he have learned? Only that he could behave foolishly with impunity. If he is sent down from Oxford, he can still succeed in life – he has his father's example in front of him, after all. Now, Mrs Parsons will shortly be arriving with a linen cloth to grace our humble table. I understand that we are to be regaled with a boiled leg of mutton and vegetables, cold game pie, and a cabinet pudding. I hope you will join me in a glass of Burgundy, to toast the recovery of the Leonardo!'

All went according to plan, and the next day a delighted – if somewhat puzzled – Arthur Clifford took possession of his valuable painting. He expressed his intention to send his thanks for Hester's intervention to Inspector Brasher immediately, and we were therefore not surprised when later that day Hester's cousin came to call.

'And so the painting just happened to appear on your doorstep this morning?' he asked.

'That is correct,' Hester said, 'There was a ring on the bell, but by the time I answered it – our housekeeper had the morning off – the street was clear. As I was only in dressing gown and slippers, it seemed foolish to race off in pursuit, as the person could have gone left or right. The Leonardo was wrapped in plain brown paper done up with stationer's twine, with no clue as to who had left it.'

'Well – I said this was a rum case at the start, and I've been proved right. Why in heaven's name do you think someone left you such a treasure?'

'I can think of only one explanation. I imagine that the thief got wind of my involvement in the case, and knowing something of my reputation, they decided to return the painting before their inevitable discovery.'

Albert chuckled. 'Hester, I can forgive you your vanity, given that you've come up with the goods. Mind you – I can't help feeling there's more to this business than you've told me. However, there's that old saying about letting sleeping dogs lie, which I think in this case I agree with.'

3. The Case of the Missing Professor

Looking through the records of the cases in which Hester and I were involved over the years, it is evident that several of the most dramatic were brought to us – directly or indirectly – by Mr Jonathan Carroll. He was a friend of my late father; they attended Rugby School together, and went up to the same Oxford college. Although their careers had subsequently moved in very different directions – my father's to a rural curacy, Jonathan's to a senior post in the Foreign Office – he and his wife had always taken a benevolent interest in my welfare. And, since my residence at 12 Newsome Street, Jonathan had also developed a healthy respect for Hester's talents as a consulting detective.

Thus, when Hester received a note from him one morning in early May, 1885, it did not come as a great surprise to either of us.

My friend passed the letter to me across the breakfast table.

'This was delivered by messenger at eight o'clock this morning,' she said. 'Dated today, on Foreign Office notepaper. Mrs Parsons has informed me that the messenger was a polite young man, dressed like an office clerk. Mr Carroll has evidently had this sent round from Whitehall. Dear me, he must have been at his desk at an unnaturally early hour! What do you make of it, Ivy?'

I scanned the brief message. Jonathan said that he had taken the liberty of arranging an appointment that evening between Hester and me and a gentleman from the War Office, Mr Gilbert Wilson. Mr Wilson was to call on us at seven o'clock – if that was inconvenient, we could send a note to him at 66 Pall Mall, specifying an alternative time. I read out the concluding sentence:

'Rest assured that I would have called upon you myself, if I were not impossibly busy at present. I will not elaborate further, except to say that

I have asked Mr Gilbert to seek your advice and assistance on a matter of great importance. Yours, etc …'

I passed the paper back to Hester. 'It seems that Jonathan has introduced us to what promises to be an interesting case. What do you think Mr Gilbert wants?'

Hester smiled. 'I will not hypothesise in the absence of evidence. However, there is one indication. Are you aware who occupies 66 Pall Mall?'

I shook my head.

'It is a War Office establishment, and houses the Directorate of Military Intelligence. I believe that the current director, Colonel Hubert Crawshaw, reports directly to Jonathan on matters of national importance. Whatever Mr Wilson wants from us, I suspect that it is not a request to recover a stolen bicycle.'

Our housekeeper, Mrs Parsons, had arranged to visit her niece in Ealing that evening, so when we were summoned by the distant pealing of the electric bell, Hester and I both descended the stairs to greet our visitor.

We ushered Mr Wilson into the hallway. He was a tall young man of no more than thirty years of age, with an air of confidence and affability; a typical product of the better sort of English public school. Hester insisted on taking his silver-topped walking stick and tall crowned bowler hat before we accompanied him upstairs to our rooms. He carried a brown leather briefcase.

'Do sit down, Mr Wilson,' Hester said. 'Mrs Parsons is not here to make us tea, but can I offer you something a little stronger?' She pointed towards the bottles that stood upon a low table near the fireplace. 'Miss Jessop and I keep a modest supply for those of our clients who are not strict teetotallers.'

Our visitor seemed pleasantly surprised. 'Well – that is very hospitable. A small whisky and soda, perhaps.'

As he settled in his chair and raised the tumbler to his lips, I observed him closely, whilst making every effort not to be too obvious in my scrutiny. His clothes – a tight-fitting morning coat, slender pinstriped trousers and high starched collar – indicated a man who had both the means and the inclination to be at the forefront of fashion. As Hester spoke, I noticed that his eyes darted round the room as if absorbing every detail.

'Allow me to introduce you to my secretary and colleague, Miss Ivy Jessop,' Hester said, nodding in my direction. 'No doubt Mr Carroll has informed you that Miss Jessop and I work as a team. It is hardly necessary to say that any information that you give us will be treated in the strictest confidence. Now, if you will tell us exactly how we can help you, I would be most grateful. You may wish to begin by explaining whom – or what – you represent.'

Wilson took a card case from the pocket of his waistcoat, extracted a card and passed it to Hester. She read it and then handed it to me. The name *Mr Gilbert Horatio Wilson* was embossed in a fine copperplate print, and under it was inscribed *Personal Assistant to Colonel Crawshaw.*

Wilson cleared his throat. 'I will explain everything. Colonel Crawshaw is my superior at the War Office, and I am here on his behalf. The facts are these. We are most anxious to trace the whereabouts of Ambrose Dixon, a sixty-eight-year-old gentleman who is Professor Emeritus at the West Kensington Technical Institute. For the last six months, he has been engaged in work on behalf of the War Office, and been based at Aldershot army camp. He was last seen twenty days ago, on the evening of Friday the seventeenth of April, by his housekeeper in London. It is the professor's habit to lodge at the camp during the week, and travel home to his house in Bloomsbury at weekends – usually, he goes back on a Friday, but sometimes on a Thursday. He was supposed to return to Aldershot on the following Monday, but did not arrive. We have, of course, interviewed his housekeeper, who informs us that the professor did not come down to breakfast on the Saturday morning. When she knocked at his bedroom door, she received no reply and when she entered, found it empty, although his bed had been slept in. He had taken no clothes, luggage or other belongings – he also left his bank book and a small sum in cash behind. She has not seen or heard from him since. We have spoken to his bankers, and the professor has withdrawn no money since his disappearance ...'

Hester interrupted; 'And have the Metropolitan Police carried out their investigations in the manner usual to such circumstances? Surely they would be your first port of call, rather than a private detective such as myself?'

For a moment, Wilson's urbanity seemed to desert him, and a fleeting expression of discomfort disturbed his features. 'Given the sensitive nature of the case, it was decided that the War Office would carry out its own enquiries. Several competent investigators from our department have been employed upon the task. I can assure you that we have done all that the police would have done. I have been authorised to give you this photograph of the professor – it was taken just over a year ago.'

Wilson opened his briefcase and took out a cabinet photograph of Professor Dixon amongst a group of colleagues wearing academic dress. He had a somewhat old-fashioned full beard, streaked with grey, and wore a pince-nez secured by a chain. His eyes were piercing and intelligent. Hester took the picture and Wilson continued.

'Unfortunately, Professor Dixon is reclusive to the point of eccentricity. He has an elderly sister in Islington whom he last saw in early March this year, and no other known friends or relatives to whom we could talk. He normally spends his weekends in his study or library. We found nothing in his London house or Aldershot quarters that might give any clue as to his whereabouts. His former colleagues at the West Kensington Institute – where he still has a small office, and occasionally uses the laboratory facilities – have not seen him since the end of January this year.'

Hester frowned. 'I can quite see your difficulty. But precisely why is it so urgent that the professor be found? Is foul play suspected? He does not seem a person who would accrue many enemies. And it is as yet no crime in England to disappear without notice, should one wish to do so.'

Once more, our visitor betrayed a fleeting anxiety. 'We believe that Professor Dixon has in his possession a document that absolutely must not fall into the wrong hands. I am afraid I am not authorised to tell you more. If you can find the professor, I am sure that we can recover the document. Are you able to help us with this matter?'

'Very possibly,' Hester said. 'However, in order to do so I will need to speak to your superior. I am sure Colonel Crawshaw will be happy to tell us the rest of the story. Ivy, if you would be good enough to consult our diary?'

I reached for the slim leather volume and took it down from the bookshelves. 'You have a meeting with Inspector Brasher at Scotland Yard in the morning, to discuss the Simpson case. The afternoon is free.'

Hester stood up. 'Very well. Mr Wilson, if you could inform Colonel Crawshaw that we will arrive at 66 Pall Mall tomorrow at three o'clock,

I would be grateful. Perhaps he could send us a message if that is inconvenient? Now, another whisky before you go?'

Wilson pulled a wafer-thin gold watch out of his waistcoat pocket. 'Alas, I have another appointment to keep. But thank you for your kindness. I will relay your message to Colonel Crawshaw; I am sure he will be glad to see you at that time. Oh – and one further thing. If you are successful in locating the professor, please ensure that I am the first to know. It is most important that you give the information directly to me, with no intermediary. The desk clerk at 66 Pall Mall will always be able to find me.'

After we had shown our visitor to the door, Hester turned to me with a smile. 'What did you make of him, Ivy?'

'A very polished gentleman,' I said. 'And you?'

'He is certainly an interesting study – and not entirely what I might have expected. However, I now understand why Jonathan recommended that Colonel Crawshaw should seek our help. The only two people who had any significant contact with Professor Dixon appear to be his sister and his housekeeper. If all the personnel employed by the War Office are like Mr Wilson, I can see why those two ladies might have been less than forthcoming. Jonathan must think that our feminine charms will achieve more than official gravitas can. And now, if you will find me the file on the Simpson case, I will refresh my memory before meeting Albert tomorrow morning. When I see him I shall mention another matter, which I need him to look into.'

I knew better than to ask Hester precisely what she had in mind. Her cousin, Albert Brasher – a Metropolitan Police inspector – was in the habit of consulting her about particularly intractable cases. I could see that, on this occasion, he would be asked to return the favour.

Having heard nothing to the contrary from Colonel Crawshaw, the following afternoon Hester and I took a hansom from our lodgings and were soon on our way to Pall Mall. As we stepped down outside the impressive frontage of number 66, Hester consulted her pocket watch.

'It is almost three o'clock. I wonder how long Colonel Crawshaw will see fit to keep us waiting? I would guess fifteen minutes.'

'Why fifteen minutes, Hester?' I asked.

'Any sooner would suggest an undignified desire to see us. Any longer would be too obviously impolite.'

In the end, we waited in an oak-panelled anteroom until twenty past three before being ushered into a spacious office. As Hester later remarked, on our way back to Newsome Street, Colonel Crawshaw bore a striking resemblance to the German chancellor, Otto von Bismarck; an impression reinforced by a decided air of self-importance. He dismissed his attendant with wave of his hand.

'Do sit down, ladies. As you know I am Colonel Hubert Crawshaw – but you have the advantage of me. Which of you is Miss Lynton?'

'I am Miss Hester Lynton – this is my secretary and colleague, Miss Ivy Jessop. Now, I am sure that Mr Wilson has passed on to you my request for the fullest possible information regarding Professor Dixon, if we are to help your department find him.'

Colonel Crawshaw smiled graciously. 'He has, but I am afraid that I can tell you no more than Wilson has already confided. You know the circumstances of Dixon's disappearance, and are aware that he has a document in his possession which the War Office is most anxious to obtain. Of course, we are not asking you to find the document – the professor will tell us where it is, if we can locate him. I suppose you will start by interviewing Dixon's housekeeper? Our men got very little out of her.'

Hester stood up. 'Colonel Crawshaw, I am not in the habit of having my time wasted. Other, more deserving clients may have use for my services. I was asked to help you by my friend Mr Jonathan Carroll. I understand that Mr Carroll is your superior, and that as the head of Military Intelligence you report directly to him. I will have to tell Jonathan that you are unable to cooperate fully with my investigation. Come, Ivy – we can find out own way out.'

This time, it was the director who got to his feet. His face was flushed, and I could see that he was grappling with an unusual experience – being reprimanded by a woman.

'Miss Lynton, I apologise. Please be seated. You are, of course, quite correct. I will tell you everything. The professor's field is industrial chemistry, and over the years he has done important work for the War Office – most notably, the design of a very effective type of signal flare, now in general use by the British Army. Since last November, Professor Dixon has been developing a new and very powerful explosive, using the ordnance laboratory facilities at Aldershot. The first large-scale test took place on the morning of Friday the seventeenth of April – the day of the professor's disappearance.'

'And was it successful?' I asked.

'Remarkably successful – as you can see.'

Colonel Crawshaw slid open a drawer of his desk. He took out two large photographs and passed them to me. Hester stood and looked over my shoulder. The first photograph showed a substantial windowless brick-built structure with a flat roof, about the size of a small cottage. A soldier stood next to it, to indicate the scale. The second showed the remains of the building, which would have been unrecognisable had we not seen the first illustration. Jumbled brickwork surrounded a crater, which must have been at least twelve feet in diameter.

'That was the result of the detonation of just five pounds of Dixon's new explosive,' Colonel Crawshaw said.

'A suitable weight for a field-gun shell,' Hester said.

Colonel Crawshaw nodded. 'Indeed. Now, you can see how concerned we are at the professor's disappearance. Without Dixon we have no means of obtaining the formula for his new munition.'

Observing my puzzled expression, the director continued. 'Professor Ambrose Dixon is a brilliant man, but he is also reclusive and eccentric. He has always insisted on carrying out his researches completely unassisted and unobserved. He kept all his notes and papers in a safe in his laboratory, locking them up at the end of the day. When he did not arrive at work on Monday the twentieth of April, after waiting until noon I ordered his safe forced open. It was empty.'

'The contents must amount to a good deal of paperwork,' Hester said. 'Hardly convenient for a fugitive to carry around.'

'He may not have needed to. In the case of his last project – the signal flare – when Dixon had completed his researches, he recorded the final formula for the chemicals used and the key features of the manufacturing process on three sheets of foolscap. If he has followed the same method this time, he could have hidden, or indeed destroyed, the bulk of the papers and kept the essential details on his person. Incidentally, you need to be aware that Dixon's eccentricity extended to personally typing his most important papers – having first rendered them into a personal code.'

'But surely some indication of the composition could have been gained by an examination of his laboratory – what chemicals he had ordered, and so on?' I said.

Colonel Crawshaw seemed surprised at my suggestion. 'That is an excellent point, Miss Jessop. However, it seems that Dixon might have anticipated such an investigation. A very large variety of chemicals was ordered by him over the last six months, including many with no conceivable application to the manufacture of explosives. He has been careful to open and partly use all of the shipments. There are really no clues to be had in that direction. Of course we also have the residue of the test carried out on the Aldershot range, but I have been assured that no chemist could reconstruct the original compound from the oxidised traces that remain.'

'Thank you, Colonel Crawshaw, that has been most helpful,' Hester said. 'Incidentally, after Mr Wilson left us yesterday it occurred to me that I may have met him before. Has he been in your employment long?'

'He has been my personal assistant for just over a year. He applied for the post having returned from South Africa. A very competent young man, and an old Etonian, like me. His employers in Cape Town provided a glowing testimonial. Where do you think you may have met him?

'I thought it was at a reception some years ago, but I am probably mistaken. Now, if you can supply us with the information that your investigators have gathered thus far in their interviews with the professor's servants and with his sister, and anything they may have unearthed regarding his habits and friends, we will trouble you no longer. Ivy and I will start with a visit to his London address.'

That evening, after we had both had the opportunity to read through the investigators' files that Colonel Crawshaw had provided for us, Hester threw down the last report with annoyance.

'Really, Professor Dixon must be one of the most boring men in London. I suppose it was too much to hope that he had an expensive mistress maintained at his expense in Belgravia – or that he was an enthusiastic anarchist or revolutionary. However, I had expected more than this. The last time that he travelled further than his London house or Aldershot laboratory appears to be on the sixth of March, when he went to spend the weekend with his sister, Mrs Clark, in Islington – that is, unless we include his regular attendance at church on Sunday mornings. As Mr Wilson has already informed us, Dixon appears to have no friends or other relatives. The key to solving this mystery is to discover the professor's motive for disappearing with the formula.'

'And what is your opinion, Hester?' I asked.

My friend took down her long ebony cigarette holder from the mantlepiece and opened the wooden box containing her favourite brand. Although I could not pretend that I liked the smell of Turkish tobacco, I could hardly complain; Hester had few other habits that might be considered objectionable and she invariably smoked when a more than usually difficult problem was presented to her agile mind for analysis. I could not help smiling at the incongruity of the spirals of pungent smoke that surrounded her elegant features. After a few more contemplative puffs, she answered my question.

'Any kind of theory would be premature, given our current lack of knowledge. This is what I propose. Tomorrow morning we will visit Mrs Cooper, the professor's housekeeper, in Bloomsbury, then we will seek out the vicar of his local church – as it seems that no one from the War Office has spoken to him. After that, we may need to see the professor's sister in Islington. Ah – are those Mrs Parsons' footsteps that I hear approaching? I have reason to believe that she has provided a sea bass for our dinner. If it is true that fish enhances the mental processes, then she has made a fortunate choice, given the task that faces us.'

The professor's address turned out to be a well-kept Georgian townhouse. A small flight of stone steps led up to the glossy front door, framed on each side by a neatly clipped box tree. I was just about to ring the bell when the door opened, to reveal a stout, sombrely-dressed woman of about fifty years of age with a large wicker basket over her arm.

'Mrs Cooper?' Hester asked. Before the woman could reply, Hester continued. 'I can see that you are about to visit the shops. We had come to consult you on a matter regarding your missing employer, Professor

Dixon, but I would not wish to interrupt your errand. Perhaps my colleague and I could return to see you this afternoon?' As she spoke, Hester held out her card.

I had often observed how my friend's natural good manners and thoughtfulness, offered to all irrespective of social standing, achieved much more than might have been gained by a more forthright approach.

'Yes, I'm Mrs Cooper.' The housekeeper took Hester's card and squinted at it myopically. She read the inscription aloud, with the deliberation often seen in those whose literacy is not the strongest.

'"Miss Hester Lynton … Consulting Detective, 12 Newsome Street, London". No, miss, you are kind, but I'm happy to see you now. My bit of shopping can easily wait. If you have anything to tell me about the professor, I'll be glad to hear it.'

At Hester's insistence, Mrs Cooper took us into the kitchen rather than the drawing room, and before long the three of us were comfortably seated around a large pine table, enjoying a cup of strong tea. Hester introduced me to the housekeeper, then took out a pocketbook from her handbag.

'I must apologise for the intrusion, given that you have already spoken to a gentleman from the, erm, government. If you could just confirm the facts as I understand them, I would be grateful.'

Hester summarised what we had already learned from Gilbert Wilson and Colonel Hubert Crawshaw, regarding Professor Dixon's disappearance.

Mrs Cooper took a fortifying sip of tea. 'Yes, that's all true, miss. I haven't set eyes on Professor Dixon since that Friday night – the seventeenth of April, as you say. There's only me and the housemaid, Elsie Pine, that lives in – I do all the cooking, what there is of it. Then there's the cleaner, Mrs Strettle, who comes in four mornings a week – she does the washing as well. If you want to speak to Elsie or our cleaner …'

Hester shook her head. 'That will not be necessary. Now, I understand from the gentlemen who visited you that when you examined the professor's rooms after his appearance, you found that he had taken no luggage, extra clothes or other belongings with him?'

'That's true, miss. No *outdoor* clothes, at any rate. Although I have since realised that some of his things seem to have gone. I suppose he must have taken them.'

Hester's eyes narrowed, and she leant forward. 'Tell me exactly what is missing. It could be very important.'

The housekeeper looked a little flustered. 'Three sets of his linen undergarments, two nightshirts and a dressing gown. Oh – and his smoking jacket.'

Hester glanced at me quizzically. 'I see. And where does the professor keep his luggage?'

'He keeps his leather suitcase – the one he uses when he travels to and from Aldershot – in his dressing room. It's still there. The rest of the luggage is kept in the box room on the second floor, but none is missing. The government gentlemen checked on that, too.'

Hester turned towards me. 'Colonel Crawshaw's men seem to be very competent. Now, Mrs Cooper, you have been very helpful. I have just a few further questions for you before we leave you in peace. Firstly, how did the professor's mood strike you on the Friday evening? Did he seem at all anxious, or behave in any way out of the ordinary?'

Mrs Cooper put down her teacup and thought for a moment. 'That's rather hard to say, miss. You see, Professor Dixon is a such a quiet man, it's hard to say what he's thinking. Although he did do something a bit strange a couple of weeks before he disappeared, now I come to think of it. He normally gives me £15 cash in advance on the first of every month for all the day-to-day household expenses – and the wages for me, Elsie and the cleaner – and I keep all the accounts, showing what's been spent. But last time, on the first of April, he told me he wanted to change the system. He said he had arranged with his bank – Hepplewhite's – that I should collect the £15 directly from them. He gave me a letter that I had to show to the clerk.'

'That is interesting. Now, I understand that Professor Dixon spends most of his time at home – that is, when he is not at Aldershot. Are you aware of any visits he paid in London in the two weeks before he disappeared? Please think carefully.'

'Well, miss … let me see. He always went to the ten o'clock service at St Timothy's on Sunday mornings – that's the church on the corner of Gower Street. And the week before he disappeared, he came back to London on Thursday evening, because he had an appointment with his doctor on the Friday morning.'

Hester nodded. 'We know about his regular church attendance. As for his medical appointments – would you by any chance know the name of his doctor?'

'As it happens, yes, miss. It wasn't his *regular* doctor – that would be Dr

Smethwick, who has a practice near here. The doctor he saw that Friday is called Sir Steven Lansdowne. I remember it because I'd been given a message from him for the professor, and I thought it strange that a doctor should be a titled gentleman, but the professor told me that in Harley Street it was not unusual. It wasn't the first time he'd seen him, either.'

'And do you know the reason for his doctor's appointment?' I asked.

'Yes, miss. The professor made no secret of it. He's suffered from lumbago for years. It was so bad last winter that he even used a walking stick for a while. Dr Smethwick prescribed him a tonic, but it didn't seem to do much good.'

After we had thanked the housekeeper and were ready to leave, she paused with us at the doorway.

'Begging your pardon, miss, but there is something I'd like to ask you. Should I keep taking the £15 that the professor allows me each month? What if he never comes back? Me and Elsie can't hardly live here for ever, it wouldn't seem right to be earning his money for nothing.'

'You are an honest woman,' Hester said. 'My friend and I are seeing the professor's sister later today. I shall ask her to write to you, but I am sure she will wish you to continue living here and looking after the house for at least the next few months. After all, Professor Dixon might return at any time. He would not wish to find his house cold and empty.'

The Reverend George Wilkes turned out to be an amiable clergyman who was happy to discuss his parishioner.

'I am sorry to hear that Ambrose Dixon has gone missing,' the vicar said. 'I guessed something must have happened, as it is most unusual for him to miss a service. And you are looking into his disappearance? I must admit I have not been questioned by lady detectives before – or gentleman detectives, come to that.'

'Never fear,' Hester said with a smile, 'we are not here to arrest you. Now, concerning Professor Dixon. Did he give you any cause to think that something was amiss?'

'You are fortunate that his faith is Church of England, rather than Roman Catholic like his sister! That is, I am not bound by any secrets of the confession. As a matter of fact he *did* confide in me the last time I spoke to him – after the morning service the last time I saw him, on the twelfth of April. He asked me a question of an ethical nature. He phrased it hypothetically, but it was clear that it pertained to his own situation. If someone had made a discovery which could be of great benefit to their country, but could also – if misused – cause great harm, should they conceal what they had found out? I told him that he should pray for guidance and then do what he felt right. No doubt you two ladies will consider that to be rather an evasive answer.'

'Not at all, Reverend,' I replied. 'After all, you have directed Professor Dixon to the highest possible authority. Who could have done more than that?'

When we secured a hansom outside St Timothy's church, Hester asked the cab driver to take us to Harley Street.

'We have no appointment, but I am hopeful that Sir Steven Lansdowne will agree to see us. We will wait if necessary. Tell me, Ivy, what do you make of our interviews with Mrs Cooper and the Reverend Wilkes? Have they illuminated our case at all?'

It was a habit of Hester's to ask me for my theories about a developing case, whilst at the same time remaining very uncommunicative about her own conclusions. Perhaps some would have found this trait to be irritating – however, I was always happy to tell her my thoughts, and flattered myself that in some cases they provided a stimulus to Hester's rather more profound ruminations.

'Here is my hypothesis, Hester. Ambrose Dixon was clearly worried about the nature of his researches. A signal flare is one thing – a new and enormously powerful explosive, quite another. He must have considered for some time the need to cover his tracks – hence his clever purchase of a large variety of chemicals. I believe that following the shockingly successful test of his invention, he finally decided that the army should *not* have the formula. He has therefore destroyed all records of his work, and left London for ever. Why, I expect that even as we speak, he is half way to the Orient or the Americas. He has no one, except possibly his sister, to regret his absence. He knows that if Colonel Crawshaw and his men catch up with him, he will be placed under great pressure to reveal his secret.'

Hester turned towards me and clapped her hands. 'Bravo, Ivy! You have certainly captured a large part of the truth. However, there are some other aspects of the story which have yet to be understood. For example: why, according to Colonel Crawshaw's men, has Dixon left all his money in his London bank? A fugitive would surely arrange to withdraw it and take it with him. And why should he take only his underclothing and nightwear with him? He can hardly be travelling to the Orient in his dressing gown. However – I see we are turning into Harley Street. Perhaps Dixon's lumbago specialist will be able to help us penetrate these murky waters . . .'

An enquiry at the first medical establishment that we came to soon directed us to the house occupied by Sir Steven Lansdowne. Having sent up Hester's card, the immaculately dressed and somewhat aloof receptionist told us that the doctor would be happy to see us shortly. After we had taken our seats in the comfortably furnished foyer, Hester drew my attention to the pictures displayed on the opposite wall. They comprised mainly paintings and photographs of Queen Victoria. I noticed that one large photograph showed the queen and a group of men in dark morning suits; she appeared to be accepting a scroll from one of them. But before I could say anything, we were shown upstairs to the consulting rooms.

Sir Steven was a tall, sparsely built gentleman in his early fifties, with that pleasant informality of manner often associated with those who have risen to the top of their chosen profession and no longer have to bolster their status with any unnecessary *froideur*. It helped that he had heard of Hester's reputation, which even at that relatively early stage in her career was becoming known to the public.

The doctor gestured for us both to sit. 'You must be Miss Hester Lynton,' he said to my friend. 'My secretary described the lady who sent up her card. And of course, Miss Ivy Jessop. I have heard of your work, Miss Lynton. Your overturning of Lord Huntingdon's conviction was marvellous.'

Hester smiled. 'Thank you, Sir Steven. The case certainly excited the press. I am afraid that the combination of a violent murder, a peer, a jealous wife and an attractive governess could hardly remain private. However, the matter that we have brought to you today is less sensational. It concerns a patient of yours, Professor Ambrose Dixon. I understand that you last saw him on Friday, the tenth of April?'

The doctor's demeanour underwent a subtle change at the mention of his patient, and he addressed Hester in a more guarded tone.

'Much as I would like to help you, Miss Lynton, you will – I am sure – understand when I say that the information I can give you about my patients is strictly limited, for reasons of professional confidentiality. I can certainly confirm that I saw Professor Dixon on the date you mentioned. That is really all that I can say.'

'I understand your position completely, but let me put the matter to you in another way. If a patient announced at the end of his appointment that it was his intention to go home and murder his wife and family, I have no doubt you would inform a constable. Confidentiality is not absolute. In this case, the information that I seek concerning the professor is of the highest national importance. Indeed, the welfare of our queen and country may depend upon it. Now, I could suggest that you take a cab with Ivy and me to Windsor Castle, where a person of the very highest authority could repeat my request. However, if you can place your trust in me, I can assure you that anything you tell me will be used only if absolutely necessary.'

Hester's solemn words had an immediate effect on the doctor. He left his chair and paced nervously across the room.

'Windsor Castle! I would not wish for the world to trouble Her Majesty on such a matter. Tell me what you wish to know.'

Hester caught my eye as a flicker of amusement registered in her features. 'Thank you. I understand that you were treating Professor Dixon for lumbago?'

Sir Steven laughed. 'Lumbago! What on earth gave you that idea? No, don't answer – let me explain. I am a neurologist, and Dixon was referred to me earlier this year by his local physician. Dixon was suffering from aphasia – a difficulty in finding the correct words. It is a particularly irksome condition for the patient, since intelligence itself is not affected. In Dixon's case, he retained the ability to write fluently, at least up to the time that I last saw him.'

'And were you able to identify a cause?' Hester interjected.

The doctor nodded solemnly. 'Yes. Ambrose Dixon had a rapidly growing brain tumour, almost certainly of the temporal lobe. When I last saw him, he had begun to develop a range of other symptoms, making the diagnosis certain. I was my sad task to inform him that the prognosis was a severe one. I told him that by early May he should expect to be physically incapacitated, and could not expect to live much beyond the end of that month. He took the news stoically – a surprisingly common reaction – settled his bill, thanked me and bade me farewell. And that is the last I heard of him.'

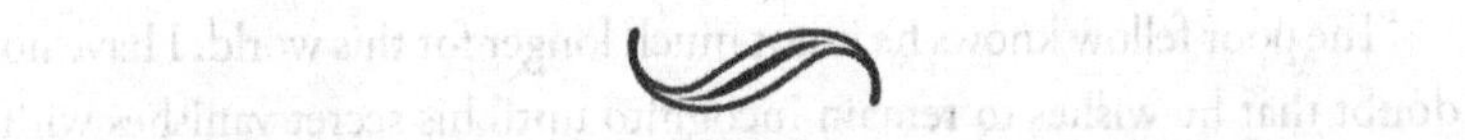

Once we were seated in a cab and on our way back to 12 Newsome Street, I turned to Hester.

'Tell me, what would you have done if Sir Steven Lansdowne had taken up your offer of a visit to Windsor Palace? The queen might have found our unexpected arrival inconvenient.'

Hester chuckled. 'I would have made some excuse and taken him to Whitehall instead. I was relieved that my ploy worked as well as it did.'

'You refer to his collection of pictures?'

'That, and the photograph. I recognised two of the figures in the scene – both eminent physicians. I would wager that if we saw that photograph again, we would also recognise Sir Steven amongst the bystanders. I imagine that the queen was being given some kind of honorary distinction, or pledge of loyalty. At any rate, it was obvious that Sir Steven is an enthusiastic royalist. I guessed that an appeal to his loyalty to the monarch might produce the desired result.'

'And what do you propose as the next step in our investigation?' I asked.

'This evening, I would like you to look through our collection of business directories and gazetteers, and compile a list of the dozen or so most exclusive nursing homes within the London area. Then, tomorrow, I would like you to visit each of them in turn.'

'To ask them if Professor Ambrose Dixon has recently been admitted as a patient?' I asked.

Hester shook her head. 'By no means! Enquire whether a clean-shaven gentleman in his late sixties – probably wearing spectacles – was admitted between Friday the eighteenth and Monday the twentieth of April. The name he gave will *not* have been Dixon. I will leave it to you to think of a suitable pretext. Obtain the men's details if you can, if any fit the description, but on no account speak to any of them. I do apologise for giving you such an onerous task, but it is not one that I can entrust to anyone else.'

'Not at all,' I said, 'I shall be happy to help. But why clean-shaven? Dixon has a full beard.'

Hester looked at me with amusement. 'Exactly! That is precisely why he will have shaved it off, and no doubt also abandoned his pince-nez.'

'And why do you think he is in a nursing home?'

'The poor fellow knows he is not much longer for this world. I have no doubt that he wishes to remain incognito until his secret vanishes with him. Remember the items that he took with him – probably packed into a carpet bag he bought for the purpose. For a man who anticipates being confined to his bed and armchair, dressing gowns and a smoking jacket will suffice. He must have opened a bank account in his assumed name, and paid in enough to cover his stay, which sadly will not be lengthy.'

The next morning, armed with the addresses of eleven superior nursing homes in London and shod in comfortable walking shoes, I waited for Hester to appear before starting my investigations. She had received a note from her cousin, Inspector Brasher, first thing that morning, but had not revealed the contents. I was used to Hester's secrecy in such matters, which I had learned was the result of a desire to marshal her facts before revealing them, rather than any reluctance to trust my confidence.

When she emerged from her bedroom, I could not help a sudden start of surprise, even though her uncanny facility for disguise was well known to me.

The grace and femininity of an attractive twenty-eight-year-old had been transformed into the stooped figure of an ill-dressed and somewhat grimy looking woman in her fifties, wearing a stained black bombazine dress and a man's cord jacket, her complexion tinged by the florid bloom of the habitual drinker. That portion of Hester's glossy brown hair that was visible under the rim of a battered black hat was now streaked with grey.

'Why, you look positively disreputable!' I exclaimed. 'Your talents are a great loss to the theatre. If I shared your powers of deduction, I would conclude that you were seeking information better gained by a bottle washer or skivvy that a correctly brought-up young lady.'

'You are quite correct. I expect to be back before eight tonight, and have asked Mrs Parsons to prepare a welcoming supper for us at that hour, and to open a bottle of wine. I suspect that we will both be in need of refreshment.'

I arrived back at 12 Newsome Street at seven o'clock that evening, pleased with what I had accomplished but sufficiently footsore to order up a hot mustard bath from our housekeeper. It was not until half past seven that Hester appeared, entering the room to see me bathing my feet contentedly. She retained her slatternly disguise.

Hester pointed at the steaming liquid. 'If that is one of Mrs Parsons' mixing bowls, remind me never to eat her Dundee cake again! I believe that I have just time to change before dinner. I insist that we do not speak a word about the results of your investigations today until the lamb chops and marmalade pudding have been eaten, and the claret thoroughly explored.'

I agreed with Hester's suggestion, and so it was not until the table had been cleared and we were sitting in our favourite armchairs with the remnants of the wine in front of us that I told her what I had discovered. I took out my pocketbook from my bag and laid it open upon the side-table that stood between us.

'Only two establishments met the criteria that you gave me. In the first, Chesterton's Nursing Home in South Kensington, they admitted an elderly gentleman on Monday the twentieth of April. However, as he was accompanied by his wife and family, that would seem to rule Professor Dixon out. The second, Thrushcross Private Hospital in Camden, received a new patient on Saturday the eighteenth of April. He has no family. He gave his name as Mr Harold Bessemer, and his age as seventy-one.'

Hester got to her feet. 'Excellent, Ivy! What reason did you give for your enquiries? Such places are naturally guarded when asked for information by complete strangers, no matter how ladylike.'

'When I approached each establishment, I introduced myself as the companion of Lady Northwaite. I explained that her ladyship was seeking an elderly gentleman known to her as Horace Blenkinsop, although she suspected that Blenkinsop may be a false name. I gave the dates of admission that are of interest to us, and explained that I deeply regretted not being able to give any further details regarding Lady Northwaite's interest in the gentleman. When Miss Lewis – the proprietor of Thrushcross Hospital – gave me Bessemer's details, I asked if we could visit tomorrow morning to speak to him, as he was probably the person Lady Northwaite seeks. She was happy to give her permission.'

'Really, Ivy, you have excelled yourself! You are the kind of naturally honest person who makes an excellent liar, although I would have preferred not to have the obligation to assume yet another disguise. Fortunately, the new hat and dress that I was forced to buy for my invitation to Downing Street last spring are still very presentable. I shall ring for Mrs Parsons, and ask her to hire a carriage for us from Lambert's first thing on Monday morning, then we will make our way to Camden in suitable style. Incidentally – is there a *real* Lady Northwaite?'

I smiled. 'There is – she is thirty years old, and lives quietly in Dorset with her husband and three children. We will have to hope that no word of our little deception ever reaches her. And speaking of deceptions – I suppose it would be too much to ask what your disreputable counterpart managed to discover today?'

'My dear Ivy, you know me too well. I can certainly say that my descent into the lower ranks of society brought some interesting results. Hopefully, all will be resolved very soon.'

By eleven thirty that Monday morning we were seated in the new barouche that Hester had hired, driven by a smartly-dressed coachman in a silk top hat and silver-buttoned livery. We pulled up outside the Camden private hospital, and it was not long before the proprietor, Miss Lewis, led us to a private room on the first floor.

Miss Lewis paused before opening the door. 'After your secretary called, I explained to Mr Bessemer that he might have a visitor. He is a very sick man, my lady. He seems to understand all that is said to him, but can communicate very little – just a few words, and those with difficulty. When he arranged to be admitted he insisted on paying his bill up to the end of June this year. However, I fear that he will not live beyond the end of May. Of course we have the name of his solicitor – there are no other persons to contact – and will refund the balance to Mr Bessemer's estate.'

Miss Lewis ushered us into the sick room, and at Hester's polite request she left us, asking that we not tire Bessemer with our visit. The patient was propped up in bed with a collection of pillows, facing a large picture window that looked out over pleasant lawned grounds. He was clean-shaven, and wore gold-rimmed spectacles. He inclined his head slightly when we entered, an evident invitation to be seated in the two chairs at his bedside. Although he was much changed from the photograph Gilbert Wilson had given us, it was quite apparent that this was the man we sought.

'Professor Ambrose Dixon?' Hester asked. 'I have a request to put to you, Professor. I promise that I will be brief, and that after I have received your answer – if you are willing and able to speak – I make my solemn promise that I will leave you and never reveal your whereabouts to another soul. I speak for my companion, also.' Again the professor nodded, and Hester continued.

'My name is Miss Lynton – I am a consulting detective, and Miss Jessop is my assistant. I have been commissioned by the War Office to discover the whereabouts of the formula for the new explosive that you have developed. It may be that you have destroyed all traces of your research, in which case my task is at an end. However, it is my hope that the formula does exist – it is an unusual man or woman who can contemplate the utter destruction of their unique creation. Here are my arguments for your revealing it.

'Firstly, I understand that you are concerned about the destructive power of your discovery. However, consider the probable circumstances of its use. England will never instigate a continental war. Only when England or its allies are threatened by an aggressor will your weapon be used. In such circumstances, this new ordnance could make the difference between victory and defeat – a defeat that might easily lead to an invasion of these shores.

'Secondly, there is indisputable evidence that at least one of the European powers is currently conducting an extensive programme of military research.

This research includes the refinement of more powerful explosives, but also the development of new and deadly poisonous gases. England has no such programme under way, and therefore your invention could be our only hope of tipping the scales in our favour if the worst happens. I believe that you have retained a copy of your formula, no doubt cleverly concealed. If you are a patriot, I beg you to help me locate it.'

As Hester spoke, I observed Professor Dixon closely. His expression appeared more animated, and a gleam of interest had returned to his eyes. His lips trembled, and Hester immediately lowered her head towards him to catch any words he could utter.

'Caro …' he said. 'Caroline. Bring James … Bring James …'

It was clear that the effort of speaking was too much for him. His chin lolled towards his chest, and Hester rang the bell cord, which hung above his bed. Soon Miss Lewis arrived, accompanied by a nurse. They assured us that we could expect no more from their patient that day, and so, reluctantly, we left them.

On our way back to Newsome Street, Hester announced her intention to visit Professor Dixon's sister the next morning.

'I will post a letter to Mrs Clark this afternoon, warning her of our arrival. According to the file passed to us by Colonel Crawshaw, she is an elderly lady and does not often leave home. I suggest we arrive at eleven o'clock in the morning. I recall that the file also stated her Christian name; it is Caroline. If she can direct us to the mysterious James, then our search may be nearing its end.'

'Should we inform the colonel?' I asked. 'He may wish to speak to the professor himself. As far as one could tell, Dixon seemed convinced by your appeal to his patriotism.'

Hester turned to me with a sombre expression. 'I hardly think that military intelligence would learn much from badgering the poor man. It is clear that his days are severely limited. Let us report to the colonel when we have made some more progress. I have asked Miss Lewis to send me a telegram immediately if the worst happens, via my good friend Miss Lynton, 12 Newsome Street. If you are in agreement, I will also not mention to Mrs Clark that we have located her missing brother. Seeing him in his current state would upset her and do him no good. We will, of course, be sure to contact her when he finally succumbs to his illness.'

When we reached Mrs Clark's address in Islington the next morning, we were pleased to find that she had received Hester's letter via the first postal delivery and was at home waiting for us. Colonel Crawshaw's report had given us her age – at seventy-eight, she was ten years older than her brother. Her house was in a secluded terrace, very comfortably furnished in the style fashionable thirty years ago.

The elderly parlourmaid who ushered us into the sitting room was of a similar vintage. After the usual exchange of greetings, Hester apologised for our visit, coming as it did after she had already been questioned extensively by Crawshaw's men.

'I will come straight to the point, Mrs Clark. As you know, your brother has not been seen since the seventeenth of April. We suspect that he knows the whereabouts of an important document – it is vital for the interests of this country that we find it. Since you were last spoken to on this topic, a further item of information has emerged. We think that your brother may have given the document to a friend or family member for safe keeping, someone called James – a Christian name or surname. Does "James" mean anything to you?'

At that moment, the parlourmaid brought in a tray of refreshments, and it was not until tea and cake had been distributed that our hostess answered.

'I am afraid not, Miss Lynton. My neighbour and good friend, Mrs Jenkins, has a son called James in the navy – but that is hardly relevant, as Ambrose has never met him.'

Hester smiled brightly, but I knew her well enough to sense her disappointment. I put down my teacup.

'I believe that your brother last visited you on Friday the sixth of March?'

'That is so. He had left Aldershot on Thursday that evening, came to me on Friday, and returned home to Bloomsbury on Saturday, before luncheon.'

'And what do you do during his visit? Did you go out at all, perhaps to the theatre or a restaurant?'

Mrs Clark shook her head. 'Goodness me, no! We are both very quiet people and rarely go out into society. Cook made us an excellent boiled knuckle of veal and baked apple pudding on Friday for dinner. On Saturday morning we sat in the gazebo in the garden, as the weather was so pleasant.

Really, Miss Lynton, I have already given all this information to the government gentlemen who spoke to me shortly after Ambrose went missing. They also carried out a thorough search of the house and garden.'

'We will not take up your time for much longer. Can I ask – did your brother seem at all anxious when you met? Was his behaviour unusual in any way?'

Mrs Clark frowned in concentration. 'Well – he was not anxious, just rather preoccupied. He talked a good deal about his faith – Ambrose is a very devout Christian, although not given to any excessive demonstrations of piety. He was upset when I married Albert – my late husband – and converted to the Catholic faith, but that was many years ago. After dinner that Friday we read a few verses from the family Bible together – it had belonged to our father.'

'Was that your usual practice?' Hester asked.

'Oh, yes. I too take a great comfort from religious observance. Our father was an Anglican clergyman, so of course we were brought up in a devout family. I remember that when we parted that evening, Ambrose took the Bible up to his room to study further.'

'I see. Now, there is just one more favour I would like to ask of you. I know that the gentlemen from the government who visited you carried out a thorough search of the house. However, if you would allow Miss Jessop and me briefly to examine your brother's study, I would be most grateful.'

A moment later, Hester and I were inside Ambrose Dixon's study. It was a large room, and more sparsely furnished than I had expected, until I reminded myself that all his work was now done in his Bloomsbury house and his laboratory at Aldershot.

Hester lifted down and examined in turn a number of pictures that hung upon the walls of the study. She ended with a large mezzotint, which hung over the leather-topped desk in one corner of the room. She turned it so that I could see the back of the frame.

'Do you see this, Ivy? I would date this print at around 1800, and the frame is of the same age. And yet the backing board has been very recently removed, and then secured back in place with strips of gummed paper. It would be pointless to subject this house to a further search. The gentlemen from military intelligence have clearly been very thorough. If they have looked here, they will have looked everywhere else with as much care.'

I frowned. 'I am no doubt being very stupid, but is it not possible that Ambrose Dixon removed the board and hid his formula behind the print himself?'

'I think not. Every picture in this room has been taken apart and searched in the same way. If Dixon had hidden his formula in this manner, he would have dismantled *one* picture, not all of them. I think we have exhausted the possibilities of Mrs Clark's house. It is time that we returned to Newsome Street to decide upon our next course of action.'

After saying our goodbyes to Mrs Clark, we hailed a passing hansom and took our seats. However, we had not driven a dozen yards before Hester opened the trap door in the roof and the cab man drew his horse to a halt.

'Wait here, driver, I shall not be long!' Hester called out. 'Ivy, I'll be back in a few minutes.'

True to her word, Hester soon returned, panting slightly. In her hands she held a large black book. She spoke to the cab man – I did not catch her words – and we set off once more.

Hester turned towards me with a serious expression. 'This is Professor Dixon's Bible,' she explained, putting it in my hands. 'I shall explain everything when we are at home together. I have asked the driver to make a small diversion. I will leave you at Clerkenwell, and return by myself. When you arrive at Newsome Street, I have asked the driver to walk with you to the front door, and see that you get inside safely. Please tell Mrs Parsons she is on no account to admit anyone until I return. Do not alarm yourself, Ivy. I am only taking precautions against what I believe to be an unlikely eventuality.'

As it transpired, I was admitted by Mrs Parsons without incident, and passed on Hester's message. I placed Professor Dixon's Bible carefully on our dining table – overcoming a strong urge to examine it further – and waited anxiously by the window, looking down into the busy street until after about twenty minutes a hansom stopped outside our door and Hester alighted, carrying a parcel wrapped in brown paper, about the size of a large hat box. It was some time before she entered our rooms.

'My apologies for keeping you waiting,' she said. 'I have been talking to Mrs Parsons – she has agreed to undertake a little project for me.'

I had learned, over the years, not to quiz Hester about her schemes before she was ready to reveal them – which she took great pleasure in doing, once a favourable outcome had been achieved. I therefore did not ask her about her concern for my safety on my recent return to Newsome Street, or about the task that she had given Mrs Parsons. The Bible, however, was a matter on which I could not remain silent.

I pointed to the large black volume. 'You will be impressed to learn that I have not examined it at all. Do you think we will find the formula slipped between its pages? The Book of Revelation might be the place to start looking.'

Hester chuckled. 'Alas, no. It is clear from the of Professor Dixon's bookshelves that every volume has been looked through during the search of the house. However, I am convinced that this Bible holds the key to the puzzle. Think back to when the professor spoke to us. "Bring James" were the words he said. But remember that the poor man suffers from aphasia. I am sure that the words he *wanted* to say were "King James". Now, the King James Bible is another name for the Authorised Version – the Bible that Dixon and his father before him would have used, as members of the Church of England.'

'That is very ingenious. But surely it is just as likely that Dixon could have been referring to some other person – someone of whom his sister was unaware?'

Hester stood up, walked to the window and looked down into the street before answering. 'Possibly, but there is more to consider. Normally, if someone referred to their Bible, they would use that word, and not make reference to the version. However, there were two different Bibles in Mrs Clark's house, as I confirmed when I returned to collect this one. As a Catholic, Dixon's sister used the Douay-Rheims Bible. Dixon was trying to tell us which Bible held the secret.'

'I am still puzzled. Why could we not have both returned to Mrs Clark's house, and examined the Bible at our leisure, instead of hurrying home with it?'

'Because I am certain that we were followed to Islington by a four-wheeler. It was waiting at the end of Newsome Street when we set off, and I saw it again just before we turned into Clotherton Road. If my return to the house had been seen, I did not wish to linger there any longer than is necessary. Whilst we are on the subject – come to the window, Ivy, but do not stand too close to the glass – and observe the man standing about ten yards away, outside number fifteen. What do you make of him?'

The man in question was dressed like a down-at-heel loafer, no more than thirty years of age, puffing upon a pipe. He wore stained and baggy cord trousers, a crumpled jacket, and a grubby muffler.

'He appears to be a common idler – perhaps out of work, or passing the time before a late shift. A labourer of some kind?'

'That is certainly the impression he wishes to create. But look again. Do you see his boots? They are muddy, but of a superior quality, more suited to the salon than the builder's yard. And he has been very recently shaved by a good barber, not at home in front of the mirror. Depend upon it, that is a young man of the upper middle classes. There he goes again, puffing heartily on his pipe! A genuine pipe smoker does not try so hard to give an impression of an express locomotive leaving Paddington Station. If I am not mistaken, he is there to keep an eye on our comings and goings. I am happy for him to do so for the present, so let us turn our attention to Professor Dixon's Bible.'

We soon reassured ourselves that there was nothing between the pages. Then Hester took out a large magnifying lens from her desk drawer, and looked carefully at the substantial leather covers on the front and back, both outside and in. The yellowed endpapers and inner linings did not seem to have disturbed since the book was printed some seventy years ago.

Then, something caught my attention. 'Lend me your glass, Hester,' I said. 'Do you see? The edge of the back cover has a fine line upon it.'

'You are quite correct!' Hester exclaimed. 'Here – let me get my paper knife. It has an edge sharper than anything in Mrs Parsons' kitchen. Yes – this cover has been slit open with a fine blade, something has been inserted, and then the cover gummed together again. Let us see what lurks within …'

After a few minutes of careful dissection, the answer lay in front of us. There were three sheets of fine quality thin paper, covered in an incomprehensible mix of typewritten characters, as if a typist had struck the keys at random.

'The formula!' I exclaimed, somewhat redundantly. 'Should we not go to the Directorate of Military Intelligence immediately, and give it to Mr Wilson or one of his colleagues? If some mysterious stranger is indeed tracking our movements, it will hardly matter if he knows that we are going to the War Office, as we will have by then achieved our objective.'

Before replying, Hester took up the three sheets of paper and placed them in a large brown envelope, which she put in a drawer of her desk.

'My dear Ivy, I understand your sense of urgency, but in this instance, I must ask you to indulge me. I have my reasons, believe me. I would prefer that we remain here at home until tomorrow morning, and then hand the formula over. Besides, I am expecting a visitor later today, and would not like to be out when our caller arrives.'

The rest of the day passed without incident, other than the disappearance of the suspicious observer who had placed himself on the street. As Hester pointed out, this did not mean that we were no longer being watched, as the busy thoroughfare outside our door was rarely free of passers-by.

At about seven o'clock that evening, I took a letter down to the hallway. I had just placed it in the tray ready to be posted on the following day when I heard a muted noise coming from the direction of Mrs Parsons' private parlour, as if someone was tapping in a picture nail. A moment later, our housekeeper opened the door into the hall – she had an uncanny talent for knowing when Hester or I had entered her domain.

'Mrs Parsons!' I said. 'If I had Miss Lynton's powers of deduction, I would conclude that you have just received a picture of one of your many nieces and nephews, and have secured it above your mantlepiece!'

'Oh no, miss … that is, if you could give a message to Miss Lynton, I would be obliged if you could tell her that I have just finished the little job she gave me.'

When I relayed this message Hester seemed delighted, and went down to speak Mrs Parsons. When she returned, she spoke solemnly.

'As I mentioned to you earlier today, I expect us to have a caller this evening. I must ask you to promise me one thing. Whatever our visitor says to me or to you, do not say or do anything – leave the talking to me. And do not be alarmed at anything that may occur.'

'Hester, you intrigue me! However, I should be accustomed to surprises by now. Trust me to remain as still as a statue, unless your mysterious client produces a tarantula or rattlesnake from his pockets.'

It was just after eight o'clock when we heard the distant ringing of the electric doorbell. Our housekeeper had a standing instruction to bring up any visitor who presented a card, and a few moments later the door opened to reveal Mr Gilbert Wilson, as stylishly dressed as when he had last called upon us.

Hester was all smiles. 'Why, Mr Wilson!' she cried. 'How kind of you to call upon us. Do sit down. Would you like some tea – or a glass of something stronger?'

Wilson seemed less affable than he had been on the last occasion he spoke to us. 'Not on this occasion, Miss Lynton. I will come straight to the point. Am I right in thinking that you have discovered the whereabouts of Professor Dixon's formula – and if so, do you have it in your possession?'

'You are correct on both counts, Mr Wilson. It is now safe with me, and I intend to hand it personally to Colonel Hubert Crawshaw at the War Office, tomorrow.

Wilson forced a smile, looking like someone who has just received an unwanted gift and does not wish to offend their benefactor. 'That will not be necessary. If you can just give the document to me now, I will make sure Colonel Crawshaw is given it tonight.'

Hester shook her head. 'I am afraid that is impossible, since I am determined to present the formula to him in person. There is surely no urgent reason for Colonel Crawshaw to receive it?'

Wilson leaned forward, lowering his voice and adopting a menacing tone. 'Now you listen to me, Miss Lynton. I *must* have the formula now, and I *will* have it, whatever you say.' As he spoke he reached into an inner pocket of his well-cut lounging jacket and produced a heavy rubber truncheon, which he held across his knees.

'You have a choice,' Wilson said. 'Either you bring me the formula immediately, or I shall quickly render you and Miss Jessop unconscious and search your rooms from top to bottom. I have no desire to harm either of you – if you give me the formula, I will leave immediately. However, be aware that both front and back doors to your house will be watched until midnight. If you attempt to escape and give the alarm before that hour, you will be dealt with severely.'

I could not help a gasp of surprise at Wilson's shocking statement. I pride myself on my steadiness in a crisis – like Hester, I despise a panic-stricken man or a woman who cannot keep a cool head – but even so, I felt a cold chill through my body. We had entertained unpleasant clients before, but I could not remember such a brutal threat being made in our rooms. Instinctively, I looked towards the desk drawer that contained Hester's pearl-handled revolver, which – despite my objections – she always kept loaded. Hester caught my eye and shook her head. Then she turned to our visitor.

'So, Mr Wilson – it is clear that you are not the man you pretend to be. Tell me, are you proud to be a traitor to your queen and country?'

Wilson's complexion reddened slightly. 'You have been given a choice,' he said. 'What is your reply?'

Hester sank back in her chair, a look of sullen defeat upon her features. She pointed to the top drawer of her desk. 'In there,' she said. 'In the large brown envelope. Tell me – were you the man who followed us to Islington? I hope you did not harm poor Mrs Clark.'

Wilson removed the papers from the envelope and scanned them briefly before replacing them and putting the envelope in his pocket. 'Mrs Clark is perfectly well. She told me that you had borrowed her brother's Bible – the rest was easy to surmise. Now, ladies, I am sure you will excuse me. Remember, if you remain indoors until midnight, no harm will come to you.'

For some moments after Gilbert Wilson's departure we sat in silence. Then I spoke to my companion.

'I suppose we should leave the house at midnight, and search out a policeman?'

Hester's response was surprisingly cheerful. 'Oh, I do not think so, Ivy. Wilson will be well on his way to Europe by that time – the night mail boat from Dover to Paris leaves at a quarter to twelve. We will report to Colonel Hubert Crawshaw in the morning. I suggest we arrive at the Directorate of Military Intelligence at eleven o'clock. That will give me time to send a telegram to Jonathan Carroll, requesting his presence at the meeting. And please do not distress yourself. I do believe that this is one of those occasions where things might turn out for the best after all, despite appearances.'

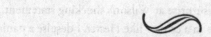

The next morning brought us unwelcome but not unexpected information, just as we were about to leave for Pall Mall; a telegram from the proprietor of Thrushcross Private Hospital, telling us that 'Mr Harold Bessemer' – Professor Ambrose Dixon – had died the previous evening.

'I will visit his sister later today and give her the sad news,' Hester said. 'Meanwhile, we must prepare to give Colonel Crawshaw an unpleasant shock.'

It was not long before we were both seated in the colonel's impressive office; he rose to greet us, as did Jonathan Carroll, who had evidently agreed to attend. I had mixed feelings about Jonathan's presence; as Colonel Crawshaw's superior, he had of course been responsible for involving Hester and me in the case. It would surely be embarrassing for Jonathan to hear of our failure in front of his subordinate. However, I had every trust in Hester's judgement.

Without further ado, Hester described everything that had taken place up to the events of the previous evening, when Gilbert Wilson had disappeared with the formula. On more than one occasion during her narrative the colonel seemed intent on interrupting, until a gesture from Jonathan dissuaded him.

As she concluded her account, Hester looked at them both with surprising cheerfulness.

'I expect you are already aware that Mr Wilson is absent from his duties today, Colonel Crawshaw?' she asked.

Colonel Crawshaw got to his feet, red-faced with anger. 'Indeed – I received a message to say that he was unwell, and would remain at home. At home, indeed! He'll be half way across Europe by now. Why in the name of … why the blazes didn't you raise the alarm last night? Of all the …'

Jonathan interrupted him. 'Do sit down, Colonel Crawshaw. Exciting yourself will do no good. I know Miss Lynton and Miss Jessop very well, and something tells me that there is more to this case than we have yet been told. Hester, I am aware that you enjoy springing surprises, but I must insist that put your love of the dramatic aside, and tells us anything else that you know. The national interest demands it.'

Hester smiled. 'Very well. Can I start by asking Colonel Crawshaw if he had any inkling of Wilson's true character?'

'None whatsoever. As I believe I told you on a previous occasion, he is an old Etonian – in fact he was in the same house as me, although many years later – and came to us from South Africa with the most glowing testimonials. He had no family; he was an only child, and both parents died some years ago.'

'That was most convenient. And how do you know that he was, as he said, an Eton old boy?' Hester asked. 'After all, anyone can claim to have attended a school.'

'We are not quite that stupid,' Colonel Crawshaw sneered. 'Gilbert Wilson entered Eton College in 1865, and left to join the Rhodesian police force in 1871. Mr Lawson, his housemaster, confirmed it. We wrote to him before confirming Wilson's appointment.'

'I am sure that a boy of that *name* attended the school,' Hester said. 'But did one of your officers visit Eton with a recent photograph of Wilson to show to the staff who remembered him? And did you question Wilson about his old school – I'm sure there are plenty of arcane Etonian traditions and practices which you could have quizzed him about?'

For the first time, Colonel Crawshaw looked disconcerted. 'Well … no, I did not. Were you suspicious of him? If so, you should have reported the fact immediately.'

'I was suspicious of him from the moment he entered our rooms last Wednesday. He was dressed like a young man of wealth and fashion, rather than a mid-ranking government employee. His silver card case – and the cards within – were of the highest quality. He could have obtained perfectly respectable alternatives at a tenth of the price. Did you notice his pocket watch, Ivy?'

I thought carefully. 'A thin gold watch, I think.'

'Correct. In fact it was a fine Swiss timepiece. When Wilson then asked us to deliver the formula directly to him if we discovered it – rather than to Colonel Crawshaw – I decide to ask my cousin, Inspector Albert Brasher of Scotland Yard, to do a little investigation of Wilson's finances on my behalf. Albert discovered that Wilson has no private income, but that he regularly deposits large sums of money into his bank account – a total of £800 during the last twelve months alone. At that point. I decided to pay a visit to Wilson's house – disguised as a washerwoman – Albert had obtained the address for me.'

'And what did you discover?' the colonel asked.

'It turned out that Wilson occupied a very pleasant town house in Marylebone. I struck up a conversation with the housemaid, with the result that I spent most of the day scrubbing floors and cleaning fireplaces.

I was rewarded with tuppence, a large glass of her employer's sherry and a cheese sandwich. And, of course, with a good deal of gossip, since no one knows a household as well as the servants. For an assistant at the War Office, Gilbert Wilson seemed fortunate to be master of an extensive establishment. There were three resident servants in addition to the housemaid, and he entertained his friends liberally. There was also a certain young lady – believed to be a dancer at Rosing's Music Hall – who was a *very* frequent visitor, with the convenience of her own key.

'The next time I saw Gilbert Wilson he was in a carriage, following Ivy and me as we went to see the professor's sister. It was only a fleeting glimpse, but I was sure it was him. It was not hard to deduce from all this that he was either a foreign agent, or at any rate was in the payment of a foreign power; that he had heard about my abilities and was confident that I would retrieve the formula; that he would find out from Mrs Clark that I had borrowed the professor's Bible and that he would later call upon us at 12 Newsome Street.'

Jonathan looked puzzled. 'I see all that, Hester. What I do *not* understand is why – given what you knew – you did not immediately take the formula to the War Office, then arrange for Colonel Crawshaw's men to lie in wait in your rooms to arrest Wilson!'

Hester continued. 'I agree that the formula needs to be placed in the hands of the British government, although in the circumstances I would prefer to give it directly to you, where I can be sure that it is safe.'

As she spoke, Hester reached into her handbag and took out a large brown envelope, which she passed to Jonathan. He reached inside and drew out three sheets of paper, covered in what appeared to be random groups of typewritten letters and numbers, and spread them on the table next to him. Colonel Crawshaw leapt from behind his desk and bent over the table.

'Let me anticipate your questions and explain everything,' Hester said with a smile. 'When I thought it likely that Wilson would call upon us and attempt to steal the formula, I decided that it would be an excellent idea to give him what he wanted. In that way his masters – in whichever European capital they reside – would no longer use all their formidable resources to obtain it. I had already learned from Colonel Crawshaw that Professor Dixon typed up his most important papers in code. Therefore, on my way back to Newsome Street, I called in at Harrods and bought a

Remington 2 typewriter. I instructed Mrs Parsons in its operation, and asked her to compose three sheets of gibberish – random groups of letters and numbers up to seven characters in length. I felt it safe to assume that Wilson had not seen any of the professor's encodings before, and would accept it as genuine.'

As Hester spoke, I realised that the mysterious tapping I had heard coming from Mrs Parsons' quarters had been the final strokes of her typewriting task.

'Wait a moment, Miss Lynton,' the colonel said, raising his index finger. 'How are we to know that the formula that you have now given us is in fact the genuine one?'

I felt my face reddening at the implied accusation of dishonesty, but Hester appeared unperturbed. 'That is a very fair question, colonel. However, the matter is easily resolved. You are aware that every typewriting machine produces its own characteristic and unique imprint?'

Colonel Crawshaw frowned uncertainly, and I noticed that Jonathan appeared to be enjoying Hester's command of the situation.

'Each of the metal letters has its own minor imperfections, reproduced in the print and easily visible under a magnifying glass. You need to send word to the commanding officer at Aldershot, and ask him to send the professor's typewriter – under escort – to Mr Carroll. Jonathan can then compare the sheets I have given him with a sample typed on the Aldershot machine. I think he will find their characteristics to be identical.'

Jonathan rubbed his hands with satisfaction. 'An excellent suggestion! Colonel, I will keep the formula for the time being and ask one of my staff to send for the typewriter, although I believe the verification of these papers to be a mere formality. Meanwhile, please say nothing of this matter to any of your officials – let them think the formula is still missing. It is clear that we need to take a close look at the bona fides of everyone currently employed in military intelligence. Gilbert Wilson may not be the only self-styled public schoolboy of dubious provenance in your department.'

It was not until several days later that Jonathan's onerous duties allowed him to make an evening call at 12 Newsome Street. Hester had, in the meantime, made her promised visit to Dixon's sister, and after passing on the sad news of her brother's death, had reassured that lady that Dixon served his country exceptionally well. It came as no surprise that Dixon had left instructions for his sister, which included generous provision for his servants at Bloomsbury.

Once Jonathan was comfortably seated with a glass of whisky in his hand, he spoke to both of us with the expression of a man very satisfied with life.

'Ivy … Hester – you will be pleased to know that the papers you recovered from Dixon's Bible were indeed typed on his Aldershot machine.'

'Then we must hope that they comprise the formula for his new explosive – and not a secret recipe for cabinet pudding,' I said.

Hester laughed. 'Excellent, Ivy! Tell me, Jonathan, have your men deciphered the document yet?'

'Hardly – I only gave them the original this afternoon, but I expect them to make short work of it. Dixon's expertise lay in chemistry, not cryptography. The code he used for the compound used in his signal flares was one of simple substitution. No doubt this will be the same. However, one thing is certain. Whoever is now poring over Mrs Parsons' inspired creation is going to have a thankless task.'

'And what of Colonel Crashaw's vetting of his subordinates?' I asked. 'Have any more imposters been exposed?'

Jonathan put down his glass. 'Not as yet. I am afraid that the colonel is a chastened man, and no longer takes anyone's word for granted. Let us hope he does not investigate *me*, and discover that I was born in Bavaria, and that my real name is "von" something or other …'

After Jonathan had left us, Hester placed a Turkish cigarette in her long ebony holder, lit the end with a vesta and drew in the smoke contentedly.

'Do you expect the British army to deploy Dixon's explosive immediately, or conserve it for a future emergency?' I asked.

Hester gazed at me enigmatically through a rapidly dissipating blue haze. 'Perhaps neither,' she said. 'True, Dixon chose a simple code for his relatively benign invention of a much-improved signal flare. However, I suspect Jonathan has underestimated the professor's cryptographic skills. Someone who is brilliant in one field often excels in others. If Ambrose Dixon was determined to make the decoding of his fearsome invention as difficult as he could, it is possible that the cypher will remain a mystery for ever.'

4. The Mystery of the Locked Room

Once Hester's name and reputation as a consulting detective gradually became known to the general public, some of our most interesting cases came from approaches by clients who felt that the official police force was either unwilling or unable to help them, as on one wet summer evening in September, 1891.

Hester had received a telegram at noon, saying no more than that a Mrs Lucy Millar intended to call upon us at half past six on a confidential matter, and would be grateful if we could receive her, if we were at home. Since there was little else to occupy us that evening, at five minutes before the appointed hour I stood at the window and looked down on Newsome Street in anticipation of our visitor. The normal throng of pedestrians, carriages and tradesmen that filled our busy street during the day had dissipated, and when our visitor appeared in the gathering dusk she had the pavement almost to herself in the driving rain. It did not require much deductive effort to identify her, since she stopped and took out a pocketbook from under her caped and hooded Ulster, no doubt to confirm our address.

'Our mysterious client has arrived!' I exclaimed, and a moment later Hester was at my side. As Mrs Millar – for I assumed it was she – continued her progress towards our door, Hester turned towards me.

'What do you make of the lady?' she asked.

'She seems anxious to find us,' I replied. 'Do you see anything else of note?'

Hester smiled. 'She is clearly a well-organised, practical and independent woman, and in comfortable financial circumstances. She lives in the country, but no more than an hour's travelling time from London. Her business with us is both serious and urgent.'

At that moment, we heard the muffled sound of the electric doorbell.

'Hester, whilst Mrs Parsons is taking our visitor's wet coat, do tell me your reasoning,' I asked.

'It is very straightforward. Her journey here alone demonstrates her independence; her arrival within minutes of the appointed hour and use of a pocketbook, rather than a scrap of paper, shows practicality and organisation. Her boots are of good quality, but too sturdy for town; that and her practical raincoat demonstrate that she is a country dweller – but given that she could well have had a wasted journey, she can hardly have come very far. That she come to us at all signifies the seriousness of her problem – and to do so without a prior appointment signals its urgency. And she is prepared to pay our fee, so is not short of money. But I hear her tread upon the stairs – let us see how the reality matches our speculations.'

It came as no surprise to me that Hester's character sketch of our client appeared correct in all respects. Hester put her at her ease with the natural kindness which was one of my colleague's most endearing features, and our visitor introduced herself as Mrs Lucy Millar, of Lampton House, near Maidstone. I put her age at no more than thirty-five, with that healthy complexion that is rarely achieved by the town-dweller. She wore a well-tailored tweed jacket and skirt, and lacked only an accompanying gun-dog to confirm her credentials as a stalwart of the more affluent rural classes.

After Mrs Parson had delivered a tray of tea and cake, Mrs Millar – at Hester's invitation – began her story.

'It is best that I explain everything, and you can then decide if you are able to help me. I am a widow; my husband died two years ago, and I have two sons, who are both fortunately at boarding school and as yet know nothing of what I am about to tell you. I live at Lampton House, a large rural villa on the outskirts of Maidstone. Two days ago – last Sunday evening – one of our maids, Hetty Lawrence, tried to go into the library to see to the fire before bedtime – just after eleven o'clock – and was unable to enter, as the door was locked from the inside. She called and got no reply. I should say that I share the house with two others: my sister, Miss Adeline Cormac, and my brother, Mr Frederic Cormac, who is five years younger than I. We sent for Higgins – the butler – and he arrived with

Frederic. At my insistence, they broke down the door. A terrible sight lay in front of us. Poor Adeline was slumped stone dead at a writing desk in one corner of the library, surrounded by blood. Of course, we had the police sent for immediately. They found that she had a paper knife in her hand – it is kept in the library writing desk for our general use – and that her throat had been horribly cut.'

Hester leaned forward and placed her hand on Mrs Millar's arm. 'What a terrible tragedy,' Hester said. 'Pray go on, if you are able.'

I could see the effort that our visitor made to contain her emotions, but after a few moments she continued.

'I cannot fault the thoroughness with which the constabulary have carried out their investigation. I naturally assumed at first that a vile murder had been committed, and they questioned me – and my brother – very thoroughly regarding any enemies that poor Adeline may have had. However, my sister was a gentle, quiet person – forty years old, five years older than me – whose life revolved round our local church and a number of charitable bodies. Given that nothing had been stolen, there seems no possible motive for such a crime. I can quite see how the police have determined upon suicide, given the note that they found next to her body …'

I could not stop myself interrupting. 'A note? I suppose you have not been able to bring it with you?'

'No, but I have seen it, and made an exact copy of the wording.'

As Mrs Millar spoke, she reached into her handbag and took out the small leather-bound pocketbook she had consulted earlier. She passed it to me, and Hester read the entry over my shoulder.

I cannot go on living a lie. It is best ended now. Please forgive me.

'Was the original in your sister's handwriting?' Hester asked.

Our visitor nodded. 'I would swear to it in a court of law. Adeline had a very distinctive writing style – we used to tease her about it when we were children.'

'And have you any notion at all of what this note might have referred to?'

It might have been my imagination, but I thought that I could detect a moment's hesitation before our visitor replied.

'None whatsoever. As I said, my sister had a retiring nature and was the last person to become involved in any intrigue. Can I add that there is one further reason for the police deciding that she must have taken her own life. As I said, the door was locked from the inside and the key remained in the lock. There are three windows in the library, which look out across the front lawn and were shuttered and bolted on the inside, as it was a foul, rainy night. Even if Adeline *had* been murdered, it is impossible to see how the culprit could have left the room and secured it behind them. The police have examined the room very thoroughly, and there is no other exit, hidden or otherwise.'

Hester stood up and refilled our tea cups. 'That is all very clear, Mrs Millar. Now, how exactly can we help you in this matter? The police appear to have done all that can be done.'

Our visitor looked at us with an expression of quiet determination. 'Despite the evidence, I simply cannot believe that my sister would take her own life. For one thing, her strong religious principles would totally forbid it. For another, when I sat down at dinner with her a few hours before she died, Adeline seemed in good spirits, and she was the last person in the world capable of disguising her emotions. I would like you and Miss Jessop to come down to Lampton House tomorrow – shall we say at mid-day? – to determine the truth of the matter. However poor Adeline died, it was not by her own hand, believe me … but the police cannot be persuaded otherwise.'

After Hester had agreed to undertake the investigation, and we had said goodbye to Mrs Millar, my friend sat in silence for some moments. When she spoke to me, it was with an unusually solemn air.

'Ivy, as you have now achieved such a commendable level of skill at the Marylebone shooting range, I should like to make you a present of my revolver. Henceforth you are to consider it your own. On the occasions we go armed on one of our adventures, it is hardly fair that you should never carry a weapon.'

As she spoke, Hester opened a drawer in her writing desk and took out her pearl handled .22 revolver, which she passed to me, together with a small box of cartridges.

I was taken aback by Hester's generosity. 'That is most kind, but I could not agree – I know how attached you are to that little weapon. Was it not a gift from Major Lynton?'

Hester nodded. 'It was, and do not forget to follow my father's advice, which is always to carry it loaded. As he used to say, if the situation does not warrant a loaded gun, then it does not warrant a gun at all. As to me, you will see that I am well provided for. I bought this for myself last week – what do you make of it?'

Hester reached into the drawer again, and took out a large handgun, which she passed to me to hold. It felt very heavy.

'The Mark 1 Webley service revolver,' Hester said, with a note of pride in her voice. 'Standard issue for the British Army, with a .455 cartridge – it rather dwarfs my old pistol. You must try this out the next time we go to the range – the recoil is not as severe as one might expect. I have bought a new and rather unfashionable handbag to accommodate it when required. I will be taking the Webley to Maidstone, so you can take your new revolver and have no fear of being the only sharpshooter in the town.'

Our train from Victoria Station to Maidstone the next morning took just over one hour, and by ten o'clock we had deposited our travelling bags at the Old Bell Hotel. Hester had insisted that we went prepared for a stay of several days, as it was clearly a case of particular complexity. We had already enjoyed one piece of good fortune: before her return home on the previous evening, Mrs Millar had told us that the police officer in charge of the case was Chief Inspector Harold Grimes. Several years ago, when he was an inspector in the Metropolitan Police, we had been able to give him some valuable assistance, and I was sure that he would remember us. Out of courtesy our first visit was to the central police station, where the chief inspector agreed to see us immediately.

'Miss Lynton! And Miss Jessop! It's very good to see you again, very good indeed! I well remember that case you helped me with – the Bermondsey fraudster. Did my career no harm at all. Now, I don't think it's difficult to guess what's brought you here today. Miss Cormac's suicide, I'd wager? A terrible tragedy. Mrs Millar isn't happy. I suppose you're working for her? Well, I've no objection. A fresh eye on the case can do no harm.'

Hester laughed. 'I see you are as sharp as I remember, Chief Inspector. You are exactly right. If you or one of your constables can accompany us to Lampton House, I would be very grateful. And if we do happen to discover anything of interest, you shall be the first to claim the credit. Ivy and I have had quite enough exposure in the newspapers of late.'

Grimes insisted on accompanying us himself, and ordered a police carriage to take us to the scene of the tragedy. On the way there, Hester asked him to tell us what he knew about the deceased's brother and sister.

'You'll have met Mrs Millar,' Grimes said. 'Her husband died in a riding accident just over two years ago. She's only thirty-five, and was left with two young sons. At the time of the accident she and her husband were living in Canterbury, but she moved back to her family home – Lampton House – after the accident. She's a strong-minded woman, and is involved in a good deal of charity work. Her sister, Adeline Cormac, had never left the family home – lived there all her life. Neither parent is living, and when her father died five years ago he left Lampton House and the bulk of his capital to Miss Cormac.'

I frowned. 'Was that not somewhat unusual? I would have expected his son to be the main benefactor.'

'Frederick had a good position in a London bank at the time, and Lucy's husband was comfortably off. Under the terms of Cormac's will, they each receive a generous monthly allowance for their lifetime. I suspect that Adeline's father felt that his unmarried daughter required the security of her own establishment.'

'And what are the provisions of Adeline's will?' Hester asked.

'I have spoken to her solicitor. The house has been left to her sister, Mrs Lucy Millar. All the capital that Adeline inherited from her father – a large fortune, I might add – has been divided equally between Lucy Millar and her brother, Frederick Cormac. I rather wish that the money had gone to some penniless relative, who would then have a very powerful motive for murder. But here's the house – just the sort of place I'd buy if I were a man of means!'

The carriage turned a corner and down a short gravelled drive to Lampton House. It was a detached Georgian residence, and although modest in size, its exterior was charming. Although just a mile or two from Maidstone, its setting amidst fields and woodland gave the house an air of rural isolation. Grimes did not take us to the main door, but to a rear entrance intended for tradespeople, where a constable stood guard.

'There's been a good deal of interest from the newspapers, as you might imagine,' Grimes said. 'We've had several reporters bothering the family. There's another policeman guarding the entrance hall. I have made a brief statement – that Miss Cormac has been found dead, and that the police are investigating the matter. Of course, everything will have to come out at the inquest. If you would like to follow me, I'll take you to the scene of the tragedy.'

'I understand that you have informed Mrs Millar that you think the cause of death was suicide?' Hester asked. 'She told us about the locked room, and the note you discovered.'

Grimes nodded. 'I felt it only fair to give her notice of the likely outcome. Mrs Millar is convinced that her sister would not kill herself, but I'm afraid that experience has taught me how often people act out of character. Here's the library – let me show you inside.'

As Grimes spoke, he took a large cast-iron key from his pocket and let us in. The room that we entered appeared part library, part study. A desk stood in one corner, and several comfortable chairs were arranged to receive the light from three large sash windows, which overlooked the lawned garden beyond. The walls were equipped with floor-to-ceiling shelves, filled with collections of sombre leather volumes which, I suspected, were now retained for decorative purposes, rather than for the amusement of the modern reader.

Hester turned to examine the heavy oak door through which we had entered the library. It was easy to see where new wood had been used to repair the damage to the frame, caused when the door was forcibly opened.

'The carpenter was called in as soon as possible, to make repairs,' Grimes said. 'I've kept the key. The butler has a spare, if needed.'

After spending some moments kneeling by the lock, and using the key to open and shut the bolt, Hester rose to her feet and walked to the windows. The heavy internal shutters could be secured by bolts at the top and bottom.

'You are sure that these shutters were bolted at the time Adeline Cormac died?' she asked the chief inspector.

'Very sure. The fact was noted by Mrs Millar when she entered the room, and later confirmed by the butler and Frederic Cormac.'

I indicated the desk in the corner. 'Is this where poor Miss Cormac was found?'

'Correct. It's no one's desk in particular – used by the family to write letters, and so on.'

Hester took me by the arm. 'Ivy, I am sure you will not mind if I ask you to play the part of the victim. If you could just take a seat at the desk – thank you. Now, Chief Inspector, how exactly was the body positioned? Ivy will very kindly try to duplicate the scene.'

Grimes seemed uneasy. 'Well, if Miss Jessop does not object … The, erm, victim was found with her forehead touching the desk, bent forward – and both arms stretched out, in front – like this, miss – that's exactly right. There was blood everywhere – as you know, she'd cut her throat. The paper knife was in her right hand. I've checked – Miss Cormac was right-handed.'

'And what about the note?' Hester asked.

'She'd pushed that to the far edge of the desk, so there was no blood on it.'

Hester walked slowly round the table, scrutinising it carefully. 'Ivy, you can resurrect yourself now. That was very helpful. Perhaps I could see the knife and the note later today, Chief Inspector?'

Grimes smiled broadly, and reached into the briefcase that he had brought with him.

'I can do better than that – I thought you'd want to see them. Here's the knife.'

Hester took it from him and carefully touched the blade against her thumb. It was an attractive item, with a bone handle decorated with copper bands. Even my inexpert eye could see that its original purpose had been nothing as benign as opening the post.

'My goodness!' she exclaimed. 'This is as sharp as a razor. How long has it been in the family? If I'm not mistaken, it's Italian – eighteenth century.'

'It belonged to the late Mr Cormac,' Grimes said. 'And here is the note.'

Hester took the piece of paper from him, held it up to the light for a few moments, then passed it to me. The wording was exactly as Mrs Millar had transcribed it: *I cannot go on living a lie. It is best ended now. Please forgive me.* It was written in a peculiarly ornate, old-fashioned copperplate style. The sheet was somewhat smaller than the normal letter size, and the line was written at the very top, the space below being blank.

'This is an interesting document,' she said. I knew Hester well enough to detect that in spite of her bland comment, there was a suppressed excitement in her voice.

'Tell me, Chief Inspector,' she continued. 'If it is true that Adeline Cormac committed suicide, then the clue to the reason must lie in this note. It surely suggests an intrigue of some kind – as if she is giving a message to a lover. Have your investigations looked at that possibility?'

Grimes pursed his lips. 'We have indeed, and I can tell you that few people appear to have led as blameless a life as Miss Cormac. Her small circle of friends were almost all members of the congregation of the local parish church, St Cecilia's in Maidstone. Even the servants can't come up with a breath of gossip, which is a rarity in my experience. However, I've another explanation for the note – and her suicide – which I think the coroner will agree with, in the circumstances.'

Hester looked surprised. 'Really? Then do enlighten us.'

'The poor woman was touched in the head – off her chump. Kept it well hidden, of course, but then she gave in to it. She probably *thought* she'd done something wrong – imagined a man was involved. I'm not surprised. She was a spinster of forty with no prospect of marriage or children. Very unnatural.'

I could not help laughing. 'Really, Chief Inspector, it seems that Hester and I are in grave danger! We are not many years younger than Adeline, and our status as childless spinsters is well established. It's as well you have forewarned us that insanity threatens …'

As the pink-faced Grimes began to mumble an apology, Hester interrupted him.

'You must excuse Ivy's satirical sense of humour, Chief Inspector. We are both extremely grateful for your time and trouble in indulging us. Now, if you can spare me just a few more minutes, we will leave you to your duties.'

With those words, Hester once more knelt down by the door. She took her handkerchief from her bag, rolled one corner of it into a cylindrical shape, and carefully inserted it in the keyhole. At that moment, a man's head and shoulders appeared round the part-opened doorway.

'Oh – Chief Inspector Grimes! I was not expecting you. And …'

The man's voice tailed off as he looked down at Hester, who was still on her knees, and was examining the end of the handkerchief, which she had withdrawn from the keyhole. She got to her feet and dusted down the front of her dress before speaking to the new arrival.

'Mr Cormac, I presume? Do accept my apologies for invading your home without prior warning. I am Miss Lynton. I am here – as is my colleague, Miss Jessop – at Mrs Millar's invitation, to investigate the tragic death of your sister.'

'Then I can't object, can I? Lucy's got some bee in her bonnet … but never mind. Of course I've heard your names before – Lynton and Jessop, the female detectives! I must say, I would have expected two severe matrons in cycling breeches – not the charming ladies I see before me.'

Hester nodded slightly in response to Cormac's compliment, and I imagined that her assessment of him was similar to mine. His carefully oiled hair was parted in the centre with geometrical exactness, his left cheek slightly contorted to keep his monocle in place. His complexion was ruddy, but had the blotched and veined appearance suggestive of a fondness for the spirits bottle, rather than the open air.

Hester forced a smile. 'I am afraid we are about to compound our ill manners by leaving you before we have had a chance to talk – but we have arranged to meet your sister. Perhaps we could find you here later today, or tomorrow?'

'Of course, of course. Always happy to oblige the ladies. I won't be going up to town for the next few days, so call upon me at any time. I'll be in my workshop this afternoon, if you need to find me. It's in the old stable block behind the house. Come to that, feel free to look me up any time you are in town. I'll jot down my address for you.'

'How kind of you,' Hester said. 'Ivy and I are always happy to make new acquaintances.'

I was surprised at her uncharacteristic response to Cormac's presumptuous suggestion, but guessed that she had her own reasons for her behaviour. He scribbled his address on a sheet torn from his pocketbook, which Hester carefully folded and stowed away in her purse.

We said our goodbyes to Chief Inspector Grimes, having first obtained his permission to call upon the police surgeon in Maidstone who had examined Adeline's body. Before seeking out Mrs Millar, I asked Hester about the significance of her investigation of the lock.

'Did your handkerchief reveal anything of interest?'

Hester glanced down the corridor to make sure that we were unobserved, then carefully took her handkerchief out of her bag. One corner was still rolled up after its insertion into the keyhole, and she held it out towards me. I could see the dark stain on the white linen very clearly.

'What is that?' I asked.

Hester sniffed at it delicately. 'Oil. Someone wanted to make sure that the key would turn easily in the lock. And do you see this, Ivy?'

She pointed to the tip of the handkerchief, and I could just make out the pattern of tiny, shining particles which clung to the oily material, like silver dust. Before I could question Hester, she continued.

'I cannot be sure what this means, but it is certainly interesting. No doubt all will become clear in due course. Meanwhile, we must keep these matters to ourselves for the time being. Now, let us seek out Mrs Millar.'

A maid confirmed that Mrs Millar was waiting for us in the parlour, and we were soon comfortably seated around a blazing fire. She rang for sandwiches and cake in lieu of luncheon, and when these had arrived she asked if we had made any progress in our investigation.

'We have already examined the scene of the tragedy,' Hester said. 'Chief Inspector Grimes is an old acquaintance of ours, and has been extremely helpful. We did not call you to the library, as I suspect it would be distressing for you. While we were there, we met your brother – he seemed surprised to see us.'

'That is understandable, as I have not seen Frederic since yesterday morning, and have had no chance to tell him about your impending visit. He spends a good deal of his time in London – he has a set of rooms there and prefers town life to our provincial society. Miss Lynton, Miss Jessop – I will be quite frank with you. Frederic and I do not "get on", as the vulgar saying has it.'

'When you called upon us at Newsome Street last night you mentioned that Frederic was employed by a London bank when your father passed away,' I said. 'Is that still the case?'

'Not at all! He has not worked there – he was a broker at Canning and Wheatley – for, let me see, over two years. He only started there at father's insistence, and since father died, Frederic has received a generous allowance irrespective of whether he chooses to work or not. He chooses not.'

It was Hester's turn to ask a question. 'Your brother mentioned a workshop. Is he engaged in manufacturing?'

'Hardly!' Mrs Millar laughed. 'He got it into his head – let me see, it would have been about six months ago, in April – that he could make his fortune by inventing a new type of bicycle brake. Frederic has always had a practical bent – he made some ingenious mechanical toys when he was a child – but of course father did not encourage it, as an artisan's occupation is hardly appropriate for a gentleman. He's equipped the old stables at the back of his house for his experiments, although not much seems to have come from it, apart from the destruction of some perfectly good bicycles.'

Hester took another slice of sponge cake, which I have to admit was the equal of anything baked by Mrs Parsons. 'Mrs Millar, before I ask you some further questions regarding your late sister, I would be grateful if you could explain to me the whereabouts of everyone when your sister's body was discovered last Sunday evening. You have already explained that you were called by the maid just after eleven o'clock, when you gave orders for the study door to be forced. Where were you when the maid called?'

'I was in my room, preparing for bed. I had been there since ten thirty.'

'And what about Mr Frederic Cormac?'

'He was in the billiard room, where he had been since dinner. He heard the noise from the study and joined us there until the police arrived – we sent the groom into Maidstone to call them out.'

Hester took her notebook out of her bag and jotted down a few lines. 'Thank you. Now, with reference to your sister, I need to pursue a line of questioning which you may find distasteful, for which I apologise. The solution to this case lies in the note that was found upon Adeline's person. When you called on us at Newsome Street last night you denied any knowledge of what the note might have referred to. I ask you again, is there the slightest possibility that something might have been preying on your sister's mind? You may rely upon our absolute confidence.'

Mrs Millar paused for some moments before replying. 'Well, there is perhaps something, though hardly enough to have generated such a dramatic statement. As you know, Adeline was a very devout Christian, and worshipped at our local parish church, St Cecilia's. Last year, our vicar retired and he was replaced by the Reverend Algernon Lewis, an energetic young man of thirty with a wife and two children. He had served in a parish in London. Although she is a committed Christian, Adeline has always been troubled by doubts – unnaturally so, I believe, and related to her nervous disposition. She had numerous conversations with the Reverend Lewis upon the subject – Mr Darwin's theories were particularly disquieting for her.'

'Tell me, where did they meet?' I interjected.

'Here, at Lampton House for tea, on a number of occasions. Mrs Lewis and I would talk about the children whist Adeline and the vicar had theological discussions. I believe they also often talked after church services – my sister particularly admired the Reverend Lewis's sermons. Let me be frank. Adeline was forty years old, yet in many ways she had the emotions of a naïve schoolgirl. I believe she was besotted with the new vicar. It was "the Reverend Lewis this" and "the Reverend Lewis that" all day, until I had to tell her to curb her enthusiasm. Frederic made something of a joke of the matter, which mortified her. But any suggestion of impropriety would be nonsense.'

Mrs Millar paused, understandably embarrassed.

'Thank you for being so frank, Mrs Millar,' Hester said, 'I am sure that your interpretation of the matter between your sister and the Reverend Lewis is correct. However, I must warn you that there is every possibility that the coroner may believe that although their relationship was entirely innocent, Adeline was under a delusion that she was in some way guilty of misconduct, and committed suicide whilst her mind was disturbed. That would explain her words: "I cannot go on living a lie."'

Mrs Millar shook her head. 'But surely you do not think my sister took her own life, Miss Lynton?'

Hester got to her feet. 'My opinions are not pertinent at present. I intend to establish the facts – and the facts will determine exactly what took place behind the locked door of the study last Sunday evening. Now, if you could ring to ask your butler to spare me a few minutes of his time, there are one or two things I would like to discuss with him. We can talk in his parlour, I think.'

My considerable experience of working with Hester had made me aware of her methods, and I was therefore not surprised that she chose to interview the butler, Higgins, in his own room. We declined his offer of further refreshment, and Hester began by making some anodyne enquiries about his length of service and the number of servants in the establishment. After thus putting the butler at his ease, Hester continued.

'If you could describe what you saw last Sunday night, I would be grateful.'

'Very well, miss. I was here in my sitting room, and just after eleven o'clock Hetty Lawrence – one of the housemaids – said that I was to go to the study straight away. When we got there, Mrs Millar arrived with Mr Frederic. The study door was locked – I got down on my knees and could see the key in the lock. Mrs Millar told us to break down the door, and inside there was poor Miss Adeline, dead as stone. Mr Frederic waited by the door and Mrs Millar went to tell the groom to ride into Maidstone and fetch the police.'

'And what did you do until the police arrived?' Hester asked.

'Mrs Millar sent me to wait at the end of the corridor, with Hetty, to make sure that none of the other servants got past. The police were here very quickly – we're only a couple of miles from the police station. When the sergeant saw what had happened he sent word for Chief Inspector Grimes to come.'

'You have been very helpful,' Hester said. 'I have one more question for you. The chief inspector told me that he had taken the key for the study, but that you had a spare. Is that correct?'

'It's true, miss. Those old locks always have spares – and just as well, for it would be the Devil's own job getting one made, if you'll pardon my language. There are two spares for each door on that corridor.'

'And could I see them?'

'They are on the keyboard in the pantry, Miss Lynton – I'll get them for you.'

We seemed to be waiting a long time for Higgins to return. When he did so, it was clear that something was puzzling him. He held out a large cast iron key on the palm of his hand. Attached to it with a length of twine was a yellowed paper label, *Library*.

'Well – I don't understand it. There is only one key. Yet I'm sure there were two.'

'Could the key have been put onto the wrong hook?' I asked.

Higgins shook his head. 'I've just been through them all. No, it's missing, for some reason.'

Hester smiled. 'No matter. Please go not concern yourself. No doubt one of the maids has mislaid it.'

Mrs Millar had kindly arranged for her own carriage to take us back into Maidstone, although out of respect to her feelings we did not tell her our destination: the town mortuary, where Grimes had told us we could expect to find Dr Brandon, the police surgeon. As we travelled the short distance into town, I turned to address Hester.

'Do you find any significance in the missing key? I can quite see that if the study door had been locked with no key inside, then someone who might be in possession of a spare could have locked it after leaving. But the study door was locked from the *inside*! A spare key could not have been used from the outside to do that.'

Hester frowned thoughtfully. 'It is nevertheless possible that the missing key provides a clue. The evidence thus far, I agree, does not explain it. The carriage is slowing up – ah, here is the mortuary. A new building, by the look of it. Let us hope that Grimes is right and that the police surgeon is here.'

The town mortuary was indeed only a year or so old; the date *1889* was carved into the stone lintel above the steps, which led up the glazed entrance door. A stern-faced, uniformed porter became much more helpful when we stated that Chief Inspector Grimes had directed us to see Dr Brandon. He had, we were told, just that minute completed a post mortem, and at that very moment the surgeon – a tall, middle-aged gentleman in a tweed suit – came up to the desk. Hester quickly explained the reason for our visit.

'If it is possible to see the deceased, we would be most grateful,' she concluded. 'I promise you that we will not take up too much of your valuable time.'

I could not help smiling at this excellent example of Hester's powers of ingratiation. Whilst capable of the most forthright assertion when needed, she usually obtained her ends with a more subtle approach.

The doctor nodded appreciatively. 'Normally, that would be out of the question. I would not be willing to expose two refined ladies such as yourselves to the harsh realities of the autopsy room. However, I am aware of your standing in your profession, and as Chief Inspector Grimes has sent you with his blessing – by all means, follow me.'

A few minutes later we descended a flight of stone steps into a basement, lit by a row of skylights in the roof. The walls were lined with gleaming white tiles, and the flagstone floor was washed clean. The air was chilled, as was no doubt the intention of the designer of the facility. A strong smell of carbolic acid filled the air. Dr Brandon walked to the side of the room, where a row of three sheeted corpses lay upon trestle tables. He took hold of the cloth that covered the right-hand corpse, and pulled it down to expose the head and shoulders.

It was, of course, not the first time that Hester and I had encountered a dead body during the course of our investigations, but there was something particularly poignant about the bloodless, scrubbed face of the poor woman exposed in front of us. Her thin features and her fine fair hair gave her appearance a fragility that was compounded by the ghastly wound below. She had suffered a very deep – and obviously fatal – cut to the right side of her neck. Hester leaded forward to inspect the lesion.

'This must have severed the right carotid artery,' she said. 'I suppose death would have been very rapid?'

'Indeed,' the doctor replied. 'A matter of seconds. I have not undertaken an examination of the internal organs, as the cause of death is so obvious.'

'And were there any other marks or injuries upon the body?' Hester asked.

'Well, there is one bruise. I will, of course, include it in my report for the coroner. But I cannot imagine it has any bearing upon Miss Cormac's death. I would imagine she had some small accident in the preceding day or two impacting upon the biceps brachii. But look for yourself.'

The doctor pulled the sheet further down, exposing the arms of the corpse in the manner of a low-cut evening dress. The front of the right upper arm showed a wide, reddish-purple bruise.

'An unusual place to knock oneself accidentally,' I observed.

'That is true, Ivy,' Hester said. 'Perhaps she fell onto some hard object. However, as Dr Brandon says, that could hardly have been the cause of death. Thank you, Doctor, that has been most helpful, and we must take up no more of your time. Ivy and I will show ourselves out. We will convey our thanks to Chief Inspector Grimes.'

After returning to the Old Bell to enjoy an early supper, it was Hester's suggestion that we should attempt to call upon the Reverend Algernon Lewis after he had taken the evening service at St Cecilia's. Thus, just after eight o'clock we arrived at the vicarage – a pleasant villa on the outskirts of the town – and presented our cards. The maid showed us into the vicar's study without delay.

The Reverend Lewis was a fresh-faced, strongly-built gentleman who looked younger than his thirty years. When we introduced ourselves it was clear that the vicar was uneasy in his mind. He stood with our cards in his hand, frowning slightly.

'Miss Lynton ... Miss Jessop – you are very welcome. Do sit down. Forgive me if I do not offer you refreshment, but I feel that our conversation will be best uninterrupted. I am aware of your standing in your profession, and can think of only one reason for your visiting me; the tragic events of last Sunday at Lampton House. I know that the police are investigating Adeline Cormac's death; surely they do not suspect foul play?'

Hester lowered her voice. 'I have been asked by a family member to carry out my own investigation of the matter, with the approval of the police. I would like to show you – in the strictest confidence – a note, which was found at Miss Cormac's side after her death. This is a transcript, but there is no question that the original is in the deceased's own handwriting.'

Hester opened her pocketbook at a page where she had copied down Adeline's last message. The vicar read it, his face registering shock and surprise.

Eventually, he spoke. 'And what have the police made of this?'

'I will speak plainly,' Hester said. 'There is some suggestion that Miss Cormac had feelings for you that went beyond those proper between a parishioner and her vicar. She may have had the misguided belief that these feelings were reciprocated, and that she needed to atone by taking her own life. I do not think that anyone supposes anything irregular took place between you, but I would like to hear your view on the matter.'

The vicar sat down heavily in his chair. 'You have spoken plainly, so I will do the same. I had begun to feel that Miss Cormac was seeking me out too frequently. My wife and I visited Lampton House on a number of occasions, just as I would visit the family of any other parishioner, but Miss Cormac would also try to buttonhole me after church services. For the last few weeks I have taken the precaution of never seeing her alone, but unfortunately I was not the only one who had noticed her – how shall we put it – fixation. There was a regrettable incident two weeks ago last Sunday – I shall tell you, because you will probably hear of it anyway, as you are investigating the case. It was after the Sunday morning service. Somewhat to my surprise, Frederic Cormac was amongst the congregation – his church attendance is very irregular. I was bidding goodbye to my parishioners, and as Mrs Millar and Miss Cormac were taking their leave, Frederic Cormac made some *sotto voce* comment to Adeline about "saying goodbye to her sweetheart". She was visibly upset and I challenged him. I told him that if he had anything to say that concerned me, he should come out with it like a man, rather than whispering behind his hand like a schoolboy.'

Hester chuckled. 'My goodness! I see you are a believer in directness, Reverend. And how did he respond?'

'He looked angry, but held his voice. It was just as well, because I would have knocked him down for tuppence. However, if he holds any grudge, he may well have the last laugh. This business about poor Adeline's note is bound to come out in the inquest. Although we both know that I have done nothing wrong, that is not how the bishop is likely to view the matter. This could be very serious for me.'

Hester stood up. 'I would not be too despondent, sir. I believe that there is a strong possibility that the true facts of the case will soon emerge. Meanwhile, say nothing to anyone on the subject. I will make sure that you are told of any significant developments. Your statement has been most helpful, and we will take up no more of your time.'

The next morning, Hester took the early train back to Victoria Station, informing me that there were some matters in the case that required her presence in London.

'If all goes well, we will have a delicate mission to undertake this evening,' she said. 'It will require us to stay at the Old Bell for one further night. You may return to London with me for the day, or wait here for my return – whatever you wish. I shall be back by six o'clock this evening.'

As a journey back and forth from the metropolis seemed pointless, I opted to remain in Maidstone for the day, which I spent happily exploring that historic town. At Hester's appointed hour of return I was waiting for her in our room at the hotel.

Hester was characteristically punctual, arriving just a few minutes after six. She carried with her a large, cheaply-made suitcase, which she deposited with a heavy thud onto the floor.

'I hope you have not decided to extend your stay in Maidstone indefinitely!' I laughed. 'You seem to have brought a month's supply of belongings with you.'

'I have, in fact, brought some items for *both* of us,' Hester said with a smile. 'Although they will not equip us for any venture into sophisticated society, they will do well enough for the expedition that I have planned.'

My friend showed me what she had brought: two similar outfits for each of us, all second-hand, consisting of hard-wearing trousers – corduroy and moleskin – Norfolk jackets, mufflers and flat caps.

Hester pointed to the latter. 'I have bought large sizes, so our hair should be concealed quite easily,' she said. 'Let us hope the previous owners were not too allergic to bathwater. I have borrowed a key from the porter, who has let me have a key to the hotel side entrance – as well as the loan of two bicycles for the evening. A half sovereign did wonders for his cooperation.'

Although I was well used to Hester's habit of revealing very little of her plans until they were well advanced, this mystery was too much even for me.

'No doubt all is to be revealed very shortly,' I said with a smile. 'However, knowing where we are going would be very welcome. I take it that we will not be attending the mayor of Maidstone's soirée?'

'Hardly,' Hester chuckled. 'I intend us to pay a visit to Frederic Cormac's workshop. I suggest we leave the hotel at eleven o'clock this evening. In the event that anyone should see us, we will hopefully be mistaken for touring cyclists returning home for the evening. There is a full moon, which should let us see our way. I suggest we leave our bicycles before we get to Lampton House – I noticed that there is a track behind the grounds which should allow us to approach the old stable block without attracting the attention of anyone enjoying a late evening stroll.'

'Tell me, Hester,' I asked. 'Do you feel that you are now close to solving the case?'

'I believe that I now know *what* happened in the library at Lampton House last Sunday, and *why* it happened. All that remains is to supply the third piece in the jigsaw: *how* the deed was accomplished. Let us hope that tonight's expedition supplies the answer. Incidentally, I would be grateful if you could put your revolver in your handbag. If my theory is correct, we may find ourselves dealing with very determined criminal.'

All went according to Hester's plan, and by eleven thirty that evening we were directly behind that old stable block where Frederic Cormac had his workshop. Close by, Lampton House was in darkness save for the yellow light of an oil lantern shining through one of the servants' windows in an attic room. A window in the side of the stables was not overlooked by the house, and the clear moonlight meant that we could see something of the inside, despite the grimy condition of the glass. A bicycle lay in pieces against the opposite wall, and several pieces of machinery surrounded a large work bench.

'The door is at the front – too easily seen from the house,' Hester whispered. 'This window offers the best way in. Unfortunately, we will have to cause some damage, but if we take some tools away with us when we leave, Cormac will think he has been burgled.'

Hester took a short jemmy from her bag – a tool I had seen her use before – and inserted it within the window frame. With a small effort the wood splintered, and the window could be swung open. A few seconds later, we had both scrambled inside.

The front windows had been recently cleaned, and admitted enough moonlight to make the interior visible.

Hester ran her fingers down the centre of the workbench, then held her hand up to the light.

'This is very dusty,' she said. 'If Cormac did visit his workshop on Wednesday afternoon, he could not have done much work on his new type of bicycle brake. Ah – here is a brake he has removed from one of his bicycles.'

Hester picked up the brake mechanism, which appeared no different from any other. Next to it was a metal slab, with a series of holes drilled into it. The holes were small, being no wider than a grain of rice. Hester picked it up and hefted it in her hand.

'Cast iron. Why would one want to drill holes in it, I wonder?

Hester lifted a canvas cover from the bulky mechanism that occupied one end of the bench.

'Is this the machine that has been used for the process? Perhaps not – it looks more like a lathe to my inexpert eye. But to use the popular phrase, I believe that we are getting warmer.'

She pointed to the contents of a wooden tray nearby.

'Do you see, Ivy? Those are screw-cutting taps and dies, if I am not mistaken. And some long, thin, metal rods. This is most interesting. Do you suppose ...'

Hester was unable to complete her question, for at that moment the outer door to the workshop was flung open, and a man stepped into the room. He held an oil lamp in one hand, and the glare from the reflector momentarily dazzled me. It was Frederic Cormac, and in his left hand he carried a double-barrelled shotgun. He put the lantern down on a bench next to him, and pointed the shotgun towards us.

Hester spoke calmly. 'Well done, Mr Cormac. I see that you must have noticed some movement in your workshop and concluded that a burglary was in progress. I must plead guilty to breaking in – and am happy to do so, if you wish to send for the police. You have, of course, committed no crime in apprehending us.'

'A nice try, Miss Lynton.' Cormac's lips curled in an unpleasant snarl. 'But if you think I'm going to let you and your little friend walk out of here, you are much mistaken. I found you here because I was expecting you. I saw you meddling with the door lock in the library – then you made the mistake of asking Higgins about the spare keys. He told me straight off when I asked him what you'd had to say – he's an old fool and suspects nothing. Just throw your bag at my feet, missy – gently.'

Hester did as Cormac ordered, and her handbag landed next to him with a heavy thump. He bent down and rummaged within it, his eyes still trained upon us. Then he withdrew Hester's Webley revolver and placed it carefully on the workbench beside him.

'You see, I have heard of you before, Miss Lynton. Not a very ladylike weapon, I have to say. I suppose you think you know all about this case, now?'

As he spoke, I caught Hester's eye, and moved my hand towards my bag. She gave a barely perceptible shake of the head, so I went no further in my attempt to retrieve my pistol – but told myself that I would do so the moment that Cormac's attention was off us.

'I certainly know *most* of it,' Hester said. 'Although I am curious about one thing. How did you persuade poor Adeline to write her letter to the Reverend Lewis? Surely the last thing she would have wished would be to end her connection with him.'

'That was simple.' As Cormac spoke his eyes glinted with an unnatural strangeness, and in that instant I had a glimpse into his diseased mind which made me cold with fear.

'I told her that if she did *not* write her letter – to my dictation – I would personally see the diocesan bishop – and Lewis's wife for good measure – and tell them that Lewis was conducting an illicit liaison with my sister, thereby disgracing them both. Of course, I only gave her the opportunity to write the first few lines from my dictation.'

The truth of the 'suicide note' was then plain to me. Adeline had started to write a letter to the Reverend Lewis, as Cormac had described, using the Lampton House notepaper. Then he had taken the incomplete letter from her and cut off the headings and the salutation, leaving only the words that she wrote at the beginning – and trimming the rest of the paper around it.

Cormac addressed me directly. 'Miss Jessop, there is a trap door to your right. The brass ring is flush with the floorboards. Kindly pull it open and lay the door flat on the opposite side.'

After I had done what he asked – with something of a struggle – I saw that a set of stone steps led down into a dark cellar.

Cormac stepped back and pointed his shotgun directly at me.

'This is what I propose,' our captor said. 'The two of you will go down those steps, whereupon I will close the trapdoor and secure the fastening to prevent you getting out. I will then make my escape – I will leave the country as soon as I can. I'm sure that if you bang on the trap door for a day or two someone will eventually find you – or you can starve to death, for all I care. Now, down those steps you go. Miss Jessop first, I think.'

My momentary relief in thinking that Cormac was to leave us unharmed was soon dispelled by Hester's next words.

'Come now Mr Cormac, you can hardly expect us to believe that. Ivy, stay where you are. Here is my analysis of the situation: you intend to kill us, and then dispose of our bodies at some later stage. Would you have told me about Adeline's note otherwise? If you shoot us where we stand, there is every likelihood that the shots will be heard at Lampton House, and if anyone then investigates, that would be the end of your scheme. However, once we are safely in the cellar, then you could follow us down, shoot us where the sound will be safely muffled, then return to retrieve our bodies at your leisure.'

'Very clever!' Cormac snarled. 'But you see, I have another plan. If you don't go down the steps I'll shoot you here, push you both in the cellar, and if anyone comes I'll blame poachers for the shots and say I was after them myself. So down you go, Miss Jessop, or else.'

Hester laughed, and folded her arms. 'You do realise that Chief Inspector Grimes is observing your every move through the window behind you?'

Cormac swivelled round, and at the same instant – for I had been rehearsing the move in my head – I pulled the revolver from my handbag, pointed it at Cormac as he turned back towards us, and pulled the trigger. Despite the small size of the weapon the sound in the enclosed confines of the workshop was deafening. Cormac screamed and clutched his right arm, keeping hold of the shotgun with one hand. A moment later Hester stepped forward and snatched the weapon from him, knocking him to the floor with the butt.

'Well done, Ivy,' she exclaimed. 'Those hours at the shooting range have not been wasted! I will guard our prisoner here – he will not bleed to death from that little bullet – whilst you get help from Lampton House. I do not want to risk escorting such an unpleasant gentleman there in the dark, even in his current, rather damaged, state.'

Less than an hour later we were sitting in the parlour of Lampton House with Chief Inspector Grimes, a restorative tumbler of whisky and water in front of each of us. Two of his constables had returned to Maidstone in a police carriage with Frederic Cormac, whose wound – as Hester had predicted – proved no threat to his life.

'Miss Lynton and Miss Jessop, I must congratulate you,' Grimes said. 'I could suggest that it might have been better to have flushed out Cormac with my help, but that would be churlish of me. That was very fine marksmanship, Miss Jessop. I could hardly have objected if you'd shot

Cormac stone dead, but as it is, we have every hope that he will admit to everything in the hope of clemency. There's no possibility of him escaping a hanging, however.'

I mumbled my embarrassed thanks at the chief inspector's compliment, as Hester interjected.

'Somehow I do not think you will get a word out of that reprobate,' she said. 'However, I believe that everything about the case is now apparent, and will be very pleased to explain all to you.'

My long friendship with Hester had taught me that she liked nothing better than to exhibit her powers of deduction, and had to suppress a smile at her obvious pleasure at the prospect of revealing all.

'Tell me first, how did Cormac lock the library door from the outside after he'd killed his sister?' the policeman asked.

Hester topped up her glass. 'That was the cleverest part of his scheme. He took full advantage of his talent for mechanical ingenuity. He must have thought of it back in April, if not before, because that was when he set up his workshop in the old stable block – ostensibly to develop a new type of bicycle brake. In fact, it was to give him the excuse to set up some machinery and construct the device he needed to lock the study door behind him. At some time prior to the murder, Cormac took a spare library key from Higgins's keyboard. They are old cast iron keys, and although it is a brittle metal, cast iron is surprisingly easy to drill. Cormac used a bench drill and metalworking tap to thread a small hole in the end of the key; he practised on some scraps of cast iron first. Then, he used a die to put a matching thread onto the end of a long thin rod. He took the specially adapted key to the library with him, and after he had killed Adeline he placed the key in the lock and shut the door behind him. He then screwed the rod into the key-end from *outside* the door, turned it so that the door was locked, then unscrewed the rod. No doubt he practised the whole method beforehand, when he was alone in the library, to make sure that all worked as planned. Of course, after the body was discovered, Frederic replaced his customised key with the original, to make sure that no one noticed the tampering – he had ample opportunity to make the switch when left alone to guard the door.'

'So that was why you discovered oil in the lock,' I said. 'Cormac had oiled the mechanism to make sure it turned smoothly. But what about the silver dust you found?'

'Drilling and threading creates some fine detritus,' Hester said. 'Some of it had clung to the key and rod during the process. What we saw on the handkerchief was powdered cast iron, not yet sufficiently exposed to the air to be oxidised. When I learned of Cormac's technical talents, it seemed likely that some kind of mechanical contrivance had been used to lock the door after him.'

The chief inspector took a large gulp of his whisky. 'Amazing, Miss Lynton. His motive must have been the money he stood to inherit on Adeline's death?'

Hester nodded. 'Absolutely. I went up to London this morning, and spoke to Cormac's last employer, the manager of the Canning and Wheatley Bank – someone I have met professionally before. He remembered Cormac as a most unreliable employee. Even better, he could direct me to one or two of Cormac's many creditors; in short, the man owes a very great deal of money, and the chickens were shortly coming home to roost. Without the inheritance from Adeline, her brother would have been a ruined man.'

'There is one further thing,' Grimes said. 'How was Cormac able to persuade his sister to write a suicide note? Surely she would have screamed the place down!'

Hester explained how the note had been dictated in the guise of a letter, then trimmed to size after Adeline had been killed.

'If she had known what was in her brother's mind, and called out for help, his whole plan would have been ruined,' Hester said. 'Thus, the ghastly method chosen for her death. He could not have forced her to take poison, for example, without risking an uproar. I believe I know what took place in the study that evening.'

Hester pulled an upright chair away from a side table and placed it in front of us, then stood behind it.

'Ivy, would you be so good as to take a seat?' she asked. 'Thank you. Adeline thought she was being bullied into writing a letter – nothing worse. When she had written the desired words, her brother snatched the unfinished letter from her. He then moved behind her, picked up the paper knife with his left hand – I noticed he was left-handed when he wrote down his London address for Ivy and me – wrapped his right arm round his sister, holding her tightly enough to cause the bruising to her upper arm identified in the post-mortem. I suspect that the paper knife had been sharpened beforehand by Cormac in his workshop, in preparation for his vicious attack.'

Hester extended the index finger of her left hand and placed it across my throat, seizing me from behind as she had described.

'You will recall that the right carotid artery was severed,' she said. 'As you see – exactly what you would expect from a left-handed attack from behind. Adeline was right-handed and was found with the knife in her right hand – if she had cut her throat herself, the *left* artery would have been severed. Thank you, Ivy, that was most helpful. By the way, Chief Inspector, you will recollect the posture in which the body was found – bent forward, you told us, with her arms stretched out in front of her? If she *had* cut her own throat I suspect the body would have fallen down awkwardly, and not in such a neat pose. However, that is a minor matter. You have more than enough to ensure that Cormac keeps his appointment with the hangman's noose without such trivial details.'

Before we took our leave of the chief inspector, Hester had one more thing to add.

'I would consider it a great favour if you could have a private word with the Bishop of Maidstone. Although the Reverend Lewis is entirely innocent in this case, there is a saying about mud sticking which is sadly all too true. If you could stress Lewis's blamelessness, and the kindness he showed to the deceased, I would be very grateful.'

Such was the lateness of the hour that Mrs Millar – profuse in her thanks for the light we had shed upon the true facts of her older sister's death – insisted we spend the remainder of the night at Lampton House. The next morning, we collected our belongings from the Old Bell Hotel, and it was not long before we were enjoying the luxury of a first-class railway carriage to ourselves, en route to Victoria Station.

'One thing still puzzles me,' I said. 'Why did Frederic Cormac set up his workshop so close to home? If he had rented a manufacturing space in London, no clue to his scheme would ever have been found.'

'A more public arena would have meant that his metalworking experiments might have been noted by other craftsmen. Then, if Chief Inspector Grimes had looked into Cormac's enterprise he might have deduced his clever scheme. No, on the whole I think Cormac felt safer with his enterprise closer to home. Unfortunately – for him – he must have thought that dismantling his workshop immediately after Adeline's death might have been suspicious. He probably planned to leave the matter for a week or two before getting rid of the incriminating machinery. Incidentally, I have asked the chief inspector to take the credit for solving the case. I hope you do not object to your skills as a marksman – or rather markswoman – being concealed from the public.'

'Not at all,' I said with a smile. 'In fact, I have a small confession to make. My shot at Cormac's arm may have saved him for the scaffold, but it was entirely unintentional. I simply followed the advice given to us by Sergeant Morris at the shooting range: "Always aim for the centre of the target, whether it's a funfair bulls-eye or an axe-wielding maniac". I was just a little inaccurate.'

'Quite accurate enough for our purposes,' Hester said. 'I cannot bring myself to feel sorry for the man, but I dare say he would have preferred to have been killed outright than to spend his last days contemplating his dreadful fate. It often occurs to me how inadvisable it is to ignore a natural talent in favour of a status supposedly more desirable in society. If Frederic's father had allowed his son to make a career of his mechanical aptitude – rather than forcing him to stultify in a bank – he might have been remembered as one of Britain's foremost inventors, rather than the perpetrator of a particularly ingenious and malevolent crime.'

5. The Adventure of the Diamond Necklace

It was a cold November evening in 1895 when Hester and I first met Lady Ellen Talbot. *Burke's Peerage* told us that she was twenty-five years old and the eldest daughter of the Earl and Countess of Nantwich. Other than that – as neither Hester nor I were *aficionados* of the society pages – we knew nothing of her.

The young woman who was shown into our sitting room by Mrs Parsons was immaculately dressed in a fashionable yellow and heliotrope silk dress, and was both graceful and assured in manner. Yet, beneath her delicate features I could detect a distinct unease. She had left her winter coat and hat downstairs with Mrs Parsons, and accepted our invitation to draw her chair closer to our blazing fire. After the usual introductions, Hester invited our visitor to state her business.

'Miss Lynton ... Miss Jessop – I have come to you because of your reputation for confidentiality. The matter upon which I seek your assistance is one which requires the utmost discretion. Should any word leak out, the consequences for me would be grave indeed.'

Hester smiled reassuringly. 'Believe me, Lady Ellen, my practice as a consulting detective would not survive for long if secrecy was not absolute! You may speak freely in front of us.'

Our client seemed rather happier at those words.

'Very well. I am engaged to marry the Duke of Walton – our wedding is to take place in April of next year. A situation has arisen, which threatens that happy event. Two months ago I was given a present by the duke – a diamond necklace, which had belonged to his late mother. It is undoubtedly a most valuable item, but its true significance lies in its provenance. The duke is twelve years my senior, and man of strict principles and loyalties. The loss of the necklace would be a grave blow for him.'

'It is missing?' Hester asked. 'What are the circumstances?'

A slight but perceptible flush perfused our visitor's flawless complexion.

'A most unfortunate occurrence. Last Thursday – five days ago – I attended an evening supper party at the London residence of Sir Howard Lawrence, the banker. I left somewhat early at nine o'clock, pleading a headache. However, rather than returning home I then went to the house of an Italian gentleman and his widowed sister, with whom I am acquainted, in Portland Place – Signor Angelo Baraldi and Signora Maria Calvino. Signor Baraldi is an importer of olive oil. My father and mother would disapprove of my friendship with them, and so when I returned home I let them assume I had been at the Lawrences' all evening. I had taken the necklace to the Lawrences' party in its case, and put it on as I arrived. When I left, I put it in its case, which I kept in my handbag, and did not wear it when I visited Angelo – that is, Signor Baraldi. Then, when I returned home to our town house in Wimpole Street I discovered to my dismay that the case was empty!'

Hester looked puzzled. 'You will forgive my question, but why did you not immediately inform the police?'

Lady Ellen lowered her eyes. 'Because the necklace could only have been stolen when I was at Signor Angelo Baraldi's house. It would be hard – very hard – to explain my presence there. You see, when I arrived, I discovered that the signora was not in fact present that evening, and that I would be alone with her brother. To put it bluntly, there would be a scandal.'

'Ah – I see now,' Hester said. 'And what time did you arrive home?'

'A little before eleven o'clock that evening. I have my own key to the side door.'

'Is it at all possible that you might have accidentally left the necklace case at your friends' house?' I interjected. 'I suppose you have asked the signor and signora if they have seen it?'

Our client clasped her hands nervously. 'Of course – I called there on the following day, and spoke to both of them. They were adamant that the necklace had not been left there. Signor Baraldi suggested that I might have left the necklace in the cab that took me back to Wimpole Street, but I am certain that I did not.'

'Could you describe the item for us?' I asked.

'It is a choker, with strands of alternate length – there are seventy-three diamonds in all. It is unique, I believe.'

At that moment Mrs Parsons arrived bearing a tray of tea and cake, which she left on our dining table for us to serve ourselves. Hester stood up and took charge of the teapot.

'There is one thing that I must ask you, Lady Ellen,' she said. 'If we are to recover the necklace, it is essential that you are frank with us. Do you think that it is possible that Signor Baraldi took the necklace from its case during the course of your visit that evening?'

'That is exactly why I have come to you,' the young woman said. 'I think that it is more than possible – I believe that it is *probable* that Angelo stole my necklace, knowing that it would be impossible for me to accuse him without ruining my reputation and my plans to marry the duke. I am afraid that I have had evidence before of his flawed character – evidence that I foolishly chose to ignore. I even believe that I know where the necklace is now – not that the knowledge will be of any help in recovering it. Last Thursday was not the only time that I visited the signor and his sister. On a previous occasion – two or three weeks ago – I overheard a conversation between the two of them; I confess to lingering outside their drawing room when they believed me to be elsewhere in the house. Angelo had passed a small package to Maria, and told her – lowering his voice – to "take this to our safe deposit box after lunch". Then at luncheon, when I asked Maria what her plans were for the day, she told me that she had some business to transact at Weatherhead's Bank in the Strand. As she spoke, her brother gave her a brief but unpleasant glance, as if he disapproved of her giving me that information, and Maria remained silent for the rest of the meal.'

'That is most interesting,' Hester said. 'Tell me, do you feel that Maria Calvino is happy in her brother's household?'

Lady Ellen shook her head. 'I believe she is not. She once told me that she was living in London when her husband died – she has no children – and would have liked to return to her parents in Palermo, but had no money. I understand that she assists her brother in his business affairs – running errands and so on. I also believe that she is a little afraid of him.'

'Thank you, that is very clear,' Hester said. 'How much would you be prepared to pay for the return of the necklace?'

'I am a wealthy woman in my own right, Miss Lynton. I would pay a great deal to regain the necklace; up to £1,000 if necessary.'

I could not help a smothered gasp escaping me. That was an enormous sum.

'Just one final question, if I may,' Hester said. Is Signor Baraldi always in London, or does he ever travel in connection with his business interests?'

'He is often away from London, but never for more than a few days. I believe he is to travel to Paris later this month, but I do not know the exact date.

'Well, we shall see what we can do. Leave the matter in our hands. I will let you know – discreetly, of course – if there are any developments. Let me take you downstairs and we will retrieve your coat and hat.'

When Hester returned she seemed deep in thought, and I was not surprised when she sat down in her favourite chair and placed a cigarette in her long ebony holder. Five minutes must have passed, during which time she did her best to fill our room with the strong aroma associated with the Turkish brand; a sure sign that Hester was struggling to find the solution to a difficult problem. Finally, she got to her feet and moved across to stoke up the fire.

'I will see Jacob Carpenter tomorrow morning,' she said. 'I have a task to which his talents are well suited. There is also a commission which I would like you to undertake for me, Ivy. It is not too onerous, and I am sure that you will not object to a little dissimulation in a good cause.'

I readily agreed to my friend's request, and therefore the following morning I took a cab to the Strand in search of Weatherhead's Bank, where Hester had asked me to rent a safe deposit box, assuring me that I could use my own name. When I had asked the reason for this, she explained that we needed to know how the bank's system operated before we could lay our own plans. The clerk was very welcoming, and the procedure could not have been more straightforward. After completing a form – on payment of the five-guinea annual fee – I was given a box number, a letter of authorisation and a key. The procedure for placing or retrieving in item in the box was then explained to me. On arrival at the bank I would need to show my letter and key, and sign the depositors' book. I would then be led to a small anteroom furnished with a desk and chair, and my box would be brought to me, to be taken back to the strong room after I had finished with it and rung the bell.

When I got back from my errand, Hester had just returned from her visit to Jacob Carpenter. Jacob was a former policeman, and the proprietor of a private detective agency whose bread-and-butter work consisted of finding missing persons, following the spouses of suspicious husbands and wives, and similarly tedious, time-consuming investigations. Hester had used his services on a number of occasions in the past.

'Jacob's men and women will keep a sharp eye on the movements of Angelo Baraldi,' Hester said. 'The moment Baraldi leaves the country, Jacob will inform us.'

'Surely by then he will have disposed of the necklace, and it will be too late?' I said.

'That is, of course, a possibility, but I think it unlikely. Baraldi cannot be certain that Lady Ellen has not told the police of her suspicions. For all he knows, there may be a net closing around him, waiting to find the necklace in his possession. He seems a cool customer, and I think more likely to do the sensible thing and wait until the affair has died down. He does not appear to be short of money – leaving the necklace in the safe keeping of his sister for a year or so would be his easiest option. No, I think the solution to this case lies with his sister, but we must wait until her brother is safely out of the way before we spring our trap. Incidentally, Jacob was able to tell me some interesting things about that gentleman. Although outwardly a respectable merchant, Signor Baraldi has a sinister reputation. Not only does he prey on wealthy young women, but he is also an associate of that shadowy criminal organisation, the *Mantello Rosso* – the Red Cloak. You will no doubt remember the ruthless methods they employed in the case of the Bloomsbury medium. Now, as there is no more to do in this matter until we hear from Jacob, I suggest we turn our thoughts to happier topics. There is a performance of *Rigoletto* at Covent Garden tonight, and if you are agreeable, I will reserve a box for us.

It was not until a week later that a that a telegram arrived for Hester after breakfast, giving us the news that we had been waiting for. *AB left Dover for France this morning. J Carpenter*. Hester clapped her hands with glee.

'Now we can act!' she said. 'I will go to the post office immediately, and send Signora Calvino a telegram. I will explain everything when I return.'

When Hester reappeared half an hour later, she opened her pocketbook and showed me a transcription of the telegram that she had sent to Maria.

Go to 12 Newsome Street today and collect item from Mrs Jones who is expecting you then take item to bank deposit box. Will explain all when I return. Angelo.

'Perhaps I am being obtuse, Hester,' I said with a frown. 'I can see that we can now expect Maria to come here hoping to receive something from "Mrs Jones". But how will that help our recovery of the necklace?'

'Because when Maria arrives, she will have with her all that is needed to access her safe deposit box. It will then be our task to persuade her to retrieve Lady Ellen's necklace.'

I said nothing. Much as I admired Hester's abilities, it seemed to me somewhat optimistic to expect Maria to undertake an action so obviously contrary to her brother's wishes. Evidently, Hester had great confidence in her powers of persuasion.

After Mrs Parsons had cleared away the remains of our luncheon, I thought I could detect some signs of anxiety in Hester's demeanour. It was after all possible that Maria Calvino might have decided not to carry out the instructions in the telegram.

'Do you think Maria would have found it odd to have received a telegram dispatched in London, when she knew that her brother had left for Dover?' I asked.

'Perhaps, if her brother had been a reliably conventional man involved in nothing more than the importation of olive oil. However, I am sure that she knows his dealings are rather darker and more inscrutable than that. He might well have changed his plans at the last minute – or even got a confederate to send the message on his behalf. No, on balance I believe that she would be more afraid of *not* doing as he has asked. I would have much preferred to have sent her a written note, but as I have had no samples of Baraldi's handwriting to copy, that was alas impossible.'

I could not help smiling, remembering the occasions upon which Hester had demonstrated an uncanny ability to imitate the handwriting of others – I had more than once suggested that if the demand for consulting detectives were to collapse, she could very easily turn her hand to forgery.

It was at that moment that the distant sound of the electric bell reached us. Our housekeeper had been given instructions to show our caller up to "Mrs Jones" and a few moments later there was a knock on our door.

Our visitor was a slender woman in her early thirties, dressed in a smart tailor-made jacket and skirt, with neatly coiffured dark hair. In physical appearance she was, in fact, very similar to Hester – although her demeanour had none of the forthright confidence of my friend.

'Signora Maria Calvino? Do take a seat,' Hester said. 'I am aware that you came here in search of a Mrs Jones. I am afraid that I have a confession to make. My name is Hester Lynton, and this is my friend and colleague, Miss Ivy Jessop. I thought it possible that our names would be familiar to you; I am a consulting detective, and Miss Jessop assists me. I therefore gave the name of Jones, to ensure that you came as requested. The telegram you received was sent by me – not by your brother.'

'Then I have been brought here under false pretences!' Maria cried. 'I must leave immediately.' Her English, I noted, was excellent, although spoken with a slight accent from the land of her birth.

'At least let me explain,' Hester said. 'Then I promise you that you will be free to go if you so wish.'

Maria subsided in her seat without further comment, and Hester continued.

'Believe me, I regret the need for my deception, but I had little choice in the matter. The situation is as follows. I am aware that there is a safe deposit held in your name at Weatherhead's Bank in the Strand. I assume that you use it on your brother's behalf. As you may know – or may perhaps have guessed – some of the objects stored in that box are stolen. There is one item in particular, which I intend to recover on behalf of a client, and I would like you to help me. Am I right in thinking that Angelo gave you a small package to deposit at the beginning of this month, shortly after Thursday the thirty-first of October?'

Maria shook her head violently. 'I'm afraid that is quite impossible.

He did give me a package to deposit at that time, but I know nothing of what is in the box – I use it as my brother orders. How can I trust you? You'll have to wait until Angelo returns home, and ask him.'

'You do not perhaps understand the situation in which your brother has placed you,' Hester said. 'My client does not wish to involve the official police in the matter, but if necessary I will have summon them. They will obtain the necessary legal permissions in order to examine *your* safe deposit box – remember, it is held in your name. When the stolen items are discovered you will be charged with complicity in the theft, and almost certainly convicted. As it is a first offence, the judge is likely to be lenient. I would imagine that a sentence of two or three years will be deemed sufficient.'

Maria said nothing, but I could tell from her frightened expression and pale features that Hester's words had filled her with dread.

'There, is however, an alternative course of action open to you,' continued Hester. 'Would you like the opportunity to return to your family in Palermo?'

Our visitor's eyes widened with surprise. 'Of course – I can think of nothing better. But I, have no money, and my family are very poor. I could not return and be a burden on them.'

'You would not need to be. My client is willing to pay a large reward for the item that has been stolen from her. If you help us recover it, then I will pay you £1,000 and make sure you return safely to Italy.'

'With such a large sum, I would be a very happy woman,' Maria said. 'I would be able to buy a house in Palermo for me, my mother and father and older sister to live in for always. What would I have to do?'

Hester stood up and folded her arms. 'Come with Ivy and me to Weatherhead's Bank. Ask for your safe deposit box. Inside, you will find the package that you deposited at the start of this month. You will need to give it to us.'

Our visitor stood up and walked to one of the windows overlooking Newsome Street. She looked carefully up and down the highway before turning to face us.

'I would like nothing better than to go back to Italy, but I believe that to do what you suggest would put me in great danger. For some weeks now, I have been certain that when I leave the house – for any purpose – I am followed. There are two men in particular who have been constantly at my heels. I have not mentioned this to Angelo, as I thought that they were probably *his* men, employed because Angelo does not trust me. If they saw me entering and leaving the bank when I have had no orders from my brother, I would be afraid for my life.'

As Maria spoke, I could see Hester watching her closely.

'I have an idea,' Hester said. 'Signora, when you have used your safe deposit box, was it always the same clerk that you spoke to, and who asked you to sign their record book?'

'No – it is a large bank, and there seem to be several members of staff who carry out that duty.'

'Excellent! Then this is what we will do. You came here expecting to be given a package to deposit, so I assume you have upon your person your letter of authorisation and key?'

Maria nodded.

'Very well,' Hester said. 'Miss Jessop has rented a box in that very bank, so we know the procedure well. However, as she is known to the bank and I am not – and I resemble you more that Ivy does – I will take it upon myself to go in your place, giving your name. If you could just demonstrate your signature on this notepaper ...'

I was not at all surprised by the speed at which Hester mastered Maria's signature.

'Very well,' Hester said when she was satisfied with her efforts. 'This is what I propose. We will all three leave this house together, taking a four-wheeler. We will go first to Weatherhead's Bank in the Strand, where I will retrieve the necklace. After that, we will visit the *Banca Nazionale Italiana* in Oxford Street, where we will open an account in your name, signora. I will pay in a cheque for £1,000 and withdraw £50 in notes for your immediate expenses. I assume there is nothing at your house in Portland Place that is absolutely essential for you to retrieve? Good – I think it best that you do not return there. Our final journey will be to Clerkenwell, where Jacob Carpenter has his office. Mr Carpenter is a private detective – a former sergeant in the Metropolitan Police who can be trusted absolutely. He will make all of the arrangements for your journey to Palermo. Until you are ready to leave, you will remain under Mr and Mrs Carpenter's protection – they have a comfortable spare room where you will be completely safe. They will require no payment – I will settle their bill later. Now, before we start our expedition, I insist on ringing for Mrs Parsons and ordering tea and a plate of sandwiches. It would not do for one of us to faint with hunger en route.'

Suitably refreshed, the three of us were soon making the short journey to the Strand. When I had hailed the four-wheeler in Newsome Street I noticed a smart new hansom cab waiting a hundred yards or so from our front door, and as we crossed Oxford Circus I peered through the rear window – there was the hansom again. The driver wore a Norfolk jacket and bowler hat, resembling a private vehicle owner more than a London cab driver. After the second sighting, I mentioned it to Hester.

'It is probably nothing,' she said. 'But when we turn into High Holborn I will ask our driver to stop. There will be a long stretch of road behind us, and if we are being followed by the vehicle you observed, it will be impossible for our pursuers to hide.'

According to plan Hester signalled for us to halt, just after we had passed Chancery Lane. She jumped down from the carriage and crossed the road, looking down the route we had just travelled.

'The cab you described is not visible,' she said. 'I will ask the driver to continue.'

When we reached Weatherhead's Bank, Hester stepped down from our vehicle.

'Ivy, I should like you and the signora to remain here, in the carriage,' she said. 'I should not be too long.'

When Hester had been inside the bank for fifteen minutes or so, I took out my pocket watch. Although it was only half past three, the sky was already darkening in the winter twilight. Then, I noticed a large closed carriage draw up beside us, the blinds drawn down to obscure the upper half of the windows. Two heavily-built men in cloth caps and mufflers stepped out simultaneously, one from each side of the vehicle. Before I could utter a word, they had wrenched open the doors of out four-wheeler, grabbed Maria and me by the arms, and bundled us into their own carriage, which then drove off at great speed.

'Scream out and it'll be the last sound that you make,' one of the men said in a harsh, low voice. As he spoke, he took a stubby black rubber cosh from an inside pocket of his greasy corduroy jacket. Neither man was easy to see clearly in the twilight with the blinds half closed, but the one who had spoken had an expression of feral shrewdness that made me suspect he was the leader. The other, his creased morning coat stretched over bulging shoulders, had that air of incipient incomprehension often indicative of limited mental powers.

I turned to face the signora, who was sitting rigid and pale faced with terror. 'Maria, do not be frightened,' I said. 'These gentlemen wish neither to rob us, or do us harm.'

The rough with the cosh snorted. 'Oh yes, and how do you know that, Miss High-and-Mighty?'

I looked at him calmly. 'If robbery had been your motive, when you bundled us out of our carriage you would hardly have left our handbags behind. As to harming us, you could have attacked us in the street and fled, rather than undertaking a hazardous abduction. It seems to me that you must be taking us ...'

'Just shut yer gob,' our kidnapper cried. 'Or me an' Alf'll shut it for yer!'

The pace of the carriage slowed, and we continued our journey in silence. My speculation – rudely interrupted by the gentleman with the cosh – was that we were being taken somewhere for questioning, or held as bargaining chips. It did not need Hester's extraordinary powers of reasoning to deduce that our kidnapping was associated with the signora – had she been followed to our rooms at 12 Newsome Street? It was clear that such speculations would be of no use until I had further evidence. I could not help smiling at the thought of poor Hester's reaction to our abduction; she would no doubt have emerged from the bank to find our cabman distraught, and at this very moment would be applying her considerable intellect to a strategy for our rescue.

After perhaps half an hour, the carriage bumped down what I guessed was a cobbled street. A moment or two later it halted, and we were pulled out, none too gently, by our captors. The outside air had that damp, faintly mouldy tang associated with the lower reaches of the River Thames; that and the row of tall, somewhat dilapidated brick warehouses suggested to me that we were near the river.

Maria – still thankfully silent – and I were hauled across the road and into an adjacent warehouse. We were taken down a long passage with several rooms leading off, then pushed into a large, unlit room on the ground floor. It was dusty and bare apart from a few broken barrels and baulks of timber in a far corner.

Our friend with the cosh – which had now been put back in his pocket, no doubt in recognition of our helplessness – paused as he was about to leave.

'Don't worry, ladies, you won't be left alone for long. The boss is comin' to see you in an hour or so. Better decide now that you'll tell 'im everything – 'e's not a man to be crossed.'

The two kidnappers pulled the door shut behind them, and I could hear the clunk of the heavy lock being closed.

I led Maria to the pile of lumber, and made a seat for her on an upturned barrel. There was little I could do or say to comfort her, and so once her sobs had subsided somewhat I made a careful circuit of the room. I soon realised that escape was impossible. The faint lighting came from two windows high up the wall, impossible to reach, and the door was strong enough to withstand a rhinoceros. No, there was only one option available to us. I returned to Maria's side and whispered for some minutes into her ear. At first she shook her head violently – but as I explained that my plan was our only hope, she reluctantly agreed to play her part.

Ten minutes later, the scene was set. Maria was sitting on the floor in the corner of the room, her back against a broken barrel, with pieces of lumber scattered close by her. I knocked loudly on the door of the room.

'Help!' I shouted. 'Maria has fainted! She needs a glass of water – come quickly!'

My scheme was dependent upon only *one* of our captors answering my summons, and I felt a surge of disappointment as both hove into view. It seemed to my eyes that they were walking a little unsteadily, and when they opened the door there was a sudden smell of beer.

'Don't worry, Alf,' the more intelligent man said. 'You go back and finish that booze. I'll get the little lady some water.'

He locked the door after himself, then returned a few minutes later alone, carrying a tin mug. When he re-entered the room I was standing next to Maria, wringing my hands. Maria sat with her head back, breathing heavily.

'Oh sir, do hurry,' I said. 'Poor Maria is unwell – but if you give her a sip of water, I am sure she will recover.'

The kidnapper crouched down and held the mug to Maria's lips. As he did so, I stepped behind him, out of his line of sight, and soundlessly picked up the short, heavy wooden stave I had earlier selected. I brought it crashing down on the back of his skull with a dull, sickening thud.

Our abductor fell forward without a sound. With Maria at my side, I moved swiftly through the door and down the corridor. This was by far the most dangerous part of our plan, since I could hardly hope to cope with the other gentleman without the element of surprise. We retraced our steps and found, to our relief, that the key had been left in the lock of the outside door. We stepped into the street and for good measure I locked the door behind me, tossing the key down the road into the darkness. A dim and distant gas light was all the illumination we had.

'Now what?' said Maria. 'Shall we try to find a policeman?'

I sniffed the air. 'I have a better idea – let us walk in this direction, away from the Thames. We are sure to strike a main highway, this close to central London. Then we can hail a cab.'

'But we have no money!' Maria cried. 'Our bags were left in the four-wheeler.'

I smiled, and reached under my skirt, taking out a cloth purse from a hidden pocket in the lining. 'A ruse that dear Hester taught me,' I said. 'Always have some spare cash on your person. There are five pounds here – more than enough to return us to 12 Newsome Street in style.'

It was just after six o'clock that evening when we reached Newsome Street and I rang the bell. We were both shivering after our journey, and the beginnings of a snow shower swirled around us. The door was opened not by Mrs Parsons, but by Hester. I could see the expression on her face turn from anxiety to relief as she saw us both on the doorstep.

'Ivy! And Maria! Thank God, you are both safe. You are unharmed, I hope? Come upstairs quickly. There is a fire blazing, and I will ask Mrs Parsons to bring us something hot to eat. I have been beside myself with worry. What has happened to you? The driver of the four-wheeler witnessed your abduction. No, don't answer that question. You must put on some warm dry clothes – I have some that will fit the signora very well – and have a hot whisky and lemon to drive out the cold. Then you must tell me everything.'

It was not long before Maria and I were seated close to the glowing fire, well wrapped up and nursing the bowls of steaming pea and ham soup provided by our housekeeper. It did not take long to recount all that had taken place since our abduction.

Throughout my monologue, Hester remained uncharacteristically silent. As for Maria, it was apparent that tiredness was rapidly overtaking her – assisted by her consumption of a large tumbler of hot spirits – and at Hester's suggestion, I directed her to the guest bedroom, promising to wake here before we retired for the night and to explain what was to happen.

When I had finished my story, Hester paused for a few moments, deep in thought, then reached across to clasp my hand tightly.

'My dear Ivy – if anything untoward had happened to you, or indeed to Signora Calvino, I could never have forgiven myself. I have been monstrously stupid. When I saw that there was no one following us down High Holborn I should have realised that there could have been more than one person on our track. But, thanks to your daring escape, it may be that this whole affair will turn out happily after all. You have told me about your adventure – let me turn the tables, and tell you of my discoveries at Weatherhead's Bank.

'My plan to obtain Maria's safe-deposit box worked perfectly. The elderly clerk barely glanced at my signature, and soon I was left alone with the deposit box. I confess that my hand trembled as turned the key and opened it. It contained some small leather-bound ledgers and loose papers of various kinds – with an object wrapped in tissue laid on top. I unwrapped it – it was very obviously the necklace that had been taken from Lady Ellen Talbot. Then, I spent a moment or two looking through the notebooks that filled the rest of the box. They seemed to be a record of accounts, but not laid out in any convention of bookkeeping. My instincts told me that I should take them – after all, it would be obvious from the missing necklace that someone had raided the box. I therefore swept the contents into my bag, returned the box to the clerk and hurried back to the pavement – to find the driver of our four-wheeler distraught. He described your abduction, and after taking his details – in case he is required as a witness – I let him leave the scene.'

'And you then reported the incident to the nearest police constable?' I asked.

Hester shook her head. 'Actually I did not. Let me explain. My assumption at that time was that you and the signora had been kidnapped by someone acting in the interests of Angelo Baraldi, or even by that gentleman himself, if he had already returned to England. If so, it seemed to me that they would soon discover that when they were busy driving you away, I was taking possession of the diamond necklace. Now, what do you suppose they would do next?'

'Well – contact you, demanding the return of the necklace, and threatening to harm Maria and me if it was not forthcoming?'

'Bravo, Ivy! Those were my thoughts exactly. My main priority was to ensure that both of you were safe. Therefore, to instigate a noisy and probably unprofitable police hunt across London was the last thing that I wished to do. It would only have scared your abductors – with possibly fatal consequences. I therefore decided to wait until I was contacted, however frustrating such a course of enforced inaction would be. However, after I had returned to Newsome Street and spent an hour going over Baraldi's ledgers, things took on a very different complexion. Some of my assumptions have been sadly misguided.'

I smiled. 'Hester, if there was some mechanical device capable of recording the human voice, I would like nothing better than to capture those words, if only to confront your later denials – but please, continue.'

'Very well. On careful scrutiny the accounts books – for that is what they are – show money collected, and money subsequently paid out to someone identified as "JK", over the last five years or so, from December 1890 to the present. Considerably more has been collected than has been paid out. Fortunately, I also found a letter inside one of the books, addressed to Baraldi, acknowledging a payment. This letter was signed "Karnkraft." You remember my mentioning Baraldi's association with the *Mantello Rosso*? Well, the leader of that organisation, at least in England, is a gentleman by the name of Dr Johan Karnkraft. Of Swedish nationality, he has lived in London for many years.'

I frowned. 'I have never heard of him.'

'Very few people have heard of him – that is part of his genius. It would not be an exaggeration to say that he is one of the cleverest and most dangerous criminals in London; he is careful never to be directly involved in his schemes, but to remain, malign and spider-like, at the centre of a web of intrigue. I am sure that that he is the "JK" listed in Baraldi's accounts. I have therefore developed the following hypothesis. Let us suppose that Baraldi has been defrauding Dr Karnkraft of some of the profits of his criminal activities, and the doctor has become aware of this. We might then assume that the men who abducted you did so on the orders of the doctor, thinking that you were confederates of Baraldi, and could be made to confirm that he has been siphoning money from the profits of his fellow criminals. As soon as I had come to that conclusion, I sent word to Dr Karnkraft, inviting him to call upon me here at seven o'clock so that I could provide the evidence against Baraldi that he needed, in return for your freedom.'

'And now that we have returned safely, do you still intend to see the doctor?' I asked.

'I certainly do. He can no longer bargain for your release, but there is another favour that I shall be asking of him in return for Baraldi's account books. I expect his arrival imminently. If you could ring for Mrs Parsons to collect the dishes, we must tidy this room to ensure that it is a fitting setting in which to receive such a celebrity of crime. Do not be deceived by the man's bland exterior. I will have my pistol close to hand, and I suggest you do the same.'

The gentleman who was shown into our rooms at the appointed hour bore little resemblance to the arch-villains of popular melodrama. He was a little below the medium in height, between fifty and sixty years of age, and wore a long frock coat of fine grey worsted. His beard was neatly clipped in the style favoured by the Prince of Wales, and his plump, pink face bore a disarming smile.

'Miss Lynton, I am very pleased to see you again,' he said. 'It was some years ago, I believe, that we exchanged a few words. At the Russian ambassador's reception, if memory serves me correctly. And Miss Jessop – we have not met, but of course I know of your sterling work as Miss Lynton's colleague. You must tell me why you have summoned me here so urgently. Is there some problem with which I can assist?'

I glanced quizzically at Hester. If, in accordance with her theory, Dr

Karnkraft had a few hours earlier arranged for my abduction, and had subsequently been informed of my escape, his affectation of bonhomie was marvellous.

Hester appeared not the least nonplussed. 'Do sit down, sir. You are a busy man, and I shall pay you the complement of being perfectly frank. Miss Jessop and another lady were abducted earlier today. Fortunately, they were able to make their escape, as you can see. I assumed that you knew something of the matter. Is that not the case?'

Our visitor's expression of surprise seemed genuine.

'I assure you, I know nothing of this business,' he said.

'Very well,' Hester said. 'The proposal that I am about to make to you is in any case not affected by your responsibility – or otherwise – for today's attempted kidnapping. If you will hear me out, I will explain. I am aware that you have – how shall we put it – a professional connection with Signor Angelo Baraldi, the olive oil merchant who lives at Portland Place with his widowed sister.'

'I will not deny it.' As Karnkraft spoke, his manner seemed rather less friendly.

'Good. A number of documents have recently come into my possession – account books, by the look of them – which relate to Baraldi's business dealings. There are many references to someone designated "JK" – yourself, I believe – suggesting that he has been paying you less than was due. Baraldi is currently in Europe – if his movements accord with his past habits, I expect him to return within the next few days. At present, he is unaware that his ledgers are missing. I have no use for these documents. I am happy to give them to you to use as you think fit, in exchange for your solemn promise.'

'And what would that be, Miss Lynton?'

'Signora Maria Calvino, Baraldi's sister, is a poor woman who was forced to take shelter under her brother's roof. He has used her to open accounts for him, run errands and generally assist with his business dealings. She knew nothing of his activities and did not profit from his, erm, *enterprises*. She now has the means to return to Italy, and to have no more to do with her brother. She knows nothing, and there is therefore nothing to be gained by silencing her. If I give you Baraldi's papers, can you promise me that you will not pursue the signora?'

Karnkraft threw out his arms in a gesture of innocent surprise.

'I assure that that I have no interest in interfering with Signora Calvino's plans.'

'Very well,' Hester said. 'There is one more thing. I wish you to say nothing to anyone about our conversation. In return, Hester and I will keep silent about your visit, and the documents you receive from me.'

'And am I now allowed to see these mysterious records?' the doctor asked with a smile.

Hester went to her writing desk and reached into the bottom drawer, retrieving a canvas bag containing several small leather-bound ledgers which she passed to Karnkraft. He spent a moment or two looking through them. His face was immobile, but nevertheless I thought I could detect a gleam of excitement in his eyes.

Suddenly, our visitor got to his feet. As he did so, my hand slid under the cushion next to me, and I grasped the handle of my little .22 revolver. My movement had not escaped Karnkraft's attention.

'Do not alarm yourself, Miss Jessop,' he said. 'I have to say that these items are certainly of interest to me. Miss Lynton, if you will allow me to leave with them in my possession, I repeat that Signora Calvino is free to do as she pleases – and our meeting today will remain secret.'

Hester smiled. 'Then it seems that we are in agreement. However, I must mention one more thing. Should any accident or other misadventure befall Miss Jessop, Signora Calvino or myself, then my solicitors have been instructed to release a document to the police, which will inevitably result in your arrest.'

Karnkraft nodded, and turned to the door. I confess to a feeling of some relief when that gentleman left us.

'Do you still intend to ask Jacob Carpenter to make the arrangements for Maria's return to Palermo?' I said.

'Certainly. We will continue our interrupted errands tomorrow morning. We will open the account for Maria at the *Banca Nazionale Italiana*, and then deliver her to Clerkenwell where Jacob and his wife will take charge of her.'

'And the necklace? Are we to return it to Lady Ellen?'

Hester pursed her lips. 'Not immediately. There is a final scene to be played out in this affair. When Angelo Baraldi returns to England – almost certainly within the next few days – he will find that both his sister and the contents of the safe deposit box are missing. Whether he detects our own part in the case is another matter, but I would not wish Lady Ellen to have her necklace back until the case is resolved. If my suspicions about Dr Karnkraft are correct, I would not like to be in Angelo's shoes when he returns. We will, at any rate, wait for a few days before contacting our client. It is after all little more than a week since she first consulted us.'

The following day we took Maria Calvino to the Italian bank as we had planned, then gave her into the safe keeping of Jacob Carpenter. Two days later, just as Mrs Parsons had cleared away the remains of our dinner, we heard the electric doorbell ring repeatedly.

'Someone is evidently very anxious to see us,' Hester said, picking up her capacious leather handbag and putting it down on the chair next to her. 'I wonder if it could be ...'

My friend had no time to finish her sentence, for we heard the muted protestations of Mrs Parsons and a rush of footsteps upon the stairs – followed by the crash of our door as it was flung open.

A powerfully-built man in his thirties stepped swiftly into our rooms. He had the olive skin of a southern European, and his black hair glistened with a sheen of Macassar oil. His three-piece suit was a little too small for him, the blue serge cloth stretched across his shoulders.

'Have a care, sir!' Hester said jauntily. 'That door was manufactured for the entry and exit of *homo sapiens*, not prize bulls. You may sit down if you wish, but pray do it quietly. I presume we have the honour of addressing Signor Angelo Baraldi, importer of olive oil and sometime member of the *Mantello Rosso*?'

Our visitor remained standing, his arms handing down at each side, fists clenched. When he spoke, his words were heavily inflected with an Italian accent – which, out of respect for my readers, I shall not try to reproduce on this page.

'Think you're very clever, don't you, lady? I got home today – and found that Maria is missing. But you know that already, don't you? Fortunately I have a very loyal housekeeper. She told me that when Maria left the house last Tuesday, she'd asked my housekeeper how long it would take to get to Newsome Street – and said I'd told her to meet a "Mrs Jones" at number 12. Now, the real occupant of 12 Newsome Street is the consulting busybody, Hester Lynton. A coincidence? I don't think so. Where is Maria? It will be the worse for you both if you do not tell me. I fear no man – or woman.'

As Baraldi took a step forward, Hester reached down into the leather handbag on the chair beside her, and calmly withdrew her Webley service revolver, levelling it at our visitor's burly torso.

'Well-developed muscles come off second-best when matched against a .455 bullet,' Hester said. 'I believe the British Army chose the Webley because of its reputation as a man-stopper. Please do not tempt me to use this – the noise in this enclosed space would be frightful, and might upset Ivy's delicate hearing. I really see no use in prolonging this conversation further. Please leave, and close the door *quietly* behind you.'

Angelo's expression was both sullen and menacing. 'Very well, I'll go. But you mentioned the *Mantello Rosso*. I freely admit to being a member of that organisation – and I tell you that you and your companion will never be safe from us.'

'Then we will have to take our chances. Forgive me if I do not tremble.'

Hester accompanied our unwelcome visitor downstairs – no doubt wishing to spare Mrs Parsons the task of letting such an unprepossessing person out – then returned to our sitting room. No sooner had she stepped inside than there was a sudden commotion from the street below. We both hurried to the window and looked down. A smart black landau, drawn by two horses, had halted outside our door, and Signor Baraldi – his hat lying in the pavement – was struggling violently in the gaslit street with three men, whilst the carriage driver looked on from his seat. One of Baraldi's assailants struck him violently on the head with a short, stubby object – its precise nature was impossible to make out from our vantage point. Baraldi collapsed, and was hauled into the landau, which drove off south towards Westminster and the Thames at high speed. The few passers-by looked on impotently.

I gripped Hester's arm with excitement. 'Should we call the police?' I asked.

Hester raised her eyebrows quizzically. 'Oh, I think not, Ivy. One of the onlookers will be sure to do so. Let us not confuse matters. I would like to avoid any official involvement with this case, if possible.

'And who do you now think was responsible for kidnapping the signora and me?' I asked.

'Almost certainly Dr Karnkraft. But if it *was* Baraldi, I think it unlikely he will trouble us further.'

The next day, Hester sent Mrs Parsons out to buy all the morning editions of the papers, and scoured each one, with no result. I did not ask what she was searching for, although I had a strong inkling.

That evening, Hester repeated the process, this time with more success. 'Aha!' she cried, thrusting the *Pall Mall Gazette* under my nose. 'See – at the top of the page. *Body Found Near Vauxhall Bridge*.'

We scanned the report – police were trying to identify the body of a well-dressed man in his thirties – contusions on the skull suggestive of foul play – Italianate complexion – appeal for information.

'That is Baraldi, for certain,' Hester said. 'The *Mantello Rosso* have dealt with their disloyal associate. It is only seven o'clock. Let us pay a call upon Lady Ellen immediately, and give her the good news. You have considerable powers of dissimulation, Ivy – see if you can come up with a plausible reason to give to the earl and countess, if we encounter them. I will put the necklace in the inside pocket of my jacket – it would not do for it to be snatched out of my hand by some opportunistic thief the moment we leave the house.'

During the subsequent journey, I thought hard about a suitable excuse for our unannounced visit. It was not until we reached the imposing Wimpole Street residence of the Earl and Countess of Nantwich and their daughter that I hit upon a suitable story: the news that a mutual friend had been admitted to St Mary's Hospital with pleurisy. Perhaps fortunately, I did not have to employ it, for when Hester presented our cards the solemn-faced butler immediately ushered us upstairs into a small drawing room, which I assumed was the private salon of our client. It was not long before Lady Ellen joined us.

'I gave Thomas instructions to admit you straight away if you were to call,' she said. 'That is, without troubling my parents. As it happens, they are both out this evening. Please tell me you have some news about the necklace! I had dinner at the Savoy with my fiancé last night, and he was very concerned that I was not wearing it.'

'Then the duke will be delighted to see it round your neck the next time you meet!' Hester chuckled, reaching inside her jacket pocket.

Lady Ellen pounced upon her diamonds with a cry of joy. 'This – this is wonderful!'

Then a shadow of concern passed over he features. 'But – does Signor Baraldi know that you have retrieved it – that is, if he was responsible?'

'Oh, he was certainly responsible,' Hester said. 'However, I have reason to believe that he will never trouble you – or anyone else – again. His body has been found. I dare say it will be confirmed in the newspapers in a day or so.'

Lady Ellen sat down. 'Dead? I would not have wished *that* upon him. Well, I am conscious that I have had a lucky escape. Now, if you have no objection, I should like to settle my account with you.'

Hester smiled. 'I am afraid it is a rather large sum. I took you at your word, and offered £1,000 for the return of the necklace. With other expenses and our fee, a cheque for £1,050 will be satisfactory.'

Our client walked to her writing-desk and took out her cheque book. 'I shall pay it gladly. I feel as if I have awoken from a nightmare, and shall be forever grateful to you both.'

Both Hester and I thought that our meeting with Lady Ellen would be the end of the matter, but there was one postscript to the case: the arrival, two weeks later, of a small wooden box, dispatched from Sicily. The contents, carefully wrapped in straw, were a Parma ham; a large jar of olives; several strong cheeses; a flask of Chianti and a bottle of grappa. No card or message was enclosed, but there was no doubt in our minds as to the sender.

Hester chuckled. 'We must keep this treasure trove a secret from Mrs Parsons. These delicacies are inimical to her concept of a respectable cuisine!'

6. The Case of the Kidnapped Schoolboy

It was in the nature of the service that Hester provided to our clients that those who sought our help were nearly always individuals confronted by a dilemma which they felt unable to encounter alone. There were, however, some exceptions to this general rule, as illustrated by the occasion when Mr Samuel and Mrs Martha Arnold called upon us in the autumn of 1888.

The couple who presented themselves in our sitting room that Thursday afternoon were in their forties, although the gentleman looked somewhat younger than his wife. Both were carefully dressed in the conservative fashion favoured by the English middle classes when undertaking a serious matter of business, whether with their solicitor, bank manager or – in Hester's case – consulting detective. As their letter requesting a meeting had given no indication of the reason for their visit, other than that the matter was both urgent and confidential, Hester invited them to give a full account of what lay behind their journey from Putney to Newsome Street.

Samuel Arnold spoke first. As he did so, he glanced at his wife with an expression of thinly-disguised annoyance.

'I suggest that Mrs Arnold tells you our story, since she is the instigator of our visit here this evening. I will be quite frank, and tell you that in my opinion this consultation is inadvisable. However, I must let Martha explain all.'

He wife took a sip of coffee and returned her cup to the tray that Mrs Parsons had earlier provided. She appeared white-faced and tense, but spoke calmly and quietly.

'As you know from our letter, my husband and I live in Putney at Flexbury Villa, a detached house overlooking the heath. We have a son, Daniel, who is nine. Last Monday morning – the eighth of October – he did not appear for breakfast, despite the maid having knocked on his bedroom door at half past eight. He attends a local preparatory school as a day pupil, but as this week the school is on holiday, he is allowed to sleep in an hour longer. Eventually, I entered his room to find it in disarray. Most of the bedding had been flung onto the floor, the wardrobe doors were open and his new winter coat was not on its peg. As you can imagine, I did not know what to think. I was hurrying downstairs to tell Samuel what had happened, when our housemaid, Elsie, met me in the hallway with a letter. The envelope had evidently been pushed through our letterbox by someone other than the postman, for the envelope had no stamp or address, just *Mr and Mrs Arnold* on the front. I have the letter here. I have made a copy, so you may keep this original. Incidentally, we found that the kidnapper had gained entry to our house through a window at the rear.'

Martha Arnold took a sheet of paper from her handbag and handed it to Hester, who beckoned me to read it over her shoulder. The note was written in ink in capital letters:

I HAVE DANIEL. IF YOU WISH TO SEE HIM AGAIN TELL NO ONE. MR ARNOLD MUST BRING TWO THOUSAND POUNDS IN BANKNOTES IN A CANVAS BAG TO CHARING CROSS STATION PLATFORM 3 ON FRIDAY 19TH OF OCTOBER AFTERNOON AT 3PM AND WAIT UNDER THE CLOCK. I WILL DELIVER DANIEL SAFELY TO HIM IN RETURN FOR THE MONEY. NO TRICKS OR POLICE OR DANIEL WILL DIE.

Hester gasped. 'Why, this is shocking! That was three days ago – I take it you have not seen Daniel since he disappeared?'

'We have not,' Mrs Arnold said.

'Then I have to ask you both, why have you not informed the police? They have far more resources that I have in order to catch whoever has carried out this wicked deed ...'

'If you will allow me to interrupt, Miss Lynton,' Mr Arnold said. 'Are you aware how many such cases of child kidnapping the Metropolitan Police have investigated during the last five years, and what the outcomes of those investigations were?'

'I am afraid I cannot say, Mr Arnold.'

'Then I will enlighten you. During that period there have been four such cases, if you discount those that proved to be false reports. Of those four cases, the bodies of two children were recovered; one child has never been found but is presumed dead, and one child was returned safely to his parents. I am not a betting man, Miss Lynton, but these seem very poor odds to me. I have therefore persuaded my wife *not* to involve the official police force. It is a very large sum of money, but we will be able to raise it in time to pay the ransom, and indeed we would be prepared to pay it twice over to get our son back. However, Martha insisted that we consult you in this matter. I have to say that if your interference in the case results in any harm coming to Daniel, I for one shall never forgive you.'

Hester smiled. 'Well, I certainly cannot take on this case if you disapprove of my involvement, Mr Arnold. I am used to obstruction from my adversaries, but to have it also from my clients would make a case far too burdensome. Clearly, you have a choice. Either you agree to your wife's request to involve me fully in the matter, and promise your personal cooperation, or Mrs Arnold will have to follow her instincts and report the whole business to the police. What is it to be?'

Arnold's face reddened with annoyance. I suspected that he was not used to being put in his place by a female. Eventually, he mastered his emotions and spoke.

'Very well, Miss Lynton, if you put it like that then of course I will agree to help you in any way that I can. How do you propose to act in the case?'

'That will depend upon what we find at Flexbury Villa. Ivy and I will need to meet with you there later this afternoon, as time is of the essence in this matter. However, I can tell you that my prime objective in the case is to ensure the safe return of Daniel. The capture of the criminals responsible will be a secondary matter. Please continue with your efforts to raise the £2,000, as the ransom may still be needed. Now, before you go, please tell me if there are any other family members resident at your home, and give me details of your servants.'

Mrs Arnold appeared reassured by Hester's evident command of the situation.

'The only other member of our family is my daughter, Emily Hunt – from my first marriage, to the late Harold Hunt. Emily is nineteen years old and studying at the South London College of Science, but lives at home. We have told her everything that has occurred, and she has promised to say nothing to anyone – Emily is a very sensible young woman, and is to be trusted completely. As to the resident servants, we have a very small establishment. Mrs Norris, our housekeeper and cook, has been in service with me for more than ten years. Our housemaid, Elsie Leonard, is only sixteen but an excellent worker. Two local women come in daily to help with the heavier work, and we employ an elderly jobbing gardener, who works at several houses in our locality …'

Samuel Arnold interjected. 'My wife and I cannot conceive that any of our servants could have been involved in this dreadful business. Clearly, some criminal has plotted this outrage.'

'And do you have any idea who might have been responsible?' I asked. 'Someone you know, perhaps?'

Mrs Arnold spoke hesitantly. 'Well – my husband disagrees, but I did wonder if the old gypsy woman whom I saw near the house last weekend might have had anything to do with it. It was on Saturday afternoon. I was looking out of my bedroom window, and she was staring over the hedge into our garden, but some instinct must have made her look up. She saw me looking at her and hurried off.'

Once again, a flicker of irritation could be seen in Arnold's features. 'Really, my dear, the idea is absurd. I cannot imagine that such a woman – ignorant, uneducated – would carry out such an abduction and write such a note. Now, if a joint of beef had gone missing from the kitchen, that would be a different matter.'

Hester nodded. 'Very well. I have two further questions, and will then detain you no further. What is your occupation, Mr Arnold? And what is the financial position of the family? Forgive my bluntness, but it is an important point.'

'Of course. I am a critic and essayist, and contribute regularly to the literary magazines. My wife is a member of the Colman family, and has inherited a considerable sum from the mustard trade.'

'Thank you. I may have some further questions for one or both of you later today. If Ivy and I could call at Flexbury Villa at five o'clock this evening, that would be very helpful. We will return to Newsome Street before dinner. I will show you downstairs myself, as I detect evidence upon the air that our housekeeper is baking one of her delicious sponge cakes, and I would not wish to be responsible for any interruption of her culinary alchemy.'

Once our two visitors had departed, I picked up the printed ransom note and held it out for Hester to read again.

'What do you make of it?' I asked.

Hester sighed. 'Very little. The pen, ink and paper are of unremarkable quality. The hand that has formed these capitals is literate, but to attain that they may just as likely have attended a board school as Eton College. Block capitals are so much less revealing that cursive handwriting.'

I chuckled. 'Why, Hester, you disappoint me! I thought at the very least you would be able to tell me the age and nationality of the writer, and the breed of dog that they own.'

'You are facetious at my expense, I see. However, the couple that brought us the note make an interesting study. Let me turn the tables and ask you what you made of them.'

'It seems to me that Samuel Arnold has found a way to live a congenial life without working,' I said, 'and has a wife who appears happy to support him in his indolence.'

'Indeed. However, that does not help us in our current task. I will feel happier when we have been to Flexbury Villa and had the opportunity to survey the scene of the abduction. It will also be informative to speak to Miss Emily Hunt – she sounds an interesting young woman.'

At the appointed hour we arrived in Putney, and our hansom deposited us outside Mr and Mrs Arnold's home. Flexbury Villa was a pleasant, red brick dwelling that appeared to date from the early years of this century, set well back from the main road and overlooking the heath. The young woman who answered the bell was Elsie Leonard, the housemaid, who confirmed her name after a polite enquiry from Hester. As she showed us up to Mrs Arnold's sitting room, it occurred to me that some reason must have been given to the servants for Daniel's sudden absence.

After Mrs Arnold had greeted us and sent Elsie away to bring us some refreshments, she informed us that her husband had been called away to a meeting with a magazine editor, but hoped to return before we left that evening. After accepting his apologies, Hester turned to our hostess with a smile.

'Your account of the case earlier today was most helpful, Mrs Arnold. However, there are a number of other points that I wish to explore. Firstly, do you have a recent photograph of Daniel that I could borrow?'

'Of course.' Mrs Arnold went to a nearby shelf and returned with a framed cabinet photograph, which she handed to Hester. 'This was taken a few months ago, last June. The young lady with Daniel is Miss Helen Walker, his governess. We were on holiday in Brighton.'

Hester passed the photograph to me. It had been taken in a photographer's studio, against a seaside backdrop. Daniel was a cheerful, healthy looking boy, somewhat self-consciously attired in a sailor suit. Miss Walker could not have been more than twenty-five years of age, and the characteristically dowdy costume of her profession could not disguise her remarkable prettiness.

'But I thought Daniel was educated at a local preparatory school?' I asked.

'Indeed, but only since this September. Miss Walker left her post at that time, but I am happy to say that she is now employed by a very pleasant family in Southampton. She had been Daniel's governess for two years, and he thrived under her care. The poor boy was at first most upset at her leaving, but I believe that his new friends at school have more than compensated for his loss.'

'Thank you,' Hester said. 'Now, if I may turn to another matter. You must forgive my directness, but how readily are you able to lay hands on the £2,000 in banknotes demanded by the kidnapper? It is a substantial sum.'

Our client seemed momentarily embarrassed. 'I am afraid that I have had to sacrifice some very valuable family jewellery in order to obtain the money. The sale – to a reputable Bond Street jeweller – should provide us with adequate funds in time for the ransom to be paid. Samuel was quite correct when he told you that I had inherited a large estate from my late father, John Colman, the mustard manufacturer. However, I was widowed and remarried before my father passed away, and he did not approve of Samuel. He wished Samuel to join the family business, but Samuel did not wish to be involved with the mustard trade. As a result, the terms of father's bequest to me were very limiting. I have the house in trust for my lifetime, but it cannot be sold. In addition, a generous allowance is credited to my account every year. However, if I require a capital sum I have to apply to the trustees. Naturally I call upon them as little as possible. My daughter Emily is anxious that I do so on her behalf, in order for obtain the funds for her to train as a doctor at the London

School of Medicine for Women; I was minded to agree, but Samuel absolutely forbade it. He believes strongly that medicine is an unsuitable occupation for a genteel young woman.'

'Indeed!' Hester exclaimed. 'He should be thankful that Emily has not set her sights on setting up as a consulting detective, which I have no doubt he considers even more disreputable. If I could speak to Emily before we go back to Newsome Street, that would be very helpful. Now, if you could show Ivy and me to Daniel's bedroom – the scene of the kidnapping – I would be grateful.'

As Hester and I had expected, the disarray of Daniel's bedroom had been carefully tidied up. Mrs Arnold explained that the servants had been told Daniel had left for a short holiday with his uncle, and would return at the end of the following week. After a brief examination of the room, Hester spoke to our client.

'When you and your husband spoke to us this morning, you mentioned that Daniel's coat had disappeared with him. I imagine that he had been made to put it on over his night things. Were any other items of his clothing missing?'

Mrs Arnold appeared puzzled at the question. 'Oh yes – a complete outfit. Let me see … his school flannel trousers and blazer, a cotton shirt, socks, a set of undergarments … and a pair of shoes, or rather boots. His sturdiest footwear that he uses for country walks.'

Hester caught my eye, but I was unable to guess what lay beneath her quizzical expression.

'And was anything else taken from his room?' Hester asked.

'There was one thing – I am almost certain that it was in his room when he went to bed, for he refuses to sleep without it. His father disapproves, calling it a childish habit. I refer to Daniel's stuffed rabbit, Reginald, that he was given at the age of two. Since then, the two have been inseparable.'

'And, er, Reginald has vanished?' I said.

'Indeed. Of course, he may have been mislaid in the garden or in one of the outhouses, I suppose.'

'Very possibly,' Hester said. 'Now, if you can lead us to the window that the kidnapper forced open, I would like to examine it.'

Shortly afterwards we were shown into a small parlour at the rear of the house, which was not used by the family. Although it was clean and tidy, its mediocre furnishings and musty smell indicated its unoccupied status. The sash window had been forced from its mountings, and fixed back in place with several nails.

'The carpenter is coming next week,' Mrs Arnold said. 'My husband has nailed it shut in the meantime.'

As she spoke, I noticed that Hester was examining the inner window sill very closely. I stepped next to her.

'What do you make of that, Ivy?' she asked.

Her pointing finger indicated several shallow indentations in the paintwork beneath the window.

'I suppose that is where the kidnapper climbed into the room,' I said. 'Marking the sill with their shoes.'

Hester said nothing, but I could see that she was deep in thought. After a few moments she asked Mrs Arnold to take us to her daughter, who was waiting for us in the drawing room. After she had shown us in to the room, Mrs Arnold left us, excusing herself to carry out some necessary domestic duties.

We found Emily Hunt seated at a writing desk in the far corner of the room. She made as if to rise from her chair, but Hester signalled for her to remain seated.

'No, no, Miss Hunt – I can see that you have a chemistry textbook in front of you, and I would not wish to disturb you. We will draw up these armchairs beside you – thank you, Ivy. I am Miss Lynton and this is my friend and colleague, Miss Jessop. I understand that you are aware of the reason for our visit.'

Emily put down her pen and notebook. I was gratified to see that she did not conform to the derogatory stereotype of the frumpish bluestocking, but was charmingly costumed in a floral tea gown, her thick brown hair loosely pinned behind her head. The look of sharp appraisal that she directed towards Hester and me left us in no doubt as to her acuity.

'Certainly, Miss Lynton. I have to say that upon this occasion I am in agreement with my mother, and would have been happier had the police been informed of Daniel's kidnapping. However, my step-father is adamant that we should simply pay the ransom – although he has agreed to your involvement, I see.'

'That is correct. Miss Hunt, we will not keep you from your books for long, but there are just one or two matters which I would like to raise with you. Firstly, have you yourself noticed anything that could possibly be described as suspicious, in relation to your step-brother's kidnapping?'

Emily pursed her lips. 'There was something, but I am not sure that I should tell you. I mentioned it first to my step-father – my mother was out at the time – and he told me that I should not mention it to my mother, as it would only upset her.'

'Well, Miss Hunt, we could wait until your step-father returns home,' Hester said. 'But I assure you that he would give you permission to tell us what you saw. If you could do so now it would help greatly. I promise that we will say nothing to your mother.'

'Very well. It was last Saturday afternoon, at about four o'clock. I saw a gypsy woman at the end of our drive – I believe mother had seen the woman earlier. However, when I saw the woman she was talking to Daniel, who had been sailing his toy boat on the fish pond nearby. Before I could reach them their conversation had evidently finished, because Daniel returned to the pond. I walked over to him and asked him what had occurred. He told me that "the gypsy lady" – that was what he called her – had asked him about his boat, and whether he had ever taken it to the seaside. However, although I did not question what he told me, I suspected that he was not being entirely truthful. Then, after Daniel was taken from us, I told my step-father the whole story – but he did not think it important.'

'That is all very clear,' Hester said. 'Now, if you will forgive me trespassing on a family matter, I understand that you wish to enrol at the London School of Medicine for Women, but that your parents will not fund your studies there?'

'You are quite correct. However, if my step-father was not so disapproving of my ambition, I believe mother would obtain the money for me. I have already met with the dean, Dr Garrett Anderson, and she has promised my admission once I am able to afford it.'

'And if the funds are not forthcoming?'

Emily smiled. 'There are other ways to obtain money besides asking one's parents. I am, after all, only nineteen, and if necessary my ambitions may have to wait a while before they are fulfilled. It is even possible that I will seek employment in the family business, and endure the mustard trade for long enough to amass the necessary savings. My step-father could hardly disapprove of *that*.'

After thanking Emily Hunt for her cooperation, and saying our farewells to Mrs Arnold, Hester and I left Flexbury Villa and set off on our journey back to Newsome Street. As our four-wheeler left Putney and headed north of the river, Hester sat in contemplative silence. Eventually, I decided to interrupt her reverie.

'Well, have you come to any conclusions?' I asked. 'The behaviour of the gypsy woman seems to me to provide a good starting point for some further investigations. Should we return tomorrow to make enquiries in the neighbourhood? She may be a well-known itinerant, and we could discover her whereabouts.'

Hester stared out of the carriage window as we crossed the Thames.

'I do not think that will be necessary. In fact, it is my intention to write to Mr and Mrs Arnold, and recommend that they pay the ransom exactly as requested in the note that they received on the day of the kidnapping.'

'You surprise me, Hester! Have you therefore given up all hope of solving the mystery?'

Hester laughed. 'On the contrary, I believe that the "mystery", as you call it, has already been solved. The evidence is very plain. However, I hope that all will become clear on Friday of next week, when you and I will await Mr Arnold's appearance at Charing Cross Station. There are one or two little things which I shall have to arrange beforehand, but there is plenty of time to put them in hand. I do hope you will be able to join me that day, as I anticipate an interesting afternoon.'

It was clear to me that Hester had no intention of letting me into her secret until the appointed time, and therefore I waited patiently until the day of the ransom payment arrived. We arrived at Charing Cross Station at twenty minutes to three, but instead of heading for the concourse, Hester took me to the station master's office, where two gentlemen in ready-made tweed suits were evidently expecting us.

'Ivy, I must introduce you to Detective Sergeant Higgins and Detective Constable Brown, of the railway police. They have kindly agreed to assist us today. They will be waiting on the platform side of the ticket barrier. You and I will wait in the main concourse until Samuel Arnold goes through the barrier and shows his ticket. I will then signal to the sergeants, who will stop Arnold to question him. I have already given them Arnold's description, so there is little chance of their choosing the wrong passenger.'

We soon occupied our positions according to Hester's plan. Much as I would have liked to know more of her scheme, there seemed little point in asking her, as all would doubtless soon become clear.

At ten minutes to three Arnold appeared, carrying a stout canvas bag. As he crossed the concourse to the ticket office, he looked nervously behind him, but Hester and I had been careful to place ourselves well to the right of the station entrance. Once Arnold had shown his ticket and passed through the barrier the two plain clothes detectives took him to one side. As they did so, Hester hurried towards them, with me close behind.

Arnold had his back to us and was at first unaware of our presence. Sergeant Higgins showed Arnold his warrant card.

'Mr Samuel Arnold? May I see your ticket, sir? The one you just presented to the collector.'

Arnold took his ticket from his wallet and passed it to the detective.

'Is there some problem, officer? I bought this just a few minutes ago.'

The sergeant peered at the ticket. 'Ah – a single ticket to Dover on the boat train. Well, sir …'

Sergeant Higgins did not have the opportunity to finish his sentence, as at that point Hester stepped forward.

'Why, Mr Arnold! How pleasant to see you again. Can I ask why you have a ticket to Dover, when it is your avowed intention to return to Putney with your son?'

Arnold looked at Hester with an expression which mingled incomprehension and fear. The he looked round as if considering an escape route, but the two detectives moved closer to him, and he evidently realised that such an attempt would be futile.

'As you seem unable to answer my question, let me answer it for you – you intended to abscond with the ransom money. Now, you are an intelligent man, Mr Arnold. I am sure you realise that your full cooperation from this point on will count in your favour when you are sentenced for your crime. Where is Daniel?'

Arnold hung his head dejectedly. 'Very well. Daniel is here, at Charing Cross Station. He is waiting at platform 7, where the Dover train departs in ten minutes.'

Hester smiled broadly. 'Excellent! Ivy, if you and the two officers come with me, we will follow closely behind Mr Arnold. Lead the way to platform 7, sir – and say nothing to warn your accomplice. That person has seen none of us before, and should not take fright unless you give us away.'

After we had crossed the bridge and were walking down the broad flight of steps which led to platform 7, I could see that the Dover train had already arrived. Clouds of steam intermittently arose from the large locomotive at the head of the carriages; carriage doors were left open; porters were bringing luggage on trolleys and carts and groups of travellers were taking their seats. In the midst of all this bustle I noticed a small boy – yes, it was Daniel. He was carrying a stuffed toy rabbit, and was standing next to a fashionably-dressed young woman, whose charming features I recognised from her photograph. It was Daniel's former governess, Miss Helen Walker.

Samuel Arnold led the way, whilst we followed closely behind. I noticed that the two detectives were making great play of talking cheerfully together, and not looking towards our destination. When the young woman saw Arnold, she called anxious to him.

'Samuel! Have you brought the money with you, my dear? I shall take Daniel to the stationmaster myself before our train leaves.'

The boy caught sight of his father and rushed towards him. 'Daddy! Miss Walker and I have had a lovely holiday. *Must* I go home now? Can't I stay with you?'

Sergeant Higgins stepped forward. 'Miss Helen Walker, I am a railway police detective. You and Mr Samuel Arnold are under arrest for the kidnap of Daniel Arnold. It is my duty to inform you that anything you say will be taken down and may be used in evidence. I will need to ask you and Mr Arnold to accompany us to Charing Cross Police Station.'

After Hester and I took Daniel back to Flexbury Villa – along with £2,000 in banknotes – he would say nothing to his mother about his adventure, other than that he had enjoyed 'a lovely holiday' and that the rest was a great secret. Fortunately, he seemed not to comprehend the seriousness of his father's trip to the police station. However, Hester visited him in his room just after he had gone to bed, and I thought it possible that he had been rather more forthcoming with her.

Later that evening Hester, Mrs Arnold, Emily and I were seated in the drawing room in Flexbury Villa in front of a blazing coal fire. A tray of drinks stood on the table between us, Mrs Arnold having forgone her usual abstinence from alcohol in the current unusual circumstances. Her happiness on being reunited with her son had been a joy to behold, and I could not help thinking that the prospect of a permanent estrangement from her husband was not as unwelcome as it might have been for others in her circumstance.

'The main facts of the case you know,' Hester said. 'However, I thought it best for us to meet this evening, so that any questions you may have can be answered before Ivy and I leave for town.'

Mrs Arnold took a sip of brandy and water. 'What I do not understand is how you came to the conclusion that my husband was involved in this conspiracy,' she said.

'My suspicions were first aroused when you and your husband called upon us at Newsome Street,' Hester said. 'You will remember that your husband was adamant the police should not be involved, and quoted some statistics to support his case. If memory serves me right, he informed me that only one of the last four kidnapping cases had been successfully concluded. Now, the Metropolitan Police is not in the habit of publicising its failures, and so either Samuel had gone to an inordinate amount of trouble to obtain his figures, or he had invented them. In either case, he was obviously very frightened of an official investigation.

'However, it was the examination of the scene of the kidnapping that convinced me all was not as it seemed. It is not unusual for a child to be snatched from his or her bed by a kidnapper, but for them to be carefully dressed in a suit of clothes is less common. Daniel had also had the opportunity to take his favourite toy with him. It suggested to me that the kidnapper was someone who knew the house and who knew Daniel. This suspicion was confirmed when I saw the scene of the forced entry to the house. The marks on the sill under the damaged window showed that the sash had been levered open from the inside – probably by a jemmy of some kind. Everything therefore pointed to the kidnapper being a member of this household. If we discount the servants, there were three possibilities: Mrs Arnold, Miss Hunt and Mr Arnold.'

The simultaneous surprise shown by Martha Arnold and Emily Hunt was amusing to behold.

'But why on earth should I kidnap my step-brother?' Emily exclaimed.

'You had a very strong motive – to fund your ambition to train as a doctor. As to Mr and Mrs Arnold, well, it seemed unlikely that they would go to such lengths to obtain money, when they have a perfectly adequate income from Mrs Arnold's trustees. However, when I saw Daniel's picture with Miss Walker, another motive suggested itself. His former governess is a very attractive young woman. Mr Arnold would not be the first man of his age to become besotted by one such as Helen Walker, and the money would have enabled the couple to start life anew. Arnold would have known that it would take some time to raise £2,000 – hence the demand for the ransom by the nineteenth of October, rather than an earlier date. I decided to test my theory by arranging for Mr Arnold to be intercepted at the station, and his ticket checked. If he had purchased a platform ticket, it was probable that he was innocent, and on his way to meet the kidnapper. However, his ticket to Dover showed that he had another plan in mind. He was to meet Miss Walker, and the two would flee with the money. The only thing that may mitigate their crime is their treatment of Daniel. Miss Walker had planned to leave him with the stationmaster on some pretext – Daniel is an intelligent boy and knows his name and address, so he would have reached home safely – eventually.'

'But what happened to him after his disappearance?' Mrs Arnold asked. 'He will tell me nothing.'

Hester chuckled. 'That is because he was sworn to secrecy by his beloved governess! However, there was one other witness who had fortunately not taken a vow of silence. I persuaded Daniel that Reginald, his toy rabbit, could tell me everything without breaking any promise, and Daniel kindly interpreted for that animal. According to Reginald, he and Daniel had a "super holiday" with Miss Walker in Southampton, including a trip to the Isle of Wight, a visit to a funfair and numerous ice creams. Reginald also solved the mystery of the gypsy woman. It was Helen Walker in a somewhat melodramatic disguise – she needed to persuade the little boy to let his father take him away that night. She revealed her true identity to Daniel, who treated the whole business as an exciting game.'

'Goodness!' I exclaimed. 'Let us hope Reginald is not called upon as a witness. Meanwhile, Mrs Arnold, you have £2,000 to dispose of. I suppose there is no chance of your reclaiming your jewellery?'

'Even if it were possible, I would not do so. Emily, I will open an account for you. The money will be more than adequate to fund your chosen career. You must waste no time in contacting Dr Garrett Anderson to confirm your enrolment at the London School of Medicine for Women. When I have succumbed to decrepit old age, it will be most reassuring to know that there is a sympathetic physician in the family.'

7. The Puzzle of the Whitby Housemaid

Although the large majority of the investigations that Hester and I undertook were in London and the home counties, some of the most memorable occurred far from the metropolis. Of these, the puzzle of the Whitby housemaid is notable for the peculiarly disturbing nature of the case – one of the most bizarre we had ever encountered.

By the summer of 1890, both Hester and I were feeling the after-effects of a long and gruelling enquiry that taken us to some of the most dangerous reaches of the criminal world, and had only very recently been resolved. We therefore decided to decamp for four weeks to the picturesque seaside town of Whitby, where we obtained a private suite at the Dolphin Hotel on the East Terrace. This establishment offered fine views across the River Esk to Whitby Abbey on the hillside opposite, and was a good starting point for the explorations which we had planned, both on foot and in a trap hired from our hotel.

Our fellow guests included a pleasant couple from Aberdeen, Mr and Mrs McDonald, and in the second week of our holiday we joined them, at their invitation, for an evening lecture at the Whitby Theatre Society. The McDonalds were friends of the guest speaker, Mr Bram Stoker, who was himself enjoying a holiday in the town, and had agreed to entertain the audience with some stories of his celebrated employer, the actor Mr Henry Irving.

At the beginning of his lecture, Stoker informed us that he was the business manager of Irving's Lyceum Theatre in London, and that he and his wife were enjoying a well-earned rest in Whitby after completing a demanding theatrical tour of Scotland. Stoker had evidently mastered the secret of public speaking – to combine brevity with entertainment – and his thirty-minute talk was both interesting and informative. Refreshments were provided after the lecture, and as Hester and I sat drinking coffee with the McDonalds, Stoker came towards our table. He was a burly, genial man in his early forties, and spoke to his friends with a smile.

'Mr and Mrs McDonald, I must apologise – you have heard all my anecdotes of Irving before, I am sure. But you have made two friends, I see.'

Mr McDonald nodded. 'Indeed. May I introduce Miss Hester Lynton, and her secretary and companion, Miss Ivy Jessop?'

As we rose and shook hands, I noticed a change in Stoker's expression. I could guess the reason; despite her preference for anonymity as far as was possible, Hester's name – and indeed mine – had inevitably been associated with a number of sensational cases over the years, and was no doubt recognised by Stoker. However, he made no reference to the matter, and the remainder of our conversation was taken up by a mutual account of our enjoyment of the sights and sounds of Whitby.

It was as Hester and I were walking back to the Dolphin Hotel after the lecture – the McDonalds having gone their separate way to a restaurant near the pier – that we heard rapid footsteps behind us. It was Stoker, who waved a greeting.

'Ladies, if I might have a word ... my apologies for pursuing you, but I did not want to speak in front of the others.'

Hester smiled. 'If this is to be a lengthy conversation, you are welcome to return to the Dolphin hotel with us; they will serve us coffee in the lounge.'

'Thank you, but I would not dream of imposing upon you both. I have come to offer my own invitation. Would it be possible for you to visit my wife and me tomorrow, at our lodgings? You can name your own hour. We are staying at Mrs Veazey's guest house, at 6 Royal Crescent, and have a private sitting room where we can talk. I will be frank with you; I am aware of your professional reputation, and an issue has arisen upon which I would dearly like your advice. Of course, I will understand if you do not wish to disturb your holiday. If that is the case, tell me now, and consider the matter closed.'

Hester took a step towards Stoker and spoke to him in a serious tone. 'Not at all. We will at any rate be very glad to hear what you and Mrs Stoker have to say. After that, I promise you I will help if at all possible. Shall we say four o'clock tomorrow afternoon?'

For a moment I was tempted to point out to Hester that the purpose of our visit to Whitby was to enjoy a respite from work, not to embark upon another case. However, the enthusiasm and curiosity evident in my friend's expression signalled that such an attempt would be fruitless.

The following morning was bright and sunny, and we spent it in a delightful trip with our hired horse and trap to the picturesque fishing village of Robin Hood's Bay, some seven miles to the south of Whitby. During our return journey Hester and I speculated upon the reason that might lie behind our invitation to the Stokers' lodgings later that day.

'Do you think he is consulting us on a personal matter?' I asked.

'I would very much doubt if the problem is his own,' Hester said. 'He has only been in Whitby for the last seven days – hardly enough to become involved in anything obscure enough for my talents. A simple theft, for example, would have been reported to the local constabulary. I think it likely that he has been approached by someone else, and is requesting our help on that person's behalf. Very possible his landlady, Mrs Veazey.'

I frowned. 'And what leads you to that conclusion?'

'His fellow holidaymakers are more likely to have left their problems behind them that to have taken them to Whitby. As to the locals, Stoker will have had few opportunities for any real intimacy – his landlady will be the person he has spoken to most frequently. His suggestion of a meeting place for our discussion is also instructive. Why meet at his lodgings, when a private conversation could be assured outdoors in the sunshine? I suspect that Mrs Veazey will be a party to our conversation. However, we will know everything before long. A stroll to the Royal Crescent will be most pleasant this afternoon.'

At the appointed hour we reached the Stokers' lodgings. The term 'guest house' seemed rather too modest for the fine terrace at 6 Royal Crescent. We were welcomed by a smartly-dressed parlour maid, who was expecting us, and taken to the private sitting room where Mr and Mrs Stoker were waiting together with another woman, who might have been sixty years of age. I was immediately impressed by the poise and attractiveness of Florence Stoker – a lady who looked ten years younger than her husband – and was not surprised to learn later that she had been a celebrated society beauty.

Florence introduced the older woman as Mrs Veazey, the landlady and owner of the guest house. She struck me as an unpretentious businesswoman typical of her rank in society, one whose achievements were the result of hard work and efficiency.

Once coffee had been served and the tray removed by the servant, Hester asked the Stokers to tell us of their concerns. Florence leant forward, lowering her voice.

'I am so grateful, Miss Lynton, that you and Miss Jessop have been kind enough to see us. As you have probably guessed, it is our landlady's problem that we would like to bring to you. We have explained to Mrs Veazey that you are accustomed to looking into such matters. Perhaps you would like her to explain?'

'Of course,' Hester said. 'Do take your time, Mrs Veazey. Ivy and I are in no hurry. Please tell me how we can help. And please do not concern yourself with my fee – I charge only what those who consult me can easily afford.'

I have often observed how Hester's innate kindness was instrumental in putting her clients at their ease, and the landlady, who had previously appeared rather nervous in our company, became visibly more relaxed at Hester's considerate words.

'Well, Miss Lynton, it's like this. One of my housemaids, Lucy Dillot, had been in service here for over three years – then all of a sudden, she gave her notice. She left here about a month ago, on the fourteenth of July. She's only nineteen, so perhaps that is why she got it into her head that she needed a change and decided to throw over a good situation. She'd got a position as a maid at Renfield Place, with Dr Elias Acland. It's a large house not far from here, near the bottom of the Abbey steps, on the east side of the river. Now, ten days ago I'd gone to the shops to order some mutton – I don't trust the butcher to choose the joint himself – and I saw Lucy walking down Baxtergate. She was carrying a shopping basket, as if she'd been sent out on an errand. Then, when I caught up with her and wished her a friendly good-day – I don't hold with having airs and graces, and looking down on anyone just because they're in service – she looked so pale and ill, I was quite shocked, so I made her come with me to the quay coffee house for a sit down. I asked her if all was well, and she said it was, but there was something in her eyes that made me think otherwise. Then, when I said that she was welcome to move back to the crescent to work for me, she seemed positively frightened. In the end all

I could do was to make her promise that if she felt I could help her in any way, she would call on me – or write to me, if she preferred. And then we parted …'

Hester interrupted. 'Tell me, Mrs Veazey, what do you know of Lucy's family?'

The landlady hesitated for a moment before answering.

'Well miss, she came to me three years ago, when she was barely sixteen. As for family – the poor girl lost her parents at an early age and was brought up by her aunt and uncle in York. Then when her aunt died, her church in York – she is a Methodist – found her a place in service.'

'And does she visit her uncle?' I asked.

'Oh no – she has nothing at all to do with him now. Some kind of family falling-out. I didn't think it right to pry into her reasons.'

Hester nodded. 'I quite understand. Now, is that all you have to tell us?'

'Not quite, miss. I felt it my duty to speak to her new employer, Dr Acland, just to let him know that I was worried about Lucy. So the day after I'd met Lucy in town, I called at Renfield Place and asked to speak to the doctor. I was met at the door by Abraham Killock, who told me right off that his master didn't see anyone without an appointment.'

'Killock is another of the servants?' Hester asked.

'Yes miss. He and his wife – Susan – came to Whitby along with Dr Acland, when he moved here from London five years ago. He'd worked in a London hospital, so people say. As far as I know they're the only servants who live in, apart from Lucy. Dr Acland did employ a local woman as cook when he first arrived, but the poor woman passed away last year. Susan Killock does all the cooking now, I think. They did have a young lad at the house, but he left just before Lucy started working there. Susan is housekeeper – Abraham acts as butler and general handyman. They're a strange couple, like their master – keep themselves to themselves – anyone who tries to speak to them barely gets the time of day. Anyway, that same day I posted a letter to Dr Acland, explaining that I'd like to talk to him about Lucy if he could spare the time. This is the reply I got. It was then that I spoke to Mr and Mrs Stoker to ask their advice.'

Mrs Veazey took a letter out of her handbag and passed it to Hester, who after reading it passed it on to me. It was a very brief note, written on heavy paper with the address of *Renfield Place* embossed as a heading. I reproduce it here in its entirety.

Dear Mrs Veazey,

Thank you for your communication of the 4th inst. I wish to inform you that it will not be possible for me to speak to you regarding my servant, Lucy Dillot, who I can assure you is in no need of your assistance. I regret that I am unable to correspond further on this matter.

Yours etc, E. A. Acland (Dr.)

'Hardly the friendliest of letters!' Hester exclaimed. 'It does not reflect well on Acland's manners. You have given us a very clear account of the case. Now, I have just one or two questions. Do you recall the name of the cook who died whilst in Acland's service?'

Mrs Veazey thought. 'Let me see – Mrs Arkwright ... no, Mrs Arbuckle, that was it. She was a widow with grown-up children.'

'Thank you. And the young man who worked at Renfield Place before Lucy took up her post?'

'That was William Walker. His mother lives in Whitby, she owns the draper's shop in Cliff Street.'

'Excellent. Well, Mrs Veazey, I certainly think you are right to be concerned about Lucy's welfare. Rest assured that Miss Jessop and I will look into the matter right away. We will let you and Mr and Mrs Stoker know immediately if there are any developments in the case.'

Just before three o'clock on the following afternoon, Hester and I set off on the short walk to Renfield Place. Hester had posted a letter to Dr Acland the day before, after we had left Mrs Veazey's guest house, requesting an interview at that time and saying that she would understand if the doctor had made other arrangements and was not at home to receive us. Hester's letter said nothing about our reasons for seeking a meeting.

Dr Acland's house, one of five in a terrace at near the foot of the steps that ran up the hill to the ruins of Whitby Abbey, was an imposing building over five floors. Seen close to, the frontage of Renfield Place had a subtle air of neglect compared to its neighbours; the steps leading up to the portico had not been scrubbed for days, and the black enamel paint on the front door was streaked with salty grime. That was hardly surprising,

I thought, given the small establishment employed by the owner.

I assumed that the servant who answered the door was Abraham Killock. He was slight, weasel-like man dressed in a Norfolk jacket that had seen better days, together with ill-matched patterned waistcoat and wrinkled moleskin trousers. Hester took my card from me, and passed both of our cards to Killock.

'Please take our cards up to Dr Acland,' Hester said. 'He is expecting us to call.'

Killock stood his ground, staring at our cards and turning them over in his hand with the suspicious air of someone who has just been given a foreign banknote. Finally he turned round with a shrug, and sauntered down the hallway in silence.

Hester chuckled. 'I wonder why Dr Acland saw fit to bring his servant up from London? It cannot be because of Killock's social graces. The post of stableman would suit him better. Perhaps his wife makes up for his failings.'

Killock returned with rather more alacrity than he had departed.

'If you'll just follow me, missus, master will see you now,' he mumbled.

We were shown into a large room on the first floor that had the appearance of a grandiose study, although it too would not have passed muster under the eyes of an efficient housekeeper; cobwebs clung to the cornices and the large windows were dulled with dust. A number of heavy tables were covered with an assortment of papers and books, together with some glass retorts and other chemical apparatus that would have looked more at home in a laboratory than a gentleman's study.

Dr Acland stood in the centre of the room awaiting our arrival, his hands clasped behind him. He was a striking figure, tall and thin, with pale features that contrasted with the darkness of his hair. He wore an old-fashioned, loose-fitting black frock coat and a black silk neckerchief swathed round a high collar. I would have placed his age at no more than fifty, although he had the kind of sparse physiognomy that often changes little over a decade. He observed us with evident sharpness and intelligence.

'Miss Lynton, Miss Jessop – I received your note. Welcome to Renfield Place. I am of course familiar with your names. Do take a seat. Tell me, have you moved permanently to Whitby? And in what way can I help you? I assume you have come regarding a professional matter, rather than to pass the time of day discussing the weather.'

Hester smiled. 'I am grateful that you have agreed to see us. To answer your first question, Ivy and I are here to enjoy a holiday, and will be returning to London at the end of the month. Regarding your second question, you have correctly deduced that we are looking into a matter for a client and seek your help.'

Once we were seated, Acland took his place in an armchair opposite us. He leant forward, his eyes narrowing.

'Now, ladies, you must let me hazard a guess as to the reason for your visit. I am something of a recluse, so I suspect that your enquiry relates to my own establishment rather than the affairs of another. Let me see – have you come regarding my young housemaid, Lucy Dillot? I know that her previous employer has some concerns about her.'

'I see that my role as consulting detective has been usurped!' Hester laughed. 'You are quite correct. Let me recount what we have been told.'

Hester then went on to describe Mrs Veazey's encounter with Lucy, and concluded as follows.

'My client wants merely to reassure herself that Lucy is quite well, and happy in her circumstances. I have seen the letter that you sent to Mrs Veazey. Would it not be possible for you to reconsider, and to meet with the lady? Of course strictly speaking she no longer has any responsibility for Lucy, but nevertheless she feels some duty of care for her former servant.'

Dr Acland sat back in his chair, his palms pressed together in ecclesiastical fashion.

'Let me explain, Miss Lynton. I am sure my note to Mrs Veazey must have seemed rather brusque, but there is a reason for it. A vacancy arose in my household in early July, when a young man left my service, and so I placed an advertisement in the *Whitby Gazette* for a replacement. Lucy Dillot was one of a number of applicants, and after Mrs Killock – my housekeeper – had spoken to all of them, Lucy was appointed. Lucy was a well-trained and obliging servant, but it quickly became apparent that she was a most anxious young woman. Fortunately, as a medical man I was well placed to help her. Lucy exhibited some pronounced neurological abnormalities, leading to episodes of hysteria and amnesia. However, ladies, I do not wish to confuse you with the medical technicalities. Suffice it to say that when Lucy came to me she was already quite unwell.'

I could not help smiling at Hester reaction to the doctor's words; my friend detested any kind condescension from the male sex.

'Not at all, Doctor. That is most interesting. I have some familiarity with William Gower's work in the field. Tell me, what appeared to be the precipitating circumstances behind Lucy's hysteria? Did you identify any physiological cause?'

Dr Acland struggled to disguise the annoyance typically experienced by the professional who feels that a layman (or, even worse, a laywoman) is trespassing upon their area of expertise.

'I will explain, but please do not repeat that I am about to say. The fact is, Lucy Dillot had suffered a most unfortunate experience at the hands of one of Mrs Veazey's male guests. Nothing actionable had occurred, or could be proven, but she had felt both threatened and vulnerable. Naturally, after that she wished to leave Mrs Veazey's employment, hence her move to Renfield Place. I do not believe that Mrs Veazey knows anything of the matter, and Lucy is most anxious that nothing is said to her former employer.'

'I am very sorry to hear that, Doctor,' Hester said. 'You have my assurance that our conversation will go no further. May I ask whether you have treated poor Lucy for her anxiety? I ask only so that I can assure Mrs Veazey that she is in good hands, and receiving the best of care.'

Dr Acland seemed mollified by Hester's words.

'Thank you. I have prescribed a regime of light work only, and a nourishing diet of my own devising. I have also prescribed a solution of cocaine, combined with regular mesmerism, to lessen her anxiety. She has proven an excellent hypnotic subject, and I have every hope that within a few more weeks the memory of her upsetting experience will cease to trouble her, and she will be able to play her full part in the household.'

At those words, the doctor pulled out his pocket watch and consulted it. 'Now, ladies, if that is all, I will ask Killock to show you out. I hope I have been able to offer you some reassurance, and that in turn you will be able to tell your client that she has no reason to fear for Lucy's welfare.'

After leaving Renfield Place Hester and I decided that some fresh air would not come amiss, and so set off up the long flight of steps to the headland and Whitby Abbey. We had undertaken the same walk on several previous occasions and each time were impressed by the magnificent view from the Abbey ruins down to the town and harbour below.

Hester pointed to the Abbey behind us. 'Oh that we were artistically inclined, Ivy. Those picturesque ruins almost demand to be painted. Although I suspect they would look rather less appealing at night.'

'Not for enthusiasts of the Gothic style,' I answered with a smile. 'I would imagine that Horace Walpole or Ann Radcliffe would have liked nothing better than a moonlit sojourn in such surroundings. Now, you have said nothing yet about our encounter with Dr Acland. What did you make of the fellow?'

'Let me put it like this,' Hester said. 'If Lucy was my sister, I would not be happy for her to remain under the doctor's roof. However, our investigation currently suffers from a fatal weakness; we have too little information, and without it, further speculation is idle. I suggest that we divide our labour as follows. I will send a telegram today to Professor Wilkins-Blyth at the Chelsea Hospital to find out more about Dr Acland. The professor is a former client – you will remember the Gillespie case – and I am sure he will do his best to help us. Then tomorrow I will discover what I can regarding Acland's late cook, Mrs Arbuckle. Perhaps at the same time you could have a word with William's mother, Mrs Walker? It would be interesting to discover why her son left Acland's service, and where he has gone since.'

The following day we carried out Hester's plan, and after breakfast I walked the short distance to the small shop on Cliff Street which bore the sign *S J Walker and Son, Drapers*. A tall woman in a long brown dustcoat stood behind the counter. She was no more than fifty years of age, but with the lined features and sombre countenance of someone who had borne more than their share of troubles. Was she a widow, I wondered, continuing a business founded by her husband? Or had she started the enterprise herself?

'Mrs Walker?' I said. 'You must excuse my intrusion – I can return at another time if you wish. My name is Miss Ivy Jessop. I am undertaking some enquiries on behalf of a friend, Mr Jenkins, who is anxious to contact your son William. Your son very kindly lent my friend five shillings some months ago, and now that Mr Jenkins is well again, he wishes to repay the debt. Mr Jenkins is an elderly gentleman, unable to call upon you himself.'

Mrs Walker self-consciously brushed her hands down her coat, and looked at me anxiously.

'William, you say? You'd better come to the back room. You'll have to excuse me if the doorbell rings and I have to see to a customer.

The room into which she ushered me was furnished with a small deal table and two chairs, hemmed in by bolts of cloth of all types and colours.

'I've no stove in the shop,' Mrs Walker said. 'So I can't offer you tea. William said nothing to me about Mr Jenkins – is he a local man?'

'An occasional visitor to Whitby,' I said, anxious not to be drawn into a discussion about my imaginary friend. 'He knew that William was employed in town, but no more than that – apart from the fact that his mother had this shop, hence my visit. I must apologise again for calling upon you unannounced.'

'That's alright, miss. But I'm afraid I won't be of much help to you. I haven't seen William since he left Dr Acland's house at the end of June, seven weeks ago. Let me explain. Dr Acland called on me in the first week of July. I was surprised to see him – he don't go out much, hardly at all. Friday the fourth, it was. He told me that I ought to know that William had gone to another post at the Excelsior Hotel in Liverpool! Well, I could hardly believe it – that he'd go without even saying goodbye.'

'Did Dr Acland give any reason for your son going so suddenly?' I asked.

'Yes. He said that William had got talking to one of the managers who worked at the hotel, on holiday here, who offered him a well-paid job as night porter, and said William could travel to Liverpool with him that day. William worked as a groom and gardener for the doctor, so I suppose he was trying to better himself. But why he couldn't have called in to say goodbye to me I don't know. I don't mind telling you, I was worried sick – but then I got a letter in the post from William a few days later. I've got it here, if you'd like to see it. I'm afraid William's not much of a scholar, like me, but it's plain enough to make out what he says.

I took hold of the small sheet of notepaper that Mrs Walker passed to me. The words upon it were printed roughly, and the orthography was semi-literate. I have reproduced it – as far as is possible – on the opposite page.

7 July

Derest Mother

Ive started work at the Exzelsore here in Livopol and am ernig a good wagis.

Im sorry I didernt say goodby

I will cum to see you when I hav my holyday

Youre loving sun,

William

I handed the note back to Mrs Walker, thinking that it would be useful to show it to Hester – but I could hardly request the loan of such a personal item. Instead, I made a concerted effort to remember William's words, including his eccentricities of spelling.

'You have been very helpful, Mrs Walker,' I said. 'I will relay what you have told me to my friend; he may decide to send William his money care of the hotel. I do hope that you see William before too much time has passed. Now, before I go – I noticed that you had a very fine-looking pair of grey suede gloves in your window. I should like to try them on, if that is in order.'

Five minutes later I left the shop with my purchase neatly wrapped in brown paper. They were indeed very elegant gloves, but I confess that I had bought them mainly to create a favourable impression with the owner; she would be much more likely to receive me willingly a second time – if that became necessary – now that I had added to her profits.

It was later that afternoon when Hester re-joined me at the Dolphin Hotel. She poured out a glass of sherry for each of us and asked me to outline my findings.

I explained to Hester all that had taken place in my interview with Mrs Walker, and I also presented her with a piece of paper on which I had transcribed – from memory – William's letter to his mother. When I had completed my account, Hester walked to the window with William's words in her hand and stared out across the harbour to the Abbey ruins on the headland opposite. After a few moments, she turned round to face me.

'The note that you have memorised is most interesting. You have reproduced the defective orthography remarkably well. I will keep this copy, if you have no objection. It arrived by post, you say?'

'That is what Mrs Walker told me, yes. "I got a letter in the post from William" were the exact words that she used.'

Hester chuckled. 'Really, Hester, your extraordinary mental powers are wasted as my assistant! You should set up on the stage as "The Amazing Memory Woman". But regarding young William, it is a pity that we do not have the envelope in which his letter arrived.'

Quite why possession of the envelope would have helped us was a mystery to me, but before I could ask Hester to explain, she had embarked upon an account of her own investigation.

'I will spare you the details of any little subterfuges I had to indulge in to obtain my information,' Hester said with a smile. 'The facts are these. Mrs Arbuckle – her first name was Betsy – died on the fifth of December, 1889. She was fifty-three years of age. The death certificate gave the cause of death as acute anaemia, although according to her medical man, Dr Sedgefield, her general health was sound, and her rapid decline came as something of a surprise.'

'You have spoken to her doctor?' I asked.

'Yes, Dr Sedgefield was most helpful. His opinion of his fellow professional, Dr Acland, is not so high, however. He considers Acland – who apparently had a senior post in a London hospital before retiring to Whitby – to be stand-offish. We will hopefully learn more of Acland when I receive a reply to my telegram. I am hopeful that a letter will arrive tomorrow. Until then, I fear there is little more that we can do.'

'And is the case at all clearer to you, given what we have now learned?' I asked.

Hester nodded. 'You know me well enough to understand that I would not wish to theorise whilst some of the details are as yet unknown, but I have every hope that this case can be resolved very soon. And for the sake of young Lucy, the sooner the better. Now, if you will excuse me, I must walk to the post office. I have another telegram to send.'

The following morning proved to be both busy and rewarding. After breakfast Hester received two replies following her enquiries; a letter from Professor Wilkins-Blyth regarding Dr Acland, and a reply to the telegram which Hester had sent the previous evening. She passed the latter to me.

From Howard Spinks Manager Excelsior Hotel Liverpool. Regret no knowledge of William Walker he has never been employed at the Excelsior

'What do you make of that?' Hester asked.

'Perhaps he had other reasons for going to Liverpool, which he was not prepared to divulge to his mother. A romantic entanglement, perhaps, of which she would disapprove. Hence his letter to her pretending he was employed at the hotel.'

'Very possibly. Now, let us read what Wilkins-Blyth has to say about Dr Acland. He seems to have written at some length. No doubt he still feels in our debt for the help we were able to give him regarding the Harley Street poisoner.'

After reading the letter through with some care, Hester passed it over to me. It was, as she had remarked, somewhat lengthy – the professor seemed to have a predilection for verbosity – and I will record only the essentials here. Until five years ago, Acland had been a respected surgeon with a considerable private practice, as well as a place on the staff of St Bertram's Hospital in Spitalfields. He had attempted – with some success – experiments in the transfusion of blood; he had undertaken research in the field of anaesthesia and was responsible for some significant developments in the administration of chloroform narcosis. However, a scandal arose, which resulted in his departure from the hospital, and it was only due to the lack of any real evidence that he avoided a criminal prosecution. He had treated poor patients at St Bertram's without charging a fee – but had been using them as subjects for untried and dangerous anaesthetic procedures. At least two of his patients had died from the administration of nitrous oxide in a new and unorthodox manner. Dr Acland was a bachelor, with no known family in London, and Professor Wilkins-Blyth knew only that he had left London abruptly when his employment was terminated.

I was about to ask Hester's opinion concerning the disturbing contents of the professor's letter when there was a knock upon our door. The maid that entered told us that a gentleman had arrived at reception – a Mr Stoker – and was anxious to see us. We asked that he be shown up to our rooms, and a few moments later he was sitting opposite us, evidently keen to share some news.

'Not fifteen minutes ago Mrs Veazey received a letter,' he said. 'It was brought to her door in a sealed envelope not by the postman but by Tom the butcher's boy, who delivered it on behalf of Lucy Dillot. She gave it to him yesterday, but he had no time to bring it round then. She has sworn him to secrecy, and I believe he will do as she asks. Lucy is a pretty girl, which perhaps explains Tom's willingness to act as courier. Here, read it for yourselves.'

Lucy's letter was short and to the point. She asked Mrs Veazey to meet her in the Abbey ruins at midnight on Sunday the seventeenth of August – tomorrow evening – to ask her advice. She said that she should be sent no reply, but would go to the Abbey regardless, in the hope that she could be met.

'The question is, ladies, should Mrs Veazey agree to meet Lucy?' Stoker asked. 'My own view is that I should go instead, but naturally I would wish to have your opinion. Have you been able to shed any light on the case since we last me?'

Hester smiled. 'Let me answer your questions in order. Firstly, can I suggest that Mrs Veazey does meet Lucy as requested – but that Ivy and I accompany her. I do not wish to give offence, but I believe that three women are more likely to reassure her than one man. You need not be concerned about our safety, as Ivy and I are well used to such clandestine outings. Regarding your second question; I am optimistic that the mystery behind Lucy's troubled state of mind will soon be resolved. More than that, it would be premature to say.'

Stoker readily agreed with Hester's plan, and so a little before midnight on the Sunday evening Hester and I called to collect Mrs Veazey, who was expecting us, and set off down the deserted streets towards the Abbey steps. Fortunately, the full moon made a lantern unnecessary.

I noticed that Hester was carrying a small wicker basket, and asked her what it contained.

'A collection of jam jars, which the hotel kitchen has kindly lent me,' she said with a chuckle. 'If a policeman should ask us our business, I shall explain that we are three lady naturalists, out seeking specimens of *Hepialus Humuli* – the ghost moth. It is a little late in the year for their appearance, but I doubt that a constable would know that. He will put us down as harmless eccentrics, I am sure.'

As it turned out, Hester had no cause to use her elaborate excuse, and we had soon climbed the steps and entered the Abbey ruins. As we did so, the sound of a church clock striking the hour could be heard from the harbour below. I confess that it was not a spot where I would have wished to linger alone, but with Hester and Mrs Veazey at my side, and with my revolver stowed in the pocket of my dress, I felt more than able to meet any eventuality. Hester had left her Webley service revolver behind in London – an omission I suspected she was beginning to regret.

Mrs Veazey and I concealed ourselves behind one of the inner walls of the Abbey, whilst Hester peered through the broken stone tracery of a nearby window, which gave a good view of the path from the town. At first it seemed that our expedition might have been fruitless, as by ten minutes past midnight there was no sight of the young servant. I walked silently and cautiously towards Hester, who turned round and put her finger to her lips. Over Hester's shoulder I could clearly see the caped and hooded outline of a small figure, illuminated by the light of the full moon. Hester moved out of the shelter of the ruins and beckoned the person to join us. She did so, and when she removed her hood we could see that it was Lucy Dillot. I could also see that under her cloak she wore only a thin nightgown.

We retreated further inside the Abbey, where we sat down on a group of flat stones. The moonlight barely penetrated this interior section of the ruins, but there was enough light to make out Lucy's features, which appeared strained and nervous.

'You'll forgive me bringing my two friends, I'm sure,' Mrs Veazey said. 'The fact is, I felt I needed some support. This is Miss Lynton, and this is Miss Jessop. They're from London, and can be trusted.'

Lucy looked at us anxiously, but did not speak.

'Rest assured, any secrets you may have are safe with us,' Hester said. 'Mrs Veazey told us about your meeting in town with her at the beginning of August. Is there any way that we can help you?'

'I want to know what I should do. You'll find my story strange, but every word is true,' Lucy said.

The landlady was about to speak, but at a glance from Hester she remained silent, and Lucy continued.

'It was Susan – Mrs Killock, the housekeeper and cook at Renfield Place – that talked me into moving. She told me that I'd get five shillings a week more at Dr Acland's, and that the work would be very light, as they have two daily women in to do the rough cleaning, and very few visitors. That was true enough, but as for the rest … it started after I'd been there for about a week, and caught a bit of a chill. Nothing at all serious, you understand. Well, Dr Acland insisted that I take his medicine for it, and I did for a day or two and it seemed to make me better. But whether it was the medicine or not, after that I didn't feel quite right in myself. I worried about everything, and couldn't sleep. So then Dr Acland asked if he could mesmerise me. I agreed, and each evening before bed I go to his study. I stare into his eyes and he asks me to count to twenty, but I never seem to reach the end of the count, and five or ten minutes later – I can tell by his mantle clock – I wake up again. This happens every evening, except Sundays. Mr and Mrs Killock have the day off then, so perhaps the doctor is too busy to treat me. I still take Dr Acland's medicine every morning with my breakfast. Mrs Killock reminds me if I forget.'

I glanced at Hester, whose face expressed concern.

'And are you still anxious?' Hester said.

'That's the funny thing, miss. It's only that the thought of having to be in service anywhere but Renfield Place that makes me feel frightened. It's as if I'm a prisoner who is free to leave, but can't.'

'Fascinating,' Hester said, as if to herself. 'And have you had any other unhappy experiences at Renfield Place?'

'There are two things, Miss Lynton. The first is the nightmares, which seem to be getting worse and worse. They're always the same. I'm lying on my bed, unable to stir. My bed is moving – somehow – along the corridor that leads to Dr Acland's workshop, and I try to sit up, but can't. The bed stops at the door, then I wake up. It sounds foolish, I know, but I feel that there is something horrible waiting for me on the other side of the door …'

I interrupted Lucy. 'And the corridor and workshop door that you dream of – do they exist in the house in real life?' I asked.

'Oh yes, miss. I've been down there myself several times, to another cellar where the wine is kept, but I've never gone into the workshop.'

'And the other thing you wanted to tell us?' Hester asked.

'It's this strange mark. Dr Acland says that I must have bruised my arm without noticing it.

Lucy slipped her cloak below her shoulders and pulled up the sleeve of her nightdress to reveal her upper arm. There was an irregular circle of dark bruising an inch or so in diameter, the centre of which looked black. Hester drew Lucy away into a patch of brighter moonlight and studied the mark closely.

'What colour is this patch in the daylight?' she asked.

'Purple and yellow, like a bad bruise, she said. 'And red in the middle, although there is no wound to be seen.'

'And when did you first notice the mark?' Hester asked.

'After I'd been here for about a week – about the same time as I caught a chill.'

Hester nodded. 'I am hardly surprised that you are seeking help,' she said. 'Mrs Veazey, what do you think Lucy should do? I have my own opinion, but you know her better than I.'

Up to this point Mrs Veazey had appeared rather overawed by what had occurred, but now she seemed very sure of her opinion.

'I don't think Lucy should spend one more night in that dreadful place,' she said. 'She should come back home with me now, and tomorrow I'll take her to Dr Sedgefield to have that nasty thing on her arm looked at. If you ask me, it's a rat bite. I've seen them before.'

At these words Lucy leapt to her feet, her eyes wide with terror. 'No, that's impossible! I can't leave my place in Dr Acland's house, please don't ask me to.'

Hester walked over to the young woman and took her arm. 'Please don't distress yourself, Lucy. A few moments ago you asked us to advise you what you should do about your upsetting experiences. Let me make a suggestion. Let Miss Jessop and me accompany you back to Renfield Place. You must say nothing about meeting us this evening; if your absence was noticed, say that you were gripped by the urge for a late-night walk – it will be assumed that you were meeting an admirer, but that cannot be helped. I promise you that before the week is out, your situation will be much improved.'

Lucy sighed. 'Well, miss, if you're sure – I can put up with a few more days, I suppose.'

Our return journey proved uneventful; during the few minutes it took to reach Renfield Place, Hester asked Lucy to describe, in as much detail as possible, the internal layout of the house. After we had reached the bottom of the Abbey steps, Lucy whispered softly to us.

'There's a small window at the side of the house which I have left off the latch. I came out that way and I'll get back in through it.'

'I will accompany you, while Mrs Veazey and Miss Jessop wait here,' Hester said.

A few minutes later Hester returned alone, and we walked with the landlady back to the Royal Crescent. On the short walk back to our hotel I asked my friend the question that had been troubling me ever since we had taken Lucy back to Renfield Place.

'Hester – should we not have insisted that Lucy return with us? I am very anxious at the thought of her staying for much longer in that sinister household.'

Hester stopped and turned towards me, her serious expression illuminated by the moonlight.

'No more anxious that I am, I assure you. There is clearly something seriously amiss. However, it would hardly have been practical to force poor Lucy kicking and screaming into town. Here is my proposal. Tomorrow night, you and I will visit Renfield Place, long after all members of the household have retired to bed. I have asked Lucy to leave open the window that she used tonight; she has told me how to find it. I am convinced that there is some wickedness in Dr Acland's household, and because it would be impossible for the official police force to take action without any concrete evidence, will have to do our best to discover the secret ourselves.'

I chuckled. 'It will not be the first time that we have posed as lady housebreakers. I will see if the Whitby shops can furnish us with a dark lantern and some suitable clothing. What a shame that we did not anticipate this adventure when we planned our holiday – you could have packed your service revolver!'

All went according to plan, and thus twenty-four hours after we had parted from Lucy, Hester and I found ourselves outside Renfield Place once more. It was just after midnight, and the small seaside town was devoid of any sign of human existence – in marked contrast to the streets of the metropolis, where that anthill of humanity is never entirely still, whatever the hour of day or night. Hester had decided not to tell Bram Stoker about her plans; when she had spoken to him earlier that day about our encounter in the Abbey ruins, she said only that our investigation was progressing well, and might shortly reach a conclusion.

Hester put her finger to her lips, and pointed to the narrow path that led down the side of the doctor's house to the small garden behind it. Halfway down the path we could see the small window that Lucy had described. Hester pulled it open, and we were just able to worm our way inside. Earlier, I had bought us some second-hand workmen's clothes for us to wear on our expedition. It was just as well, since the usual garments of a respectable woman would have both impeded our progress and threatened our dignity.

We found ourselves inside what seemed to be a small kitchen storeroom, shelved on two sides and stocked with bags of flour, jars of pickles and other such comestibles. Hester pulled the window shut behind her. I took out the dark lantern from my carpet bag, lit it, and adjusted the aperture to release a thin ray of light. I followed Hester's silent footsteps through the large, old-fashioned kitchen, dominated by a cast iron range that would not have looked out of place several decades ago.

Using the information provided earlier by Lucy, we soon arrived at the stone steps leading to the cellarage below. This part of the house was evidently more ancient than the upper storeys; the walls on each side of the corridor at the bottom of the steps were roughly hewn granite, and covered with an unwholesome sheen of damp. Shortly afterwards, the door of Dr Acland's workshop appeared before us.

Before I could take another step, Hester laid her hand upon my arm to stop me. She pointed towards the bottom of the door, from which appeared a glimmer of light. Thus far, the whole house had been in complete darkness, and I immediately wondered if the room in front of us was occupied. My unspoken question was soon answered, as the sound of indistinct voices came from the workshop.

The corridor continued past the workshop door, and beyond it was another door, half open. With mutual purpose Hester and I hurried towards it and entered the room – it was empty apart from some empty tea chests and piles of sacking. I closed the shutter on my dark lantern – it was not a moment too soon, for we heard the door of the workshop open. Once the footsteps of those that had emerged had receded down the corridor, back towards the steps, Hester looked round the door. I did the same, a moment later. Although seen from behind, it was clear that two of the three figures were Dr Acland and his servant, Abraham Killock. The third was a woman, but all we could see of her was her dowdy dark dress and grey hair, knotted in a bun. I guessed that it was probably Killock's wife, Susan.

When they had disappeared from sight, Hester whispered to me.

'We have time to make a brief examination of the workshop before they return, if you are willing to come with me.'

'Could they not have retired for the night? It is well after midnight.'

'Hardly – if so, they would surely have extinguished the cellar light. But come, we are wasting time.'

Without more delay we entered the workshop, Hester leading the way. I have seldom seen my friend as shocked as she was by the scene that we encountered, and I am sure that my expression was as surprised as hers.

The large room – about twenty feet square – was illuminated by three oil lamps set in recesses in the granite walls. Several deal tables and a low bed occupied one side of the room, and were covered with a variety of glassware and other apparatus unfamiliar to me. 'Workshop' was something of a misnomer, as the room resembled a scientific laboratory. However, it was the bizarre sight in a far corner of the room that froze us. A young man, his shirt sleeves rolled up, was slumped in a heavy oak chair – he was unconscious, his wrists bound to the chair arms. A bloodstained bandage was tied round his upper left arm. A shallow dish was on the floor next to the chair, containing a coil of rubber tubing, one end of which terminated in a clear glass jar. The jar was half full of blood.

Our temporary paralysis vanished as we sprang towards the young man. Hester put her hand upon the victim's neck, placing her index and middle fingers upon the carotid artery.

'A weak pulse, but he is alive,' she said. 'Let us undo his hands.'

We had hardly finished releasing him when the young man sat up, his eyes open. He looked wild-eyed at each of us in turn, then – clearly realising that we were not his tormentors – called out to us urgently.

'For God's sake, help me!' He cried. 'I've been kept here, and the doctor's been …'

Before the poor fellow could finish his sentence he stopped and listened, an expression of terror upon his features. We heard the sound of raised voices outside, rapidly approaching the workshop door. There was no possibility of concealment, and so we both stood for a few seconds, waiting for the door to open.

'I suggest you take out your pistol,' Hester said to me.

I reached into the pocket of my dress. 'Here, you have it,' I said. 'You are the better shot, if it comes to it.'

Hester said nothing, but took the weapon from my hand just as the door opened. Once again I was struck by surprise. Dr Acland and Mr and Mrs Killock came into the room, as I had expected – but Mr Killock and the doctor were supporting another, semi-conscious figure between them. It was Lucy Dillot, wearing a plain white nightdress.

All three stood still as they saw us in the room. The doctor and Killock released Lucy – none too gently – and she slid to the floor, her back against the wall.

Dr Acland gave us one brief startled look and then quickly regained his composure.

'Miss Lynton! Miss Jessop! What in high heaven are you doing in my house, waving a pistol like burglars? If this is a joke, I am bound to say that it is in very poor taste.'

Hester smiled. 'Much as I would be interested hear any explanation for all of this,' – Hester used my pistol to gesture around the room – 'which you might have to offer, I have a far better suggestion. You and the Killocks will wait here with me, whilst Ivy goes to summon the constabulary. Then, if your subsequent innocence of any wrongdoing is proven, Ivy and I will be happy to pay the penalty for invading your privacy.'

Again, a flicker of anxiety passed across the doctor's features, but was soon repressed.

'Of course you must rouse the police, if you think it necessary,' he said. 'But first, at least let me show you this letter from the hospital in York, which I think will explain everything.'

As he spoke he moved towards a filling cabinet, which stood several feet away, turning his back on Hester as he pulled open the top drawer and reached inside it.

'Dr Acland . . .' Hester began – but before she was able to complete her warning he spun round to face her, a revolver in his hand. Before he could discharge it, the youth in the chair next to us threw himself towards the doctor. Then, there was the deafening sound of the doctor's weapon, and a glass jar behind us shattered – his bullet had missed. For a few frantic seconds the pair wrestled upon the floor, the young man's fear metamorphosed into unexpected energy. Before Hester or I could act, a second shot rang out and Acland lay still upon the floor.

It was unnecessary to examine the doctor to detect any sign of life, since the small entry wound in his left temple made that possibility quite untenable.

The following morning, Hester and I made a visit to Mrs Veazey's guest house at 6 Royal Crescent, where we found Mr and Mrs Stoker finishing their breakfast. We asked Mrs Veazey to join us, and after first assuring them of Lucy Dillot's safety, gave all three of them a brief account of what had taken place the previous evening.

'After Dr Acland was shot, I kept guard over the Killocks whilst Ivy went to the police station,' Hester concluded. 'Sergeant Potter then roused Dr Sedgefield, the local medical practitioner, who returned with them. Fortunately, neither Lucy nor the young man we discovered in the laboratory are in any serious danger; Dr Sedgefield has admitted them to the cottage hospital. I told the sergeant everything that had happened, and he took the Killocks into custody. He is sending for Chief Inspector Crowthorne from the Durham constabulary, who should arrive here in Whitby by mid-day, when I shall be able to give him a detailed account of the whole business.'

Florence Stoker lifted the lid of the silver coffee pot, which stood amidst the detritus of their breakfast. 'There is enough left for everyone,' she said. And as we all accepted her offer, Florence – dismissing Mrs Veazey's attempts to take on the task – filled cups for all of us.

Florence settled herself down with her coffee. 'Well, I hope that I can speak for my husband and Mrs Veazey as well as myself – I confess to being quite mystified regarding what has been happening at Renfield Place. Or am I wrong, Bram dear?'

Both Stoker and Mrs Veazey signalled their agreement.

'I have some tenuous ideas,' Stoker said. 'But I would plead with Miss Lynton to give us a definitive explanation. I am sure we can all keep a confidence.'

Hester thought for a moment, then appeared to make a decision.

'Very well,' she said. 'But nothing I say must leave this room. I have every hope of persuading the chief inspector to do what he can to keep the sensational elements of this case out of the newspapers, and I would not wish word to reach the press through any other channel.

'The central issue is this case is the recruitment of Lucy Dillot into the service of Dr Acland. The doctor's motive might seem obvious; that is, he was in need of a housemaid. However, we were led to believe that the vacancy that arose in Acland's household was due to the fact that William Walker had left his household. And yet, as Mrs Walker told Ivy, William was employed as a groom and gardener. A housemaid is hardly a logical replacement. It is therefore apparent that Dr Acland wished Lucy to be working at Renfield Place for some other reason.

'At this point, I became interested in William Walker's story. His sudden departure from Renfield Place seemed peculiar – and when Ivy discovered the letter that he had written to his mother, my suspicions were raised. I have a copy here, if you would like to examine it.'

Hester took my transcription out of her bag and passed it to the Stokers and Mrs Veazey.

'The letter is not so much semi-literate, as a parody of misspelling,' Hester said. 'Even a person with very limited language skills is likely to be able to spell at least one of these: "work", "wage", "goodbye", "come" and "have". The forger is trying too hard.'

'But would not Mrs Walker have noticed if her son's handwriting had been imitated?' I asked.

Hester smiled. 'Not if the writing was a reasonable likeness. I doubt Mrs Walker received much of an education, and the less familiar one is with the written word, the harder it is to spot an imitation. There is, of course, the fact that she received her son's letter through the post – unfortunately we do not have the envelope – but that difficulty can easily be got round. I imagine that whoever forged William's letter also produced a convincing simulacrum of a letter franked by the post office – old stamps are easy enough to come by, and a smudged franking can easily be imitated. Then, the forger just pushed the envelope through Mrs Walker's letterbox late one night, and the recipient naturally assumed it had come in an early post. As Ivy knows, the manager of the hotel in Liverpool where William was meant to be working had never heard of him.'

Stoker looked puzzled. 'So where had William gone?'

'He went nowhere. He never left the house. He was the unfortunate young man that Ivy and I found unconscious in Dr Acland's workroom. Oh, there can be no doubt about it. Mrs Walker was sent for by Dr Sedgefield; she is at her son's bedside as I speak. Fortunately, the lad is likely to make a full recovery from his horrible ordeal ...'

Now it was Florence Stoker's turn to interrupt. 'You say "horrible ordeal". What was happening to poor William? What was Dr Acland doing to him, and to Lucy?'

'Ah. That is the crux of the matter. Ivy and I have discovered that Dr Acland was forced to leave his previous post due to an unfortunate predilection for conducting unauthorised – and dangerous – experiments upon his unwitting patients. It seems that in his forced retirement the habit had not left him. Although it was experiments in anaesthesia that caused his professional downfall, Acland was also researching the transfusion of blood. This is a most risky procedure and is normally never attempted unless the patient is *in extremis*. However, even someone with as slight an understanding of medicine as myself could see that, when Ivy and I entered the doctor's laboratory, poor William's blood was being drained from his body.'

'And what about Lucy?' Stoker asked.

'She too was being abused in the name of medical science,' Hester said. 'The regime of drugs and hypnotic suggestion to which she was subjected by Dr Acland made her terrified to leave his employment. His statement to us regarding her previous nervous illness and its causes was nonsense; she only became unwell after the doctor began to mistreat her. As Ivy and Mrs Veazey can confirm, the poor girl had an unpleasant wound on her arm. This was caused by the insertion of a cannula into her vein. A cannula is a thin tubular device designed to allow blood to be fed in or drained out. However, I cannot gain the credit for my certain knowledge of this fact. Before Ivy and I left Renfield Place last night, I took the chance to look briefly through the papers in Dr Acland's filing cabinet – which now awaits a full examination by the police. In brief, Acland's ghastly experiment was as follows: he would regularly draw blood from Lucy and from William, so that they were both near the point of death. Then, he would inject Lucy's blood into William, and vice versa, thereby reviving them. Of course, there was one great flaw in his methodology. If we assume that by some chance Lucy's and William's blood were particularly compatible, then merely repeating the process would prove nothing.'

'Then we are lucky he did not find another subject!' I cried.

Hester looked sombre. 'I believe there *was* at least one earlier victim of Acland's criminal irresponsibility – his late cook, Betsy Arbuckle. Remember that she was in good health until she died suddenly of acute anaemia. However, nothing can be gained by trying to unravel that episode. Dr Acland has already paid the ultimate penalty for his crimes, and the only judgement he now has to face needs no court of law to administer.'

Fortunately, Chief Inspector Crowthorne proved to be a most competent officer, and Hester's desire to avoid sensational publicity was achieved as far as it could be. There was every hope that Lucy Dillot – now free of Acland's stupefying drugs and mesmeric influence – would soon be able to return to her position at Mrs Veazey's guest house, and to the joy of his mother, William was also making excellent progress back to health. Hester and I were able to enjoy the rest of our holiday in Whitby in blessed peace and quiet, and it was not until the day before our planned return to London that a final footnote was added to the case, when Bram Stoker called upon us in the afternoon.

'Miss Lynton, Miss Jessop,' he cried. 'I will not interrupt your packing – I call only to wish you a safe journey, and to insist that you visit the Lyceum Theatre before too long. Mr Irving will be delighted to meet you.'

I smiled. 'We shall be happy to do so. And do you and Mrs Stoker plan to stay for much longer?'

'We will be leaving for London next week. Our holiday has been rather more stimulating than we anticipated,' – here we all smiled – 'but I believe that it may prove useful in an unexpected way. For some time I have been planning to write a novel – something sensational, with a Gothic flavour – and Whitby will make an excellent location for part of it. The rest I shall set somewhere in Eastern Europe, I think. I have a friend in London who knows the Carpathian Mountains very well. I am sure that Professor Van Helsing will be able to help me.'

8. The Case of the Russian Icon

When searching through the extensive collection of notes that Hester provided for me, I was often struck by the wide variety of people who had approached us during her career as a consulting detective. Indeed, on encountering one of her clients for the first time, they were as likely to be a vagrant as a viscount. However, the woman who sought our help in the case of the Russian icon fell into neither of those extremes, but occupied that middle ground of solid, respectable humanity who form the backbone of our British character and nation.

It was just after breakfast on a fine but rainswept April morning that I first caught sight of her. Mrs Parsons had just cleared away the breakfast things, and I had walked to the window to idly gaze down upon the pedestrians making their way along Newsome Street. One in particular caught my attention.

'Why, Hester, come and see!' I called to my friend. 'I believe that someone has come to call upon us. There – the woman in the black overcoat.'

Hester looked over my shoulder as I pointed. The woman in question had just turned the corner on the north end of the street, about fifty yards away. She was splashing unconcernedly through the puddles gathering on the pavement, holding a large umbrella over her head with one hand, and peering at a small piece of paper in the other, in between glances at the doorways that she passed.

'I see that your powers of deduction are in good order this morning,' Hester said with a smile. 'But could she not be searching for any householder along the street?'

I shook my head. 'The other houses nearby are all private establishments – and at nine o'clock in the morning she will hardly be making a social call at an address she has not visited before. But what do you make of her, Hester? Is she an Austrian princess in disguise, come to consult us about her missing tiara?'

'You are being facetious! However, there are one or two inferences that could be made.'

Before Hester could elaborate, a rough-looking idler – of a type not often encountered in our part of London – stepped directly in front of the woman we had been observing. He thrust out his hand impudently, evidently begging for a few coppers. She did not fall back, but instead furled her umbrella, waved it threateningly, and mouthed some angry words at him which, perhaps fortunately for my readers, we were not able to interpret. With the other hand still clutching her note she pointed down the road, and her disreputable interlocutor turned on his heel and slouched sullenly away in the direction indicated.

'Most instructive,' Hester said. 'Now, I would hazard a guess that our client – if that is what she turns out to be – is a widow, and the proprietor of a successful business that brings her into frequent contact with the lower orders; very likely a public house no more than a mile or two away.'

'But why a widow? And why a nearby public house, come to that? I asked.

'As to the first – she is a fine-looking woman in her fifties, and there is enough evidence to see that as a young girl she must have been strikingly attractive. It would be somewhat unusual for her not to be married – and if her husband was alive, he would probably have wished to accompany her this morning. As to the second – her dismissal of that ruffian showed the confidence of the experienced publican or landlady in repelling undesirables. Of course, if her business – whatever it turns out to be – was not close by, she would have taken a cab on such a wet morning. However, I hear the sound of the bell below. We can put aside further speculation, as I suspect that our curiosity will soon be satisfied.'

Shortly afterwards, the same woman was shown into our rooms. Mrs Parsons had taken her coat and umbrella, and was sent away with orders to bring coffee and muffins.

Our visitor was soon put at her ease by Hester's usual kindness and consideration. Her name, she told us, was Mrs Eliza Ward, and having heard something of Hester's reputation, she wished to consult us concerning a recent difficulty she had experienced.

'Of course, Miss Lynton, you've got a business to run the same as me, so I'll be happy to pay your fee, if you can help me,' she said with refreshing directness. 'I have only myself to rely on, since my late husband died last year, and so you won't mind my asking you about your charges. I read about you in in the papers last year, helping Lord Brinksfield find his collie dog.'

Hester leaned forward reassuringly. 'I only charge what my clients are well able to pay,' she said. 'I suggested we discuss my fee after we see whether Ivy and I are able to assist you. Do tell me exactly what it is that you require.'

'Well, it's like this. My late husband, Jack, was in the merchant navy before we married and we bought a public house with our savings when he retired – the Royal Oak, just half a mile or so from here on the Marylebone Road. You may have seen it?'

'Indeed we have,' I said. 'Do you remember, Hester, we visited it with Mr ... that is to say, a client, last winter. A very pleasant and welcoming establishment. There was a splendid Georgian oak settle by the fireside.'

Mrs Ward smiled with pleasure. 'That's the place all right. I didn't serve you myself, or I would have remembered. Anyway, my husband was a collector of sorts, and we've a back room half full of his curios. Ships in bottles, African spears, old paintings, that kind of thing. Now that he's passed away I've been having a bit of a clear-out and selling it off – not for the money, for I've a good business, but to get some more space. Last month, I took an old painting to Mortenson's – the antique and curios dealers in the Tottenham Court Road – to see what I could get for it, as I've sold them things before. The painting was of a flat-faced man with a beard, with lots of decorations all round it. Not something I'd want over my fireplace. Mr Mortenson himself had a look at it, and told me that as it was in poor condition, and not very well done at that, he could not offer me more than ten shillings, which I took for it. Then, ten days ago I was walking down Oxford Street with a friend, Mrs Harris, just window shopping. Wonderful things they have there. Lo and behold, there on display in the Mablethorpe Gallery was my old picture, looking no better that when I'd sold it to Mortenson. And the price was £250!'

'Did you speak to the gallery?' Hester asked.

Mrs Ward shook her head. 'No. I didn't even say anything to Maisy – Mrs Harris. I didn't go back to Mortenson, either. Why warn him I'd found out that he'd swindled me? Instead, I had a chat with a nice young solicitor's clerk who usually comes into my public house on Saturday evening with his friends for a glass or two. I had a confidential word with him – not naming names – to ask if buying something far too cheap was against the law. He told me that that it wasn't, and I gave him a glass of port for his advice.'

'I am afraid to say that the young man was perfectly correct,' Hester said. 'Mortenson has done nothing illegal, however disreputable his conduct. Now I must ask you; how do you expect us to help?'

Our client sighed. 'I really don't know, Miss. It seems to me that *something* ought to be done. Just think if I'd been a poor woman with nothing in the world – that £250 might have meant everything to me! The man's a disgrace, and should be taught a lesson. If my Jack was still alive, Mortenson would know all about it, I can tell you.'

Hester caught my eye. I nodded – we really should try to help.

'Well, well,' Hester said. 'We will see what we can do. Leave the case with us, and say nothing to anyone about the matter. Now, about the picture. Can you describe it for us?'

I will not weary my readers with the somewhat convoluted way in which Hester was able to discover, from her patient questioning of Mrs Ward, that the apparently nondescript picture was in fact a Russian Orthodox icon of Christ, painted on a wood panel, undoubtedly of great antiquity. Eventually, Hester found a steel engraving of a similar icon in one of the many reference books we keep in our rooms.

'Yes, like that, only not as sharply drawn, and mine was in colour,' our client said. 'And is mine really worth £250? Even in its dirty state?'

'I am afraid so,' Hester said. 'I think we can excuse it some grime, as it appears that for ten shillings you sold Mr Mortenson a picture that was painted around 500 years ago. Now, Mrs Ward, I would like you to return home and to try to put this whole business out of your head, and to mention it to no one. Rest assure that I shall contact you before the month is out, with news of any progress we have made in the matter.'

Hester remained indoors for most of the rest of the day, idly turning the pages of the newspapers, intermittently pacing round our room and gazing out of the window, deep in thought. I knew her well enough to understand that she was searching for a way in which to address Mrs Ward's grievance, and I was careful not to interrupt her thoughts with unnecessary chatter. Then, after the tea things had been taken away, Hester placed a Turkish cigarette in her ebony holder, and the room was soon so full of fragrant smoke that I excused myself on a spurious errand, and left the house for a half-hour walk.

On my return, I found Hester preparing to leave.

'I am about to pay a visit to the Earl of Lochaire,' she announced. I immediately recognised the name – we had been able to render him a great service a few years ago, regarding a delicate family matter.

'Is it a social call?'

'Hardly! I do not presume to move in such rarefied circles. No, the earl has something I wish to borrow for a few weeks, that is all. I will explain everything when I return.'

Less than an hour later my friend returned, a look of quiet satisfaction on her features. She was carrying a flat brown paper parcel under her arm, about two feet long by eighteen inches wide. She placed this on the table, and unwrapped it to reveal an exquisite oil painting of obvious antiquity, protected by a glazed frame. The picture showed a large public square full of people in old-fashioned costume.

'Canaletto did not always sign his paintings, but he has done so in this instance,' Hester said, pointing to the signature. 'It depicts the Piazza San Marco in Venice, painted in the 1720s. The earl has been kind enough to lend it to me for a few weeks. I hope you will be able to accompany me tomorrow evening, when I shall show it to someone who will be sure to appreciate its beauty. The hour is rather late to call upon him today.'

'And who might that be?' I asked.

'Mr Amos Clegg, the conservator at the Ronsard Gallery.'

I nodded. I was unclear to me what Hester wanted from Clegg, a man she had once taken pity on after his attempted theft of a valuable painting. However, rather than give her the satisfaction of keeping a secret, I said nothing, waiting for the next day to provide the answer.

The following evening, Amos Clegg admitted us to his house with the alacrity that might have been expected, given that Hester had once rescued him and his wife from a certain prison sentence. Hester carried the Canaletto under her arm, wrapped in oil cloth.

'It must be three years since we last met, Miss Lynton,' Clegg said. 'And Miss Jessop too – I hope you are both well. Tell, me, what can I do for the two of you? Just name it, and it will be done.'

Hester looked round the walls of Clegg's sitting room, decorated with many cleverly executed paintings, just as I remembered it.

'I recall seeing some oils in the style of the eighteenth-century Venetian school the last time I was here,' said Hester. 'Have you disposed of them?'

'Indeed I have, miss – all signed by me, as authentic copies! You could buy one for two guineas at Rollinson's.'

'That was very honest of you – and wise, given your promise to me. However, I have a task for you. Would you be able to make an exact copy of this painting – enough to satisfy an informed connoisseur – in, say, two weeks?'

Clegg frowned. He opened a nearby drawer and took out a large magnifying lens, then scrutinised the picture for several minutes.

'If I'm not mistaken, this is a genuine Canaletto. Yes, I could make you a fair copy in a fortnight. I've a few days of holiday owing to me, and it's quiet at the gallery at present. But I can't promise that the copy could withstand scrutiny by a real expert. I'll have to use a modern canvas – unless you can find me an early eighteenth-century work to paint over.'

'That will not be necessary; I am sure your best efforts will suffice. I will leave the painting with you. Please look after it carefully; I would not wish to have to compensate the Earl of Lochaire for its loss.'

'Very well, miss. And I'll take no payment for the copy. I haven't forgotten the great debt I owe you.'

During our short walk back to 12 Newsome Street, I hazarded a guess at Hester's plan.

'So, you plan to sell Mortenson the fake copy of the Canaletto, and turn the proceeds over to Mrs Ward?' I said. 'Surely you would put us at risk of arrest for criminal fraud?'

'That is certainly not my intention. Mortenson would be sure to ask one of his experts to access the painting, and despite Clegg's skill, I doubt it would pass muster. No, I intend to sell him the *genuine* Canaletto! I will hold out for at least £300.'

I stopped in my tracks and turned towards my friend. 'Forgive me for being obtuse, my dear Hester, but is there not a flaw in your plan? The Earl of Lochaire may not take kindly to you disposing of his property.'

Hester chuckled. 'I did not say that I would *give* Mortenson the painting – only that I would *sell* it to him. We must contrive to bait the hook with the original, and ensure that the fish takes the fake.'

Light began to dawn upon me. 'Yes, I see. But how will you manage that?'

'All in good time, Ivy. It occurs to me that we have not yet dined. I suggest we give Mrs Parsons the evening off, and go out for supper. Perhaps that charming new restaurant in Goodge Street? I understand that the chef learned his trade from Escoffier, so we should not be disappointed.'

Hester and I had ample time to discuss the next steps in the case whilst we were waiting for Amos Clegg to complete his copy of the Canaletto. A day or two before we had arranged to collect the copy, Hester announced that she intended to pay a visit to Mortenson's. I did not give her the satisfaction of asking for an explanation, but instead awaited her return.

Hester entered our rooms with a cheerful smile.

'Excellent!' she said, rubbing her hands. 'I have spoken to Mr Mortenson, and explained that we have a Canaletto to sell – if the right price is forthcoming. We are to take it in at two o'clock this coming Wednesday. Mortenson will arrange for one of his associates, Monsieur Louis Moreau, to examine and authenticate it. And Mortenson inadvertently supplied me with a piece of very valuable information. Monsieur Moreau spends only the first half of each week in London. From Thursday to Sunday, he stays at his house in Kent.'

Quite why this fact was of such importance escaped me, but I refrained from comment.

'Are we to operate under an alias?' I asked.

'Not at all! We can be open and honest – at least about our identities and profession. I have an idea regarding the story we should tell the dealer, but let us not decide upon that until the copy – and the original – are safely in our possession.'

A sudden and rather alarming thought then struck me.

'You will think me foolish, Hester, but has it occurred to you that Amos Clegg might have had time to make *two* copies of the original? How can we sure that he has not succumbed to temptation, and retained the original for disposal at some later date?'

Hester smiled. 'That is not foolish at all. The same possibility occurred to me. However, I have taken suitable precautions. No copy of an oil painting can ever be an exact replica. Put the copy and the original side by side, and many small differences will be apparent. I therefore spent some time noting down some trivial features of the original – for example, the exact distance between the left ear of the small brown dog in the right-hand corner of St Mark's Square and the shopping basket of a woman some distance away. I will know if Clegg tries to play any such trick upon us – although I think that for him to relapse into dishonesty would be most unlikely.'

'There is one further matter,' I said. 'Will Mortenson not think it strange that we have not gone directly to a more prestigious establishment to sell the painting – such as the Mablethorpe Gallery, where Mrs Ward's icon is now for sale?'

'That is simple answered. The Mablethorpe Gallery, and other such emporia, will not deal directly with a member of the public. They do not wish to have the trouble of distinguishing between honest and criminal sellers, or worrying about the provenance of an artefact. They deal with trusted dealers only, such as Mortenson. I wonder if they are aware of that gentleman's true character? In his twenties he had a reputation as one of the most skilful burglars in London. He was arrested several times but never successfully prosecuted. Eventually, he decided that before his luck ran out he would move into a legitimate and rather more respectable profession – that of a dealer in antiques and curios.'

At the appointed time we stepped down from our cab at Mortenson's in Tottenham Court Road. Hester was carrying a stout wooden picture box, which she had purchased the day before, and the original Canaletto was inside it. She had extracted that work from its frame the day before – it was clear from the new pins in the backboard that Amos Clegg had also taken it from its frame in order to copy it more easily and then replaced it in a fashion that would allow its easy removal if required.

The window of the long-established antique and curios dealers was narrow and stained with London grime, but the strong iron bars that protected it gave notice of the value of the articles kept within. A young clerk was expecting our arrival. He showed us up a winding stairway into a second-floor office, which was larger and brighter than the rooms below had suggested. Two gentlemen rose to greet us. The younger, a man in his forties, was the proprietor, whose clean-shaven face, lounge suit and patterned waistcoat were all in the best of taste. A half-smoked Cuban cigar rested in a glass dish in front of him; it had evidently been recently extinguished, as its sweet odour filled the room. The other, white-haired and wearing a black morning coat, appeared to be at least seventy, and was introduced to us as Monsieur Louis Moreau.

After an exchange of introductions, Hester placed her box on a large table which stood at one side of the office, and opened the lid.

'I have transported it in its frame for extra protection,' Hester said. 'However, I have loosened the backboard and ensured that the canvas can easily be removed for examination.'

'For that, I thank you,' Monsieur Moreau replied. 'Now, if I may …'

Without further ado, the Frenchman carefully removed the canvas from its frame, as Hester had done earlier. For some moments he viewed it from all angles, then lifted the canvas and placed it on a wooden board. This he carried to the front window, and studied the painting further with the help of a large magnifying lens. Finally, he carried the board back to the table, and pulled a needle from the lapel of his jacket.

'If madam will allow?' he asked. The question was clearly rhetorical, for at the same time he lifted the edge of the canvas, and inserted the needle a fraction of an inch into the side, without disturbing the painted upper surface. After replacing the needle in his coat, he addressed us with a smile.

'It gives me pleasure to say that this Canaletto, it is entirely genuine. *Magnifique*! A typical Venetian scene. I believe it is one of a series of five, painted in the 1720s. As to its value – Mr Mortenson knows the English art market better than I do. And now, with your forgiveness, I must depart for the British Museum. Today I am much in demand, you see!'

We thanked and said our goodbyes to the genial Frenchman. Then Mortenson, Hester and I sat down to business.

'I must ask you one question directly,' the dealer said. 'I am, of course, well aware of your reputation as a consulting detective, Miss Lynton – and of the valuable part played by your colleague, Miss Jessop. But how did such a valuable item come into your possession?'

Hester chuckled. 'A very fair question! But before I answer, can I be assured of your discretion?'

'I would not last long as a dealer unless my confidence could be relied upon, I assure you.'

'Very well. As a consulting detective, much of my time is spent dealing with criminal cases. However, quite frequently I am asked to carry out delicate private transactions which cannot be entrusted to a friend or relative. In this case, a client has asked me to sell this painting on their behalf – for a small commission, of course.'

Mortenson nodded. 'Yes, I understand. Some noble personage … financial difficulties … but I will not speculate. Now, as to the price …'

Hester interrupted. '£300 is the figure I am looking for, with one stipulation. I require payment in cash – more specifically, in gold sovereigns. Much as I would regret having to spend time and trouble looking for another dealer, that is my fixed price, and it will allow you to make a respectable profit. Of course, I realise that you will not have such a large sum at your premises. I therefore propose that if the price is acceptable to you, that we meet at your bank this Friday morning. I will take the painting away with me, and give it to you in the banking hall in return for your payment.

The dealer tutted. 'Dear me! You client must be in sorry circumstances if they cannot even present a cheque to their bank. I have to say that if you were unknown to me the transaction would look decidedly suspicious. However, you are a respectable woman, and I have Monsieur Moreau's word for the authenticity of the painting. Let me see … yes, your price is a fair one. Come to Brotherton's Bank in Chancery Lane this Friday, at eleven in the morning. I will ask the manger to set aside a private room for our use.'

On Friday at the appointed hour, Hester and I arrived at the bank. Hester clutched the picture box under her arm, whilst I carried a stout leather valise. This time we had secured the backboard more permanently, and under the glass rested Amos Clegg's copy of the Canaletto, rather than the original. It was a tribute to Clegg's talents that we had to make doubly sure that the correct version had been framed, since the two were virtually indistinguishable.

We were expected, and a deferential clerk showed us into a private inner room, where Mortenson sat alone waiting for us. I must confess to a feeling of great relief. If the dealer had decided to persuade Monsieur Moreau to remain in London and to be present at the exchange, then a most embarrassing situation could have arisen. However, Hester's air of honest professionalism seemed to have allayed any suspicions that he might have had.

The matter was swiftly concluded. Mortenson – as we had anticipated – had drawn up a simple deed of exchange, which Hester signed to confirm that she gave up all rights to the picture in return for the £300. I confess, I had never before seen such a heap of gold as there was upon the table. Mortenson left before us with the picture, leaving Hester and I to scoop the coins into my valise. Fortunately, we were able to secure a cab immediately outside the bank, and had only to carry our treasure a few steps over the threshold of 12 Newsome Street and up the stairs to our rooms.

After Mrs Parsons had brought up a tray of refreshments, I asked Hester the question that had been troubling me for some time.

'I am no expert in English law, Hester, but surely we have just committed a serious crime? We have brazenly sold a forgery to an outwardly respectable art dealer. I dare say that morally we have taken revenge for his shabby treatment of Mrs Ward, but surely that is no defence in law?'

Hester poured herself a second cup of coffee and helped herself to a third macaroon.

'Mrs Parsons' baking is excellent – let us hope she is not stolen from us by some prestigious hotel. But to answer your question: you are quite correct, we have acted unlawfully, and the matter cannot be allowed to rest there. That is why, after luncheon, I suggest we pay a return visit to Mortenson's premises. I am hopeful that, after speaking to that gentleman, we will be able to resolve the matter once and for all.'

The dealer was somewhat taken aback to see us again so soon, but invited us up to his office with good grace. Two clerks were working at a desk, but at Hester's request Mortenson asked them to leave. Hester placed the large valise – which she had brought with her – upon the floor next to her.

'Now tell me, ladies, how I can help you,' Mortenson said with a somewhat artificial smile. 'I hope you have not changed your mind about the sale. It is rather too late for that, now!'

'Not at all,' Hester said with a grin. 'It is just that there is a matter connected with the sale of which you should be aware. A month or so ago a respectable landlady of mature years – Mrs Ward, you may remember her – brought a valuable Russian icon to you for valuation. You may recall that you gave her ten shillings for it. Now, you and I know that £150 would have been a fair price. You sold it to the Mablethorpe Gallery, and I expect you got £200 for it – £50 would have been a good profit for you. Instead, you gave in to greed and selfishness, and in effect stole £149 and ten shillings from her.'

This time Mortenson's smile was genuine, although no more pleasant to observe.

'Ah ha!' he cried. 'In your profession, you should be more properly informed as to the law of the land. I have done nothing at all illegal. Ask any lawyer in London.'

'Correct. However, Mrs Ward has not been the only victim of malpractice on these premises. Earlier today you paid me £300 in gold for a painting of St Mark's Square by Canaletto, executed in the 1720s. Alas, the canvas you received from me did indeed depict the Piazza San Marco, but it was painted a few weeks ago in London – which rather rules out Canaletto as the artist.'

The dealer turned red with anger. 'Impossible! Why, Monsieur Moreau is a renowned expert ...'

Mortenson's voice tailed off in mid-sentence as a dreadful possibility occurred to him. Hester concluded his thought.

'Yes, just so. Moreau valued one painting, and you bought another.'

The dealer seemed to recover his spirits. 'Wait. You have not been so very clever after all. Moreau will vouch for my story. You can prove no criminal act against *me*, but I can bring down the full force of the law against *you* – and your fellow conspirator. You and Miss Jessop may well end up sharing a prison cell.'

'True enough,' Hester said. 'But here is another proposal for you which happily avoids our incarceration. If you return the forged Canaletto to me, I will refund your £300. However, there is the matter of the £150 you still owe Mrs Ward – let us not quibble about the odd ten shillings. My refund of your £300 will depend upon you refunding Mrs Ward her money.'

Mortenson stood up and thumped the table with his fist.

'And here is *my* proposal! I will send for a constable, and put you both in charge for fraud!'

'Before you do so, sir, consider this. There will be a court case – and the presence of Miss Jessop and I in the dock will ensure the maximum publicity. Your shabby, dishonest treatment of Mrs Ward, albeit perfectly legal, will make you a personal and professional pariah – you will be disgraced locally, nationally and internationally. Your business will be ruined, and there will be a demand for rotten fruit whenever there is a rumour that you are to appear in a public place. As for Miss Jessop and me, our reputations as protectors of the weak will only be enhanced. With luck, we will be discharged with a fine and a stern warning.'

Mortenson took a few paces across the room, evidently struggling with two conflicting emotions. Eventually he accepted the inevitable, and turned to Hester with an effort at politeness.

'Very well, Miss Lynton, I accept your terms. At least I will have emerged from the whole fiasco without making a loss. However, I must insist that you say nothing of the matter to anyone. I do not wish to become a laughing stock. I will send one of my clerks to fetch the forgery, whilst you give me the £300 in gold – I assume it is in the valise at your feet.'

'There is little point in my giving you £300, when you owe Mrs Ward £150,' Hester said. Instead, I will give you £150 and deliver our client's cash to her in person.'

Again, Mortenson made a creditable effort to mask his feelings, although it was clear to me that Hester had made an enemy for life.

'So be it,' the dealer said. 'Kindly count out my 150 gold sovereigns upon the desk, while I send for the painting. And I sincerely hope that it will not be necessary for our paths to cross again.'

Shortly afterwards we left Mortenson's premises, Hester's valise considerably lightened and the forged Canaletto once more in our possession. After we had hailed a hansom Hester spoke to me.

'My dear Ivy, I wonder if you will allow me a foolish gesture? I would dearly like to tell Mrs Ward about our successful conclusion of the case, and to show her the little pile of gold which she has gained. I have no doubt she will want the convenience of a cheque and I will offer to make one out to her – but the sight of her windfall will surely please her.'

'Of course!' I replied. 'Tell me, did you have that in mind when you originally asked to be paid in gold?'

'No. However, I did anticipate a rapid refund of some of Mortenson's purchase price. An exchange of cheques would have complicated matters greatly.'

It was not long before we arrived at the Royal Oak, which I remembered well from my visit the previous year. There were only a few customers at that hour of the afternoon, and we were fortunate to find Mrs Ward herself behind the bar. When she caught sight of us she speedily summoned a cheerful young woman to take her place, and led us into her private sitting room.

I will not impose upon my readers a detailed account of our explanation of our successful conclusion of the case, except to say that Mrs Ward's delight was very evident as she surveyed the small pile of sovereigns on her side table.

'I have no doubt you would prefer a cheque,' Hester said. 'I am happy to write you one, and to take away the coins, if you so wish.'

Mrs Ward smiled. 'Thank you, but if it is all the same to you, I would prefer to have the gold. Of course I have no intention of keeping such a large sum permanently on the premises. As it happens, I am travelling to Bristol tomorrow, to see my sister. It is my intention to give her the bulk of the money, and her circumstances are such that cash would be more convenient than a cheque. I will keep it safe here overnight, I assure you. But first, tell me your fee, so that I can pay the debt I owe you.'

'Of course I will leave the gold with you, if that is what you wish,' Hester said. 'But please guard it carefully on your journey. As for our fee, three pounds will be ample. I wish all our cases could turn out so well – do you not agree, Ivy?'

I have no doubt that Hester has since regretted tempting fate with those complacent words. Despite the apparent success of our mission, it was swiftly followed by an event as unexpected as it was unwelcome.

Early the following morning, my head a little fuddled by the effects of the vintage champagne with which we had celebrated our success the night before, I was awoken by the sound of a knock on my bedroom door. It was Hester, a dressing gown thrown over her nightdress.

'Ivy, I am sorry to wake you at such an early hour – it is not yet seven o'clock – but we have had a visitor who has brought some disturbing news. A young woman, Rosie Wilkins – she is employed at Mrs Ward's public house, and lives on the premises. I have sent Rosie back there to look after her mistress. We must dress quickly, and go to the Royal Oak ourselves. I will explain everything as we walk there. It will only take us fifteen minutes, and we might wait longer than that for a cab.'

We were soon hurrying down Newsome Street towards the Marylebone Road.

'Rosie went to call Mrs Ward at six this morning, as was her habit,' Hester said. 'She found the room in disarray, and her mistress lying on the floor, pale faced and with a cut upon her forehead. Rosie at first feared the worst, but when she entered, Mrs Ward sat up and spoke to her. It seems that an intruder broke into her room the night before and struck her to the ground. Naturally, Rosie wished to inform the police immediately – and to summon a doctor – but Mrs Ward was adamant that her servant should do neither. Instead, she asked Rosie to fetch us to her.'

When we were shown up to Mrs Ward's room we found her sitting up in bed sipping a cup of tea, a bandage round her forehead but otherwise seemingly unaffected by her unpleasant experience. We immediately suggested that she should call the police.

'And if I were a schoolmistress or dressmaker that is exactly what I *would* do,' Mrs Ward explained. 'However, summoning the police to a public house can have unfortunate consequences for a landlady. Even a hint of scandal could drive away my best customers. No, I would prefer that you two ladies look into the matter for me – that is, if you are willing.'

'Of course, Mrs Ward,' Hester said. 'However, you must grant me permission to hand the perpetrator over to the authorities for punishment if we succeed in identifying your assailant.'

Our client agreed to Hester's request, and was able to give us a very detailed account of her frightening experience of the previous evening. For the convenience of my readers I will summarise her story as follows. At midnight or shortly afterwards, our client, a light sleeper, was disturbed by a noise in her bedroom. She sat up to light her candle, but before she could do so the faint illumination from the gaslight outside revealed a dim figure in a black coat standing over her. She attempted to call out, but before she could do so he had sprung forwards and grabbed her throat. Mrs Ward managed to escape his grip, and a violent struggle ensued – which ended in the landlady being flung to the floor, cutting her head against the corner of her washstand in the process. She lost consciousness, and by the time she recovered her mysterious assailant had disappeared – along with the gold sovereigns, which she had hidden under her mattress. Before she could raise the alarm she fainted again, and did not wake until Rosie roused her in the morning.

When Mrs Ward had finished her story, Hester spoke to her earnestly.

'Tell me, is there anything else you can remember about your assailant? Could you judge how old he was, for example?'

'I'm sorry, Miss Lynton – I didn't see his face. There was one thing a bit strange, though ... he brought a smell with him into the room. At least, it wasn't there before, and it's gone now. Not a bad smell – a sort of sweetish scent, like that thing they burn in Catholic churches.'

'You mean incense?' I said.

'That's it, Miss Jessop. Or something like, anyway. I must say I feel a fool ... leaving all that money in my room, when Miss Lynton offered me a cheque.'

'On the contrary, any foolishness lies at my door,' Hester said. 'Rest assured we will deal with this matter, and do our best to restore the money to you. I have one final question for you. Your struggle with the burglar must have created a lot of noise. Why was no one in the household alerted?'

'Rosie Wilkins is the only one who lives on the premises,' the landlady said. 'Rosie is twenty-two years old, and I have given her a latchkey. She's sensible girl, and I don't hold with locking servants up like animals in a zoo. When she found me today, she told me that she had returned to the Royal Oak at half past one in the morning, after visiting some friends in Spitalfields. By that time, of course, all was quiet.'

Hester nodded. 'I see. Now, you have persuaded me not to send for the police, but I absolutely insist on sending for a doctor to make sure that no serious harm has been done to you. If you will give us the name of your medical man, Ivy and I will search him out on the way back to Newsome Street. Do you have someone who can help Rosie in the bar in your absence? You should certainly not be on your feet for a few days.'

'Yes, Maisy Harris used to work here at one time, which is how we became friends. I am sure she will help me.'

'Very well. We will leave you to your rest, and I will call back in a day or two, to let you know what progress I am making.'

During the short walk from the Royal Oak back to Newsome Street, Hester said very little. I noticed that her face was pale and determined, and it was clear that she was as angry as I have ever known her. When we reached our rooms, she spoke to me very solemnly.

'My dear Ivy, I have an errand to run and will be away for some time. I am afraid I have a task to perform which can best be accomplished alone. If you will wait here for me, I should not be more than an hour or two.'

Her resolution was such that I was not inclined to question her further. However, I had some inkling of her destination and purpose, which was not contradicted when I saw her take her service revolver from her desk drawer and place it in the bag she took with her on her errand.

As it transpired, Hester returned within the hour. The transformation in her temper was remarkable. She was all smiles, and it was clear that whatever had occurred had been most congenial to her.

'You will be delighted to hear that it is likely that we will soon be able to reunite poor Mrs Ward with her money!' Hester cried. 'That will make up in part for our inexcusable stupidity in leaving her unprotected last night.'

'Good gracious! What on earth has happened?'

'Let me explain. As you will probably have guessed, when I left you a little earlier today it was my intention to force Mortenson to return the money he took so violently from poor Mrs Ward. I suppose you realise that it was he who attacked our client?'

I frowned. 'Of course I thought it was a possibility. But how can you be so sure?'

'Do you remember our visit to his premises? His evident fondness for Cuban cigars gave his office a distinctive fragrance, which tends to adhere to the smoker's person. That was the incense-like smell detected by Mrs Ward. It is clear that Mortenson broke into our client's rooms, hoping that the money might have been returned to her. However, that is not evidence strong enough to convict him in court. All Mortenson needed to do was to say that he had spent the night at home alone in bed – he is a bachelor – and no one could have proved otherwise. But when I challenged Mortenson and told him I would go to the police if he did not hand over the £150, he made a fatal mistake, probably because he was a little disconcerted by the revolver I was pointing at him. He told me that he had nothing to fear from a police investigation, as he had a witness who could testify that he had been at home between the hours of eight o'clock the previous evening and nine o'clock this morning. That witness, he was happy to tell me, was a Miss Betsy Collins, a dancer at the Gaiety Theatre, Aldwych.'

'But how does that help us?' I asked.

Hester rubbed her hands gleefully. 'Because if she *was* with him between those hours, and if he did leave the house, then we have only to persuade her to tell the truth, and Mortenson is in difficulties. Who knows what else she might tell us? He has provided us with a solution to the case, if we play our cards carefully, and enjoy that degree of luck which is always necessary in such a delicate matter.'

An hour later we were at Betsy's lodgings, having obtained the address from the theatre manger en route. Luck was certainly with us thus far, for the young woman was at home, and reluctantly received us.

Once Betsy had told us that she had been with Mortenson all night, Hester's handling of the situation was masterful. Mortenson's friend was a pretty and pleasant enough young woman, but very young – she could not have been more than twenty – and clearly of only moderate intellect.

'So you see, Betsy,' Hester concluded, 'that by helping us you are also helping yourself escape from a very dangerous situation. Suppose you tell the police that Herbert – Mr Mortenson – was with you at his house for the whole night, as he told you to? You will then have committed a serious offence – lying to the police – and will certainly go to jail when the truth is discovered. However, if instead you tell us when he left the house, and repeat that in a statement for the police, then you will be in no trouble at all.'

Betsy looked frightened. 'But what about Herbert?' she said. 'What will he do to me, when he finds out I've blabbed on him?'

Hester placed her hand on the young woman's arm. 'He will do very little to anyone except his fellow convicts for the next ten years, which is the sentence he will likely receive for robbery with violence. Then, when he does come out of prison, a word from me will ensure that he never goes near you. What do you say?'

'I suppose you're right,' Betsy said. 'To be honest, I'll be glad to see the back of him. Very well – he *did* leave me at half past eleven, and returned around two in the morning. He tried to creep out without waking me, but I'm a light sleeper, and when he'd gone I looked at the clock on the mantlepiece. Very cheerful he was when he got back – drank a deal of gin before he came back to bed. I remember he said something rather strange before he turned over and went to sleep – something about having got the better of someone – an interfering cow, he called her – a lady detective. And he said that I'd enjoy helping him to spend a windfall – £150 in gold.'

'Excellent!' Hester clapped her hands. 'Now, I have a cousin who is an inspector in the Metropolitan force. We can take you to him right away, and after you have written down everything you have just told me, you will be free to go, without a care in the world – at least, as regards Mr Herbert Mortenson.'

We were lucky enough to find Inspector Albert Brasher at Scotland Yard, where Betsy provided a written statement. Hester's cousin was delighted at being presented with a ready-made case to add to his list of successes, particularly as Hester insisted on taking no credit for the matter. As a precaution, Hester, Betsy and I remained at Scotland Yard until a police wagon had been sent to arrest Mortenson. As soon as the arrest was confirmed we returned to Newsome Street by way of Betsy Collins' lodgings, where we left her.

When we had returned to our rooms, Hester sent down for tea. 'I have every expectation that the £150 will be returned to Mrs Ward as soon as the process required by justice has taken its course,' she said.

'But how can you be so sure? Mortenson could have hidden the money anywhere – buried it in Hyde Park, come to that – why should he reveal its whereabouts?'

'It is quite simple. Mortenson knows only too well that a lengthy prison sentence awaits him. He will hope – vainly, no doubt – to mitigate his punishment by admitting everything that he has done, including the whereabouts of the money. After we have had our tea and scones, I propose that we walk to the Royal Oak and give Mrs Ward the good news. And given the success with which this case has been concluded, I suggest we treat ourselves to a glass of that good lady's porter, which I recollect as being particularly fine.'

9. The Case of the Naked Clergyman

The autumn of 1887 was a particularly busy time for us, since we were involved in an investigation that required not only a constant attention to detail, but also – in view of the public position and importance of the personages involved – a degree of tact and sensitivity, which made our work all the more difficult. Thus, when Hester received a letter from a Miss Harriet Dowson of Ledbury Grange, Horsham, I expected her to politely decline that lady's plea for assistance. I was, however, mistaken.

'Let us at least hear what Miss Dowson has to say,' Hester said. 'There is something about her letter which suggests a case of more than usual interest. Who knows; it may be that we can help her without great expenditure of time and effort.'

Thus three days later our client arrived for the appointment we had offered her. The lady that our housekeeper showed into our sitting room appeared to be in her early forties, and had the characteristic robustness of the healthy country woman, combined with that forthrightness of manner often associated with an unmarried female of the middle classes who has had to take responsibility for her own path through life.

Once we had introduced ourselves, and been served with the refreshments brought in by Mrs Parsons, Hester turned to our visitor with a smile.

'Your letter was most circumspect, Miss Dowson,' Hester said. 'You mentioned that your concerns related to your father, the Reverend Alfred Dowson. I took the liberty of consulting *Crockford's*, and I see that he retired from his parish in Sussex eight years ago at the age of sixty, and now lives at Ledbury Grange. However, as that is the sum of my little store of information, I would be most grateful if you could tell me exactly which you have come to seek our help. I would ask you to be as exact and detailed as possible. And let me reassure you that Miss Jessop and I will hear your account in the strictest of confidence.'

Thus encouraged, Miss Dowson gave us a very detailed summary of the circumstances that had led up to her visit that morning; she periodically consulted a leather-bound pocketbook, and gave every impression that her veracity could be counted on. Rather than attempting a lengthy verbatim transcription of her account, I shall instead attempt to encapsulate the pertinent points for my readers.

Our client explained that she and her father were the only residents of Ledbury Grange other than the servants. Her father had been widowed for over twenty years. Since his retirement from his parish in 1879, he had been very happily occupied organizing and adding to his collection of rare topographical books on Sussex, and working in his garden and hothouse. Then, in early July of this year, Miss Dowson had begun to notice some subtle changes in her father's behaviour. To begin with these were of a minor nature, not obvious to one who did not know the reverend well. He seemed less energetic than previously, and would regularly sleep for an hour or two in the afternoon; he also became less interested in his hobbies. More recently, his conduct had become more disturbing. He had left the house in the early hours of the morning on several occasions, to wander about the grounds – he had been seen by the servants, and on one occasion by Miss Dowson when a maid had raised the alarm – but seemed to have no recollection of what had happened when challenged the next morning. The reverend had been persuaded to seek the advice of the family physician, Dr Harold Millington, but the doctor could find nothing physically wrong with his patient, and could only suggest that his behaviour might signal the early onset of senility.

Then a little under two weeks previously, early on Tuesday the twenty-first of September, an incident had occurred which led directly to Miss Dowson requesting our assistance. She had been roused by the housekeeper, Ethel Simpkins, just after two o'clock in the morning. Ethel had been woken up by sounds coming from the kitchen garden at the back of the house, and from her third-floor window she could see – plainly visible in the moonlight – the bizarre source of the disturbance. The Reverend Dowson was leaping and dancing amongst the vegetables, singing garbled snatches of song – and was doing so in a state of complete nakedness.

The butler was called from his bed, and with his assistance Miss Dowson and the housekeeper were able to lead the reverend back to his bedroom, help him into his nightshirt and settle him down for the rest of the night. As with his previous nocturnal adventures, he claimed to have no knowledge of it the following morning, and resisted all attempts to restrict his movements, such as the locking of his bedroom door from the outside at night. After this shocking development, Miss Dowson insisted on her father consulting Sir Richard Helmsley, the eminent neurologist, in Harley Street. He had been able to see the Reverend Dowson just three days after the episode in the kitchen garden. Sir Richard gave the clergyman a very thorough examination, and declared him to be – apparently – in excellent health. Sir Richard had made a point of stating that in his professional opinion there was absolutely no sign of senile decay, as all of Dowson's faculties were without impairment. Miss Dowson had therefore concluded that the mystery behind her father's extraordinary behaviour required investigation by a private detective, and hence she had decided to consult Hester regarding the case.

Both Hester and I refrained from interrupting our client during the course of her fluent exposition, and after she had finished we sat in silence for some moments. Hester was the first to speak.

'That is all very clear, Miss Dowson. Now, if you will bear with me, there are just a few questions I would like to ask you. The first is, I am afraid, rather intrusive. What are your father's drinking habits?'

Miss Dowson smiled. 'That is a very fair question, and one that is easy to answer. Every evening after dinner he retires to his study, where our butler, Moxon, takes him a single glass of port. The decanter remains on the sideboard in the dining room. On special occasions he may take a glass or two of wine – other than that, he does not indulge.'

'I see. Now, regarding the servants – if you could list them with length of service, Miss Jessop with note the details down for me.'

Our client reached into her handbag. 'I have already prepared such a list,' she said. 'You may keep it for your records.'

The document she gave us is reproduced below, in a somewhat abbreviated form: Miss Dowson was clearly a most efficient woman, and had also provided full details of when the previous cook and butler had given notice.

Butler: Henry Moxon, aged 50, began service at Ledbury Grange 6 months ago.

Cook: Señora Rosalia Caballero, 48, began service at Ledbury Grange 7 months ago.

Housekeeper: Ethel Simpkins, 56, in service at Ledbury Grange for over 20 years.

Two housemaids and a parlourmaid: in service at Ledbury Grange for 6, 8 and 12 years respectively.

Footman, coachman, groom and gardener: all four in service for over 10 years.

Gardener's boy, age 14.

Kitchen maid, age 16.

(NB A number of local women come in to clean on a daily basis.)

'That is most useful,' Hester said. 'And now I have a further question. Are you able to give me the names of the chief beneficiaries of your father's will? I imagine there is a substantial estate involved.'

Miss Dowson's expression showed the usual surprise of those unacquainted with Hester's powers of deduction.

'There is indeed; he inherited a large sum of money as a young man, from his uncle, Lord Brentford, and the estate is a very valuable one. But are you privy to my father's affairs?'

'Not at all. However, your father retired at the relatively early age, for a clergyman in good health, of sixty, suggesting a comfortable income independent of his stipend. In addition, his hobbies of collecting rare books and growing artificially-heated plants require considerable expenditure. His establishment of servants is also generous, when only two persons occupy the house.'

'Yes, I see. Regarding his will, the provision is very straightforward. He showed me a copy when it was drawn up some years ago. Each of the resident servants are to receive the equivalent of a year's wages, and £200 is to go to his old college, Brasenose. The rest – less the usual expenses – is to be divided equally between me and my sister, Mrs Julia Collins. It amounts to over £100,000 pounds, excluding the house and grounds.'

At these words I caught Hester's eye. She nodded imperceptibly – a signal which, after six years of working together, I was able to interpret as an indication that I should explore this new item of information.

'Tell us about your sister, Miss Dowson,' I said. 'You will appreciate that in a case such as this, all information is useful to us, even the seemingly irrelevant. Is she a frequent visitor to Ledbury Grange?'

A faint but unmistakable flush of embarrassment suffused our client's features.

'I am afraid Julia is no longer welcome at our house. Her husband, an insurance broker in the City, died unexpectedly just over a year ago; Julia was left a widow at the age of thirty-eight. Perhaps fortunately, they had no children. Then, just three months after her sudden bereavement, she re-married. That would have been in October of last year. Father was extremely upset at what was, to his eyes, a most unseemly rush into matrimony, one that broke all rules of decorum and mourning. I'm afraid my father is rather strict on such matters.'

'But he did not exclude your sister from his will?' I asked.

'By no means. In fact, my father made a point of telling Julia that she would still receive her inheritance – he felt a moral duty not to disinherit her just because of his personal disapproval of her actions. However, he made it very clear that he wished to have as little contact with her, and with her husband, as possible. In fact, since their remarriage neither Julia or her husband have met with my father, as far as I am aware. They have certainly not visited Ledbury Grange. Perhaps I should mention that since she left home and moved to London, Julia has in any case never felt any attraction to the countryside. I have never been introduced to Julia's new husband, although I would have no objection to meeting him.'

'What of her husband?' Hester asked. 'What is his profession?'

'He is a doctor based at the William Harvey School of Medicine in South Kensington,' Miss Dowson said. 'Dr Isaac Collins is some ten years older than my sister, and met her when he was treating her late husband.'

Hester nodded. 'You have been very helpful, Miss Dowson. Do I take it that you would like us to look into the case?'

'Yes indeed – if you think you can help me.'

'Alas, you have arrived at a time when I am heavily involved in an investigation that currently requires my continuous presence in London. Were it not for that, I would wish to travel back with you to Ledbury Grange. It is really a case which requires investigation *in situ*, rather than deduction at a distance.'

A sudden idea struck me. 'Why not let *me* go? My presence in London is not essential for our current enquiry. I could pay a visit to Miss Dowson on some pretext or other.'

Our client seemed greatly relieved at my suggestion.

'What a splendid idea!' she cried. 'I suggest an assumed surname. Perhaps Miss Ivy Green, the daughter of an older friend of mine – a governess between positions, who needs accommodation for a few weeks? I will feel so much happier to know that you are by my side. I will tell Simpkins to prepare a room for you. Come down as soon as you are able!'

I think it is fair to say that Miss Dowson's enthusiasm for my proposal was not matched by Hester, but my colleague accepted it as a *fait accompli*. After Miss Dowson had left us, we discussed my forthcoming visit to Sussex.

'I shall send Miss Dowson a telegram saying that I shall travel down on Wednesday morning,' I said. 'Is there anything in particular you would like me to look into?'

'There is one thing. If it is possible for you to discover who provided references for the two newest servants – the cook and the butler – that would be helpful. Other than that, I will just ask you to take the greatest care, and to make sure that you include your revolver amongst your luggage.'

I chuckled. 'I will conceal it carefully – if one of the maids finds it, it will cast serious doubt on my provenance as a governess! But surely you do not think that any real danger threatens?'

'I do not yet know what to think. Of course, there are several hypotheses that fit the very limited facts we have at present, but we are sadly lacking information. It would be best if you were circumspect in sharing any theories you might have with Miss Dowson, to avoid any premature action on her part. You must make sure that you write to me with your immediate observations – omit nothing, however trivial it may seem. I also suggest that you make some excuse to return to London for the day this coming Saturday, to have lunch with me. I will reserve a table at the East Room of the Criterion for one o'clock. Then you can give me your findings first hand. And a word of advice – you will need to be on first-name terms with Miss Dowson – Harriet – if you are to be convincing in your deception. Let us hope, as an accomplished governess, you are not required to entertain the household on the pianoforte after dinner …'

Thus, two days later I completed the final stage of my journey from Newsome Street to Ledbury Grange, having taken the train from Victoria Station to Horsham, and a hired carriage from there to my destination, where I arrived a little after five o'clock that afternoon. The house was a large mansion of quite recent construction – I discovered later that it had been built in the early 1860s. The red brick and stone dressed walls still had the unpatinated appearance of a recent building and there were several ornate towers and turrets typical of the Gothic style. As the carriage turned into the gravelled drive, which led up to the imposing portico, it was clear that my arrival had been observed; a gentleman dressed in black trousers and a swallow-tail coat came out to greet me, accompanied by a liveried footman. The former gave me a solemn bow as I was helped out of the carriage by the driver.

'I am Moxon, miss – the Reverend Dowson's butler. Higson will take your boxes up to your room, and one of the parlourmaids will meet you in the hall to show you your way. Miss Dowson has asked that you join her in the drawing room before dinner, which is served at seven o'clock.'

The butler opened the front door to usher me inside. He was an unassuming, slender man of average height, about fifty years of age; rather different from the tall, imposing figures usually chosen for such positions in a well-to-do household. The house – including my room – had every appearance of luxury; whilst nothing was ostentatiously gaudy, it was clear that expense was no object. I thought back to the conversation that Hester and I had with Miss Dowson regarding her father's will; it was apparent both Miss Dowson and her sister would be very wealthy women in the event of the reverend's death. However, if there were some sinister plot to do the Reverend Dowson harm, it seemed hard to see how either woman could be involved. It was surely inconceivable that Harriet Dowson would have asked Hester to investigate if she herself was involved in any wrong-doing; and according to Harriet, Julia Collins had not been to Ledbury Grange since her marriage.

When I joined Miss Dowson in the drawing room, she introduced me to her father. It seemed that only the three of us were to dine that evening, there being other guests. The Reverend Dowson was not at all how I had imagined him. His daughter's description of his aberrant behaviour had led me to expect an eccentric or feeble appearance; however, the reverend appeared to be in the best of health, and remarkably well-preserved for a man of sixty-eight. He wore a dark suit and clerical collar; this was of little surprise to me, as my late father had been a parson, and had adopted the same dress in his retirement, conscious that an ordained clergyman retains his status for life. It was fortunate that, after some polite enquires concerning my current situation (to which I had already prepared adequate answers), the Reverend Dowson showed no inclination to quiz me in detail, and when prompted by me was very willing to discourse on his twin hobbies of topographical books and hothouse horticulture. As he fell into that category of genial gentlemen who are more than happy for their own preoccupations to dominate the conversation, Harriet (as I must now call her) and I found it easy to sustain our little deception.

The dinner that was served to us by Moxon and the footman was a model of understated excellence. The cook was evidently first-rate, providing us with a delicious mulligatawny soup, veal cutlets, a boiled fowl and vol-au-vent of pears, and an iced pudding.

Our dinner was marked by an incident trivial in itself, but clearly of concern to the reverend in his role of host. When the veal cutlets had been served, the butler took up the decanter of wine and poured his master a glass. After one sip the reverend muttered something inaudible and held the glass up the gaslight – after which he sniffed at the contents, and took another small taste.

'Moxon, I believe this Burgundy is sherrified!' he said. 'Tell me, ladies, are you in agreement? It may be that my nose is at fault.'

Harriet and I dutifully took a sip. I looked towards Harriet, but she remained silent. As my long acquaintance with Hester had endowed me with some of her connoisseurship, I felt able to offer an opinion with some confidence.

'I agree with you, Reverend,' I said. 'There is certainly some evidence of mild oxidisation – just a hint of old apples. However, I believe it is perfectly drinkable.'

No sooner had the words left my mouth than I realised they were hardly in character with my assumed profession of governess. However, my host seemed not to notice the anomaly.

'Thank you, Miss Green. However, drinkable or not, I must apologise for offering you a tainted vintage. Moxon, when was this Burgundy decanted?'

Moxon's features showed a faint flush of embarrassment.

'A few hours ago, sir. Of course I take full responsibility for my error.'

The reverend frowned. 'As you are in charge of my cellar, that is surely *ad oculus*. However, we will make do with the Chablis. You can dispose of the Burgundy later – and I do not want it to reappear in the servants' hall. Do remember in future that a vintage red wine should be decanted not more than half an hour before serving.'

The butler nodded. 'Yes, sir. I will make sure that the error is not repeated.'

The reverend appeared to consider the matter closed, and it was not long before his usual good humour returned. I had earlier that evening expressed an interest in early maps of Sussex – not altogether feigned – and he took the opportunity to return to the subject.

'My topographical collection is housed in my study,' he said to me. 'Or rather, I chose to make the library my study when I first moved to this house. You are most welcome to look through it at any time – the door is not kept locked. Now, if it is maps that interest you, be sure to examine the one framed above the fireplace. Sussex in 1611, in full colour, engraved by Jodocus Hondius ...'

These and other observations sustained the conversation until the end of the meal, when the reverend addressed me with a smile.

'I hope you will not think it impolite of me if I now adjourn to my study for a glass of port. I am sure you and Harriet have much to talk about.'

'By all means, Reverend. You are quite right; it will be wonderful to be able to give my friend all my news. And thank you for such a splendid dinner!'

After Moxon had taken in the reverend his glass of port, he asked us if we wished for any refreshments. When we declined, he left us, and we found ourselves alone in the drawing room.

Harriet chuckled. 'Poor father! He will now be convinced that the duties of a governess include a familiarity with fine wine – however, as we have no prospect of a governess in this household, his misapprehension will do no harm. I must say, I was not surprised at Moxon's *faux pas*. He is very willing, but is certainly not the most skilful practitioner of his profession. Perhaps that accounts for his diffidence. I understand that he rarely appears in the servants' hall, and spends his free time in his living quarters next to the kitchen.'

'At least you are blessed with an excellent cook,' I said.

'Yes, Señora Caballero is very talented. Perhaps too talented to be a cook in an unpretentious family house. When she first arrived, her concept of a suitable dinner menu was far too elaborate.'

I sensed that there was something more about the cook that Harriet had not mentioned.

'And in other respects, is she a satisfactory servant?'

'I see you have sensed my concern. I will be frank with you, Ivy – I do have some reservations about the familiarity that appears to exist between father and the señora. She is an attractive woman, twenty years younger than he is, and her background means that she is rather less reserved than her English equivalent would be. They also have the Spanish language in common. After he was first ordained, my father spent some time attached to the Anglican cathedral in Madrid, and consequently is fluent in Spanish. Of course, I am not suggesting that there has been any impropriety; that would be quite out of character for father. It is just that their conversations regarding hothouse vegetables are more enthusiastic than one should expect. Thankfully, father is retired, so it does not matter if the bishop gets to hear of it.'

I struggled to suppress a smile. 'I am sure it is an innocent friendship. However, there was one matter regarding Señora Rosalia Caballero – and also Henry Moxon – which Miss Lynton asked me to raise with you, as they are relatively recent members of the household. Do you happen to remember who provided each of them with references?'

'Let me see … father obtained them, then passed them to me to look at. In fact I still have them in my writing desk in my boudoir. If you will excuse me, I will fetch them for you.'

A moment later Harriet returned with a manila folder. I quickly scanned Moxon's reference. It was a recommendation from his most recent employer, Dr Henry Lawrence, who gave an address in Pimlico. Señora Caballero's reference was fortunately in English, and had been provided by an English lady resident in Barcelona, where the señora had last worked.

‘Although the reverend does not usually interview prospective servants, he made a point of assisting with the señora’s appointment,’ she said. ‘In fact there were some good local candidates, but I think father was influenced by the opportunity to practise his Spanish.’

And perhaps by the prospect of an attractive woman under his roof, I could not help thinking.

‘Tell me, what brought the señora from Barcelona to England?’ I asked.

Harriet sniffed disapprovingly. ‘Her official reason is that she has an elderly relative in London that she is concerned about – however, I think it much more likely that it was some affair of the heart, possibly some unpleasantness that caused her to seek a fresh start in another country. I understand from my maid that Señora Caballero is remarkably reticent about her background. However, she is a most capable cook, which I suppose is all that matters. And her friendship with father is probably harmless enough.’

I nodded. ‘The reverend certainly appears to be in very good spirits. I take it that there have been no, erm, further *incidents* since you spoke to Miss Lynton and me two days ago?’

Harriet seemed to hesitate before answering. ‘No *incidents* as such, but there was one small thing – so trivial I hesitate to mention it. I am usually a heavy sleeper, but last night I woke just after two o’clock in the morning. There was enough moonlight for me to see the time on the carriage clock on my bedroom mantlepiece. After a few minutes, I began to fall asleep again when I heard a faint tapping sound – not on my window, but as if someone was tapping the roof or the outside wall at some distance from my room. That was evidently what had woken me earlier. I got out of bed, went to the window, raised the sash and looked out. I could see nothing, but of course my view was restricted to the one wall of the house. I decided later that the origin of the sound may well have been much closer – it would not be the first time that I have heard a mouse scurrying across the joists of my bedroom ceiling. Hector – he is looked after by the groom – is an excellent mouser, but of course he cannot be everywhere at once.’

I made some noncommittal remark, and after some further conversation – none of which was pertinent to the case in question – I made the excuse of tiredness and returned to my room. However, I did not extinguish the gas until I had written a long letter to Hester mentioning every detail of my first evening at Ledbury Grange.

When the maid brought up my hot water the following morning, I gave her my letter to Hester, with the instruction that it should be placed in the morning post. As Harriet had gone up to town for the day – to attend a meeting of the board of one of several charities she supported – I had my time to myself, and an hour or so before lunch I set off to explore the extensive grounds of Ledbury Grange.

Although the house itself was of recent construction, it was clear that it had been built on the site of a much earlier building. The high walls of the kitchen garden were constructed from ancient, roughly shaped red bricks which could have dated from the age of Queen Elizabeth, and the granite flags of the path that led into it had been worn concave by the tread of countless feet. I was speculating on the nature of the house that stood originally, and making a mental note to ask the reverend about this later, when I turned into a sheltered corner, and saw that gentleman no more than a yard or two distant, standing in front of a spread of cranberry bushes. He had forsaken his usual dark suit and clerical collar for an old tweed jacket, flat cap and corduroy leggings. He was leaning forward, in animated conversation with a tall, handsome woman of Mediterranean appearance who could surely be none other than the Spanish cook.

Thus it transpired. The señora, who had a wicker basket of cranberries in her hands, stepped back with a start. The reverend too appeared surprised, but quickly regained his composure.

'Miss Green!' he exclaimed. 'You have come to admire our kitchen garden, it seems. And I believe you have not yet met Señora Rosalia Caballero, our cook.'

The señora bowed to me in a distinctly un-English manner, but said nothing.

'That is true, we have not met – but I have sampled Señora Caballero's dishes,' I said. 'Your dinner on Wednesday was a delight, señora. Would it be possible to have the recipe for your mulligatawny soup before I leave? I promise that the secret will go no further than my housekeeper.'

She smiled warmly, and addressed me in very good English, albeit heavily accented with her native tones: an effect I shall not attempt to replicate for my readers.

'Thank you, Miss Green. As I myself obtained that recipe from an Englishwoman, I can hardly object at returning the favour. I hope you will enjoy tonight's meal; the Reverend Dowson has been kind enough to provide a goose for me, and I will not be able to blame the freshness of the cranberries for any deficiencies in the sauce.'

'I shall look forward to it,' I said. 'And now I will leave you to your harvesting. Miss Dowson has told me all about the Japanese bridge and water garden beyond the copse, and I have decided to explore it while this fine weather holds.'

As I walked off, I speculated on the words and demeanour of the cook. Although perfectly respectful, her manner had not shown the deference one would have expected from an English servant in similar circumstances. It was also clear than she was on terms of friendly intimacy with the Reverend Dowson. I wondered whether she was cognisant of the reverend's outbreaks of peculiar behaviour – and if so, whether she had any opinions about them. However, for the time being I decided that a direct approach to the cook would be unwise, since it would almost certainly expose the object of my visit.

The morning and afternoon passed without incident; however, whilst the day was uneventful, the same cannot be said of the evening, which confirmed all the concerns Harriet Dowson had expressed when she originally consulted us at Newsome Street.

I had gone to bed at just after eleven o'clock that night, and was sleeping soundly when I was suddenly woken up by Harriet, who was shaking my shoulder. She was wearing a nightgown, and the dishevelled state of her hair suggested to me that she had rushed to my room with some urgency.

'Please come with me. My father has woken up in a most disturbed state of mind. Moxon is with him now, but I thought you would wish to be present.'

Pausing only to put on my dressing gown, I followed Harriet down the corridor. The candlestick that she held cast grotesque shadows of our hurrying figures upon the walls and ceilings as we hastened to the reverend's bedroom. His room, like mine, was on the first floor of the house. Harriet spoke over her shoulder to me as we sped.

'Moxon heard father cry out, and went to his room. Once he had made sure that father was safe, he knocked on my door to fetch me to him.'

We entered to room to find that it was illuminated by the yellow light of an oil lamp, which stood on the bedside table. The Reverend Dowson was sitting up in bed, and the butler was better arranging the bolster and pillows to support his back. The reverend's eyes were wide open, and his left hand was thrust out, his index finger extended and pointing towards the curtained window.

The reverend did not turn round to acknowledge our presence when we entered the room, and Harriet placed herself directly in front of him.

'Father!' she cried. 'What is it? What has disturbed you?'

Without acknowledging his daughter's question, the Reverend Dowson leant to the left, his hand still outstretched, so that he could again see the window that Harriet was obscuring. When he spoke, his voice was unnaturally loud, as if addressing a congregation from a pulpit rather than a small group of people in his bedroom.

'The devil! The devil's face – I saw it at the window!'

Feeling rather foolish, I stepped to the window and pulled open the heavy velvet curtains. There was a half moon, giving enough light to show the grounds of Ledbury Grange which stretched beyond the house. No figure of any kind was visible.

'There is nothing there now, Reverend,' I said. Again he did not appear to acknowledge my presence, but slumped back upon his pillows, his face moist and pallid, and his eyes closed.

Harriet spoke to me in a hushed voice. 'This is his usual condition after one of his episodes of excitement. If events proceed as they have done before, he will now sink into a deep sleep, and appear perfectly normal tomorrow morning, having no memory of the night's events.'

She turned to address the butler, who had been standing impassively in the corner of the room.

'You may leave us now, Moxon. I am grateful for your vigilance, and for having called me. I shall watch over the reverend for what remains of the night. If I need your assistance, I will send for you.'

Once it was clear that her father was sleeping quietly, Harriet insisted that I return to my bedroom, whilst she stayed with him until the morning.

Harriet's prediction of her father's swift return to normality turned out to be correct. Just as I was sitting down to breakfast, the Reverend Dowson entered the dining room, greeting me cheerfully.

'Why, Miss Green! You are bright and early today. Harriet and I are to drive into Horsham this morning. Would you care to join us?'

I was about to say yes, when it occurred to me that their absence might present me with an opportunity to do some surreptitious investigation at Ledbury Grange.,

'I think I will excuse myself on this occasion,' I said. 'I have an elderly aunt who enjoys receiving letters from me – I will write to tell her all about my visit here, then take advantage of your kind offer inviting me to explore your collection of topographical works. If you intend lunching in Horsham, please tell Señora Caballero not to trouble herself with any luncheon just for me – I will make do with a cup of tea and slice of cake.'

There seemed little point in my writing to Hester describing the events of the night before, as I was lunching with her tomorrow. Thus, as soon as my hosts had left I made my way to the reverend's study. It was easy to see that its original purpose had been to serve as a library; three of the walls were lined with bookshelves, and a number of comfortable armchairs were placed throughout. A heavy mahogany kneehole desk stood under the large window at the far end of the room. The books and manuscripts placed upon it – examples of which also filled the shelves nearby – bore witness to the reverend's interest in the topography of ancient Sussex.

However, it was not his collection that interested me at that moment. I was not entirely sure what I might discover when I went through the contents of the desk drawers, but it seemed to me that there were some hidden facts in the case which might go some way to explaining the curious scenes that I had witnessed.

It came as no surprise to me that the drawers were locked. I could only hope that the reverend had taken the somewhat illogical approach favoured by many householders – to lock his desk, but to keep the keys hidden close at hand, for ease of use when he needed them. I was correct – it only took me a moment to discover a bunch of small keys, hidden inside a silver tankard on the desk.

Fortunately the Reverend Dowson's papers were meticulously organised. Several of the drawers contained an alphabetical catalogue of his topographical collection, which I could speedily dismiss. I soon discovered a more fruitful source of information – a stack of manila folders containing his personal documents and financial statements. Nothing seemed surprising in any way, although an examination of the latter showed that his sister had not exaggerated the size of his estate. Then, I found a stout manila envelope, unsealed, with the words *Alfred Dowson, his last will and testament, 5th June 1887.*

The date – just four months ago – took me by surprise. The will in the envelope must be a new one. Had Harriet Dowson been aware of its contents when she spoke to Hester and me? When I drew the document out and examined it the mystery deepened, for the front of the will – a copy of the original – was dated the fifth of January, 1879. A further sheet, which was pinned to the will, provided the solution. It was a codicil to the original, dated fifth of June 1887. The provisions of the codicil were very straightforward. In addition to the provisions already made, a sum of £2,000 was left to Señora Rosalia Caballero.

Nothing else in the reverend's papers seemed worthy of note, and so I locked the drawers, being careful to leave everything as I had found it and replaced the keys in their hiding place. I was then careful to disturb some of the maps and guide books on the nearby table, to give evidence of my supposed reason for visiting the study.

I thought carefully about the next steps to take in the case. On balance, it seemed best to say nothing to Harriet about my discovery – at least until I had spoken to Hester.

As I left the study, Moxon presented me with a telegram from Hester. She wished me to draw up a plan of the house, showing all the rooms, their occupants (in respect of the bedrooms) and the links between them, and to bring it with me to our luncheon tomorrow.

There were fortunately no further nocturnal adventures that evening, and I was able to travel up to London in the morning as arranged. By the time I arrived at the Criterion, Hester was already seated at our table. I was amused to see that amongst the packed crowd of lady diners, Hester and I appeared to be the only ones unencumbered by the bags and hat boxes that signalled a busy morning's shopping.

Hester insisted that I give her my news before she returned the compliment. Thus – after presenting her with the plan of the house that I had prepared – I told her all about the Reverend Dowson's disturbed state in the early hours of Friday morning, and my discovery of the codicil to his will.

Hester heard me in silence, then thought for a moment or two before responding.

'Tell me, did any other servants appear during the episode in the reverend's bedroom?' she asked. 'Besides Moxon, that is. The housekeeper or the cook, for example? I would have thought that sufficient noise was made to disturb them all.'

'None that I saw,' I replied. 'Of course, it could be that Moxon had got word to them, and told them not to interfere, as help was already at hand.'

'That is very likely. Now, let us look at your plan of the house. I must say, it is a remarkably well drawn document! Let me see … this bedroom on the second floor, directly above the reverend's, appears to be unoccupied.'

'Yes, I believe it was Miss Julia Dowson's, before she married her first husband and moved to London.'

Hester pursed her lips. 'I see. Ivy, when the opportunity presents itself, I would like you to examine that room. If it is kept locked, I am sure your ingenuity will find a way to locate the key.'

'What do you wish me to look out for?'

'Anything that seems unusual, or out of place in any way. There may be nothing, but it is an avenue worth exploring.'

'And what do you make of the recent codicil to the reverend's will?' I asked.

'Given what we already know about the Reverend Dowson's attraction to Señora Caballero, the explanation seems very clear! The señora came to at Ledbury Grange in March of this year – the reverend became infatuated with her, and three months after her arrival he decided to provide for her in his will, which he amended accordingly. More problematic is the possibility of a connection between the codicil and the reverend's delusional behaviour. After all, £2,000 is a great deal of money for someone in the señora's walk of life. Her salary cannot be more than £100 a year at most. Many people in her situation might wish to gain their inheritance sooner rather than later. That is, of course, assuming that the señora knows about the bequest.'

I frowned. 'But how could the señora gain from the reverend's erratic behaviour? Or indeed from instigating it in any way?'

Hester laughed. 'There, we are in deep waters! However, you have been very patient. Let me tell you about my own discoveries, which might throw further light on the case. I have investigated the references provided by the cook and the butler prior to their appointments, with some interesting results. Firstly, Moxon. Dr Henry Lawrence is no longer resident at Pimlico, but I talked to one of the tradesmen who supplied the house – a local butcher – who confirmed that Henry Moxon was indeed a servant in the doctor's household until January of this year, when Dr Lawrence retired and moved to Devonshire. However, the butcher's recollection was that Moxon was more of a general manservant than a butler.'

'That would explain his lack of finesse in the role!' I exclaimed. 'No wonder he made mistakes about serving wine and waiting at the table, if he had never undertaken such duties before. However, his ambition is understandable. He would not be the first person to exaggerate his experience in order to gain employment. He certainly has the superior manners of a butler, if not the capabilities. And what of the cook?'

'I am afraid that the testimonial provided by Señora Caballero is more problematic. The address given by her referee, Mrs Northam, was the Calle Loja – that is, Loja Street. There is indeed such a location in Barcelona, which shows up on any street guide to the city. However, when I called in at the Geographical Institute in Bloomsbury and consulted a more detailed plan of the city, it is clear that there is no *residential* development on that street, which is entirely given up to warehouses and manufacturing. Naturally, I have written to Mrs Northam asking her to contact me – it was easy enough to think of a pretext – but even if the lady does exist, it will be some days before I can expect a reply. I have to say that I think she is an invention, and that the testimonial is a fraud.'

I frowned. 'So it seems that the Reverend Dowson's cook may have been appointed under false pretences. Still, there may be nothing more sinister behind her actions than a desire to gain a good position. Should we tell Harriet Dowson or her father what we have discovered?'

'I do not think so. If the señora is involved in any wrong-doing, any premature exposure will mean that she will simply give notice and leave – and we have as yet no evidence to prevent her. I should like you to return to Ledbury Grange, and to exercise extreme vigilance. I hope to join you there at the end of the week if I can – providing Harriet is willing to invent yet another white lie to explain my presence.'

I had returned to Ledbury Grange by six o'clock that Saturday evening, and was able to enjoy a night of uninterrupted sleep. On Sunday morning, when the rest of the household decamped to the morning church service, I remained at home, pleading a headache. It seemed an excellent opportunity to examine the bedroom above me. If the door turned out to be locked, I was confident that a search of the housekeeper's quarters would provide the key.

In the event, that proved unnecessary – the door swung open at my touch. The room had the musty smell of a chamber unoccupied for some years, where succeeding winters have not been relieved by the glow of a bedroom fire. The high, old fashioned bed was not made up; there was just a bare mattress, no sheets or blankets. The rest of the room was sparsely furnished with a cane chair; an empty wardrobe and a washstand with a china jug and basin. I was about to leave when, on a whim, I knelt down to look under the bed. There was a large battered leather suitcase, equidistant from the sides, which made it difficult to retrieve. Eventually I was successful and pulled its heavy weight into the middle of the room.

When I had released the straps and raised the lid, a strong scent of camphor moth balls filled the room. The suitcase was full of sheets and pillow cases, edged and embroidered in the style of forty years ago. Without expecting to find anything of note, I rummaged through them – until, at the very bottom of the pile, my hand struck something hard. It was an object about the size of a dinner-plate, and when I withdrew it from the case, I gave an involuntary gasp of surprise. It was a mask made of a dark wood, reminiscent of East African indigenous art, with grotesque, devilish features, evidently designed to be worn over the face. However, the thin cords that secured it at each side were far longer than would be needed to tie it over one's features – each was about ten feet. It required no very great powers of deduction to realise the importance of my discovery. I walked swiftly to the sash window and attempted to raise it. As I had expected, the sash lifted easily – more easily than would usually be the case in an unoccupied room. The implication was clear. Someone had entered the room, leant out of the window and dangled the mask in front of the reverend's bedroom window, which lay directly below. Some adroit swinging of the heavy object would make it tap upon the glass, and gain the reverend's attention. I thought back to what Harriet Dowson had said to me – the mask must have been the source of the tapping sound that she had heard from her room.

I carefully replaced the mask and pushed the trunk back under the bed, hoping that if whoever was responsible decided to repeat their cruel trick, they would not notice that it had been disturbed. I was now faced with a difficult decision. Should I inform Harriet of my discovery? I remembered Hester's words – if the perpetrator got wind of our suspicions, he or she would be likely to lie low and bide their time, making the solution of the case well-nigh impossible. I decided upon another course of action. I would plead a headache, and do my best to get a few hours' sleep that afternoon. Then, when the rest of the household had retired to bed, I would stay awake and alert in my room. If I left my bedroom door ajar it should be possible to hear noise from the Reverend Dowson's room – and my window had a good view of the grounds to the rear of the house.

At midnight I was sitting near my bedroom door, my ear turned to the opening. Despite my efforts to sleep on the previous afternoon, tiredness was growing upon me, and I believe that my head had already drooped to my chest when I was brought back to my senses by a faint cry from the lawn under my window. I had left the sash half open, despite the chill October air. I dashed to the window and saw the Reverend Dowson, standing in the middle of the lawn, staring intently at the densely wooded copse beyond the parkland. I looked in the direction of his gaze and caught a glimpse of a figure shrouded in a cloak, its head covered by a cowl, as it disappeared amongst the trees. The reverend strode off rapidly in the same direction, as if to follow it.

Without hesitation, I made my way down the stairs towards the tradesmen's entrance at the rear of the house. Fortunately, the reverend had left it unlocked behind him; I had earlier learned from his sister that her attempts to persuade him to relinquish his latch key had been futile. When I reached the lawn I could see that the reverend had not yet reached the belt of woodland,

and so when I broke into a run I was not much more than fifty yards behind him when he reached the narrow path that snaked through the copse. I called out before he disappeared, but he did not slow or turn his head.

As soon as I entered the belt of trees I found myself in near darkness, and wished that I had brought a lantern with me. I was forced to stop running and proceed at a cautious walking pace. The path was, however, in good condition, and it was not long before I emerged on the other side, with the water garden and Japanese bridge directly in front of me.

Two figures were clearly illuminated in the moonlight. The Reverend Dowson, dressed in trousers and a smoking jacket which had been hastily flung on over his nightshirt; and the cowled apparition that he had been pursuing. The latter figure stopped when it had reached the centre of the bridge, and turned to face the reverend, at the same time pulling down the hood that shrouded its face. For a moment I recoiled in silent horror – the face that was exposed was that of a gargoyle, hideously distorted in a fixed snarl of rage. The reverend leapt back with a cry, his arm shielding his face, leaning backwards against the low railings that ran down each side of the concave bridge. His tormentor held him by the shoulders and thrust him towards the water. By this time I was running towards them, realising with horror that I would not be able to reach the struggling pair before the reverend was pushed off the bridge. I had drawn my revolver from the pocket of my jacket, but to have attempted to use it would have been foolhardy, as either of the pair might have been shot.

Then, help arrived from a most unexpected direction. Another figure – that of a woman in long black coat, a hat pulled low over her eyes – raced onto the bridge from the opposite side, and stopped a few feet from the struggling pair.

'Stop!' she cried loudly. 'I am a witness, and your plan is discovered. To continue is useless. The police know everything, and are on their way.'

I instantly recognised the clear, confident tones of the new arrival; it was my friend and colleague, Hester. The masked figure swung round, momentarily frozen in indecision. By that time I had reached the other side of the bridge, and added my voice to the scene.

'There are now *two* witnesses! You had best heed my friend's words, whoever you are, and give up your scheme before worse harm is done.'

By this time, the mysterious figure had edged away from the reverend towards me, so I aimed my pistol squarely at its chest.

Hester spoke again. 'Remove your mask. Remove it or be shot where you stand. Your situation is hopeless.'

At those words the figure moved closer to me and tore off its mask. It was Henry Moxon, the butler. My arm must have wavered, since Moxon took the opportunity to rush past me, down the path which lead back to Ledbury Grange. I could not bring myself to fire at him – shooting a fleeing man in the back would be indefensible.

Hester walked up to me and laid her hand on my arm. 'Let him go for the moment,' she said. 'He is no threat to us now. Let us take the Reverend Dowson back to Ledbury Grange. Fortunately, I do not believe he has suffered any injury.'

The reverend did indeed seem physically unharmed, although his mental state was one of stunned incomprehension. We returned to the house as quickly as possible, where we roused Harriet and place him in her care, assisted by the housekeeper.

'And now we should go to the butler's quarters,' Hester said.

'But surely he will have made his escape?'

'Very possibly, but an escape can take more than one form. Come, we will see for ourselves.'

Hester's premonition turned out to be correct. The butler sat slumped in his armchair, a small medicine bottle on the floor, which had no doubt fallen from his hand. Hester felt the pulse in his neck, and shook her head. A stout wooden box stood nearby, the padlock hanging open. Hester rifled through the contents, nodding as she did so, then turned to me.

'He is stone dead, alas. We can do no more here. I see the key is in the door. I suggest that we lock it behind us, and report his suicide in the morning. There is no point in rousing the authorities at this early hour now that all danger had passed.'

'But I thought you said that the police were already on their way?'

Hester smiled. 'A minor subterfuge. Now, there is still time for us to get a few hours' sleep before breakfast. Let us make sure that Harriet and her father are safe and well, then I suggest you retire to your room for what remains of the night. I am sure the housekeeper will be able to find some blankets and a guest bedroom for me.'

I was very happy to follow Hester's suggestion, and remained only for the time it took me to tell her about my discovery of the devil mask hidden in the room above the Reverend Dowson's bedroom; it now seemed clear that the butler was the person behind the malicious trick played upon the clergyman.

The following morning, after an early breakfast, Higson was sent into Horsham, returning in a four-wheeler with a police sergeant and two constables. Hester spoke to the sergeant for a few minutes – I was not party to the conversation – the police drove off with the butler's body.

'The sergeant will arrange for Chief Inspector Harris from the Sussex Constabulary to call here after luncheon,' Hester said. 'I have promised to make a full statement of the facts then. Ivy, you have been remarkably patient, and have asked me nothing since our encounter on the bridge. However, I am conscious that you deserve a full explanation. I have invited Harriet Dowson to join us in the drawing room at eleven o'clock this morning. Mrs Simpkins will serve us tea, and I will endeavour to make everything clear to you. I have also taken the opportunity to speak to Señora Caballero. She has admitted that she provided false references after she had been wrongly accused of theft by her past employer, and had therefore no hope of employment in Spain – and can prove the truth of her assertion. I have advised her to tell Harriet everything, in the hope that her position in the house may continue.'

Thus at the appointed hour the three of us were seated round a tray of tea and cake.

'Is the Reverend Dowson well this morning, Miss Dowson?' Hester said.

'Indeed he is,' she replied. 'As before, he seems to have no recollection of last night's events. He has taken breakfast in his room, and I have asked my housekeeper to remain with him.'

'Very good. I must say, I blame myself for not seeing the solution of this case more quickly. It was an inexcusable oversight. Let me explain.

'I believed from the outset that the key to case lay in the great size of the reverend's estate. Money – or rather the prospect of gaining it – is, alas, the most common motive for crime. Two people would gain from the inheritance of – or access to – the reverend's wealth. One was your good self, Miss Dowson, but I thought it extremely unlikely that you would have consulted me if you were the culprit. That left your sister, Julia Collins. But Julia had not visited Ledbury Grange since her marriage. Were she to be the driving force behind some kind of malign influence directed at the reverend, she would have needed to have acted by proxy. The most obvious characters to have been her accomplice were the newly arrived servants, the butler, Henry Moxon, and the cook, Rosalia Caballero.

'It was there that I made a near-fatal error. I thought that I had established the *bona fides* of the butler by my conversation with a tradesman who had known him in his previous appointment. However, after I had studied the plan of the house that Ivy had brought me on Saturday, my suspicions were once more aroused. I spoke to the butcher again on Sunday, and discovered that he had never actually met Henry Moxon. Moxon's orders had been taken by the butcher's boy, Tom. When I had tracked down Tom later that day, he was able to tell me that Henry Moxon – who had moved back to his native Glasgow when his employer retired – was a general servant of *no more than thirty years of age.* Clearly the "Henry Moxon" working at Ledbury Grange was an imposter. I therefore set off for Sussex immediately. I intended to keep watch in the grounds of the house that evening, and meet with the two of you on the following day. It was necessary to catch Moxon in the act, if we were to be sure that we had caught the correct suspect. There was still a chance that Señora Rosalia might have been party to whatever evil scheme had been planned, if she had known about the provisions of the reverend's will. Challenging Moxon outright would have alerted her.'

'But how did my plan of the house make you suspicious of Moxon?' I asked.

'The butler's quarters are on the ground floor next to the kitchen, on the opposite side of the house from the reverend's first-floor bedroom – and yet, Moxon said he had been roused during the night by the reverend's cry, after the reverend saw the devil mask. That was clearly impossible. But let me continue. Once I had established that the butler was not Henry Moxon, then who was he? If Julia Collins had recruited him, he could be a criminal paid to masquerade – but Ivy described the butler as a very well-spoken and somewhat self-effacing gentleman of about fifty years of age – hardly the criminal type. It seemed more likely to me that Julia's henchman had been recruited rather closer to home – someone who had planned the whole scheme with her, and who would also benefit from it.'

Harriet Dowson drew a sharp breath. 'Her husband! Dr Isaac Collins! But he works at the William Harvey School of Medicine. How could he also be living here as a butler?'

'I took the precaution of making some inquiries about your sister and her husband after you first consulted us,' Hester said. 'I learned that Dr Collins had been granted a period of sabbatical leave for the summer term, from April to September of this year. On my journey down London yesterday evening I sketched out a probable timeline of events, which you may find instructive.'

Hester took out her pocketbook, turned a page and continued. 'July 1886 – Julia's first husband dies. September 1886 – the butler at Ledbury Grange gives notice that he is leaving at the end of April 1887: a fact of which Julia was probably aware. October 1886 – Julia marries Dr Collins, who subsequently negotiates sabbatical leave for the summer term, 1887, and successfully applies for the post of butler.'

'How did he know his application would be successful?' I asked.

'He did not – but would have lost nothing in the attempt. Dr Collins is a neurologist, and specialises in pharmacological treatments of illnesses of the brain. The box in his room contains various medicines and hand-written notes. I will hand it to the chief inspector this afternoon, but I have no doubt that a thorough examination of its contents will reveal a cold-hearted intention to induce the reverend's progressive madness.'

'But why would he abandon his plan to drive the reverend out of his senses, and decide instead to drown him and fake a suicide?' I asked.

'I dare say he felt that the attempt to unhinge his mind was progressing too slowly,' Hester said, grim-faced. 'Of course if the reverend had drowned, his recent history of apparent mental illness would have made any investigation of foul play less likely.'

'Forgive me,' Harriet interjected, 'but how would the reverend's madness have helped Julia inherit his money?'

'That was the most subtle part of their plan. If Julia had been successful in invoking the Lunacy Act, and in registering the Reverend Dowson as legally insane, then she – and you, of course – could have used the provisions of the law in order to obtain access to his wealth on his behalf. It would have been her intention to use that access to extract money for herself and her husband. Of course, after "Moxon" had given his notice and left Ledbury Grange they would have had to make sure that Dr Collins was never subsequently seen by you or any of the servants, but that would not have been difficult.'

I helped myself to a further slice of cake. 'Surely Julia should now be arrested as soon as possible, before she hears of her husband's fate and flees?

Hester nodded. 'I gave full instructions to the sergeant to that effect. Of course, he will have to consult with his superiors, but I have no doubt that Julia Collins is already in custody.'

'It is difficult for me to feel any sympathy for her,' Harriet said. 'To plot someone's insanity – or worse – is a heinous crime.'

'And that may not be all of which she is guilty,' Hester said. 'When we first met, you mentioned that her first husband's death was unexpected. At that time she already knew Dr Collins, whom she was to marry just a few months later – her late husband was then his patient. With Collins' medical expertise, her husband's unexpected demise may have arranged between them. However, that will be for the police to decide. Once I have told Chief Inspector Harris all that we know, the rest will be up to him. Miss Dowson – Harriet – you will have much to do, and Ivy and I should return to London. Please accept our hopes and prayers for your father's swift recovery.'

I am delighted to say that once Moxon's – or rather Dr Collins' – malign influence was no longer present, the Reverend Dowson soon returned to his normal, equable, state of mind. A detailed examination of the papers that Collins had left behind showed that, as Hester had suspected, he had been administering powerful hallucinatory drugs to the reverend via his regular evening glass of port.

After receiving the happy news of the reverend's recovery, Hester and I expected to hear no more of the case. However, there were two subsequent events which warrant a postscript. The first was the conviction of Julia Collins, who received a sentence of ten years' imprisonment for her part in the conspiracy against the reverend; no earlier crime came to light, despite Hester's suspicions. The second was a happier event, and not altogether unexpected. The Reverend Dowson and Señora Rosalia Caballero became man and wife – and they insisted that Harriet Dowson remain at Ledbury Grange with them, provided she could submit to the unconventionality of the lady of the house presiding over the kitchen, as well as the drawing room.

10. The Problem of Oscar Wilde

It was by no means unusual for well-known public figures to grace our home at 12 Newsome Street. On one such memorable occasion, Hester and I were enjoying our leisure after a particularly busy –and ultimately successful – day in which we had concluded a difficult and lengthy investigation. I was browsing the evening papers, and Hester was reading a monograph by the eminent German graphologist Professor Franz von Dingelstedt, which analysed the similarities found in the handwriting of identical twins. The hour was late, and therefore we were somewhat surprised to hear the distant sound of the electric doorbell, announcing an unexpected visitor. Shortly afterwards, Mrs Parsons knocked on our door.

'Excuse me, Miss Lynton … Miss Jessop – there's a gentleman called to see you. He has no appointment, so I said I'd better go up and ask you.'

'Did he give his name?' I asked.

'Well no, miss. That is, I didn't ask him, because I already knew it. It's Mr Oscar Wilde, him who's been in the newspapers with that new play.'

Hester smiled broadly. '*The Importance of Being Earnest* – which Miss Jessop and I saw only last week! An excellent entertainment. Well, show him up, Mrs Parsons, show him up. Although what such a celebrated man of the theatre should want with us, I cannot imagine.'

Moments later, our caller entered our room. From the satirical caricatures which had appeared in *Punch* over the years I had anticipated a flamboyantly-dressed aesthete in knee breeches and a wide-brimmed hat. Instead, Wilde had more in common with a smart solicitor or medical man, his evening dress of conservative cut and his hair worn not much longer than any other man of his age – I knew that he was forty years old, although he could have passed for someone several years younger.

'Mr Oscar Wilde, I believe?' Hester said.

He bowed to us theatrically. 'You are correct. Miss Lynton and Miss Jessop, you must forgive this unmannerly intrusion at so late an hour. However, time is of the essence in the matter upon which I wish to consult you.'

Once seated by our fireside – it was a chilly evening – and with a glass of whisky and water in his hand, Wilde told us his story.

'I have a very large acquaintance, one of whom is Mr Edmund Trilling, a talented poet and painter, who alas has not yet had that wider recognition from the public that is vulgarly deemed to be the criterion of success. He is a young man of twenty-eight, whose parents support his literary career with a generous allowance. Three days ago, Edmund's rooms were burgled. He has a suite in Jefferson Mansions in Piccadilly. Amongst the objects taken were a number of letters – ten in all – that I had written to him over the course of the last twelve months. Trilling informed me of this immediately, but I decided that the best course of action was to do nothing, and hope that whoever had stolen the letters might consider them worthless and destroy them. For the same reason, Trilling has not reported the burglary to the police, despite the additional theft of ten pounds in cash. Alas, when I visited my club this evening, this note had been delivered for me.'

Wilde passed us a small square envelope, which had his name printed in block capitals on the cover. Hester withdrew the folded sheet inside, which I read over her shoulder. It was written in pencil, in roughly-formed handwriting.

Dear Sir,

I am delighted to say that I have found the collection of your letters which have recently gone missing from your friend's rooms, and for which you have offered the very generous reward of £200, from which I can only deduce that they are of great importance to you. I believe that I may justly claim that sum. I would be most grateful if you could bring the reward in banknotes in a briefcase, and meet me at the time and place indicated below. I will approach you and give you the letters in return for the briefcase. Please come alone, as I would not wish your letters to be scrutinised by the wider public.

Yours respectfully, Harold Cuthbertson

THURSDAY 7th MARCH, 3 O'CLOCK
THE ROUGEMONT LOUNGE
THE PELLAM HOTEL
GOODGE STREET

'Thursday – in three days' time. A clear case of blackmail,' Hester said. 'I must ask you, Mr Wilde, why you have not gone to the police rather than Miss Jessop and me? They are well equipped to catch the perpetrator.'

I seemed to me that Hester must have already guessed the answer to her question, but no doubt she had good reason for putting it to our client. At any rate, it did not seem to cause him the least embarrassment.

'The letters are, of course, entirely innocent,' Wilde said with a smile. 'However, my sentiments of friendship are expressed in such poetic terms as are liable to be misinterpreted, and could be used by my enemies – of whom there are many – against me. Were the police to be involved, it is very likely that my letters would become public very shortly afterwards, whereas I can rely on you and your colleague to reveal nothing. Do not misunderstand me – I should be very happy to secure the letters for £200. However, what is to stop the blackmailer keeping back a letter or two and repeating the whole process? No doubt the recent success of my new play has persuaded him – or her – that I am a rich man, which is far from the truth. I will not feel secure until I have the whole collection safely in my hands. I have every hope that you will be able to help me. I should add that the sentiments of admiration expressed could be construed as entirely my own. They contain no suggestion that Edmund has welcomed or reciprocated them in any way.'

'Well, we shall see.' Hester took a large magnifying lens from her desk and picked up the letter again. 'This note is a good starting place. It has several features of interest. What a shame that we cannot consult Professor von Dingelstedt, but as he teaches at the University of Heidelberg that would hardly be practicable. The main letter – from salutation to valediction – has been *composed* by an educated person, as evidenced by the syntax and diction; and yet it has been *written* by someone with little or no formal schooling. The address below has been written by someone else – probably by whoever composed the letter.' Hester held her lens over the page. 'See – the capital P in "Please come alone" is quite different from the P in "Pellam Hotel." I believe that whoever wrote the address was *pretending* to write in a rough and ready fashion – see how the sizes of the letters differ. But even the shoddiest writers usually contrive to keep their lettering a uniform size and shape.'

'And what do you deduce from these phenomena?' Wilde asked.

'Whoever sent this has gone to extreme lengths to avoid detection, Hester said. 'I think it is likely that they wrote out the first part of the letter, then paid someone to copy it out again. If the blackmailer had visited some public place to find a suitable scribe, that would account for the choice of a pencil, which is easier to carry round London than a pen and ink bottle. Note how the letter avoids a direct admission of blackmail – had it done so, it might have been harder to persuade someone to copy it. It also addresses you as "Dear Sir" rather than your name, in order to give no clue to the writer. As for the address, and the name on the front of the envelope, I believe they were added by the blackmailer, to ensure that no curious person would attend the hotel and observe the exchange. Tell me sir, did you ask the commissionaire at your club who delivered the note?'

Wilde nodded. 'I did. A street urchin handed it in – I dare say my persecutor gave him sixpence for his trouble. I must say, Miss Lynton, that your reputation is well deserved. I must include a lady detective in my next play, and save myself any imaginative exertions, since she will be based entirely upon you. What do you propose to do now?'

Hester thought for a moment. 'I should like to examine Mr Trilling's rooms. Could we meet you there tomorrow afternoon, at three o'clock? Mr Trilling's presence is not required, although I have no objection to him being there if he so wishes. I dare say he will have restored his rooms to their previous ordered state, but there may still be some features of interest for us to examine.'

At the appointed hour the following day we arrived at the entrance of Jefferson Mansions, a large apartment block, to find Oscar Wilde waiting for us.

'Mr Trilling has asked me to give you his apologies, but he has another engagement,' Wilde said. 'He has given me a key, so we can go up immediately. I will explain to the porter.'

When we entered the foyer, there was no one behind the porter's desk, but after a minute or two that personage arrived, hastily removing a cigarette from his mouth and extinguishing it in a nearby plant pot. Having explained our mission we walked up the stairs to the first floor – there was no lift – and into Trilling's suite of rooms.

As Hester had predicted, most signs of the burglary which had taken place four days earlier had been removed. Wilde took us to one of the casement windows of Trilling's drawing room, to show us how the burglary had been effected. A pane of glass next to the window latch had been replaced by a sheet of stout cardboard – obviously a temporary repair.

'Edmund found the window broken from the outside – the glass was scattered on the floor,' Wilde said. 'The glazier is coming tomorrow. The burglar must have climbed up the drainpipe to gain entry.'

Hester opened the window and peered down the wall below. 'What do you make of this, Ivy?' she asked.

She stood aside and I took her place. A cast-iron pipe passed to the left of the window, and it was clear to see how an agile thief might have climbed up it, reached across and broken the window, lifted the latch from outside, opened the casement and climbed inside. I grasped the pipe and shook – it was firmly anchored to the wall. The pipe – and indeed the whole exterior of the building – was covered with that almost invisible layer of sooty grime which is found everywhere in London, and I had to wipe my hand clean on my handkerchief.

As I did so I noticed that Hester was kneeling on the floor, examining the carpet with her magnifying lens. She then lay prone, squinting under a heavy chest of drawers which stood against the wall, close to the broken window.

Once Hester had got to her feet, she stepped over to Trilling's writing desk and pointed to the splintered wood where a drawer had been forced open.

'I assume that this was where your letters were kept?' she asked our eminent client.

'That is correct,' Wilde said. 'The ten pounds that were stolen were taken from a pocket in one of Edmund's jackets, which hung in his wardrobe.'

Hester tried the other drawers in the writing desk, all of which were locked. On the desk stood a photograph of three young men, outside what I guessed was an Oxford or Cambridge college. At Hester's request, Wilde identified one of them as Edmund Trilling. My friend then explored the rest of Trilling's suite, pausing in the dressing room. Arranged on a shelf were a dozen or so boxes of cuff links, all of which she picked up and examined, holding one pair out to me. They were made of gold, though whether the jewels that adorned each one were garnets, or something more precious, I had not the expertise to tell.

Hester placed the cufflinks back into their blue box. 'Tiffany, I believe. Edmund Trilling evidently has good taste. Well, I think we have seen enough here. If you will return with us to Newsome Street, Mr Wilde, we can discuss the next steps in the case.'

When we returned to our rooms and Mrs Parsons had brought us a tray of tea and cake, our client asked the question that was already forming in my own mind – although a long acquaintance with Hester had taught me that he was unlikely to receive a direct answer.

'Tell me, Miss Lynton – and Miss Jessop – has your visit to the scene of the crime been at all illuminating? Beyond the fact that the burglar must have a head for heights, I confess that I can deduce nothing.'

Hester looked at me. 'Ivy, what conclusions did you reach?'

'It is also likely that the perpetrator is young and athletic,' I said, 'and a man rather than a woman.'

Hester reacted with mock surprise. 'Oh indeed! The alpinist Mary Mummery might disagree with you. A woman who can reach the summit of the Täschhorn could probably ascend to Trilling's window with ease. However, you are both correct that a climb of that nature would not be a simple undertaking.'

'And what did you make of the scene at Edmund's rooms, Miss Lynton?' Wilde asked.

'There were some points of interest, but nothing that suggests a definitive solution. However, let me make a proposal. The note that you received asked you to meet with the blackmailer at three o'clock on the day after tomorrow, carrying the money in a briefcase. I suggest you do so. If the letters are offered to you, accept them without any quibbles, and hand over the case in return. Do not attempt to follow the perpetrator. Whilst I cannot absolutely guarantee that we will recover your £200, I believe there is an excellent chance of bringing this case to a successful conclusion.'

'I am glad to hear it. I will, of course, do as you say, since you know more of these matters than I. But surely we should not forgo the opportunity of identifying this person?'

'Leave that to us,' Hester said. 'I have one further request – make sure that you arrive at the Pellam Hotel no later than ten minutes to three, and find a table in the Rougemont Lounge that is well away from the door.

If you can find a distinctive-looking briefcase for the money, so much the better. Let us hope that you are not accosted by a member of your admiring public whilst you wait.'

Our eminent client having left us, Hester spent a few minutes writing, then passed the note to me for inspection.

'I will take this down for Mrs Parsons. There is just time for her to ensure that it is inserted into the personal columns of all the evening papers. What do you think?'

If the person who recently copied out a note about a large reward for missing letters calls at 12 Newsome Street this Tuesday or Wednesday evening, they will hear something to their advantage.

'It can do no harm, at any rate, I said. 'But will it not put the blackmailer on their guard?'

'Your point is a fair one, Ivy. However, we would be unlucky if that person happened by chance to scrutinise the advertisements this evening. On the other hand, the man or woman who was paid to copy the letter will surely have told all their friends about the mysterious request, and how easy it was to earn a half sovereign, or whatever they were paid. They, in turn, will report my advertisement if they chance upon it.'

By nine o'clock that evening I was beginning to think that Hester's advertisement would bring no response, and was about to say as much to my friend when the distant ringing of the doorbell signalled a visitor. Mrs Parsons had already been instructed to show up anyone that evening who was not positively drunk or dangerous, and a few minutes later our housekeeper opened the door to usher in our caller. He was a brawny, middle aged man with the appearance of a labourer, and a ruddiness of complexion which suggested he was no stranger to strong drink.

He introduced himself as Mr Sidney Croker. Hester quickly put him at his ease with the frankness and good-humour that enabled her to gain the sympathy of any client, whether high-born or humble.

'A glass of whisky and water, Mr Croker? Do help yourself. There is a sovereign for you if you can tell me all about your little adventure. When were you asked to copy the note?'

'Well miss, it's like this. I was in the bar of the Green Dragon, down Bermondsey way, last Saturday it would have been, at a corner table writing a letter for my friend Bill. His mother lives in Scotland, and as he can't write himself – he never had any schooling – I was writing it for him, for the price of a gin and water. My old mother made sure I could read and write, bless her heart, but I can't say as it's ever done me much good. Anyways – when I'd finished and Bill went to get more drinks, this young woman come up to me. She had a letter all written out neat in ink, and wanted me to do a copy for her, in pencil, for ten shillings! Course I said yes, and got the ten bob. Can't say as I remember much about it, except that there was something about a £200 reward for some letters.'

I caught Hester's eye. Her advertisement had said nothing about £200 – this was definitely our man.

'The woman – what was she like?' Hester asked.

'Young – twenty-five perhaps – with dark hair, pulled back into a bun. And she didn't speak right. I think she tried to sound like a cockney, but I'd say she was more ladylike than she made out.'

'Was she alone?'

'Couldn't say, miss. Once I'd done her letter and got paid, she went back to the bar and then left a few minutes later. There's always people coming in and out at that time of night, so she might have gone out with someone – or not.'

After Croker had left us, delighted with his windfall, Hester fell silent for a few moments.

'So your theory about the note delivered for Mr Wilde has turned out to be correct,' I said.

'In part. However, I had not expected a woman to have been at the centre of the case. I dare say we shall know more after Wilde has met the blackmailer.'

After Mrs Parsons had cleared away the breakfast things on the day of Oscar Wilde's meeting at the Pellam Hotel, Hester turned to me with a smile.

'I have one or two matters to deal with in town this morning, although I shall be back in time for luncheon. Let us discuss our strategy for this afternoon. In my opinion, if the blackmailer successfully retrieves his or her £200, they will wish to take it home with them as quickly as possible.

Our mission is therefore very straightforward; we will follow them, and therefore find out where they live.'

'You do not intend to challenge this person?' I asked.

'Certainly not in public. It is very likely that Mr Wilde's theory – that the blackmailer has retained a letter or two – is correct. Wilde's entrenched cynicism makes him an excellent judge of human nature. Were we to accost the blackmailer, the resulting fracas might involve the police, leading inexorably to the discovery of the remaining letters, which is exactly what our client wishes to avoid. No – if we can find out where the blackmailer lives, it should be a straightforward matter to discover that person's name, and to apply a more private and subtle means of persuasion.'

'And are we to follow this person together?' I asked.

Hester shook her head. 'That would be rather too obvious. We will adopt the method that we used successfully when we followed Lord Kermode to his assignation in Soho last year. I will make sure that I am seated in the Rougemont Lounge by two thirty; I will order afternoon tea, and will have the day's newspapers to occupy me – and to shelter behind. You will wait near the hotel, near enough to have a good view of the entrance. When the blackmailer leaves, I will follow closely behind, with you observing me. After a few minutes I will cease my pursuit and loiter in the street, whereupon you will overtake me and follow our mystery person, keeping at a good distance. I will follow in your train, keeping out of sight of the blackmailer as far as is possible. If you feel that the blackmailer has noticed you and is suspicious, let me once more take over the trail.'

'But Hester, what if our quarry takes a cab?'

'I have reason to think that is most unlikely. If my theory about this case is correct, we should be back at Newsome Street in plenty of time for supper. I have intimated to Mrs Parsons that something substantial would be welcome.'

After Hester left I guessed that she was engaged in some research of her own, which she was not disposed to share with me; however, I was well used to her predisposition to secrecy, which if it was a fault, was more than outweighed by her other sterling qualities.

That afternoon at a quarter to three I was able to find a useful concealment in the front portico of a dress shop, where I was able to admire the coats and hats that were on display whilst maintaining a close watch on the front entrance of the Pellam Hotel. A uniformed commissionaire stood on duty under the striped awning which sheltered the foyer to that venerable building. At ten minutes to three Oscar Wilde entered the hotel, carrying a distinctive yellow leather briefcase. I scrutinised everyone who went into the hotel, but amongst the dozen or so men and three women who entered there was no obviously suspicious character. I realised that the blackmailer might have been inside the hotel for some time before Wilde's arrival.

After three o'clock, I moved to the street corner on the opposite side of the road to the hotel, where a newspaper stall provided excellent camouflage. It seemed very likely that the blackmailer would be carrying Wilde's briefcase when they emerged, and I expected Hester to follow shortly afterwards.

Five minutes later – during which time several individuals, minus briefcase and with no Hester behind them, had left the hotel – I was momentarily frozen with surprise at what occurred. A fair-haired young woman, fashionably dressed in a dark tailored costume with leg-o'-mutton sleeves and a tall, feathered hat, stepped quickly out from the hotel awning. However, it was not her sudden appearance that caused me such surprise, but the fact she carried Wilde's briefcase in her hand. Any further speculation on my part was swiftly halted, since Hester was next to emerge, just a few yards behind the mystery woman.

I remained in my hiding place and observed my friend follow the woman down Goodge Street towards Cavendish Place. After fifty yards or so, Hester halted and entered a milliner's shop. She must have been prescient, for a second or so later the woman in the dark costume stopped in her tracks, swung round, and scrutinised the pedestrians between her and the hotel. Apparently satisfied, and pausing only to push some stray strands of her luxuriant blonde hair back under her hat, our quarry then continued her journey.

As we had previously agreed, I then led the pursuit, taking care to leave a good distance between myself and the young woman I was following. On two occasions she had ample opportunity to secure a hansom when the cabs discharged their passenger next to her, but for some reason she chose to continue her journey on foot, as Hester had predicted. As we progressed down Regent Street towards Piccadilly Circus I glanced behind me; although there was no sign of Hester, I was sure that she could not be far away.

When the woman tuned into Sackville Street I suddenly realised that we were rapidly approaching Jefferson Mansions. If that was her destination, then the case was surely moving to its conclusion. If she was a resident of the block, she could have discovered that Trilling might have valuable papers in his room. Another thought struck me; it was likely that Hester had somehow known of this in advance, hence her comment that it was unlikely that the woman would take a cab – the short distance from the Pellam Hotel to Jefferson Mansions would be better done on foot.

As the woman turned the corner into the courtyard which led up to the imposing front entrance of the apartment block, I hung back and peered round the corner so that I could see her without revealing myself. At that moment I felt a tap upon my shoulder – it was Hester, who had materialised behind me. We both saw the woman we had been following enter the building.

'What now?' I asked my friend. 'Should we pursue her inside, or wait to see if she emerges later?'

'Neither. I believe that all the essential elements of the solution to this case are now in place.'

'But surely we need to find out who she is, and attempt to recover Mr Wilde's £200?'

Hester smiled. 'I have an expedition planned for tomorrow evening, which should hopefully answer that question. In the meantime, I am sure that you will forgive me if I do not speculate further.'

After we had returned to Newsome Street, another development in the case occurred, although it did not come as a great surprise to either of us. Mrs Parsons handed us a telegram from Oscar Wilde. It read *One letter missing – what should I do?* Hester's reply – dispatched via our housekeeper – was short and to the point. *Do nothing – case progressing well.*

Hester said nothing further about the expedition that she had planned for Saturday night, and by mutual consent we paid no more heed that evening to the case of Oscar Wilde's indiscreet letters, turning our minds instead to the excellent boiled turbot with oyster sauce, haunch of venison and punch jelly which Mrs Parsons had provided for our supper.

After breakfast the next day, I turned to my friend and colleague with a smile.

'My dear Hester, much as I appreciate your enjoyment of a mystery, and your chronic inability to confirm the direction of your enquiries, I must insist that you tell me more of this evening's adventure. Am I to disguise myself as an off-duty groom or footman, in order to enjoy a cockney sing-song at the music hall? Or are we to meet the royal family at Windsor? The wrong attire would be unfortunate in either case.'

Hester laughed. 'That is a very fair question. We will be attending the Beaconsfield Club in Mayfair – I have told the proprietor, Colonel Goring, that we will arrive around midnight.'

'But that is a gambling club! And one of the most exclusive in London. Surely it is necessary to be a member in order to attend?'

'In normal circumstances, you would be correct. However, in our case, Colonel Goring will make an exception. I spoke with him on Wednesday. You will remember the case that we dealt with last year – William Harding, the young accountant falsely accused of stealing from his employer? The colonel is his uncle, and will therefore be very happy to assist us. If we leave Newsome Street at a quarter to twelve tonight, that should be early enough.'

'Will there be other ladies present?' I asked.

'Certainly. We shall be in the minority, of course, but I happen to know that a number of the colonel's most free-spending customers are female. Apparently, the Countess of Turnberry is an habituée of the roulette table. Now, if you will excuse me, I must unearth my chiffon evening dress, and ask Mrs Parsons to ensure that it looks its best.'

At midnight, we stepped down from the four-wheeler which Hester had ordered to take us to the club, and a tall, distinguished-looking gentleman, around fifty years of age and in immaculate evening dress, greeted and escorted us into the premises. I guessed that he was the proprietor, Colonel Goring.

'Miss Lynton and Miss Jessop, I am very pleased to meet you, and am at your service. Charles will take your coats, and you must let me obtain some refreshment for you – a glass of champagne, I insist. By the way, Miss Lynton, the private room that you asked for is available whenever you require it. Just mention it to one of the attendants.'

A few minutes later we arrived at the main room in the club, where the colonel took his leave of us. The room was perfumed with smoke, and the lighting from shaded gas mantles was intentionally subdued. The only exception was the roulette table, which was brightly illuminated by a large crystal chandelier above the wheel. We found a seat at one of the small tables on a raised platform at one end of the room, which gave us a good view of the table. A waiter placed a bottle of Veuve Clicquot and two glasses before us.

'Goodness! Colonel Goring is most generous,' Hester said. 'Let us restrict ourselves to one glass apiece, in order to retain our faculties.'

I sipped my drink. 'Would it be too much to ask for whom – or what – we are looking?' I asked.

Hester laughed. 'Not at all. I have discovered that the gentleman I seek is in the habit of attending this club at about this time of night – or rather I should say, early morning.'

'Is it someone we have met before?'

'No, but nevertheless you should be able to recognise him. He is ... but wait, he has just arrived, and is about to take a seat at the roulette table. And I see that he has a charming companion with him. There – the man in the velvet jacket, with the dark-haired woman in the purple silk dress standing behind him.'

There was certainly something familiar about the young man who had just taken his seat at the table. Then I realised – it was Edmund Trilling, looking some years older that he had done in the college photograph, but with the same distinctive good looks.

For some twenty minutes, we observed Trilling play. It was obvious the young woman behind him was his companion, for she watched his wagers avidly, at one point stooping to whisper in his ear.

Trilling's method – if such a term can be applied to a game of pure chance – was one adopted by many who try their luck at the roulette table. For most of the time he would bet on red or black, waiting until there was a run on one colour, and then place his money on the other. This is an intuitively sensible approach, although logically flawed. On occasion, he placed his chips on a single number, where the odds of winning were small and the rewards correspondingly great. He appeared to be neither winning nor losing a great deal. Then, for some reason, his behaviour changed. He placed a small stake on number 12 – which, predictably, he lost. Then he placed his next bet on the same number – a slightly larger amount. After ten consecutive attempts, his wager on 12 amounted to a very large sum – and the ball landed in his favour. Having collected the pile of chips he had won, Trilling and his companion walked across to the desk, to cash in his winnings.

Hester spoke to me in a low voice. 'Mathematical ignorance will sometimes triumph. Trilling has won over £200! Wait here whilst I speak to him and his companion. Then, when we leave the room, please follow us.'

I watched as Trilling exchanged his gambling tokens for a wad of banknotes which he squeezed into his wallet. Hester stepped up to him and spoke briefly. His reaction was striking. All the jollity that had previously infused his manner seemed to evaporate, and he followed Hester out of the room like a man who has seen his good fortune turn to dust. Another word from Hester and then the young woman went with them, and I quickly followed as the three entered the private room that Colonel Goring had promised to provide.

The four of us occupied comfortable leather armchairs which were arranged round a low table.

'I am Hester Lynton,' my friend announced. 'And this is my colleague, Miss Jessop. You may or may not be familiar with my name, but I am acting on behalf of Mr Oscar Wilde. Mr Trilling, I will come straight to the point. I require two things from you. Firstly, you have on your person a letter sent to you by Mr Wilde, which you must now give to me. Secondly, you owe Wilde £200. Since you have that sum in notes in your wallet, I will take that, also. In return you will be allowed to leave, and will not be prosecuted for blackmail.'

Before Trilling could answer, Hester spoke to his companion. 'I will not ask your name, Miss Whoever-You-Are, since it would be impossible for me to gauge the truth of your answer, and in any case, it is of no interest to me. You have been an accessory to a serious crime – blackmail. Firstly, you recently visited the Green Dragon in Bermondsey and obtained a copy of Trilling's note, subsequently sent to Mr Wilde. Secondly, you collected the £200 on Trilling's behalf when you met Mr Wilde in the Pellam Hotel.

Wearing a blonde wig was a little too clever, I think, and became rather obvious when you tried to tuck its bulk under your hat. You are fortunate that if Trilling cooperates you are unlikely to be prosecuted. I suggest that you think very carefully before agreeing to any more such ventures by this gentleman, whose criminality shows an unfortunate combination of arrogance and incompetence.'

Trilling sneered. 'Ha! Call me as many names as you like, Miss Lynton, but you will get nothing from me. If the police get hold of the letters, the scandal will finish Wilde, and there's nothing in them that points a finger at me.'

'In normal circumstances, you might be right,' Hester said. 'However, let me inform you that I have a cousin, Inspector Albert Brasher of Scotland Yard, whom I have consulted about this case. Albert has assured me that in order to prove the case against you – and this young woman who has assisted you – it will *not* be necessary for the letters to be made public. The judge will have to read them, of course, but not the jury. There will be rumours, naturally – I will see to it that a story goes about connecting Wilde with some fictitious actress or dancer. You will, of course, be free to state otherwise, and add slander to your crimes.'

Trilling's sneer had turned into petulance. 'Very well – but I do not have the remaining letter. It is in the hands of ...'

Hester interrupted him. 'Oh come, Mr Trilling! It is no one's hands other than yours. I cannot conceive that you would have done otherwise than keep such a valuable item on your person. However, if you wish to retain it, I am sure Inspector Brasher will be happy to arrest you.'

Trilling reached into an inside pocket, took out a letter and flung it onto the table. Hester quickly examined the contents and put in in her bag.

'And the £200?'

Trilling produced his wallet and counted out the notes.

'There,' he said. 'And I hope to God I never set sight upon you or Miss Jessop again.'

The subdued couple left the Beaconsfield Club without incident – although, despite their failure in this instance, I suspected it would not be the last time they would venture into crime.

'Shall we return to Newsome Street?' I asked.

'All in good time, my dear Ivy. I suggest that first, we return to our table and finish that excellent champagne, now that further intellectual effort is not required. Then, since we are here I will try a hand or two of whist, and endeavour not to lose our client's £200.'

The following day Hester sent a telegram inviting Oscar Wilde to our rooms, although it said nothing about the successful conclusion of the case. His joy at receiving the tenth and final letter was unbounded, and it was all Hester could do to persuade him to keep the £200 we had reclaimed.

'No, no Mr Wilde, I could not possibly accept such an extortionate fee. It would give lady detectives a bad name. I will take £10 and no more, with thanks.'

'Very well, Miss Lynton. Now, you must explain to me; how did you come to suspect Trilling, and how did you know he was to be found in the Beaconsfield Club?'

'As to the first, that is very simple. As soon as I had finished my examination of Trilling's rooms at Jefferson Mansions I realised that the burglary had been staged, in order to provide a reason for the disappearance of the letters. Ivy, did you notice the peculiarity of the markings upon the outside of the drainpipe which ran past the window?'

'But there were no markings, other than those left by my own fingers.'

'That was the peculiarity. As you yourself discovered, it was impossible to lay hands upon the pipe without removing a portion of London grime, and leaving your prints behind. If anyone *had* climbed up the pipe, then there would have been hand and foot marks in abundance. Then there was the absence of glass fragments on the carpet.'

'I can explain that,' Wilde interjected. 'Edmund has a cleaner who comes in every morning at eleven o'clock.'

'Indeed, but have you ever tried to clean broken glass from a carpet? No, I thought not. Even the most meticulous servant would not be able to remove every last speck of glass, and my lens showed nothing. One would also have expected to see a fragment or two under the nearby furniture, but there was none. I have no doubt that Trilling laid newspaper on his carpet before opening the window and reaching round to break it from outside, to save the labour of cleaning up the mess. And how can you explain that only *one* of the locked drawers in Trilling's desk had been forced open?'

'Perhaps that was the first drawer that the burglar chose, and by good fortune it contained the letters,' I suggested.

'Yes, but as we know that the burglar was also happy to steal cash – £10 was purportedly taken from Trilling's wardrobe – he would have surely broken into the other drawers, which might have contained additional money. No, the real reason was that Trilling wanted to do the least possible damage to his own property. And what else was *not* stolen?'

'Yes, of course,' Wilde said. 'The Tiffany cuff links were not taken. If he had told me that they were missing, Trilling could never have worn them again!'

'Quite. This was a burglary designed to cause as little inconvenience as possible to the victim – because the victim was also the perpetrator. If I had wanted to break into Trilling's rooms, I would have simply waited one quiet afternoon until Trilling had gone out, and that slovenly porter had disappeared for yet another cigarette, then hastened up the stairs and jemmied open Trilling's door. But let me turn to your second query – how I knew that Trilling would appear at the gambling club.

'As you can guess, as soon as I realised that the burglary had been faked, I made it my business to investigate that young man's affairs. I soon discovered that he was an inveterate gambler and owed a fellow member a large sum. He needed Mr Wilde's £200 to pay the debt. I also discovered that he was invariably at the Beaconsfield Club just after midnight on a Saturday. It had been my plan to confront him there, where he would have been able to borrow £200 from one of his fellow gamblers – albeit at extortionate rates – in order to repay Mr Wilde. By a lucky chance, he happened to win that sum himself, which made the transaction easy. His companion at the gambling club was of course the same woman who obtained a copy of Trilling's blackmail note, and who collected Mr Wilde's briefcase.'

'There is one other thing that puzzles me,' I said. 'If it is possible for Trilling to be prosecuted without revealing the contents of Mr Wilde's letters, why not have him, and his accomplice, arrested?'

Hester chuckled. 'I may have been a little optimistic in my suggestion that the content of the letters could be kept secret in the event of a trial,' she said. 'At any rate, I succeeded in persuading Trilling that he was in danger of prosecution, which achieved our objective.'

'Indeed,' Wilde said. 'Let the man go free. I for one shall have no more to do with him. The only literary effort that I would be happy to devote to him in future would be his epitaph. And now, ladies, where shall we dine this evening? I still feel that I am much in your debt, so name your venue, and let me bear the expense. Gratitude is an emotion best indulged whilst it is fresh for, like beauty, it is apt to dissipate with time.'

About the Author

Tony Evans is a full-time writer. His print publications include eighteen adaptations of classic novels published by Real Reads Ltd. His eBooks include the *Hester Lynton* mystery series and the *Jonathan Harker* mystery series. Tony has also written student guides for *Hamlet*, *Dracula* and *The Murder of Roger Ackroyd*: all published by ZigZag Education. He lives with his wife in the Yorkshire Dales.

Follow him on Twitter: @tonyevansUK

CPSIA information can be obtained
at www.ICGtesting.com
Printed in the USA
LVHW041925041121
702459LV00014B/625